COURTS & CURSES BOOK TWO

MICHELLE HELEN FRITZ

A Court of Broken Promises and Nightmares: Courts & Curses by Michelle Helen Fritz

Cover Design & Chapter Heading Art: Wanderlust Ink & Tome LLC

Cheshire Character Art: Cameo Renae

Character Art: Samaiya Art

Developmental & Copy Editing: Paranormal Depth Edits

Proofreading: Brittany Smith & Cathey Nelson

Published by Clear Spring Books LLC of Clear Spring, MD

DEDICATION

For my sons. May you always find adventure and never forget the beauty to be discovered in each new day. You are so imaginative and humorous, my handsome little gentlemen. Thank you for all the gifts you continually give me, from freshly picked flowers to warm hugs. I love you times infinity. Find your voice in this world and never stop questioning all the things.

P.S. This is my love letter to you. Whenever you miss me, pick this up and let me tell you a story.

CONTENTS

PROLOGUE

AN INVITATION

Horrifying beasts that used to exist only in nightmares now freely roamed the dark lands. Those who were once gentle and kind had been either devoured or forced to become cruel and twisted, re-created into something sinister, something truly terrifying. A Resistance was formed to fight against the swelling tide of evil, one which would need a savior, a leader who could take all of the unrest and debauchery and vanquish the very heart of evil, making something wonderful from its ashes. One who could take the darkness and embrace it as they conquered the false queen.

Femfaeascent sat upon her obsidian throne in the dimly lit chamber, fuming with formidable rage flowing through her veins like molten lava. She glared intently at the cream-colored invitation that had *no*t been addressed to her. The stationery crumbled in her tightening fist until it was nothing more than a paper ball. The faerie queen tossed it to the side as she gnashed her teeth. With widened eyes and flared nostrils, she sank further into fury.

"How dare he!" she seethed, rising from her rose-carved

throne. Vicious thorns from the four twisted feet, which ended in three sharp talons, reached out to prick her legs.

The starlight that shone down from the enchanted ceiling enhanced her ethereal beauty. Gleaming ebony hair was piled atop her head in a complicated knot and was gathered between large, onyx horns, curling inward to form a circular loop. Dark, curled tendrils were left to hang down the nape of her slender neck, caressing silken, alabaster skin free from blemishes. The most striking feature of all was her large, expressive, turquoise eyes rimmed with thick, dark lashes. Femfaeascent's full lips twisted into a sneer, which she knew frightened her Court. Her advisors were silent as the titled gentle-faeries looked elsewhere in hopes of avoiding eye contact, which would earn their queen's unwavering wrath.

She could feel the watchful gazes of her uninvited guests. The gargoyles, which had appeared from the sky not long after her reign began, were silent sentries. Lined up at the room's dark edges, their furry bodies were rigid as their intelligent eyes took in every detail. They never interfered in any of the Court's affairs, so they were largely ignored.

The Faerie Queen of the Lunar Court strode from one glittering black wall to the next. Her eyes focused over the marble fireplace where the turquoise fire burned brightly. The flames danced erratically within the grate and kept in perfect time to the faerie's racing pulse. Raising her hand, the Fae queen brought one charcoal-painted thumbnail up to her mouth to bite. Spinning in place, she turned to face her audience. Femfaeascent took in each member present and quickly cast them uselessly aside until her gaze landed upon the onyx hues of the raven's feathers that were puffed up with indignation on his mistress's behalf.

"My pet," Femfaeascent crooned as she held out her arm. The fowl took flight and gracefully flew to perch on her long, sleeved forearm and cocked its head to the side, awaiting her decree. "You have never betrayed me, and I know you never shall. I grant you the task of being my eyes and ears. Fly away to the land of the faraway kingdom where my son resides. Find him for me. I wish to pay a call upon the happy couple and their new *baby*." Her disdain at the offensive word "baby" filled the air around her with cruel intent as her jaw clenched.

The raven gave her a nod with a malicious gleam swirling within his sable gaze. Then, spreading his wings, he took flight. Femfaeascent directed her sight to follow him as he soared up to the throne room's ceiling. The Lunar Queen closed her eyes tightly once the bird had breached the glamour, and she took a deep breath.

He will not fail; soon, I shall see my wretched boy again. How dare he begin a family and forget all about his duties here. Never mind that his banishment still stands; he belongs to only me.

Femfaeascent opened her eyes and took in the glamoured, twinkling teal stars. They reminded the Lunar Court to always remember their Court was a place of dreams and nightmares, and each was equally important.

She reached a hand up to ensure the midnight crown was perfectly situated atop her head, resting on the inside of her horns. The tips of the circlet were aligned with the middle point, lining up with the faerie's nose, and were topped with a moon. The two columns that resided on either side of that were adorned with a symmetrical star each. It wasn't a fierce diadem; it had never matched her mood, nor the attire she chose to wear that was always provocative to the sensibilities of her Court.

Femfaeascent's perfect Fae hearing had captured the whispered words no one dared to utter any longer. Their queen's wrath had seen to that, but she still recalled with perfect clarity their censure.

"Scandalous..."

"A true mockery to the throne and long-held traditions!"

For what *queen* would ever clad herself in trousers made

from leather or a fitted corset top that was worn for all to see every dip and curve of her figure?

A vicious smile curled along the Fae queen's crimson lips as she reveled in the discomfort of those few stubborn faeries who still held onto their innocent ideals. Femfaeascent delighted in surrounding herself with those she could so easily offend. Their outrage and displeasure fed her darkest desires. However, not every soul before her continued to hold close to their scruples or morals. And those subjects were the Lunar Queen's favorite citizens of her Court.

Oh yes, my little retinue, I can read your hearts well enough; my beautiful darkness will eventually suffocate all of your objections away.

Femfaeascent twitched her sharpened fingertips as tendrils of the enchanted darkness seeped forth to coat the ether with a touch of intoxicating madness.

The power of the crown was an addictive force to one whose heart had long ago turned to ashes. It fed Femfaeascent its power, which it took from the Lunar Court lands. The diadem had not been given freely to the cruel-hearted faerie. Ever since her ruling era began, the Lunar Court had become a place of broken promises and nightmares.

Evil walked among those who called the kingdom their home, and it invaded nearly every soul that dwelled within its lands. It latched onto those that still retained their innocence and drove them mad. Sometimes, the savage process was slow as it agonizingly devoured one's soul. And sometimes, the metamorphosis was instantaneous, causing what was once unimaginable violence to break out, wreaking havoc on those around them.

The Lunar Court became a place of frivolity and recklessness, and all bad deeds were encouraged. There was no punishment for those who stole, murdered, or took their pleasure in using others. The queen was pleased to see the

Court delight in madness and misdeeds, and with fervor, she equally matched the crimes of her subjects. Those who were driven completely mad were her favorites to frolic with, as they were so easily led astray.

The most unexpected development had been when the madness and mayhem had begun to leech into the kingdom of the White Queen, her enemy in all schemes and endeavors. Femfaeascent vowed to ruin the White Kingdom, and the day was soon at hand. She could feel the darkness spreading, and it filled her with unending glee.

I shall rejoice, revel, and dance across the kingdom once every subject is under my control.

The queen crooked a slender finger and beckoned one of the male faeries in her cortege to come and kneel before her. The faerie, who held a crazed look in his eyes, grinned maniacally and took to his knees. With a wicked smile, Femfaeascent touched his forehead with her long index finger and closed her eyes, invading the mad faerie's mind. Images of demons swam within his sight as they brandished pitchforks and maces. They attacked the faerie's body while he screamed and thrashed against the invisible force that kept him rooted in place. The Lunar Queen would not relent as blood spilled from her victim's ears, mouth, and nose, trailing in rivulets down his once pristine shirt and waistcoat. He grew still as the echoes of his screams reverberated against the chamber's glimmering walls.

Femfaeascent's eyes flew open as she lifted her finger from the faerie's head, and he fell face forward onto the obsidian stone floor, dead. The queen threw back her head and cackled into the wonderfully oppressive atmosphere as the slain Fae's crimson blood flowed around her booted feet.

"My dear Court! It's time to paint the roses red!"

The raven had not failed his mistress. Within a fortnight, he had located his prey. Her pet allowed his queen to have use of his senses so that she could formulate her vengeful plan. The raven knew his part of the strategy was not yet completed, so he waited, watched, and listened until his mistress could be by his side.

On the morning of the christening, Femfaeascent left her kingdom through an enormous golden looking glass that allowed its owner to freely traverse between realms and enter into the mortal world. The bright sunshine hurt her eyes as its golden rays sought to burn her pale skin. She quickly summoned clouds, and the sun was hidden away.

Why has this portal been cast to this gleaming meadow? It's much too far away from the chamber in which it was to reside. I shall deal with my unfaithful friends *once I have seen* my son.

Clearing her mind from her current frustrations, Femfaeascent took a deep exhale, then linked her mind to her companion's. Within moments, she was able to trace the raven's magical essence, so she set off to bridge the distance to reach her pet. Blurs of colors whirled by in bright streaks as her speed rapidly increased with each step she took. The odors that hung upon the air were repulsive, and the grime coating the streets and buildings of the realm was an assault upon Femfaeascent's senses; her lips curled with disgust. Feeling that her familiar was close by, the queen slowed her speed and looked toward the cobblestone building that loomed before her.

The raven was perched upon a wooden windowsill, and at the queen's approach, his feathered head turned to stare at his mistress. The queen nodded a greeting as she joined the ebony bird. Together, they peered in at the intimate scene taking place within the abbey. Taking a deep breath, the faerie queen measured the well cradling the powers in her body. Femfaeascent was far away from her Lunar Court, and the farther away a Fae traveled between the realms, the weaker they became. But yes... she still had enough magic flowing within that she could easily enact a curse or two.

Smiling wickedly, the evil queen strode away from the window and entered into the holy dwelling where fear greeted her, filling her ashen heart with relish. Within mere minutes, the sorrow-filled wails of an innocent baby, now cursed for having the audacity to be born, rang through the misty morning to lay down upon the dewy grass.

1

ACROSS A CROWDED BALLROOM

The far too curious girl crept on satin-slippered tiptoes, keeping to the shadows to ensure she was not discovered too soon. The Holts were her family's nearest neighbors, their estates separated by an enchanting forest of verdant flora and fauna. It had been easy to sneak away for this one treasured evening.

As she studied the dancing couples and spied the current fashions of the country society set, Alora hoped, with all of her heart, that she would get to bask in the elegant surroundings. It was to be her first venture into such a setting, and Alora's heartbeat was racing with eagerness even though trickery had been her enabler.

She wasn't supposed to be attending the ball. Alora was much too young to taste champagne and be whirled around in her first dance, per her father's unbending dictates. Even though girls younger than Alora had experienced many such fairytale evenings, she had been denied such pleasure. Being nearly eighteen was not the same as having reached eighteen. Awaiting the momentous birthday seemed like such a daunting task, given Alora's father's steadfastness in his strict rules regarding what she may or may not do.

Earlier that afternoon, Alora had bribed the stable boy to saddle her horse, Wildflower, and leave the horse near the side balcony of her father's estate. Seeing that her directions had been perfectly followed, Alora grinned excitedly as she mounted the sidesaddle. Once she was properly settled, Alora clicked her tongue, and Wildflower took off into a canter.

The bright golden moon lit the way; even if it had been overcast, she knew the path to the neighboring estate well enough. Alora was careful to avoid fallen logs and twisted branches for her sake and that of her beloved horse. To arrive with dirt or tears marring Alora's clothing would never serve her purpose of blending into the scenery.

The long, voluminous burgundy cloak offered protection to her borrowed ball gown. Once she had learned that tonight's ball would be a masquerade, Alora hurriedly put her scheme into place.

Alora had searched through her mother's trunks that were stored in the attic until she found a gown she could spend the afternoon improving with a more modern taste and added embellishments. The vibrant blue gown was sheer, with an undergown of a darker blue. Flowers sewn with silver thread graced the hem and neckline. She had donned her own elbow-length white gloves and slippers that matched the gown.

Enlisting the aid of her ladies maid, whom she swore to secrecy, Alora had sat at her dressing table for what had felt like hours. Alora's auburn hair was styled in Greek fashion, gathered atop her head with curls that caressed either side of her oval face, enhancing her high cheekbones. With the addition of tiny seed pearls threaded through her tresses, the effect was quite stunning.

She risked criticism, and even ruination for sneaking out, but Alora feared that if she did not, another adventure would never again come her way. Since it was to be a masked ball, she had searched through her own supplies for the right materials to fashion a disguise. Alora chose a fox because her actions would be sneaky and daring.

When the glow from torches came into view, the excitement within Alora soared higher still as her heart thundered in her chest. Guiding Wildflower to the stablehand nearest the east side of the manor home, she dismounted and quickened her steps toward the front entrance. When Alora reached the massive oak double doors, which hung open, she forgot how to breathe; the sight before her was spectacular!

A chandelier lit with cream-colored glittering candles hung just inside the foyer and cast a rainbow of light in every direction. Colorful sconces were emitting their glow along the walls and marbled tiles. Feeling as if she was captured in some fairytale, Alora's skin tingled as glee flooded her senses, creating a longing to twirl about in dizzying circles. Her bemused eyes took in the prisms of color resting upon the stylish hairdos and sparkling ball gowns of the ladies and the bespeckled attire of the gentlemen. Never before had Alora seen such detailed splendor. It was almost as if magic coated the very air surrounding her.

But magic isn't anything more than make-believe.

Alora's upbringing had been stifled by the nanny and then by her governess as instructed by the overbearing wishes of her father. She was never to be out of sight and never allowed to partake in anything within her social set. Alora was suffocated at every turn and just wanted one magical evening to experience something for herself.

Adding extra chamomile leaves to her governess's tea had been unkind, but she knew that Miss Mary Prickett would never have allowed her to leave otherwise. Alora had no desire to frighten Miss Prickett with worry about her safety. There was a distinct prick in Alora's heart at the deception when she considered that Miss Prickett had never done anything to deserve such ill-treatment. Alora reached a hand up to rub the aching area of her chest. She vowed to be kinder to her companion, and while she could not blot out her actions, Alora could choose not to repeat the same mistakes.

Slipping out from her bedchamber had been easy, and Alora knew the chances of running into her father were slim. He'd been residing in his chambers on the other side of the house, and mourning his wife's death preoccupied most of Papa's time.

Her mother had passed away such a long time ago, and Alora could not bring herself to be filled with sorrow every moment of every day. Not like him. She could never aspire to love so greatly that she'd forever mourn the ghosts of her past.

Alora pushed the unpleasant thoughts of home from her mind and looked around her. She blinked and allowed anticipation to flow through her in a rushing wave. Alora wouldn't have to wait in an endless receiving line if she showed up tardy since the hosts would be off enjoying their evening amongst their guests.

"May I?" a male voice asked behind her. Alora turned and spotted Mister Morley, the Holts's butler dressed in fine navy livery.

"Of course," she replied, allowing him to assist her with removing the billowy cloak.

"The ball is underway, and the refreshments are situated along the far side of the ballroom wall," the man-servant informed her. Alora noted his kind umber eyes watching her from beneath his bird mask.

"Thank you," she replied, inclining her head toward him.

Her fox mask proved to be a wise disguise; he didn't seem to know who she was. With her courage bolstered, Alora made her way down the corridor and toward the ballroom, where the strains of music met her ears before the grandeur greeted her eyes.

She took a misstep when her knees threatened to drop her

to the floor as anxiety seized her heart. Black spots speckled her vision, and Alora quickly decided to take a detour toward the library. She soundlessly retreated back down the dark corridor that displayed gilded portraits and tall vases. Opening the door, Alora quickly shut it behind herself and leaned against it.

Oh, my Heavens!

Bringing a gloved hand to rest against her rapidly beating heart, Alora attempted to settle herself. Deep, soothing breaths soon slowed her pulse and she felt her tightly wound nerves slowly begin to relax.

Her eyes took in the gilded looking glass that hung on the wall in the opposite direction. It was a gorgeous decoration and one she had studied before; Alora knew its carved roses and rabbits well. Her reflection, staring back at her, assured her that all was well with her hair and clothing. Alora straightened, glancing at the spines that graced the shelves of books lining the wall.

Now more steady, she smoothed a hand down her gown's bodice before taking measured steps to reach the terrace doors. Alora's gloved fingers caressed the golden handles, gently turning them as she silently opened one of the doors and passed through into the outside air.

Only a few steps separated Alora from the lush garden. Rose bushes, clematis, and English ivy lined the walkway that twisted around to meet the ballroom's enormous glass doors. There was a white marble bench set a short distance away near the bubbling fountain, where a couple were seated. She was too far away to make out their faces; their masks had been removed. Alora could enter the ballroom, or she could stay in the garden.

At home, the questions of whether she *should* or *could* participate in the ball had never passed into her thoughts. But now, trepidation and the prick of her conscience were posing those questions. Stomping her foot, impatient with her fluctuating feelings, she decided that one ball, one evening, couldn't possibly cause a scandal.

With her mind made up, Alora crossed the distance, twisting the handle of the heavy door, and entered the ball. A magical scene greeted her and her breath rushed out in a stunned exhale. There were chalk images drawn onto the dance floor, which had not yet been distorted by the dancing feet that glided across it. Roses, rabbits, and teacups were artfully drawn around the incandescent wooden floor. Her heart longed for a dance partner to chalk the night away, but she didn't dare be quite so bold.

She had only wished to view the ball and those who danced; Alora had never meant to be among those dancing, so she was careful to stay along the room's edges and walls. Once or twice, she stood sentry behind tall potted ferns to see what she could spy. The gigantic room was growing warmer as the couples worked themselves through their steps.

The frescos that were painted upon the high, vaulted ceiling were whimsical. Misshapen mushrooms and large butterflies looked as if they would take flight at any moment. The golden-leafed trees were ethereal, as were the colorful flowers in shades that Alora had never seen before.

Alora straightened as a chill crept down her spine, despite the room's rising temperature. She looked around, curiosity nibbling away at her senses, but there was no one nearby and no drafts in her tiny corner. Alora turned her focus to the other side of the room. It was crowded with guests, but nothing blocked her vision from landing on the most stunningly beautiful man she had ever laid eyes on. Masculine features were on display for all to see, and she briefly wondered where his mask had been discarded. Glorious amber eyes met hers and their gazes locked. Dragonflies took flight within her stomach, and she had to remind herself to breathe. Alora's pursuer began to press through the dancing couples, never once breaking his intense stare from hers.

Reaching up a gloved hand, Alora touched her fox mask to ensure it was indeed hiding her identity. She wondered what it was about her that beckoned him.

The tall boy, for he was not yet a man, stopped before her. Dark auburn hair was cut short in the back, but the longer pieces on top and surrounding his face added to his boyish appeal. It reminded Alora of the fallen leaves in autumn.

His nose was aquiline, and his lips were… *kissable?*

He was dressed in cobalt blue breeches and a fitted tailcoat that matched perfectly. An ebony waistcoat with gold patterned roses peeked from the folds of his tailcoat. His cravat was tied into a sophisticated knot that resembled an unfurling rose. Alora sucked in a breath and slowly exhaled it.

"Hello," he greeted her as he reached for her gloved hand and bowed over it. Her pulse simultaneously sped up and slowed down.

Alora dropped into a curtsey. When she rose, she looked at her hand, which was still warmly encased within his, and felt as if the moment between them was the beginning of all of her dreams now coming true.

"Hello," she replied, attempting to hide her breathlessness.

"Interesting choice."

"I beg your pardon?"

"Your mask, I mean." He gestured to her face with his free hand.

"Ah, yes. Well, foxes are intriguing creatures, you know. They are clever and cunning. Their coats are the most beautiful shade of—your hair! It perfectly matches the highlights of gold and copper of their coats. Did you know that?" Alora could not stop staring at him. She should have been embarrassed at the boldness she was displaying, but she wasn't; Alora couldn't bring herself to rein in her feelings.

He smiled at her, and it lit up his entire face. Mirth reflected in his warm golden-brown eyes.

Clearing his throat, he said, "I did, in fact, know. But your appreciation has increased my delight. Tell me, do you enjoy hunting foxes?"

"Oh no, absolutely not. I could never engage in such an activity that harmed another. I prefer to spend my time observing the wildlife just as they are."

"Pity the foxes then. You're not endeavoring to chase them." His warm chuckle made Alora question what it was that he had found to be so amusing.

Her lips dipped into a frown as she realized that he was still holding her hand. Alora pulled it back, watching as it fell from his grasp. He tilted his head to the side, observing her with humor still etched upon his face. She felt like she was the prey and he was the hunter, but despite those feelings, she still desperately desired for him to find her pleasing.

"Am I to know your name, fair lady?"

"Only if you tell me yours first," she attempted to collect her poise.

Her rioting emotions made her feel as if she was riding a wave being tossed in turbulent currents, and yet, she still gave him a flirtatious smile. Alora had spent a good half an hour that afternoon perfecting her flirtatious face. She winked and smiled until she felt satisfied that she would be able to charm her way out of any situation that may arise.

"My name is Phillip," he said in a rich baritone.

"No last name?" she teased.

Shaking his head at her, he remained silent while a soft smile played about his lush lips.

"Very well. You may call me Alora."

"Alora," Phillip said, testing out the sound of her name.

It gave her splinters of shivers, and twinkling specks

floated in her vision. She had never drunk alcohol before, but Alora surmised that being in his presence affected her much like spirits might affect one who had imbibed too much.

"Would you care to dance with me, Alora?" Phillip held out his white-gloved hand, awaiting her response.

"I mustn't. Not here." She shook her head.

"Where then? Perhaps the garden? The moon is bright tonight. The perfect chaperone for a stolen moment or two."

Alora considered him. What harm could come from one dance in the garden where other stolen moments were being had by couples? This opportunity may never come again.

Her heart was telling her to chase this while she could. Was it not an adventure that she had longed to embark upon?

"I would love to," Alora replied as she allowed him to take her hand once more and braided their gloved fingers together. A heated current flowed through her hand and straight into her heart at the contact.

How curious! And this intimacy he displays with me is most improper, yet I cannot make myself draw away.

Phillip led them along the edges of the ballroom, and soon, they were exiting to the garden. Alora hadn't needed to match her steps to his longer stride; he had been the one to adjust to her own smaller tread as he whisked her farther into the hidden recesses of the grounds. They seemed to be all alone in the safety of the flowery paradise, with only the moon and the flowers to observe their scandalous behavior.

Alora reached up and untied her mask. She grasped it by its ribbons, not knowing what else to do with it. She had not thought to bring a reticule to store her things.

"Beautiful. You are so blindingly beautiful," Phillip stated as he gazed down at her. "Shall we?" He turned her toward him and encircled her waist with his free arm.

"We shall," Alora consented, and followed his steps.

Soon, they were gliding across the gravel ground. The smile that lit up her face could not be dimmed. He had called her beautiful; it was a moment that she knew her heart would always treasure.

They could hear the orchestra's notes as they stared into each other's eyes. With every turn, her gaze returned to his. Phillip was tall and, while Alora was not, she fit perfectly in his muscular arms. She never wanted these stolen moments to end.

Gazing up at Phillip, she noticed parts of his features that appeared almost fuzzy to her eyes. Alora blinked, and yet, the haze remained. She hadn't noticed it before. Perhaps it was just a trick of the light?

She willed her eyes to obey her. To show her what lay beneath the haze. Warmth enveloped Alora, stemming from her stomach and flowing up toward her eyes before quickly dissipating. She spied reddish-brown bushy eyebrows that were almost unkempt and bizarre. Her line of sight moved to an ear, which was completely ordinary except, of course, for the pointed tip that topped it.

Pointed ears? Curiouser and curiouser.

Alora didn't shy away from him. Phillip was handsome regardless, and she wondered if he was human or something *more*. Perhaps the fairytales of her youth were indeed true. Could he be a faerie? Some prince from a court far away? The thoughts dashed away from her mind as Phillip flashed her a dazzling smile.

"Is something wrong, sweet Alora?" he asked, seeming to notice that her attention had veered from him and their waltz.

"No, only I fear that this is nothing more than a dream. I don't wish to wake up and leave this evening forever behind. This must be just a dream?" Alora's eyes blinked three times, attempting to dry the wetness that had suddenly appeared. She felt a physical pain in her heart as the organ beat erratically.

"Do you trust me?" Phillip tilted his head to the side as he easily kept their movements in sync with the dance.

"With all of my heart," she readily answered and found that she meant every word. Alora did trust him. While it was a silly notion to give her trust so freely, she knew deep down that she need never have any fear of him. Alora let out a breath and felt the tension leave her body.

He grinned at her before replying, "I shall guard your heart then, fair maiden. This isn't a dream. There's no fear of waking. There is only you and me. And there isn't anywhere in all the realms that I'd rather be than with you locked in my arms."

Alora didn't have the words to respond to him. Phillip looked so determined, dashing, and very sincere. While his statement had been brash, boasting his self-confidence, she didn't find him conceited or cocky. Phillip's words had rang of truth and were still stirring her heart.

Back and forth, they twirled across the gravel, dancing until a high-pitched clamor alerted them to another's presence. Feeling guilty, though she hadn't done anything wrong except for sneaking out and being unchaperoned in a man's arms, she primly stepped away from him.

Alora frowned, displeased by the interruption and from the direction her thoughts had taken her.

A large white rabbit jumped out from under one of the rose bushes, shrieking at them. It became animated while it hopped in place, frantically waving its arms in the air. Had the poor creature gone mad? Perhaps it was someone's pet because it wore a collar with a white watch face hanging from it.

Alora looked over at Phillip, who was intently staring at the little rabbit, and then he glanced at her. "The hour is growing late; we should say farewell. Though I am loath to let you go."

"Forever farewell?" she questioned in a wavering voice. Alora wasn't ready for their time to come to an end. The very idea of such a parting made her feel as if claws were shredding her heart from the inside out.

"I fear that may well be the case, sweet Alora. I have recently been summoned home, and it's to a place very far from here." Regret shimmered in his expressive eyes.

"Oh. I see." She made to turn away from him when he reached for her waist. Phillip gathered her into his arms as he pulled her against his solid chest; the outburst from the intruding rabbit was momentarily forgotten as its cries fell away.

"I promise to see you again. However, I can not say when. The thought of never seeing you, never talking, never dancing, never locking gazes with you terrifies me. I fear that I shall never be the same. You have become my happiness," he reverently told her as his eyes roamed the planes of her face.

Alora felt the silent tear that coursed down her cheek, falling to dampen his waistcoat. Phillip didn't push her away; he only tightened his arms around her, letting her heart mourn. She gathered herself, looking up to meet his tender gaze. He smiled softly at her and then reached into his pocket to withdraw a handkerchief, which he placed into her palm as more tears appeared. Alora felt silly to have become such a watering pot in his presence and instantly worried that any attraction that he once felt for her had vanished.

"No more tears, not on my account," he soothed. Phillip cupped her cheek in his warm hand as his thumb gently wiped the tears away.

"No more," she told him. Collecting herself, Alora handed the handkerchief back to him, then stepped away to face what came next.

He bowed to her, tucking the linen away before offering his arm. They didn't exchange any more words as he led her toward the ballroom. She halted after taking a few steps and settled her fox mask into place, tying its laces to secure it.

Then, they linked arms once again as they neared their destination. Alora's heart was trilling as her mind dreamed of happily ever afters that may never come.

Phillip opened the door for her, letting her hand go. The cool air chilled her without his warmth. He didn't make a move to follow her in, and so, when the door softly closed behind her, she tightly squeezed her eyes shut, then did the only thing she could. Alora took a step, then another, and she kept walking, determined to reach the security of her home and her awaiting bedchamber to process the myriad of feelings she couldn't quite put a name to.

Her heart was shattering, but she was careful to keep her face neutral. Alora's eyes prickled, longing to release the pent-up tears, but she would not allow herself to let them fall. She had given her word, though she doubted that once she was home and secure in her bed, she would be able to keep her emotions at bay. That was fine with her. As outlandish as the thought was, she realized she had fallen in love within the span of one stolen evening. And though Alora wanted to keep hope lit in her heart, she doubted she would see Phillip ever again. She could not keep the fear from creeping in. His amber eyes would haunt Alora in her dreams and waking hours.

She couldn't explain the pull that she felt toward him; she only knew it existed. Her feelings were like breathing; they were something her body naturally did. Absently, Alora rubbed the aching area over her heart.

2

AN UNHAPPY BIRTHDAY

Eight Months Later....

The morning light peeped through the lace curtains as it entreated Alora to wake and greet the new day. Blearily, she opened her eyes and then frowned. Today was finally her eighteenth birthday.

The thought should have filled Alora with joy, but her heart longed for Phillip, the strange boy who seemed otherworldly. So many nights since their meeting and parting, she had dreamed of him. Alora thought of his beautiful smile and the way she felt while he held her within his strong arms. It had only been one night, but it was the most memorable moment of her entire life.

But this morning felt different. When she had awoken, her dream remained fixed in her mind and refused to fade away. How was it that one evening altered her entire life, even after all the time that had passed? Her heart ached for him, for the memory of being in his arms. Alora was utterly enchanted despite only knowing him for a handful of hours.

Alora sighed, closing her eyes for a moment as she remembered the trip home after that unforgettable evening.

She had been successful all those many months ago, returning without being discovered.

Soaring over the fields, Alora leaned forward and whispered her secrets to Wildflower as the horse's hooves pounded the dirt and greenery beneath them. Warmth spread across her chest as her stomach flipped and flopped with each new memory. When she came into sight of her father's manor house, she gently tugged upon the horse's reins to slow their pace. The last thing Alora wanted was to draw attention to herself by the sounds of thundering hoof beats. She was dismounting within minutes with the help of the bribed stableboy, who held onto the reins.

"Thank you," Alora said, beaming at the servant before turning and placing a delicate pat on Wildflower's flank. "And thank you," she whispered to the horse.

Sucking in a deep breath, Alora slowly exhaled and made her way out of the stables and into the house. Quieter than a mouse, she climbed her way up the staircase and kept to the shadows that danced along the silk-papered wall of the corridor until she came to her chamber door. Her fingers grasped at the cool knob, quietly turning it and sending up a silent prayer that the door wouldn't creak; she turned until she heard a click of the latch and pushed her way inside. Alora quickly undressed, going as fast as she could by herself, and slipped into a nightdress. A yawn erupted from her as she made her way over to the four-postered bed and climbed in. Resting her head upon her plush pillows, she lay there awake, the excitement of the ball replaying in her mind. Thoughts of moonlight kisses and strong arms had replayed over and over in her mind, making sleep nearly impossible.

As much as Alora had enjoyed that evening, she had come to equally loathe it. It was one night, and it seized her heart and rent it from her chest, leaving a gaping hole to take up residence. Nothing and no one besides Phillip could mend it. But where was he? The crushing despair made her question why she felt as if a part of her heart was missing.

The door opened, and her abigail entered and began

morning preparations by drawing the drapes. She tied the heavy, dark material to either side of the double windows where a curved hook was attached to the wall. Bright light cast the bedchamber in a glow as tiny specks of dust danced in the air.

Alora's eyes flitted over to the window as her thoughts flew to the raven, who occasionally peeped through the lead-glass panes to watch her. He often visited on her birthdays, and Alora left berries on the windowsill as a special treat just for him. Since Papa had forbidden animals inside the manor as pets, this tradition had been kept secret because she didn't willingly court her father's anger. The few times that the curious guest had been discovered by her father had nearly brought the eaves down upon their heads with his shouts of rage.

"It's a bright morning today, Mistress," the abigail commented as she moved to the dressing table to tidy up the bottles on top of it.

"It does seem like quite a fair day. No clouds in sight," replied Alora as her eyes left the window.

Tossing her coverlet aside, Alora rose while her maid hurriedly withdrew Alora's dressing gown from the wardrobe. Rushing to her mistress's side, the maid draped the dressing gown over Alora's shoulders. Nodding her thanks, Alora tied the sash at her waist.

Turning and striding to the wardrobe, the maid uttered small sounds as she withdrew the periwinkle dress Alora would wear. After gathering the rest of the trimmings, the abigail stepped toward the dressing table again and began to lay out Alora's ensemble.

Alora's father had gifted her with a new day dress just for the occasion of her birthday. Alora bounced up and down upon her tiptoes once she spied the dress again, for it was sumptuous with Brussels lace and created from the softest muslin she had ever worn. The color was stunning. Alora couldn't wait to don it.

Taking a moment to survey her lovely bedchamber, Alora's lips curved into a smile. Rich blues and soft purples decorated the papered walls and satin fabrics of her large four-poster bed and settee. A large Aubusson rug with braided edges and a daisy pattern was situated in the middle of the room. In the corner sat a small, tidied, teak desk with scrolled legs and a chair to match. Hung from the walls were landscapes painted by her own hand. Their ornate frames drew the eye to the pastures and watery depictions. Alora tried to enjoy them and keep her critical eye silent, not wanting to dwell on any perceived flaw.

She made her way to the little alcove that housed her copper tub. Her maid leaned over the tub and poured the contents from a glass bottle in.

"Thank you so very much, Phoebe. I am so thankful that Papa advanced you from chambermaid to my ladies' maid; I do not think another abigail would ever be quite as thoughtful as you." Alora's voice was filled with warmth.

"You are too kind to me. I only wish that I can prove justice in your faith in me. Now, into the tub, the water won't keep warm for too long." Phoebe straightened and placed the bottle down. She turned to assist Alora as her warm hazel eyes crinkled at the corners.

A rich aroma of crushed roses and jasmine clung to the water as Alora disrobed and sunk her body into the warm liquid. She sighed, her shoulders slumping as she rested her head against the back of the tub and relished the warmth of the steamy wisps that rose into the air.

~

The day was passing in painfully slow increments. Alora fidgeted, struggling to suppress her boredom and failing miserably.

Now that she was eighteen, all of her studies of deportment given by her governess had concluded. As Alora had learned how to dance across the floor exceptionally well in the past few months, her dancing lessons had ceased. Mister Henri had stated she was ready to take her place within Society and had taken his final leave a fortnight ago. Miss Prickett, who was her former governess, remained in her father's employ as a companion for Alora. Alora was to take her cues from the lady if she was uncertain how to respond to a situation or was hesitant when she was hostessing. With Miss Prickett being more of a wallflower, Alora didn't understand how her former governess could really be of aid to her, but nonetheless, she enjoyed the lady's company. Life would be very tiresome without her.

Alora sucked in a deep breath and huffed. She closed her eyes and slowly opened them before turning her gaze to the window. The raven had not arrived yet, and she worried for its safety. Was there a chance that Papa's hunters had finally tracked it down?

The very idea caused mist to form in her eyes. Alora wouldn't dare ask her father about it. There was nothing to be done except hope that someday she would see the raven again. It felt as if her secrets were mounting up. First, the raven, then a boy. Though the boy seemed to never be far from her mind, she only occasionally thought of the fowl.

She had no wish to be such a mulish miss, a simpering empty-headed chit who only had thoughts of boys to fill her vacant head. While she was not a great reader, Alora was far from being dull-witted. Being so entranced by a boy who hadn't bothered to keep his promise to her wasn't inspiring much confidence in her heart. What Alora needed was to find a way to fill her hours. Her paints were calling to her, and the desire to fill a blank canvas with something beautiful was a pull that Alora discovered she didn't want to dismiss.

Alora closed the book in her hands and set it aside on the table next to the armchair she sat in. She had never had a love for the written word; she had struggled to learn how to properly read, and the idea of reading aloud still gave her fright. Only gothic novels really captured Alora's attention and were worth her time.

Rising to her feet, she shook out her dress. The vibrant potted greenery lining the walls brought the scent of flora and fauna into the space. Alora inhaled and let her eyes wander over to the large bay window. The view was of the gentle hills of the lawn, and further in the distance, the vast forest rose to tower against the horizon, merging the green leaves with the light blue sky. Moving away from the cream velvet padded settee, she walked over the flower-patterned rugs and past the large ornate white marble fireplace. Its grate was free from flames as a chill had not yet entered the house.

Padding from the sitting room and through the candle-illuminated corridor, Alora came to the small room that Papa had allowed her to use for her painting. Opening the door and stepping inside, she let her gaze rove over the room. The sunshine shone through the bay windows that lined the outer pale blue wall, casting its glow onto the dark wooden floor. Her imagination created a vision of tiny faeries dancing along with the dust particles as the little creatures nodded their heads in approval of what decorated the painted canvases, which stood on wooden displays to the sides of the room.

Alora moved over to the corner where the oversized painting frock that she used to cover her clothing hung. She pulled the paint-stained garment from its peg, pushing her arms through its sleeves. Once Alora secured the frock over herself, she strode over to the stool and canvas that stood on an easel in the middle of the room.

Upon a rectangular table rested a three-tiered paint box

filled with various bottles of colors, taking up the box's dimensions on the very bottom. Different-sized brushes lay in along the length of the middle tier, while a few blank palettes rested along the top shelf.

Before her was an empty canvas, and Alora wracked her brain for what to fill the blankness with. Portraits were popular, as were landscapes, but she really delighted in filling the white spaces with garden scenes where the vibrant colors could duel against each other as they fought for dominance in beauty.

Closing her eyes, Alora drew upon her memories, attempting to focus her mind on the last time she had strolled through the garden. She always enjoyed the garden, the climbing ivy that grew along the trellis, the flowers, the crisp scent of morning dew, and the buzz of bees flitting to and fro. And while Alora loved all of those things, she found her mind wandering back toward another pretty thing she'd seen once upon a time: Phillip. Alora's brow furrowed as she tried to think back to the flowers, to the perfect shade she would concoct to capture their beauty, but instead, her mind focused on Phillip's breathtaking eyes.

Mixing the pigments onto the palette and dipping the tip of her brush into the paint, Alora let her hand create what her mind told her to. Her hand flew from the paints to the canvas over and over again as her vision came to life. Standing before her were the beginnings of a pair of amber eyes set in a handsome face.

I seem to have depicted him just as he had been. No matter how long these memories haunt me, his face will always remain untouched upon the canvas.

What to do with it once she completed it was another question. Alora couldn't hang such a work of art anywhere, or she would be questioned about its subject. She didn't want to hide it away, but it would be safer hidden from the view of others. If it were discovered, how was she to explain who the subject was? Her father would inquire where she had come in contact with such a subject, and Alora couldn't stand the thought of another fib. Papa had denied them company, and while she had often shopped in their town, Phillip's otherworldly beauty didn't seem to fit in with the ordinary townspeople.

Alora would let the oil paints dry, and then she would hide it away with a sheet for protection with no one the wiser to its presence. Under her bed wasn't an option as the mice might chew on its edges. The clothing closet wasn't a better choice either. It was likely to be found by one of the maids and she would lose her treasure; then her father would demand an explanation. It wasn't as if she had clients... women of Alora's social standing weren't allowed to earn their own wages.

Alora spent most of the afternoon closeted in her painting room while more details came to life. At some point, Miss Prickett had invited herself in; it was customary for the lady to be by her side. While Alora lost herself in her art, her companion silently read a book while lounging on the one comfortable piece of furniture the room contained. Alora welcomed the silence and the unobtrusive manner of Miss Prickett, who never ventured close enough to spy what had so inspired Alora's paintbrush to fly across the canvas for the past few hours.

She wasn't sure what time it was, but as the light shifted in the room, Alora knew that she had been at it a while. Her stomach grumbled, pinching in protest when a knock rapped at her door.

"Come in!" she called, waiting for her visitor to poke their way into her room. The door creaked, followed by the appearance of a head of graying hair, as Mister Bingley, her family's butler, graced her with his presence. His nose crinkled with disdain as he said, "It's tea time, m'lady."

"I'm really very sorry, Mister Bingley, but I'm much too

busy. If you will please leave the tea cart, then I'm quite sure Miss Prickett will prepare her own refreshments. Thank you," Alora replied, unable to part from her work. She heard a shuffle and some muttering as the butler complied.

Miss Prickett sighed and set down her book before rising and going toward the tea cart. Alora allowed Miss Prickett to enjoy the fare by herself. And when Alora finally stepped away from the portrait, she was very pleased with her efforts. She had captured him in all his stunning beauty.

Looking at the chiming clock on her fireplace mantle, Alora noted it was almost time for dinner. She untied her painting frock, then pulled it off before returning it to its peg. When Miss Prickett arose, Alora walked over to her, and they linked arms as they exited the room.

"Did you enjoy your afternoon of painting?" Miss Prickett inquired as they walked through the corridor. They passed by potted palms, and landscapes that hung in gold frames.

"I did. Did you enjoy your novel?" Alora asked, flashing a smile at her.

"Very much. How the hero rescued the heroine was breathtaking. But I cannot keep myself from pointing out all the flaws in their characters." Miss Prickett shook her head.

"We can't all possess your brilliant reasoning. Do you suppose it would have been better were the hero the one in danger and in need of rescuing?" Alora bent forward to reach for the hemline of her dress so that she could easily ascend the staircase.

"Well, now, there's an intriguing idea. I believe that would make a spectacular plot," Miss Prickett hummed in approval. She drew up her own hem, and they climbed the staircase in amused silence.

They parted ways once they reached Alora's bedchamber. Alora watched as her companion gracefully walked to her own bedchamber, then Alora passed through the open door and entered her room. Her lady's maid greeted her.

While Alora unpinned her tresses, she glided over to her dressing table to lay the pins down one at a time. When her hair was falling down the middle of her back, she allowed Phoebe to help her undress and make her ready for the evening's entertainment. Alora scrubbed her skin with a damp cloth and dried herself before allowing Phoebe to help her don her evening attire.

Once Alora was dressed and her hair arranged high upon her head, she stood before her beloved looking glass. Caressing her face was one long curl on either side. Her midnight eyes were sparkling with excitement and anticipation.

I wonder what surprise Papa has to divulge to me. He has been hinting every evening this week that he is planning a surprise. And when he has been teasing me, I can almost forget his almost permanently frosty exterior.

After expressing her gratitude to her maid, Alora strolled from her bedchamber and through the corridor to the top of the staircase. She looked to either wall that surrounded her—neither boasted family portraits, which Alora had never found odd until she had visited the Holts's home. Their ancestors all competed for attention from the many elaborate frames that lined the walls. There were portraits in every room with family members in all manner of dress. But their home lacked such warmth of family affection, and it made her long to know who her family was.

Shaking herself from her thoughts, Alora descended the staircase and wandered the corridor until she entered the drawing room. Papa and Miss Prickett were already cozily seated in the room with the warmth of the fireplace to keep them company. Alora came further into the room, taking her seat on the gold-padded settee.

The drawing room was typically a cheerful room in the absence of her father, who always seemed to scowl too much. Now his presence seemed to bring a chill that made Alora uneasy, as she longed to see him happy. He was much too young to have given up on life, clinging to the ever-present sorrow that his wife's passing bestowed him with. He still had *her.* Wasn't she enough to garner an occasional smile?

Gold and cream decorated the lavish room. It had been her mother's favorite space within their home, as the garden could be viewed from the large bay windows. In the corner near the cream-colored fireplace stood her mother's rocking chair, forevermore empty and a tribute to the lost lady of the home. Alora's heart ached with a dull pang for the mother she'd lost. There was no cheer anymore, and there hadn't been since her mother's death.

An echo of footsteps clicked against the floor as Mister Bingley came into the room. "Dinner is served."

The trio rose silently, leaving the drawing room to traverse the corridor, passing lit wall sconces and hanging landscapes until they entered the dining room. The midnight-blue papered wall contained white daisies patterned across it. The oblong mahogany table and matching chairs were padded in a similar hue of blue while they rested atop an ornate Aubusson rug, which boasted braided scrollwork with bouquets along the border, while each corner featured a golden daisy.

Alora made her way to her place, where a dark, liveried footman pulled her chair back, and she moved to sit down. Removing her white gloves, she delicately draped them across her lap, then reached for the linen napkin, which Alora shook out and placed over her gloves.

Once her father and companion were seated and Papa had given the command to begin serving, the footman began with a white soup. Alora was seated to the right of her father while Miss Prickett sat upon his left.

Miss Prickett was silent and withdrawn, as was her normal routine. Her golden hair was caught up in a severe bun that pulled the skin around her brown eyes outward at their corners. The lady's dinner gown was unassuming with its plain brown material.

She looks rather mousy and dated. I will have to ask Papa for funds to spruce up her attire if we are to be entertaining and about in Society.

Her father, Mister Featherington, addressed Alora. "My dear, now that you are eighteen, you have reached the age where traveling the continents would do you much good. I have spoken at length with Miss Prickett, who has agreed to accompany us. Your education would be greatly enhanced with the painting masters in Italy." His midnight-blue eyes, which matched her own, locked onto her.

Alora felt caught within his inquisitive gaze. To be the focus of his attention made her feel uncomfortable, her palms turned clammy, and a tightness took root within her stomach. Alora was not used to so much of his notice when he was in a serious mood. She tried not to fidget in her seat when her thoughts took a drastic turn. Alora gasped, and goosebumps pebbled on her skin.

This was terrible news. How was she to leave England when Phillip would never be able to follow? Perhaps she was nothing more than a silly girl to still cling to the idea of him, but her heart would not allow her mind to forget him.

Alora loathed to leave when he might return any day. While a part of her had been thrilled that her father was endeavoring to set his grief aside and leave the home he had built with her mother, this was too much.

How did age change one's circumstances so much so that now she would be free to travel and meet with others? Her thoughts were swirling in her mind; she had no comment to give her father.

She looked over at Miss Prickett, who was spooning soup into her small mouth. Alora shook her head at herself. She knew her companion would not be of any assistance whatsoever in swaying her father in another direction.

"Are you not pleased, my dear?" he tilted his dark head to the side.

At times, it was difficult to believe that they were father and daughter as he did not look his age. They resemble more of a brother and his younger sister. The dark clothing he wore highlighted his masculine physique, which was not fashionable amongst his peers. Well-defined bodies were for laborers, not gentlemen of leisure and wealth.

But Phillip had also possessed muscles and brawn.

While her father was not titled, he was a man of business, and because of his good judgment in investments, he was quite wealthy. Papa preferred to remain on the outskirts of polite Society, only venturing into their sphere in order to conduct his business. However, now it seemed he was willing to brave Society's delights for her benefit. He must want to match Alora with a suitor.

"I hardly know my own thoughts, dear Papa," she told him with a delicate shrug of her shoulders.

"This would be good for us all. I am determined that this will happen and we will once again be happy," he admitted, grimacing.

"I am only now eighteen. Can we not wait another year?"

"No, that is something I fear we cannot do. We must embark, and soon," Papa said, and then took a drink from his wine goblet. Alora watched the sparkles shine across the walls as the light hit the glass.

"But, Papa-"

"You must learn your place!" he bellowed as rage twisted his handsome face.

Alora's body jumped in her seat from fright at his harsh command. She had never heard him raise his voice in such a manner before. Yes, he could be cold and distant, oftentimes verging upon cruel, but never loud. She felt mist prickle her eyes as her bottom lip quivered, proving that she was still a child to react in such a mulish manner.

"Yes, Papa," she whispered. When he looked away from her and down at his soup bowl, she ventured to ask, "May I be excused?" She didn't care about the meal or the elaborately decorated cake in her honor. Her throat tightened, threatening to choke Alora as she tried to swallow. More tears gathered in her eyes and there was an ache in her heart that she couldn't handle.

Everything was to change.

When Papa nodded his head without looking at her, Alora gracefully rose and set her napkin next to her untouched soup bowl. Clutching her gloves in her right hand, she curtsied to him and nodded to Miss Prickett, then softly padded from the dining room.

Once Alora reached the mahogany staircase, she ran up the steps and kept running until she reached the fourth floor, where the empty rooms and storage were located. Her feet took her to the room where her mother's rosewood trunks were stored. Alora fell down onto her knees, wincing as pain lanced its way through her kneecaps. She threw her chest against the nearest trunk as her arms encircled it. Alora finally allowed the tears to fall as her heart squeezed painfully in her chest at the longing for her mother and the soothing words her ears would have heard. Papa had become a haunted man, and Mama leaving them ensured nothing would ever be the same again; their world had forever been torn asunder.

Tears dropped from her eyes onto the wooden trunk, taking the dust with them to collect onto her dress, forever marring its beauty. After all this time, her father wanted to move on, and she wasn't ready to say goodbye to all that she knew. She let her fears and anxieties pour from her and was exhausted by the time the last teardrop fell.

Alora straightened up, wiping at her cheeks. She was nothing but a shell, a husk of the girl she'd once been. She'd lost so much already, and it was hard to imagine what Alora had to gain from the coming changes when she had no control over what was to come.

From her peripheral vision, Alora caught sight of a dim, glowing, turquoise orb that grew brighter as the moments passed. Sparkles of dust twirled within the light that landed upon a curious wooden machine. It was made up of a wheel that rested atop a base with some sort of pointed tip. Alora's eyes widened. Her heart thundered in her chest as she felt a tug toward the orb. Pushing to her feet, she dusted the dirt from her skirts and slowly walked forward. As Alora neared it, she reached out her right hand, taking an index finger, and spun the wheel.

How have I never noticed this curious device before? What does it do?

"Touch the spindle, the pointed bit, child. That's it, just a bit closer," a disembodied voice commanded her in a hushed whisper.

Alora looked around herself, trying to discern from where the voice had come, but her gaze returned to the contraption. What harm could come from touching it? Her inner voice cautioned her not to. But what harm could possibly befall her, and what else did she have to lose?

"I know you are curious; it's written all over your face. Touch the spindle!" The voice commanded her again, a bit louder this time with a hint of impatient cruelty.

Alora lifted her hand and reached it toward the machine. She felt tingling and tightening throughout her body. She longed to touch the spindle. It was so shiny and glinted in the glowing light. Her index finger was so close to it. Alora watched her finger and hesitated.

"Touch it, I say!" screeched the malevolent voice.

With her heart thundering in her chest and her breaths shallow, Alora reached out her finger and pricked it upon the spindle. The instantaneous searing of the prick made her withdraw her hand and cradle it to her chest. She watched one crimson drop of blood fall from her finger onto the wooden floor. With a gasp, Alora fell as everything went black; her ringing ears could faintly make out the cawing of a raven and cackling laughter before a deep weariness overcame her as her brain became foggy. Attempting to blink her eyes, Alora only succeeded in closing them to the chasm of darkness that welcomed her and the cold embrace that stole her breath away.

3

WAKING UP AMIDST THE RESISTANCE

With a startled gasp, Alora awoke. She moved slightly upon the bed, rubbing the sleep from her weary eyes. Alora turned her head to the side and realized she was not actually in her bedchamber at all.

The walls were made of mud and brick. Lit lanterns hung from pegs that stuck out from the walls. The flames that danced within them burnt a turquoise color. While it was beautiful and mesmerizing to behold, the fire felt wrong to her, deadly. Something about the flame seemed to be malicious, but wasn't all fire destructive?

Off to the side was a screened-off partition, which she assumed to be a dressing area. A rosewood cabinet stood sentry and alone in one corner. There were no other furnishings in the tiny room except for the chair in which her father sat wearily watching her.

Alora peered intently at him as she tried to suppress her rising panic. Her chest was constricting while her throat felt as if it was closing. She blinked twice, but her eyes still showed pointed tips on her father's ears. The reality was too much for Alora's mind to grasp, so she pushed the unsettling discovery to the very back of her brain, resolving that if she were to panic, it would have to come later. Hadn't Phillip had pointed ears, too?

Thoughts of her birthday flooded her racing mind. The voice and the wooden machine...and the single drop of blood. Hadn't there been something else that had stood out?

The nightmares of the past three nights crept into her senses, taunting her and ramping up her fear. She felt the blood drain from her head as she recalled death, destruction, chaos, and flames. For three nights, Alora had been unable to wake herself no matter what horror played out for her to witness; each was writhing in her memories. With focused determination, she pulled herself back to the present as the crackle of fire slowly faded from her ears.

Alora reached a tentative hand up to brush against the top of one of her ears and sighed when she didn't detect a pointed tip.

At least I am still me.

"My dearest, I have failed you. I beg for you to forgive me. I was meant to outwit this curse, but I didn't fully understand its timing. I knew the Lunar Queen meant for her spell to kill you, but because she was so far away from her Court, I counted on her powers to be less than what they were. While death has not taken you away, you die a little each night with the nightmares. While your body lays in slumber, another form roams, and it's as if a physical double of you manifests. You can be hurt or even killed while your mind takes you along the journey into Wonderland and you greet its residents. That is her malediction, not a swift death as she had wished, but unending nightmares and the demise they bring for you to witness," her father hung his head in despair, unwilling to meet her gaze.

Alora surmised he couldn't fathom the idea of her dying each time she slumbered; the idea made her head spin, and she told herself to add that to her growing list of things to think about later.

"Where are we? How did we come to be here?" Alora inquired, her voice quavering.

Her father finally looked up, but instead of meeting her gaze, he looked at a spot on the wall beside her. "They call it Wonderland, for it is both wondrous and fierce. It's located in the Lunar Court, which resides in the realm of the faeries," he said as his tear-swollen eyes finally met hers.

Alora chortled; she couldn't stem the laughter that bubbled forth like a gurgling water fountain.

Wonderland? Faeries?

And then her laughter died out. Had she not wondered if Phillip was a faerie?

Is he perhaps in this Wonderland?

"I slept for three nights straight through?"

"Indeed. Nothing would wake you. Nothing, except the Faeriedust that the elf, Cormack, concocted for you. That is what finally brought you back to me."

"What of our home? Our servants? Miss Prickett? Wildflower?" Alora asked, as alarm and dread zapped along her nerve endings; horror was holding her heart within its ever-tightening grasp.

She had dreamed on the first night of an inky black dragon with razor-sharp teeth and menacing turquoise eyes. Bright turquoise flames had poured forth from its gaping maw, turning their home to nothing more than glowing cinders. Everything within its wake was destroyed.

Alora didn't want her mind to imagine what misery and fright their human servants must have endured during their final moments. And the innocent animals! Her beloved horse! The raven! They were nothing more than ashes now. What a cruel twist of fate. Did no trinket of her mother's remain? How was Alora to remember Mama without a portrait, without her precious books? She didn't want to forget her or any of those who had perished, either. Feeling like weeping, her body grew numb and icy with shock. Alora swallowed the lump of grief left in her throat and let her emotions take root. She knew that she wanted to cry for the loss of her friends and possessions, but her eyes refused to shed even a single tear.

"All gone. It's all gone now. Nothing remains, and there is nothing left to return to either." Aching despair filled her father's voice as he covered his face with his hands.

"But... it was just a dream..." Her whispered words implored her father to retract his statements even though she knew he was telling Alora the truth.

Lowering his hands, Papa replied, "You are alive, and we shall end this. We just need to figure out how to break this curse."

"Why? Why would someone hate me so much as to *curse* me? To kill those who were innocent bystanders residing on the estate? What could I have ever done to another to cause them to despise me? To enact vengeance to all I know?" Alora felt brittle as if she were made of porcelain, which was breaking apart into a million tiny pieces that she felt would never be able to be put back together again.

"No, no, no, my darling daughter! You misunderstand me! The servants and the livestock were not harmed. Once I had you settled into your bed, I sent them all away. Unfortunately, this has very little to do with you. It's all my fault. I dared to defy the wishes of a queen, and your death was her ultimate punishment for my disloyalty."

"When did she curse me? How long have you known of it?" Alora rubbed a hand over her wounded chest.

Her heart was warring with itself. Agony consumed half of Alora's being for what had taken place, but the other half of her was relieved those on the estate had not met their fiery end.

"Since your christening. I was banished from the Lunar Court where we currently are right now. Well, actually, we're below it in the hidden depth of the Lunar Court's Resistance.

But I digress since you were but a tiny babe. She cursed you at your christening. It was to be a day that brought your Mama and I such joy, and it was ruined within the blink of an eye. You cannot understand how guilty I have felt all these years, knowing what awaited you; at the will of my mother. I think that the curse slowly broke your mama's heart until one day, it just stopped beating. *It's all my fault.*" Papa bent forward as great wracking sobs shook his large frame.

Alora threw back her coverlet and was at his side in an instant. She held onto his shoulders as his tears fell. The scene before Alora latched onto her heart with vicious teeth; she wondered why her eyes couldn't summon tears.

Alora let her thoughts wander to all he had revealed to her.

A curse, an evil queen, banishment, an elf, and a resistance. Not to mention that they were in the midst of a dangerous rebellion, if that is truly what the Resistance was. There was nothing to panic over, just an ordinary English girl in the land of Faerie whose nightmares came true and whose father had pointed ears! A grandmother who desired her death wouldn't be forgotten, either; that was worth remembering. She recalled her dreams of the second night.

Large toads had leaped about with sickly-colored bile, destroying the fields that covered the estate. Little beings with pointed ears and gossamer wings carried pitchforks and slaughtered what was left of the wildlife that had made their homes upon the estate.

A chill crept up Alora's spine that made her shiver as emptiness hollowed out her bones.

Her mind remembered the third night. Aid came in the form of three knights who wore white armor. Alora was never able to view more of their faces than their eyes through the slits of their helmets.

"Vile creatures! Prepare to be vanquished!" bellowed one of the white knights as he brandished his sword in the air. With a mighty battle cry, he charged into the fray with the other two knights by his

side. They had battled back the winged faeries that sought to wound her with their tiny axes.

When they had slain their foes, the knights turned toward Alora and sprinkled her with golden-colored faeriedust. Her brows drew together as her skin began to glow. Her eyes met the eyes of one of the knights, who gave her a teasing wink.

Her dream began to lose some of its darkness. As the dream shifted, Alora dreamed of talking flowers and luminous mushrooms.

"Eat me!" begged a daisy, who wrung its leafed hands toward her.

"No, she has a bitter taste. It's me you want to nibble," boasted a gold and orchid pansy.

"She needs a bit of height to her frame. Everyone knows that a mushroom is just right for what ails you. Come and have a bite!" entreated the white and red mushroom with an evil gleam in its beady black eyes.

The talking flora and fauna had been strange but not frightening. Alora had settled down next to the chattering oddities, who spouted complete nonsense, and soon, her mind had carried her away.

Alora shook herself, bringing her attention back to the little bedchamber. This was a new world for her with unexpected creatures. While her heart hurt for her father, Papa's tears were exhaustive to behold.

Finally, when her father's tears were spent, he withdrew his handkerchief from his waistcoat pocket and blew his nose. When he was finished, he folded the linen and tucked it back into his pocket, then straightened himself.

Alora pulled away from him, giving him space. She longed to let the brokenness of her heart out, but her whole existence now was about survival. Alora didn't have time for tears, which would do her no good.

A knock sounded at the door. It opened without a moment's hesitation. In walked the three white knights from her dream. Alora's eyes widened in astonishment.

It was all real!

While she understood that fact before, faced with the truth before her now, her mind still seemed to be playing a game of catch-up.

The trio was dressed all in white; even their boots were the same shade. They had removed their helmets, and she was finally able to view their faces. Excitement danced along her spine as they swept into eloquent bows and then straightened back to their impressive heights. Each was golden-blond with striking bottle-green eyes. However, the first faerie had a tail that ended with a blond tuft of hair that was swinging back and forth. The second and third knights had horns placed on both sides of their heads. It wasn't kindness that shone from them when they gazed at her; it was respect mixed with wonder.

Alora felt as if she'd been swept up in a tidal wave as surprise washed over her.

"It is good to see you awake," Knight Number One addressed her.

"Thank you," she told him.

"We were glad to be of service to you and your father," Knight Number Two said.

"And now that you are awake, everything changes," the third knight added with a grin and a wink.

Heat flooded Alora's cheeks, creeping from her neck into her face. "Good changes? I hope."

"Changes, who can say whether they will be for the good or the bad?" asked a voice belonging to a shorter male who entered the room.

Since there wasn't much standing space, the visitors all stood shoulder-to-shoulder, except the shortest one, who came up to the stomach of the knights. He was dressed in brown from his trousers to his shirt and waistcoat with fuzzy eyebrows that resembled little caterpillars. Alora shivered with disgust, which she hurriedly pushed away because she didn't want unkind thoughts swirling around in her head.

"Don't frighten her, you old elf," admonished Knight Number Three.

Scratching his pointed ear and wiggling his bulbous nose, the elf huffed. "I'm not frightening her!"

"Alora, I should introduce these faeries to you. The elf is Cormack; the knights are Theodore, Theolf, and Remius. The knights lead the Resistance," Papa informed her.

"How did we actually get to be here?" she ventured to ask.

"We sprinkled you in Faeriedust that made your body float up from your bed. Your father held onto your hand, and together, we traveled to the realm of the faeries through the looking glass. It didn't take but a few hours, and we were here," Remius, the third knight, told her with another flirtatious wink.

"How did no one see us?" Alora tilted her head to the side in curiosity.

"A glamour, of course. Theo here is quite gifted, and honestly, it's quite easy to glamour oneself from the human eye," Knight Number Two, Theolf, replied.

"Ash rained down on us for two nights. By the third, I had begun to give up hope when the nightmares began again. But these knights rushed in and saved us. I couldn't battle and keep you safe, so I chose to remain vigilant over your bedside while the little bits of magic that still resided within me kept us safe." Her father took her hand in his and squeezed it. She had not seen this tender side of him since before her mother had died, and Alora wasn't sure what to think or how to feel.

"We should introduce you to the other Resistance members. They are all curious about you. And curious faeries that suffer from madness are never quiet for long. They shall soon become unruly, so what do you say, Princess? Are you ready to meet your subjects?" Theodore, who seemed to be the leader, awaited her response.

"Princess?" she questioned, furrowing her brows.

"Did you not know?" Remius raised his brows in astonishment.

"Of course not, you imbecile! She knows nothing of our world," Theolf scoffed at him.

"Boys," cautioned her father. "Let's not overwhelm her. We shall let her bathe and be ready to meet the Resistance."

"But, of course, Your Majesty!" Theodore bowed to him, and the other faeries followed suit. When they straightened, they bowed to Alora, to which she curtsied.

Remius cleared his throat and informed her, "Princesses don't bow to the rabble." The teasing glint in his eye nearly made her blush again. Alora wondered what was wrong with her and why it was that she couldn't seem to look away from him.

After that, the male Fae left the room, leaving Alora bedazzled and dazed. She couldn't wait to see where her part lay within this new world. But first, it was time to prepare herself and guard her heart for what was to come in this curious new realm.

4

FATE AWAITS

Alora gazed into the looking glass and touched her cheek. Her skin was soft beneath her fingertips, her skin was glowing, giving her an ethereal glow. Alora noticed her midnight-blue eyes were timidly looking back at her and were brighter. Small changes, and yet, to her, these were astounding. Was being in this new land affecting her appearance?

Alora's eyes widened when she thought, *Shall I gain a tail or horns? I think I would much rather have a tail. I could hide it away. Did all faeries have such a trait, even while looking human?*

She reached behind her and, with the back of her hand, assured herself that, as of the moment, no tail had formed. Alora's shoulders slumped as she sighed.

"You look beautiful, just like a Princess should," her father said as he softly closed the door behind himself. He came to stand behind her, and they both looked at their reflections within the looking glass.

Alora's eyes traveled to her father's pointed ears. When he noticed her staring, he wryly smiled.

"Yes, they do look different, do they not? I have grown

accustomed to not seeing them. But it is good to have them back," he said.

"Was Mama like you? I mean, was she too a.... a-"

"Faerie?" Papa prompted.

Alora nodded.

"No. I met her sometime after my banishment. She was the first joy I experienced in my new existence. She was like the sun, always shining and bright, casting warmth to all she beheld. Despite myself, I was drawn to her. She reasoned that I was not from her realm, but she never shied away from me. Instead, she grew to love me as I did her. Your mother was the other half of my soul. You only ever get one. She was mine. And for a time, much too brief as it was, we were happy. Once you were born and those pointed tips did not grace your ears, I thought perhaps we could live happily-ever-after. But it was not to be." Papa smiled softly at her.

"So I am half-faerie."

"Yes, but the magic that flows through your veins is quite a powerful force, and now we must teach you to wield it."

"If I am a princess, then that makes you what?" Alora's brows rose in question.

"I, too, am a Prince of Faerie, but the Resistance insists I am their king. My mother stole the throne; she is the Lunar Queen. The Lunar Court was not to pass to her but to her sister, who is the eldest. Then, there is the fact that my mother was not the natural child of the late king and queen. She allowed bitterness and jealousy into her heart, and it ate away all of the good that ever was, never believing she was equally beloved by either her parents or the kingdom."

"How tragic and so very sad," she mused.

To never feel as if she belonged...

"Those in the Resistance are hopeful that we can dethrone my mother and then place one of us upon that throne." There was little emotion present in her father's words.

Alora turned from the looking glass to face her father.

"But if she took it unjustly, wouldn't her elder sister take it back?"

"I have been informed that she doesn't wish to. There have been great losses on both sides of this great divide, which have saddened her. A ruler must be whole to sit upon a throne of one of the Faerie Courts, or the land will suffer. That is why this land is withering into darkness and despair; my mother's heart has turned to ash. The kingdom is infected with a blight like none before it. We must find a way to cure you and free the people and the land." Papa's fingers were soft as he cupped her cheek with one of his hands. Alora couldn't help but notice his fingers were longer now.

"Will you take the throne for yourself then?"

"I will do what is right when the time comes. In my absence, much has changed. A cleave has occurred, dividing the symbiosis into two separate kingdoms. The White Kingdom fights with the help of the Resistance. The White Queen rules for now, but she is searching for her champion who will save us all. We must offer our aid and do what we can to bring order to these lands once again. For the good of both kingdoms."

"No pressure there to succeed. What if everyone fails?" Alora felt anxious and twisted her fingers together.

"We must not," he simply said.

A tap sounded on the door, and it opened a sliver. From the slight opening, Alora spied a set of purple eyes and an elongated white face.

"Ah, here is Fate. He will be your guide and protector. He was born to serve our family and has chosen to pair with you," Papa said as he opened the door wider.

A white stallion with a pointed horn on its forehead and large wings that looked fluffy and soft stood magnificently before them. Alora was tempted to reach out just to touch one of the downy feathers. His mane was a glittering silver, as was his swishing tail. Bright eyes gazed back at her. Bending his right foreleg, he gracefully bowed before them.

"Your Majesty, Your Highness. I have waited ages to serve you. I am pleased that you are home at long last." The alicorn rose to its full height and tossed his head.

Alora's grin spread across her face as she cautiously approached her protector.

"May I touch you?" she whispered reverently.

"Of course. You may even ride me on occasion. You cannot traverse all of Wonderland yourself. My horn is yours to slay enemies with, my hooves are yours to fight or flee with, my knowledge is yours to guide you, and my wings are yours to soar however high you wish." Fate gave a whinny.

"Thank you," she said as she reached a hand out to touch his velvety nose. Alora delightfully laughed when he nuzzled her fingers, nipping at them playfully. Fate nodded his head to her. Memories of Wildflower flew through her mind, and Alora's smile withered, then died.

Wildflower! Will I never see my beloved horse again?

Alora was attempting to rein in the unanticipated sorrow that seized her lungs, threatening to suffocate her. Her father seemed to notice her struggle because he addressed her.

"We should meet with the others here. Come along, my dear; Fate awaits." Papa said as he closed the distance between them. He placed a hand against the small of her back. Alora drew comfort from the solid warmth of his hand. Taking a deep breath, she grabbed her skirts and shook out her dress. The unneeded action helped to soothe her fraying nerves.

After bathing, Alora's hair had been brushed out and twisted up with little curled tendrils left to caress her cheeks.

She had slipped into a day dress in royal blue that had golden flowers and vines sewn into its material. A gold, braided ribbon rested under Alora's bosom, which gave her high waist added elegance. Her matching slippers were comfortable.

The maid who had assisted Alora in getting ready possessed gossamer wings that reflected the lights and skin the color of amethyst. Alora had done an impressive undertaking of not ogling her maid while she was helped into the latest ladies' fashions from England.

Alora kept her thoughts and opinion to herself. She worried that she had verged upon the side of rudeness and hoped that, in time, she could present a more pleasant and gracious manner.

Allowing her father to take her arm, they exited the small bedchamber. Alora felt her heartbeat accelerate as her steps took her into a world where dreams and nightmares were created.

5

FAERIES, TROLLS AND ELVES, OH MY!

Alora and her father shadowed after Fate, who surprisingly fit in the small, dank hallways that were scented of stale air and earth. There were more black lanterns lit with the strange rippling turquoise flame. After nearly endless twists in different directions, they finally reached the glow of a large room.

It took Alora a moment for her eyes to adjust to the brighter lights. She gasped when she spied the various beings, with both pale and brilliant skin tones, that lingered in the dim corners or sat before large wooden tables with bench seats to match. Alora's eyes roamed over the tips of horns and pointed ears, over large and smaller features and imposing and petite frames. More than one tail could be seen twitching back and forth, and some of their owners seemed more human than not.

Her gaze settled on the White Knights, who were conversing with what looked to be a troll at a longer table that stood set apart from the others toward the back of the room. The troll's green body was muscled; he wore only moth-eaten brown trousers which were aged from use. The knights didn't seem to be in any danger, as no one was even looking over at them or the troll. Alora closed her mouth and swallowed, allowing her father to pull her into the dining hall.

Good gracious! Such odd creatures…

Hanging from the high ceiling were black chandeliers with silver stars dusting them. They seemed to be made from some stone, but she wasn't certain as she didn't know what materials they mined in the Lunar Court.

It was a simple room, large enough, she imagined, to house an army. Along the back wall stood a fireplace created from the same shining black of the chandeliers, with a dancing blaze housed within. Plates of foodstuffs in exotic and drab colors were set before some of those who were seated. Savory and sweet mixed together to permeate the air with a delicious aroma.

Alora felt her stomach rumble and realized she was famished. She placed a hand over her stomach, hoping others couldn't hear its unhappy grumbles.

Fate led them, weaving between the rows of tables to the large table at the back of the chamber, and stopped. Once her father halted their steps beside the table, the trio of knights looked up. Remius bolted from his seat to stand before them and cast a roguish smile toward Alora.

"What a vision you are, my Princess," said Remius, bowing before her and her father.

The other knights followed his action, each gaining their feet at a more sedate pace, but she noted the troll did not stand to greet them.

"Thank you, kind sir," she said, pleased at the attention.

"We are discussing an attack on the southern border," Theodore informed them with a heavy frown as his tail peeked from behind him.

"I want to know all about it, gentle-faeries," her father stated. He gestured to the bench, and Alora took a seat on it. "We shall discuss this over a meal. Alora hasn't eaten anything yet."

Alora was flustered and tried to stem the rising blush; she was ravenous but disliked being the center of attention, especially when bodily needs were spoken about. If she were a princess, she must become accustomed to unwanted attention and keeping to the shadows while simply observing was no longer a choice. There were worse fates than receiving unwanted notice, such as death, which was a final ending to all unfulfilled dreams, or even villainous fire-breathing dragons who could melt the flesh from one's bones.

Theodore's hand rose into the air, signaling to a female faerie who wore a torn and stained apron. She nodded her head and then scurried away through an opening in the mud wall, which Alora had not spotted before. *How curious.*

The White Knights sat on the other side of the table while Alora took her seat beside the troll. When his hulking form shifted on the bench, the wood groaned in protest under him.

I do hope this can hold our combined weight, for I should not enjoy ending up either squished like a bug or ending up in his lap.

Thankfully, Alora's father took the empty space on the other side of her. Fate came to stand sentry at her back. Alora's nose wrinkled as the scent of stale sweat and rotting onions filled her nostrils. Bile rose up her throat as Alora desperately tried not to gag. She hoped the troll's manners were better than his stench.

The crashing of china cups brought the dining hall's attention to the chipped pieces that now lay on the dirt-packed floor. An eerily haunting voice sang out, "Welcome to Wonderland! Where the Lunar Queen will greet you with red-stained hands, and the villagers will dance until they die. A place of both dreams and nightmares where we're all touched a bit by the stinging bite of madness."

Alora located the voice, which belonged to an elf who was swaying in his chair, completely three sheets to the wind. His pointed ears were jagged, bearing raised scars. A red beard covered the lower half of his face while his clothing was torn and stained with either blood or mud, and he was shoeless.

The dining hall remained quiet after the outburst as a heaviness laid thickly in the ether. Looking around, Alora noticed no other creature seemed to be alarmed by such a spectacle; instead, they all seemed to be weighted down, lost in their own thoughts.

With determination, Alora turned her attention away from the elf and faced forward. Theodore caught her gaze, and he cleared his throat.

"Princess Alora, you have not yet been introduced to our newest member, Ickburt," Theodore nodded at the troll, drawing her attention back to their prior conversation.

She looked to her side and had to tilt her head up and up. Ickburt was massive. Up close, he was even more so, resembling a small mountain. He had substantial bulbous warts along his nose and forehead. His green eyes were studying her carefully. Alora forced a smile upon her face. Ickburt spread his lips apart and bared his yellow, sharp, pointed teeth at her.

"How lovely to meet you, Ickburt. What a charming… smile you have." Alora stated, thinking of the lessons of deportment Miss Prickett had drilled into her.

Miss Prickett… How odd she would have found all this.

Alora's heart gave a painful squeeze, reminding her that she'd never again get to discuss anything with her former governess.

"Thank you, Princess. What lovely… skin you have. Pale and thoroughly appetizing," his teeth clicked together.

Alora frowned, then looked away. What was there to say to his response anyway? "Thank you" didn't quite seem appropriate.

The serving faerie returned and placed black goblets with those same shining silver stars in front of each of them. Inside was a dark red liquid that smelled of ripened fruit and picked flowers. Alora gingerly lifted the goblet to her lips and took a small sip. The flavor exploded on her tongue. It was sweet and a bit tart, nothing like Alora had ever tasted before.

Perhaps it's faerie wine! How charming!

She was happy to make a new discovery.

"Do be a gentle-faerie, Ickburt. No salivating upon the Princess," commanded Theodore.

"I understand what her loveliness does to a faerie," Remius said as he gave her a slow wink and raised his goblet to her.

"You must take care, Princess. There are many here who would win your hand through dubious means," Theolf said, finally speaking up.

"Dubious means?" Alora questioned.

"Flirting, tricking, enticing, compelling, kidnapping...," Theolf said as he ticked off each one with his fingers.

"That is quite enough. We do not need to frighten her," spoke her father with heavy disapproval lining his words.

"True, Your Majesty, but she does need to know certain things so she can guard against them," cautioned Theodore as his brows furrowed.

"That is what I am here for!" huffed Fate, stomping his hoof in indignation.

"Yes, of course. But you cannot very well never leave her side," her father placatingly said.

"It's a good idea to have her informed," agreed Remius. "I volunteer to teach her!" His bottle-green eyes twinkled at her.

"You mean to say that you volunteer to seduce her," scoffed Theolf as he rolled his eyes.

Bringing his hand up to his heart and fixing his face into a look of sincerity, Remius said, "You wound me! I am a gentle-faerie! She is our princess; it is our duty to protect her. I will lay down my life to do so."

"As would we all," agreed Theolf as he tilted his blond head to the side.

"Surely, with everyone about all the time, I should have no need to fear," Alora replied with what she hoped sounded like a sweet tone.

"He's entirely correct," sighed her father. Alora spied the dark shadows under his eyes and the tired set of his jaw.

He has lost so much. I hope he gains while here in this unbelievable world.

The serving faerie returned with steaming bowls of a dark stew. Alora thanked her once she set the bowl down before her. Alora took in every feature the lady possessed, from her violet eyes to her long, flowing pale pink hair. Her dress was not the current fashion of empire-waisted but of England twenty years ago with its large skirts. The serving maid had tipped fingers ending in black talons but no other feature stood out as inhuman.

"I think we should employ a faerie that would never seek to woo Alora. Indeed, while he might like to offer the odd treat or cruel remark, he would never harm her," Theodore remarked and stroked his chin in thought.

"Oh, you can't be serious!" groused Remius.

"He means the tabby," Ickburt said as he brought the soup bowl to his thick lips and poured the contents into his wide mouth. When he was finished, he lowered the bowl, then used his forearm to wipe his lips.

Alora tried not to notice the drool that came away and clung to the troll's forearm. She directed her attention to the bowl before her. Alora swirled her spoon around in her dark soup, desperately attempting to retain her appetite, wanting to be absolutely certain what she was about to eat would not be something unsavory.

"Tabby…oh, you mean–" began Theolf.

"Are you certain that is the wisest choice?" Remius interrupted.

"I do indeed," Theodore spoke with resolute finality.

"I think if you say this is the best way forward, then we

should proceed," agreed her father. He was eagerly taking sips of his soup from the spoon. "Eat now, dearest; it will not harm you."

Alora softly smiled at her father and began to eat her soup. It was similar to a French onion, but it was much sweeter and had little pale yellow mushrooms diced into bits. It was delicious! While her attention was fixed on her meal, the discussion turned to the attack on the southern border.

"It was nearly as horrific as the Battle of the Slain. We have recovered those we could, but there were so many bodies that we couldn't be certain whether we rescued all of the living," Theodore commented with a heavy-hearted sigh.

"With the injuries sustained, one who was living would not have done so for long," Theolf agreed.

"That is good. I can't imagine dying after hours of languishing in that horror," her father added while he shook his dark head.

"Here comes Cormack; perhaps he'll have more news," noted Theolf.

When the little elf had seated himself next to Remius, he said, "Sad tidings, my fellows. We have lost another soul."

"Who was it this time?" queried Theodore.

"Danvers. He fought for a while, and then his heart gave out," explained Cormack.

"We're losing all our best. This cannot continue. Soon, there will be no faerie worth saving this cursed kingdom for," Remius said as he bowed his blond head.

"We have what we need now to save us all," Theolf said quietly, looking at both Alora and her father.

Alora felt the weight of his words settle upon her shoulders. What was a mere half-human girl to do that could possibly turn the tide of war in their favor? She didn't want to injure others, taking up a sword, and she didn't want to willingly choose whom to sacrifice should the need arise. Alora trusted her father to know what to do, but with Papa's absence from the Court being such a long one, she knew he was just as much in the dark as she was.

Musical notes floated through the air toward them. A faerie with horns like a ram and dressed in burgundy trousers and a fitted tailcoat was playing a lute. His ebony hair was styled short, and a lock of hair kept falling into his pale blue eyes. Another faerie joined in and began to strum a mandolin. She was petite and dressed in a saffron day dress. Her blonde hair hung in ringlets. The odd Fae characteristic that revealed her to be of faerie descent was her pert, little, round pig nose. It looked odd against the other softer features of her face.

She made her eyes move away; Alora didn't want to be impolite. The few faeries who were in the dining hall paired up and began to twirl and dance around the room. It was as though there was an unnerving mania about their wild, unhindered abandon, and Alora found herself unsure whether to applaud their gaiety or mourn for the desperation that colored their antics.

Alora slowly took in all the dancers. A few were so very human in appearance, but there was always one stark animal feature that gave their race away. Each being must have a Fae characteristic, some hidden and some on full display. Alora couldn't wait to learn more from whoever the tabby was because her list of questions was quickly growing.

"Would you care to dance, my Princess," inquired Remius from across the table.

Looking at her father for guidance, Alora smiled when he nodded his approval to her. Alora addressed Remius. "Why, yes, Sir Remius."

Remius stood from the bench and made his way over to stand behind her. Fate eyed him suspiciously, then moved aside for Alora to rise. Remius held out his hand for her to take. Alora reached over to take his ungloved hand as he assisted her from the bench.

Seems as if wearing gloves is out of fashion in Faerie. How curious.

Giving her a wicked smile, Remius led her to a space of mud-packed floor off to the side and away from the other dancers. Bringing their clasped hands high into the air, he began to twirl her about. Alora shrieked with laughter as Remius smiled brightly at her. There was a frantic madness within the musical notes that urged Alora to continue dancing; she never wanted to stop. She wondered if she were being compelled and if she would be able to stop, or if she would have to be stopped.

Alora's body felt light, as dragonflies zipped along the inside of her stomach from the intense focus her dance partner lavished on her. Remius seemed to be looking at Alora as if she were something precious and delightful to behold. Her heart longed to bask in his warmth, but something else niggled its way into her mind. A beautiful smile and amber eyes virtually made her stumble as she twirled around Remius, but his strong and capable hands steadied her. Thoughts of Phillip were intruding, commanding her attention and filling the empty spaces between where she and Remius were not touching.

Breaking away from Remius's smoldering eyes, Alora observed the other dancers. It was necessary to break this spell…this living dream…because she couldn't allow herself to entertain thoughts of another when her heart longed for the one who was so deeply embedded into her soul. Even though the one that was holding her now called to her almost as deeply as Phillip had.

One of her fellow dancers bore the head of a boar with menacing tusks protruding from the top of his mouth. His body was lean and seemed to be more human than not. He danced with a lady faerie, who wore a flowing white gown that sparkled and shimmered. She looked human if one did not notice her owlish eyes, which were too large for her face.

Another couple was composed of a male elf dressed all in teal, spinning in circles with a smaller faerie who wore a dress that looked as if it was made from sunflower petals. Could that really be petals? Anything must be possible in the Faerie Realm.

Recollections of the fairytales Mama had read to her began to flood her memory. There were always princesses in need of rescuing and princes who saved the day. Along with the evil doers who drove the plot, there had always been a peppering of sage advice: dos and don'ts for surviving the Faerie Realm.

Given their current situation, it was a good idea to brush up on those timeless tales in order to survive whatever awaited them. What if the authors of such tales were simply recording more truths than employing wild imaginings? Could those tales really have existed even if there were a sprinkling of embellishments along the way?

Alora felt goosebumps alight along her skin even though she was warm from dancing.

How sinister a part to play will I have to embrace? Can I survive in a world gone mad?

6

THE TABBY

With sore feet and swirling thoughts, Alora was escorted back to her chamber by her champion, Fate. The two traversed the hallway in the direction from which they had come just a few hours ago.

Alora had danced with several faeries who alternated between twirling her around and pulling her along in their different dance steps. Not every partner had received instruction in the popular mode of dance in London, so Alora found herself floundering to match their steps. But to the true credit of the faerie race, Alora's blundering didn't really matter as long as she was attempting to enjoy herself, which she had. She hadn't gone back to partner Remius and considered that was for the best. There was something strange lingering between them, and with the complete upheaval of her entire world, Alora didn't have the capacity to explore what that could mean for her.

Stifling a yawn behind her hand, Alora felt the pull of sleep drawing her further into its clutches. She wanted to fall into a deep slumber but dreaded what nightmares sleep would bring to her. There was, of course, the macabre thought that Alora died a little each time she slumbered.

Fate halted in front of her door and bowed his head. "There is an enchantment upon your door, ordered by your father. It will be invisible to those who hold malice within their hearts. You will be safe. Cormack left you a dose of Faeriedust so you may sleep soundly tonight. We don't have an endless supply of the potion, but for now, you should use it. Never fear; I will be guarding your door."

"Thank you, Fate. Don't you need to rest as well?"

"I can sleep standing up, all equines do, you know. And as I am a light sleeper, you really have no need to worry."

Alora opened her door and then peered inside. Turning back to Fate, she smiled before walking into the small chamber.

When she closed the door behind her, Alora took the few steps needed to reach the bed. There on her pillow rested a tiny glass bottle stopped with a cork. Alora reached for it and picked it up, shaking the golden dust within. Swirls of glittering light emanated the bottle. The tiny grains of dust seemed to perk to life with her movements.

"'Tis really remarkable, is it not, Curious One?" purred a feline-sounding voice from behind her.

Alora clumsily dropped the bottle, which landed on the bed, then craned her neck to look over her shoulder.

"If I were you, I would use more care with my things, especially potions and things that reside within glass bottles. Have you no sense of what a vial of Faeriedust that size costs? The lengths one has to go to create it isn't an easy feat either. I shudder to think of it."

Alora glanced around the chamber until she spied a lime-green, striped cat with cream-colored fur, raising a furry brow at her.

Is he scowling at me? Wait one minute… Could this be the tabby that was suggested as my tutor?

The cat lifted one front paw and proceeded to bathe from his perch on the bed. His pink tongue got caught on a tuft of hair that was peeking from between his pale, pink-padded toes. The tabby gave a fierce tug; then, his tongue was freed. Alora blinked and realized he was awaiting her reply. Arranging her scattered thoughts, she finally answered him.

"I don't have any idea of the costs of anything within this realm."

"An oversight, to be sure. One that we must rectify. For if I am to bear some responsibility for you, you really must be more informed. I will not be the sticky wicket in this game." The feline settled onto his stomach and then looked up at her.

"What game is that?" Alora questioned as she situated herself atop the bed to face him.

"Why, the game to end all games, my dear. And if there's one thing you must learn, it's that everything is a game. The queen never likes to lose; should you lose to Her Majesty, it's off with your head. So there couldn't possibly be a do-over."

"I see. So my first lesson is to never lose to the queen." Alora thoughtfully nodded.

"No, your first lesson is that Faeriedust is priceless. So please do use care when handling it. The second lesson is to avoid the queen at all costs. But before you can do that, you must have an understanding of what it is that the Lunar Queen most wants," the tabby said, huffing out a dejected sigh. He blinked his bottle-green eyes at her, and she wondered if he was irate at her.

"What does she want from me?"

"Your head, definitely. And your magic, probably. But what she really wants is to rule forever, and she can't do that effectively if there are heirs running amuck amidst her plans. And if there's one thing I excel at, it's causing chaos wherever I may." The grin he cast her way practically took up his entire feline face, making a chill ascend Alora's spine.

The cat seems to be delighted with the idea of chaos and murder. His sharp teeth are formidable foes, and I shouldn't like to be on the opposite end of his good humor.

"You must play a vital role in this Resistance," she surmised as she attempted to appear unbothered by his words, masking her face into a calm facade.

"I dabble here and there. I don't take sides if I can help it. But my mistress insists I aid in your cause, and even I have some loyalty left within myself."

"How… marvelous."

"Your education begins tomorrow. We shall teach you about the history of Wonderland, and then in the afternoon, I think swordplay would be extremely valuable. After, we shall take tea where you may meet your fellow faeries. It's always a good idea to be introduced to those you will be fighting alongside."

"Fight. There is that expectation again." Alora bowed her head. "I don't desire to fight anyone."

"You just need the proper motivation. Unless, of course, like my dear friend, Hatter, you're driven mad instead." His cream ears twitched as he grinned at her again.

"What happened to your friend?" Alora asked, hesitating for a moment before gathering herself.

"'T'was during the Battle of the Slain," the tabby began as his eyes seemed to glaze over. "Hatter watched his father perish by the hand of the Lunar Queen. She reached into the depths of his chest and wrenched his beating heart from the cavity. Then, as the dying King glared at her, she placed his heart into an obsidian box while the blood dripped down her arms. Hatter witnessed it, and when his father was dead on the bloodied ground, the queen then had her men restrain Hatter as she took her dagger and carved off the tips of his pointed ears. Hatter never even made a sound; his gaze just lingered on his father's graying corpse." The feline's voice grew strained. "I have never seen one so undone quite in the way Hatter was in those moments. When she was finished with Hatter, she had her men let him go, and he staggered away. There is none that hates the Lunar Queen more than he. Justifiably so."

Alora felt the blood drain from her face as horror seized her heart with punishing force. Her icy hands gripped each other in a vice-like grip. She struggled not to fall apart as unshed tears stung her eyes. Alora's mind couldn't fathom such cruelty, such evil. To consider that she was even related to the cruel queen and had her poisonous blood flowing through her veins was unfathomable.

"You must know that the Lunar Queen has eyes and ears everywhere. There is no place, no sanctuary, that is truly safe from her. What do you know of the Fae traits?"

Alora swallowed and found her voice. "Not much at all. I've only just come to know such a world exists."

"Every faerie is capable of changing their form to that of an animal. When in their Seelie form, there will always be one characteristic, one visible Fae trait that can't be masked away. Unless a faerie is exceptional, then they have the ability to glamour away any traits they wish to hide. The queen's Unseelie form is that of a dragon. A fire-breathing monstrosity large enough to swallow an entire cow whole. Her senses, when shifted, are unbeatable. She has better sight, hearing, and sense of smell that is unparalleled to any before her. She has no rivals, and none has as yet been able to stop her. The Resistance can only do so much, but largely, what they do is pick up the shattered pieces when she strikes. We are all losing hope and faith. What Wonderland needs is a savior, and your coming was foretold by the Oraculum, and there is no being who can change what was prophesied therein." The cat stayed silent, watching Alora as his tail ticked back and forth.

Dread, horror, unbelief, and sadness warred within Alora's body as her mind tried to make sense of what she had just been told. It was too much.

The tabby rose from his spot and leaned up to place a paw

against the side of Alora's face. "Little one, all will be as it's meant to be. There is time to learn what you must, but you must make the most of the time we have. Do not fear; you will not be alone, not in this and not ever. We, your Court, bow to you. Prove yourself and those of the Lunar Court who are still pure of heart, will follow you anywhere. I shall bid you good evening now. You have had your entire world flipped topsy-turvy, and that will take time to sort through. I will never have it be said that I was an uncaring brute, not toward you."

"Your name? What shall I address you as?" Alora felt hollowed out and hopeless as her insides twisted and knotted into ribboned bits.

"You may call me Cheshire." The tabby smirked and bowed before her with a flourish. It was as if Alora blinked and he instantly disappeared. She startled, and then a hysterical giggle leaked from her mouth.

"Cheshire..." she whispered into the air.

Alora's limbs felt heavy, and her head ached. How could the weight of one's head throw their entire body to the side? Alora let herself fall to the mattress, then drew her knees up close to her chest. She wanted to embrace the silence, but her eyes grew heavier. Alora tried to keep herself awake. She thought of the Faeriedust, but before she could make a move to reach for it, slumber dragged its clawed tips into her as it desperately attempted to pull her into its disastrous depths.

7

INTO TERRIFYING NIGHTMARES

Sleep brought torturous pain, hellish nightmares, broken promises, and despair. Had she ever been truly happy before? Everything else in her mind had gone from gray to black as she desperately tried in vain to stay awake. Alora felt the frigid fingers of slumber descend upon her and was too lost with feelings of despondency to shove them away. She wanted to fight. She needed to, but Alora was just so weary in her heart and mind. Still, she begged herself not to succumb to the burdensome fatigue.

"No, please, not this time!" Alora pleaded, but to what it was, she didn't know. "I would more happily welcome death then another moment of sleep. I can't be the reason why terrible things happen." Silent tears caressed her pale face as her eyes lost their fight to remain open.

Alora was standing in a meadow filled with violet wildflowers that weaved and bobbed in the gentle breeze kissing her skin. Taking a deep breath, she let her lungs fill with the fresh air, the warmth of sunshine, and the outdoors. Butterflies swirled around her in brilliant hues of blues, from midnight to turquoise to powder blue. The mahogany trees were topped with silver leaves that sparkled and shimmered in the radiant beams of the rose-gold sun. Alora's ears caught the sounds of ruffling feathers, but her eyes couldn't locate their source. The grass was a pale green, and the pink sky was dotted with fluffy blue clouds.

She felt peaceful, as if enfolded again in the comfort of her mother's loving embrace. This was part of the dream where nothing bad could touch her.

Walking through the field, Alora came to a dirt lane that led into the small town where thatched roofs of quaint little homes were visible. She didn't dare follow the lane in that direction because once the monsters came, and they would, Alora didn't want to witness more senseless death and the utter destruction that was certain to arrive.

So, she turned and walked in the opposite direction, along the dirt path where daisies and pansies cheerfully greeted her. Their chatter was a buzzing noise Alora tried to ignore. One persistent dandelion had its leaves wrapped around a purple and blue pansy's neck as it choked the poor dear. With a heavy sigh, for even the flowers were murderers here in her strange dreamworld, she stopped and knelt before the pair.

"Why must you hurt those around you, Mister Dandelion?" she questioned as an avalanche of sorrow crashed over her without warning.

"Because I must, the queen *commands it*!" answered the weed with glee.

"I refuse to allow this behavior to continue. So move you shall, right now!" Alora reached down and dug through the dirt until the tips of her fingers uncovered the dandelion's roots. She gently extracted them all while the weed threw insults at her.

"Trollop! Interloper! Bacon-brained imbecile!"

Ignoring the cruel weed, Alora carefully freed the pansy by prying off the weed's leaves one after the other. Then Alora picked up the dandelion, who latched onto her fingers and bit down.

"Ouch, you horrid little creature!" As quickly as she could, Alora scurried away from the group of cheering pansies and reached a small patch of dirt under a large, towering tree. There was little light that filtered through the branches and leaves. Alora was happy with her decision to replant the weed there under the oppressive tree.

She bent down onto her knees, then dug into the dirt with her stained fingers until a nice-sized hole was created that would fit the dandelion's roots. Alora tried to pull its teeth from her skin, but he just gripped harder as his teeth sank further into her flesh. Her lips pressed tight as prickles of pain dueled along her skin. Waving her hand back and forth, Alora attempted to dislodge him. When that failed to detach the beastly little menace, she reached for one of its petals and pulled it out. The dandelion instantly let her go as he tumbled stem over petals to the ground.

"You barbarian! You evil, *unfaely,* hoyden!" shouted the dandelion.

"That is exactly what you deserved! You warty, little villain!" seethed Alora as she examined the tiny teeth marks that lined her middle finger. Droplets of blood were seeping from her wounds.

"Me? *You!* We were all getting along just *fine* until you came along! Then you uproot me, displace me! Now, I am here, away from anyone to torment! How utterly revolting!"

"Serves you right as far as I am concerned," Alora told him as she quickly covered the dirt over his roots. Standing up, she dusted off her hands, taking care of her injured digit.

"And now, you'll abandon me? Just like that?" the weed called out to her.

Peering down at him, Alora smirked and wiggled her fingers at him. Then she strode away while he kept shouting at her. Alora kept walking and soon came to a small pond. She sat down before it, letting her thoughts wander.

This part of my dream doesn't seem so terrible. Well, except for the little teeth bites. But… how curious. They seem to be healing all on their own.

From her peripheral vision, Alora spied a group of butterflies flying her way. Their white wings had a rose pattern gracing them. She'd never seen such beautiful butterflies before.

Their delicate wings brushed against the exposed skin of Alora's arms and neck before fluttering to her cheeks along their journey. She was delighted to experience such a rare occurrence with the wild beauties of nature. Peace filled Alora and she sighed in wonderment as their gentle kisses continued to land upon her. She smiled brilliantly with delight and joy.

Once the last butterfly flew past her, Alora heard the beating of many pairs of wings much larger than the tinier insects and looked up at the sky in bemusement. Her heartbeat was trilling at an alarming rate as the smile slipped from her face. Above her were winged beings boasting snouts, who soared high within the clouds. They flew with various weapons, such as axes, swords, and maces, clutched within their clawed hands.

Alora wrapped her arms around herself as horror flooded her. She knew they were set on causing chaos to the beautiful land in which she now resided. The blood in her veins chilled as a shiver wracked her from head to toe.

I must do something! But how do I wake from this everlasting slumber? What if they hurt the innocent beings still residing within Wonderland? Will my waking put an end to all of this?

The winged beasts littering the sky were headed into the village. There was nothing she could do except chase after them. Alora lifted her skirts, then gave chase. She leaped over flowers that were cowering in fear as they attempted to close their petals to secure their own safety. Birds careened into the nearby trees as they, too, sought to escape whatever wrathful act was soon to be executed.

Soon, she came to the dirt path that this bizarre dream had first brought her to. From the darkening skyline, smoke from chimneys plumed into the air as families were no doubt gathering around their tables to share in their evening meals. They would have no idea what terror was to rain down upon them within moments. Alora wanted to shout in warning, but her breath was coming in pants as she lacked the air to make more than a slight shriek. A slash of pain tore through her side as she fought to steady her breathing.

Alora scanned her surroundings. The village was dotted with decorative cottages that had well-tended gardens with burbling fountains. Birdhouses in a stunning array of colors stood before each dwelling. These were not soldiers, not ruffians that had built their homes here. The darkness that leaked into the Lunar Court didn't seem to have yet made its way to this quaint little village.

When Alora finally reached the first cottage, she sprinted to a window and peered into it. Seated around a table were four faeries who each possessed various shades of blue hair. Two, who she surmised were a couple, smiled at each other as the lady cut thick slices of bread. The male faerie took the slices and slathered huge heapings of blue jam onto each piece before setting them down; one piece was placed on each of the four plates. Two children sat patiently on their chairs as a motherly figure ladled the stew into the wooden soup bowls before them. The thought of the family being among those who would soon be eviscerated made her spine stiffen with resolve. Alora would not allow such a fate to befall them.

Raising a fist, Alora pounded on the window, and immediately the occupants all turned their heads to gaze at her. The children looked at her with fear while their parents cast worried glances toward her as they whispered to each other. The male faerie rose from the head of the oblong table, and soon Alora saw the cottage's front door opening. She rushed her steps to meet the male, her feet flying over the pavers that rested atop the pale grass.

"You must flee! The danger comes from the sky and will destroy your homes, your very lives!" Alora gasped, her lungs burning as they struggled to fill with air.

"What is this nonsense?" the male asked, narrowing his dark eyes.

"Look up! Don't you see the winged creatures?" Alora asked. Her voice broke. Her eyes widened, watching as the beasts grew closer.

"I don't see anything..." he trailed off as he tilted his head to the sky. His head moved from side to side as he scanned the pinks and blues of the horizon.

Alora furrowed her brows as she directed her gaze heavenward. The hoard had completely bypassed the village. She gasped as she continued to search the sky. "I don't understand..."

"There's a ward in place, set by the White Queen. None shall pass who means us harm, neither by air nor land. Rest assured all is well." He reached a hand out to Alora and awkwardly patted her shoulder.

"Why doesn't the White Queen ward off all of Wonderland?"

"Well, she can't. This village rests against the land bordering the White Kingdom. When the ward falls, all hope shall be lost. You gave me quite the fright." The kind eyes regarded her wearily.

"I do apologize; I had no idea." Alora's shoulders sank.

"No need to fash yourself. All is well. Perhaps you'd care to join the village tea party now that you're here? Hatter is hosting. And I heard a rumor from the baker that Cheshire has returned."

"Cheshire and Hatter together? Well, now I am quite curious. Where may I find the tea party?" Alora felt elated at the thought of meeting Hatter and perhaps learning more about his tragic history with the Lunar Queen. She hoped that what she might learn from him could help in offering hope to the people of Wonderland. For surely he was as ready as any to end the terrifying reign of his aunt.

"If you follow the paved path, you will soon end up in the center of the village. Near the fountain, you'll want to turn right, and soon you'll come out into the glade. Your ears should pick up the merriment before your eyes spy the party." He squinted, bringing his head closer to her to inspect her ears. "No tipped points, no jagged edges, yet you don't seem entirely human."

"You are correct; I am not entirely human. Thank you for your help." Alora nodded her gratitude to the faerie, and putting one slipper after the other, she began her stroll to the tea party. She hoped no faerie would be cross at her for arriving uninvited. The allure of meeting Hatter and spending more time with Cheshire was just too appealing to deny.

And if Alora was slumbering, what else was she to do with herself? Perhaps princesses may do as they like in Faerie?

8

BROKEN HEARTED AND CHIPPED TEACUPS

Much to Alora's relief and pleasure, the male faerie had been correct. Alora's ears heard laughter and then shouts of glee before she came into the glade. The forest was rich with yellow grass and mahogany trees topped with silver leaves. In the midst of the grassy meadow besprinkled with periwinkle and violet flowers rested one long rectangular table with ten matching chairs. Chipped teacups, broken saucers, and dishes littered the table, their shattered bits strewn in every direction.

Seated at the head of the table was a male faerie with a bronze top hat that shimmered in the fading sunlight. Men in England wore beaver-skinned top hats, yet this faerie's topper seemed to be made of satin or silk with a lacy floral pattern. His eyebrows were bushy and unruly over his amused amber eyes.

Amber? I know those eyes…

A tidal pool of dread swirled in Alora's stomach, which threatened to make her sick as she fought the sudden dizziness that made her vision swim. She had to swallow the bile that rose to the back of her throat as her stomach churned.

His physique is that of my Phillip, but he bears a wild, crazed look about him now. However, if he is Wonderland's Hatter, and Cheshire recounted the events of The Battle of the Slain properly, that would perfectly explain everything. He's never coming back for me...

Alora silently watched the tea party. Cheshire was to Phillip's right, while a small field mouse with dark gray fur and twitching whiskers sat to his left. The remaining chairs were filled with both Seelie and Unseelie faeries. Some of the Unseelie Fae wore colorful clothing that had seen better days. Patches were sewn onto their clothing, and she wondered for a brief moment whether this was the latest fashion trend in the strange and twisted land or if all the residents lacked funds for newer attire. Were the taxes here unjustly high?

Phillip captured her attention when he suddenly stopped talking and then rubbed a hand over his chest in the spot where his heart rested. Slowly, Phillip's eyes gazed up from the table, widening before his handsome features twisted into a scowl as his eyes locked onto her. Alora suppressed a tremble as she rooted her feet in place and tried to decipher if her mere presence had angered him. The thought that he had never missed her was like a tiny dagger cutting jagged lines into her tortured heart. She had hoped their first reuniting would assure Alora of his having missed her because their time apart had been nothing but torment for her. What was she to think? Perhaps for him it had all been an empty promise.

"Let us make our Princess feel welcomed," purred Cheshire after he cast a glance at Hatter and noticed her.

The tabby leaped up into the air from his seat, twirling end over end, until he was just floating in the air before her. His smile held a hint of madness as he regarded her. "You did not take the Faeriedust as instructed. Naughty, naughty. Well, come along then; since you're here, you might as well partake in our tea and sweets. What's one more when we're having such a marvelous time?" The beautiful bronze medallion that hung from the white ruff about his neck swung back and forth as he twisted his head to look toward the table.

"I don't wish to intrude," Alora began, wishing that it wasn't too late to escape. Her heart wasn't done shattering yet.

"But you have, and now you cannot go unseen. While you slumber, you might as well sit and sip with us." Cheshire patted her cheek, then floated back to the table. He reached Hatter's left, where the tiny mouse was, and carefully scooped the creature from the chair. He looked to Hatter and said, "If you would be so kind," as he twitched an ear toward the teapot that rested before his friend.

Hatter hastily reached for the teapot and removed the lid. Cheshire dropped the mouse into the brew, and Hatter quickly replaced the lid. From the spout, Alora heard what she thought was the song Twinkle Twinkle. She felt her shoulders lose some of their tension when she surmised that, at the very least, she wouldn't be taking tea with murderers after all.

Waving an impatient paw at her, Cheshire implored, "Come along now, Curious One. We haven't all night."

Alora forced her legs to move the short distance to reach the table. The distance had not been nearly long enough when she had no idea how she was to address Phillip.

When she reached the empty chair, she sat, and when she did, Hatter hurriedly gained his feet, rushing to push her chair in. For a moment, Alora thought she felt the delicate brush of fingers play along the nape of her neck. In the next instant, the feeling was gone, leaving a chill in its place, and she wondered if she had imagined it.

She clasped her hands together in her lap. Alora couldn't make herself look at him as he made his way back to his chair. But as the voices continued around the table, she felt the weight of his gaze upon her. Lifting her chin, Alora met his weighty stare.

"I feel remiss," Hatter admitted. "I feel as if I have forgotten something. Was it you?"

"Was what me?"

"The thing I have forgotten. Displaced. Unremembered. My mind is desperately attempting to recall." He tilted his head to the side. Alora tried to spy his ears, but if they were damaged as Cheshire had claimed, she couldn't tell. The tops of his ears were covered by the wide brim of the elaborate hat.

"Perhaps, in time, you shall find the answer you are seeking." Alora swallowed to try to tamp down the bitter ash of disappointment. Phillip didn't know her, and she wondered if she would ever be able to hunt down all the splintered pieces of her heart.

"Tea?" Cheshire asked as he leaned over her and poured the brown liquid into the cup before her.

"Cheshire, where are your manners?" Hatter replied as he *tsked* at his friend.

Alora gratefully smiled at Phillip. She had not forgotten about the mouse that was hopefully still breathing while bathing in the tea water, and it seemed he had not either.

"You failed to offer her cream and sugar," Hatter remarked with a frown that sent his bushy eyebrows colliding together to form a band of auburn across his forehead, just under his hat.

"First things first, better to get the tea into the cup before offering useless questions," Cheshire hissed at him as his fluffy tail ticked from side to side.

"Actually, if it's all the same to you, I'd rather not take tea nor eat anything. I am, after all, asleep, and I have never done either of those things in my dreams," Alora spoke up.

"Ahhhh, now I see. I have forgotten your kind doesn't like bathwater." Cheshire turned to Hatter and said, "While in the

Spring Court, I was informed that humans can't stomach it. Their sensibilities are so fragile, you know."

"Indeed," replied Hatter as his eyebrows lifted and his head tilted again.

"How many Courts are there?" Alora queried, attempting to drive the conversation in another direction.

"There are six. However, now is not the time to begin your education. I do like my tea with a bit of revelry, and the Court history can be so tedious." Cheshire grinned with a gleam alighting his bright eyes.

"Yes, no one wants to converse about unpleasant things," mused Hatter. "After all, our history here in the Lunar Court has not been kind to us."

Thoughts of the loss of Phillip's father flitted through Alora's mind. Purple smudges rested beneath his eyes, which led her to believe he wasn't sleeping well. His eyes reflected a haunting brokenness that latched onto her heartstrings. Phillip seemed to be just a shell of the boy that she had once known.

"Now, back to the celebration at hand," Cheshire raised his voice above the din of those still privately conversing around them. "Today is my Unbirthday! And as such, I demand a toast." He fluttered his eyelashes at Hatter.

Hatter sprang from his chair and raised his teacup to Cheshire. "Cheers to my very dear friend, Cheshire. May we gather together again many times in the coming years to toast you! I wish you a very merry and boisterous Happy Unbirthday!" With that, Hatter brought his teacup to his lips and threw his head back to swallow the contents.

"Huzzah!"

"Happy wishes to you!"

"Many more Happy Unbirthdays to you, dear friend!"

"Here, here!"

Well wishes and shouts of agreement came from those gathered around the table. Alora finally let her eyes leave

Hatter's form and scan the other guests. There was a pelican who wore a top hat, and a green and purple striped tie hung from his neck. A lovely female faerie with alabaster skin that seemed to glow possessed gossamer wings in shades of green. Her one defining trait was the mossy green horns that curved into the air above her white hair. A male faerie with umber skin and dark hair looked her way. He blinked his large eyes at her, which, Alora noted, bulged from his eye sockets. The thought that he might sneeze made her cringe, and she tried not to squirm in her chair.

Alora hurriedly took in the next faerie's features. Midnight hair and icy blue eyes met her gaze. Rosebud lips twisted into a one-sided smile, and the teeth that resided within were sharp and shark-like. This otherworldly lady was both beautiful and deadly. The faerie smirked at Alora, then seemed to dismiss her as she turned to converse with the male beside her.

This faerie was fierce. He had the head of a lion and the body of a gazelle. The strangest bit, thought Alora, was he had the hands of a human, complete with polished and well-trimmed nails. He didn't bother to meet her eyes, and she was perfectly fine with that.

Gentle fingers encircled Alora's arm as she was pulled to her feet. She swiveled her head up to meet Hatter's eyes. He politely smiled at her.

"Time to switch!" Cheshire called as he swirled in the air, turning in circles.

The other faeries rose from their chairs and followed in his wake as he flew around the table. Hatter urged Alora by giving her a slight shove into the small of her back, coaxing her to follow so the relay could continue along its course. The breath caught in her chest as his touch caused sadness to seep through her veins like icy slush. The idea he had forgotten her caused a swell of grief to break over her senses. The crushing weight of her despair made her want to double over and let her tears fall. Perhaps from this point forward she should only think of him as a beautiful dream.

Alora hurried her steps, nearly running in order to catch up to the antics of the others. When the mad dash had taken three rounds, the guests suddenly halted. Alora realized she was only one chair away from where she had been seated. The tea party guests took their chairs as Alora sunk into her own spot. She puffed out a few pants as her lungs struggled to fill with air.

"How wonderful," cooed Cheshire. "Nothing like a good chase to get the digestion going." He turned to Alora. "Something troubling you, Curious One?" His furry brows pressed together.

"I just realized something," she quietly told him.

"Oh? Well, do share; we all like discoveries."

"Today just happens to be my Unbirthday as well," Alora was pleased with herself that she could summon such an innocuous thought from those roiling within her turbulent mind.

"Really? How extraordinary." Cheshire grinned at her.

"Happy Unbirthday to you," Hatter spoke from her other side. Alora turned her head toward him. He cast her a smile that made her heart skip a beat. She had to blink her eyes several times to keep the tears at bay.

"Thank you," she replied demurely.

"It's our Happy Unbirthday today as well!" chimed a child-like voice from further down the table. Alora had to lean forward to catch sight of the speaker.

Two identical twin boys sat side-by-side. They wore orange-striped long-sleeved tunics, and atop their bald heads were the oddest hats she had ever seen. The headwear was cylindrical in shape with curious little propellers that capped them. The brown hats were an outlandish choice, but given the wearers, perhaps it wasn't such an odd choice after all. They were both portly, and their skin had a rosy hue to it.

Their hazel eyes seemed to glow with secrets and mischievousness. She wouldn't want to find herself alone with either of them.

"Yes, yes, we do know," Cheshire remarked with a wave of his paw and an exaggerated roll of his eyes.

"Happy Unbirthday to you both," Alora nodded to them.

They nodded back as they happily munched on pink-frosted cookies.

Alora cringed when she realized no one seemed to mind that the plates of cookies and cakes had been previously eaten from or that the teacups before them had been drunk from. Disgust made her stomach clench.

None shall find me noshing on a single thing this evening. Thankfully, I can blame the fact I'm not altogether here at the moment. I do hope all is well with my slumbering body. Would I know if it were not so?

"You've just met the Tweedle Twins. Your life will never be the same again," remarked Cheshire in a deadpan manner.

"I demand an epic story. Who shall be the one to entertain us all?" Hatter asked.

"I shall," came a muffled voice.

"Who's there?" Hatter leaned over to look under the table and then behind him.

"Down here," rang the small voice.

Hatter looked at the teapot with a glare, and then his face brightened. He inclined his head to it. "I forgot." He reached for the teapot and lifted the lid, then, reaching inside, smirked. When Hatter withdrew his hand and opened his palm, the gray mouse sat with drenched fur and twitching whiskers. Drops of dark tea leaked between the slits of Hatter's fingers, falling onto the stained tablecloth.

"Poor creature." Alora wondered why the little mouse hadn't seemed to mind his ill-treatment.

"Nonsense and furballs, he is quite well. Who doesn't like

a well-steeped blend?" Cheshire's grin grew broader as his eyes lit with delight. He licked his feline lips.

Did faeries eat each other? Hopefully it was frowned upon during tea time.

Gazing around the table at the silent faces all directed toward them, Alora realized they truly didn't give a thought to the creature's comfort at all. Had darkness coated their hearts in cold steel? Were they even friends? From the faraway, crazed look in their eyes it seemed as if harm was the expectation, not the exception.

Cheshire began to lick a paw as Hatter shook the mouse gently, dislodging drops of tea from its fur. But still, that was not a kind thing to do.

"All better, now you are right as rain. I am ready to hear your story. Will it be about a writing desk and a raven?" Hatter inquired.

"How about the one about the walrus and the carpenter? It's a lovely tale now that the steadfast friends are reacquainted," piped up the mouse.

"Why were they separated?" Alora asked.

"Well, he can't begin at the middle before he's even gotten to the beginning. Now, do be patient," Cheshire instructed her with a peevish tsk of his tongue.

Alora sat back against her chair and folded her hands in her lap. She unclasped her fingers and gave herself a hard pinch, stopping herself from flinching at the burning pain. She was still asleep. Alora pushed away the crushing disappointment of not being remembered. There was nothing more that she could do except experience all she may while lingering in the strange dream form that her tangled curse demanded.

9

THE WALRUS AND THE CARPENTER

The gray mouse scrambled up an upturned teacup and perched upon it. Clearing his throat, he began his tale.

"The Walrus and the Carpenter met quite unexpectedly one day. Both were residents of the Summer Court, but on opposite sides, they built their individual homes. The Walrus preferred swimming in the ocean's depths, hunting his prey of unsuspecting oysters. The Carpenter spent his days toiling under the rays of the blistering sun crafting fine seafaring vessels. On the day when fate would introduce them, a great storm blew through the heavens, throwing down hand-sized hail and icy rain. The sky turned a murderous shade of violet while the white-capped waves rose to tower above the coastline, tossing and shoving everything that bobbed along the water's surface.

"The Carpenter had begun his day repairing the dock to which he sailed his ships. He had just replaced the last wooden board and was hitting the last nail to secure it into place when a great roaring wave picked him up and dragged him down into its watery depth. The Carpenter feared he would find this to be his watery grave, for he could neither tell up from down; so much churning had muddled his senses. When the last bubble of air escaped his mouth, his eyes caught a hulking mass separating the water to reach him. Not knowing what the creature's intent was, the Carpenter closed his eyes and let oblivion carry him away." The mouse paused to rub his pale pink nose, then sneezed. Alora hoped he hadn't caught a cold from his tea bathing.

"That's a terrible tale indeed, but what happened next?" asked the lion-headed male as his large humanesque hands wrapped around a teacup. His grip seemed to be tightening, and his knuckles turned a bright white.

"Did he get eaten?" questioned one of the Tweedle twins as he grinned and the skin surrounding his eyes crinkled.

Alora canted her head to stare with widened eyes at the pair of twins. It was horrible to take pleasure from death. The faeries' everlasting bloodlust gave her fright as goosebumps appeared along her skin.

Hatter chuckled and said, "It's as if you've never heard this tale before."

"To be fair, it does tend to change here and there depending upon who is telling the tale. Our apologies, my mousy companion; please do continue." Cheshire leaned his head upon his front paws that rested on the tabletop and proceeded to purr loudly. The mouse rubbed his little paws together, his black beady eyes glimmering.

"The Walrus knew a storm was brewing, so long had the whims of the sea become known to him. He dived deeper into the murky depths, scanning the ocean bed for his favorite feast. The seething water kept ripping his body away from his treasure, much to his ire and dismay. When his final attempt to reach his dinner failed and his strength faded away, the Walrus let the waves carry him where they wished. His body sailed along in a new direction, and soon, another crashing wave dragged him under.

"Before his chocolate-colored eyes was a fully-clothed

faerie who had just breathed his last breath. The Walrus lunged for the male with his flippers and held onto him by his waist. The Walrus gave a great kick, and up the pair rose from the ocean depths. It was a battle of wills, the bedraggled pair against the raging storm who wanted the water to devour them. With flagging strength, the Walrus bested the waves, and soon, the pair reached the shore. The Walrus dragged the unconscious faerie up and onto the sand. He dropped the faerie and-"

"Died. There he died. Yes, that makes for a perfectly dreadful ending," the other Tweedle twin interrupted with flickers of glee shining maniacally within his hazel eyes.

"So much death!" Hatter sadly remarked as he rubbed his chin with the fingers of one hand. Alora felt her heart warm as she absently held a hand to the neckline of her dress.

Phillip doesn't seem to relish in the violence as the others do. Perhaps there remains a glimmer of the boy I once knew.

"No. No one died just then. May I continue?" The mouse asked his audience as he blinked at them.

When no one made another peep, he cleared his throat. "The Walrus dropped the Carpenter in the sand and fell down alongside him, greedily gulping in mouthfuls of air. When the faerie beside him still didn't wake, the Walrus smacked him with a flipper across his pale face. At last, the Carpenter made a noise as he heaved water from his lungs in sputtering bursts. When he regained his breath and sat upright, he asked his rescuer where they were. When the Walrus replied that he didn't know, the two agreed to explore the new island in which they found themselves.

"Slowly the winds began to die down as the waters calmed, and then the sun peeked down on them from the pink clouds. The Walrus decided to cast his Unseelie form away and take on a more humanesque appearance. The pair set out on foot to discover what they may. When it became apparent that the island was small and uninhabited, they agreed to construct a hut from the trees and leaves around them. Now, because the Carpenter was a builder at heart, he wasn't pleased to just make do; he wanted to build a hut that was comfortable. The Walrus readily agreed as he was used to the finer things and wanted to make their abode cheery. The Walrus was a wonderful aid and very useful with the crude tools his new friend had fashioned."

"One should always be useful when one can," interrupted Cheshire. "What happened once the pair had their little hut constructed?"

"They built, and sometimes it was just the Carpenter building as they had to eat. So, often, the Walrus was off to hunt in the sea, retaking his Unseelie form. The bounty he would return with always was a feast, and the two would eat until they were close to popping." The mouse scrunched his nose. "One day, the Walrus returned early from his adventures and rushed to meet his friend, who was busily constructing a bakery. He had already built a fine row of houses and a small market for shopping, just in case anyone else should find their way to their home. They had paved walkways from crushed seashells that had washed ashore and lamps from the sea glass they gathered to light their way by night. When the Walrus found his friend, he quickly told him of his plan for guests and another feast, but one unlike any they had yet partaken of. The Walrus only truly loved to eat oysters, and it had been forever since he had filled his portly belly with the fine fare. The Carpenter wanted to please his friend, so he happily went along with the subterfuge. He took the next few hours to finish the bakery, which, with the help of his friend, turned into a bistro.

"One long wooden table sat ready with enough seats to entertain many guests. Lit lanterns cast a soft glow from the amethyst flames across the room, which was the perfect picture of cozy dining. With everything in place, the two dined on leftover crab soup and seaweed salad. The next morning dawned fair and bright as the excited mood of the Walrus was infectious to his friend. The Walrus set out to convince his guests to leave the seabed and come ashore with him while the Carpenter stayed behind to set out dishes and utensils. He had water boiling and fresh coconut milk waiting. The Walrus gave his best smiles and assurances to the little oysters to convince them that adventure awaited. They were tired of always being at the bottom of the sea and were excited to see what lay beyond the water. They gleefully hopped right into the closely braided net their new friend had carried along with him. When they reached the shore, the Walrus rose from the waves with a triumphant gleam in his gaze. When the Carpenter caught sight of him, he rushed to open the double doors of the bistro and gave the oysters a grand bow."

"And here is where the fun begins," purred the lion-headed faerie.

Alora leaned forward in her chair with curiosity.

"The Carpenter and the Walrus ushered their tiny friends into the restaurant, and when the Walrus inquired whether they'd like to help with dinner, his question was met with cheer. The oysters wanted to enjoy all there was dwelling on the land. They were eager to follow behind the Walrus as he tread into the kitchen. The Carpenter was the last to enter, and he closed the doors to the kitchen silently behind him. With a few hurried movements of the two hungry friends, they scooped the tiny beings into the steamer that rested in the large boiling pot of water and held the lid tightly shut. They dined that night on oysters, and from that evening on, they chose one night a week to lure more friends from the watery depths to fill their bellies."

"How awful, those poor unsuspecting creatures," gasped Alora as she brought her arms around herself to warm her chilled skin.

"Yes, there is that. But such is the way of life," spoke the ebony-hued faerie.

"Quite so," agreed Cheshire, his pale pink tongue edged from his mouth to wash his paw.

"Is that the end of the story? How did they escape the island?" asked the whiny voice of the twins in unison.

"That is a story for another day. It's time to switch seats!" shouted the beautiful female faerie with a shark-like grin.

Every faerie leaped up from their seats, and this time Alora rose quickly to her slippered feet. She followed the line of parading faeries with Hatter just behind her.

"I do know you. I can't quite recall when we met, but I feel as if it was a monumental meeting. Do you remember it? Our first introduction?" Hatter adjusted his topper, holding onto it as they rounded the corner of the table.

"I do. I shan't ever forget it," she confessed as she looked back over her shoulder at him.

"Would you be so kind as to be patient with me as I try to remember?" Hatter guided her elbow, steering her into the chair she had halted before. When he scooted her wingback chair toward the table, he leaned down and peered intently into her eyes. Alora was careful not to blink or break the intense stare in any way.

"I will always give you the time you need," she whispered, barely able to draw in her next breath.

"Thank you, my Princess. You see, I am not quite me, not the me I used to be. I fear I'm losing myself more and more each day. I fear what will soon become of me when I can't recall anything." He smiled sadly at her and then rose to his full height.

Alora watched as he straightened his brown greatcoat, then turned toward his seat. When he had seated himself, his brows furrowed as his gaze fixed on something across the table. She yearned to pull his hand into hers. Hatter looked as if he might break at any moment.

"Oh dear, Curious One, you're waking up," Cheshire caught her attention. His head was tilted as he observed her.

Turning her head to look at Hatter, Alora's vision faded, and she felt a pulling sensation tugging at her core. Her skin took on a transparent sheen as sharp-edged sorrow squeezed her heart in a tight fist.

No! Not yet, I am not yet ready to say goodbye to Phillip. Not when I've only just found him!

She felt like someone had reached inside her and savagely plucked out her heart.

"Farewell, Princess. We will meet again," were the last words she heard as Hatter's handsome face disappeared.

10

NO MORE DREAMING

Alora blinked, squinting against the low light, taking a moment to allow her eyes to adjust. Beside her small bed stood her father with a frown marring his face.

She felt disoriented. It had been the afternoon while she dreamed, and now it felt as if the late night hours were courting her to slumber once more. It was as if her body had not had any rest at all as a fog circled around in her confused thoughts.

"No more dreaming for you, Alora. Did no one give the Faeriedust to you?" he irritably asked. Alora eyed his fist, which was wrapped around the bottle.

"Yes, but I forgot to take it."

"That cannot happen again. We must keep you safe, and that can't be done if you are hied off to who-knows-where," Papa admonished her as he held the bottle out to her.

"You're right. I will do better." Alora hid her yawn with the back of her hand before reaching for the potion. She unstopped the cork and let the tiny grains of golden dust fall onto her tongue. Warmth accompanied by a tingling sensation rushed through her body.

"Rest now. You won't dream anymore tonight." Her father

leaned over to press a warm kiss to her forehead. He retrieved the Faeriedust and reinserted the cork into the bottle.

Alora felt the peaceful embrace of slumber claiming her once again. It had been so long since her father had tucked her in.

WHEN ALORA AWOKE NEXT, SHE LAY STILL AND SILENT UPON HER bed. Her ears couldn't hear any sounds of movement from behind her chamber door. Not knowing what time it was bothered her. She was used to sunlight, whether pale or brilliant, waking her at home. Here, there was no chance of basking in the warm rays of the sunshine, not while she was underground in the Resistance. Her thoughts turned to Phillip, and her heart gave a painful squeeze.

He had not known who I was! All this time, I have been clinging to his promise of returning to me, and he had forgotten all about me. But, there were times last night that his eyes met mine and that tugging sensation seemed to pull him toward me. I would give him all of eternity to remember me if only my heart could bear it.

Alora tossed her coverlet aside and slowly sat up. She swung her legs over the bed, where her feet felt something fuzzy beneath them. She couldn't recall having slippers before.

When a croak sounded from beneath her probing feet, Alora threw herself backward on the bed and drew her knees up. Her heart was racing as her breaths became ragged. Alora concentrated on taking deep breaths, feeling her pulse settle into a calm, rhythmic beat. When she grew brave enough, she leaned forward and peeped over the edge of the bed.

Black eyes stared back up at her from where they were set on a small green face. Alora noticed the pair of white slippers the tiny tree frog rested upon. There were bright yellow stripes along its back, and the creature looked to be no bigger than the size of her palm.

"How did you get in here?" she wondered as she stretched her legs over the bed's edge and cautiously rose. When the little frog just blinked up at her, Alora slipped her feet into the awaiting slippers, then bent down to pick up the curious being from atop her left slipper.

"You look perfectly harmless, and Fate said no one could come into my chamber if they meant me harm. What am I to do with you? This is hardly the right place. Don't you want to find a nice pond or perhaps a lovely tree?" Alora gingerly held the frog in her hands as she met its beady gaze.

The frog croaked at her. It seemed content to rest within her palms. Alora shrugged her shoulders. "Very well. We'll see to you in a bit. Right now, I have to get dressed. My schedule is rather packed today."

Alora looked around the room. Her furnishings were sparse, not leaving her much choice as to where she should set her companion down. "How about the foot of my bed? It's as good a place as any, and I'm not liable to step nor sit on you there. Yes, that makes sense." Alora set the frog down on her blanket, then took a few steps to reach the floral wash basin that rested on the small table behind the burgundy screen.

Though she didn't want to cause the little one offense, she decided to wash her hands. But then she wouldn't want to use the same water to cleanse her face. Alora didn't know what to do. If the frog was Unseelie, it wasn't likely to carry disease.

Alora observed her hands. Noticing her oval looking glass that rested next to the water basin, she leaned over to it. She gazed down into it and scanned her face. It didn't look dirty. Perhaps one day of not washing her face wouldn't hurt. Alora would just wash her hands with the lavender soap.

Once she had seen that her hands were thoroughly

scrubbed and dried, Alora set about cleaning her teeth. She noticed a small bristled brush and tin of paste beside the floral pattern basin. Unscrewing the cap from the tin, she brought it up to her nose to sniff. It was minty, and some other elusive scent came to her, reminding her of the Christmas tree Papa had allowed her to bring into the manor last Yuletide. Examining the side of the tin, Alora read the word "Toothpaste". Switching her focus onto the tiny brush, she gingerly dipped the tip of the bristles to skim the top of the paste. Then she lifted her hand and began to gently scrub her teeth. As the paste was rubbed in, tiny blue bubbles tickled her gums until Alora pulled the brush from her mouth. Spitting out the remnants of the paste into another small bowl, she wiped her mouth with the folded cloth beside the basin. Alora had little choice in rinsing off the paste, so she set the cleaning instrument down beside the basin, hoping the maid would see it there.

Coming out from behind the screen, Alora reached into the rosewood cabinet to choose a day dress. A lovely pale green gown with a darker underskirt caught her attention. The tiny embroidered green leaves and flowers made it absolutely divine.

She searched the shelf her silk slippers rested upon and, to her delight, found a pair that seemed to match the dress.

It took some finagling and some awkward backbends, but Alora was able to unlace the back of the prior day's finery. She spotted a small basket in the corner of her dressing area and let the dress fall from her hands into it. Quickly removing her underthings, she donned fresh garments, then let the gown slip over her shoulders and down her slim form. When the hem reached the tops of her feet, Alora reached over her shoulders and secured the small seed pearl buttons that held the garment in place. Her hair was another matter to deal with and she found the task to be quite daunting. Alora wasn't used to styling her own tresses.

Making her way to the chair, she passed by the cabinet and withdrew a silver-plated hairbrush with engraved foxes. Studying the little animals, she found them to be an odd choice, but the more she gazed at them, the dearer they grew to be.

When she sat down, Alora pulled the pins from her heavy locks, placing them atop her lap. She took care that they wouldn't slip from the satin material of her lap to the dirt floor beneath her. How she had not dislodged the pins while sleeping was a mystery. She mustn't have moved at all.

Alora ran her fingers through her hair to disentangle it before she began to brush it. Her fingers snagged on a few knots at the ends of her tresses. Picking up the brush, she rhythmically began to tame her hair. When shining curls hung over her left shoulder, she wearily eyed the pins.

Her thoughts were interrupted when a light rapping sounded on her chamber door. Alora looked at the frog and then at the door. Hairpins were gathered in her lap, and she didn't wish to lose any of them.

"I suppose it's too much trouble to ask you to get the door?" Alora smiled at the frog.

"Princess?" came a muffled feminine voice from the other side of the door.

Realizing she knew the voice, Alora replied, "Do come in!"

When the door creaked open, the lady's maid with amethyst skin peeped her head into the room.

"May I enter, Princess?" the maid met her gaze.

"Of course! You're just in time to save me," Alora remarked.

"I shall be glad to be of assistance to you," she said as she moved into the room and curtsied before moving to stand behind Alora.

"I have the pins here in my lap," Alora gestured as she gathered them into her hand.

"It won't take long to create the perfect coiffure. You've such lovely hair," spoke the maid as the edges of her gossamer wings caught Alora's eyes.

"Thank you," Alora felt the maid's fingers twisting her curls into submission. "Do you know where that frog belongs?"

"Oh gracious, I don't. I have never seen it before. How did the little fellow get in here, I wonder?" the maid asked as she shifted her attention back to pinning her mistress's hair in place.

"I have no idea. I awoke, and there it was. Do you think it is a boy?" Alora continued to hand the pins to the faerie one at a time.

"Perhaps?"

"Would it be terribly rude of me to ask what your name is?"

"I don't believe so. My name is Meara, Princess," the maid replied as she pushed a few more pins into Alora's hair, then stepped back. She came to stand before Alora to inspect her hair from the front. When she nodded her approval, Meara spoke again. "Is there anything else you require?"

"Oh! If it's not too much trouble, could you please bring a new water basin with clean water? I used the one that's there to wash my hands after touching the frog."

"I shall see to it, Princess. Any other tasks?"

"I suppose not; thank you so very much, Meara." Alora stood, then looked back at the bed to the frog. "I suppose I shall just have to take you with me."

The tree frog blinked at her.

"I guess that means you have no objection," Alora patted the sides of her dress. "It's appalling that men's fashions have so many pockets, and yet we ladies have none."

"You could take a reticule and let Froggy hop into it," supplied the maid as she straightened up the chamber.

"Excellent idea! Thank you!" Alora exclaimed before she

padded over to the cabinet and riffled through one of its drawers. Her fingers found satin and lace. Alora withdrew a pale green bag with a long braided cord. She made her way back over to her bed and placed the opened purse before the frog, who dutifully jumped into it.

"That was easy!" she remarked and cinched her bag before she straightened up. She let it hang from her wrist, hoping that Froggy wouldn't become sick by the motion of swinging back and forth. Perchance the steady rhythm would lull it to a blissful nap.

Meara nodded at her, then said, "Cheshire is in the library awaiting you. He had a small breakfast prepared."

"You have a library here?" Excitement swelled in Alora.

While she didn't love reading, she did find that some libraries contained art in murals or statues. And that was where her love of libraries resided. Not within the books that lined the wooden shelves. Alora felt trepidation creep into her heart. If she were to begin her studies in the library, then surely reading would be in order. How she would endure endless hours slogging through tomes, she wasn't certain.

A memory flashed before her.

"I give up! I cannot make the words make sense. They won't stop moving about the pages and behave," Alora wailed to her mother as tears coursed down her cheeks. She was so frustrated and tired, and her head ached fiercely. Reading was supposed to expand her knowledge of the world around her. She longed to lose herself in the adventures her mother used to read to her. But every time she held a book and peered down at its pages, the letters transformed themselves into twisted shapes as they ran around the pages. Try as hard as she could, her eyes could never untangle them or make them quit moving. At the age of ten, it was past time for Alora to be reading. She longed to be normal like those around her, but her mind would not be made to comprehend the squiggly lines. The words seemed so foreign to her, taunting her efforts and wasting her time.

Alora's chin was gently lifted by her mother until their eyes met, and her mother spoke. "Dearest, this is not a lost battle. We simply have to discover what unlocks this puzzle for you. You have a keen mind, and there's not one thing that is wrong with you. For you, my love, are smarter than you know and braver even still. It takes bravery to keep toiling when all seems lost. I have spoken with Papa, and he has arranged a private tutor for you who specializes in reading difficulties. We shall soon have this all sorted out. So let's dry those tears and take a deep breath or two." Mama pulled an embroidered handkerchief, scented of honeysuckle from her sleeve, then delicately wiped the tears from Alora's face.

Alora hiccuped as she tried to calm herself. The beaming and loving emerald gaze of her mother made her feel warm and toasty. Her Mama was the most intelligent woman she knew. And if she believed in Alora, then with help, Alora could overcome this reading obstacle, making them all proud of her, herself included.

"Fate is waiting to escort you to the library for today's lesson with Cheshire," Meara informed her while she made the bed.

Meara's voice brought Alora back to the present. Alora blinked as her heart sank. Her memory of that tender moment with her mother made her heart sore, mourning for the woman who meant the whole world to her.

It was silly to still wish for the trinkets her mother had loved, to still have something tangible to hold within her hands that her mother had. But… Mama had created her, and she was her mother's greatest joy. There was comfort in that knowledge. So Alora turned her thoughts to the library. There were treasures awaiting her discovery… but they were underground. It wasn't likely to contain any great treasure.

"Does everyone know my schedule?" Alora was feeling morose and strived to pull herself from her dull ruminations.

"Those that are to serve you do," stated Meara.

"I see," said Alora as she opened the bedchamber door, seeing Fate standing before her. Her champion bent one front leg and bowed to her. The light reflected from his silver horn as he straightened.

"That really isn't necessary," Alora told him.

"It really is, my Princess," he replied.

"Well, lead where you may; let's get our day begun." Alora felt a little unsettled to be tutored by Cheshire, who could be both vain and cruel at times. Still, she had seen compassion and a wealth of knowledge from him, too. Who knew how the lessons would progress? Well, she certainly wouldn't if she balked at going. And if Alora had to beg him for more time to glean what the words in any assigned work told her, so be it. When she was nervous, the difficulty came back, and reading aloud was tortuous. Alora had overcome her reading obstacles with grace and courage.

It's time to unlock more of the mysteries surrounding the Lunar Court, and who better to instruct me in history than one who likes to gossip?

11

A TUTOR WITH STYLE AND SASS

Trailing behind Fate, Alora looked to the wall sconces that burned with the turquoise flames and to the earthen walls. She hoped the walls would hold. What was to stop them from caving in? Suffocation followed by death was nothing to just idly dismiss.

They seemed to walk for ages without passing a single soul. The corridor began to broaden out to an arch. Within the arch were three glittering ebony doors. Each door bore a knob in the shape of a shooting star and was cast from the same glittering material the chandeliers of the dining hall had been created from. The strange doors looked like wood; the planes were engraved with clouds, stars, and constellations.

Her protector halted in front of the door on the left. Fate nodded his white head, then shook out his silver mane as he flexed his fluffy wings, which had been tightly enfolded against his back. The hallways were not large enough for his wings to spread out, and she hoped that having his appendages tucked away didn't bother him. It must be dreadful to have them continually bound.

"Inside this door is the enchanted library. It's a curious room filled with old tomes and scrolls. You'll find every decree ever dictated and all the laws governing the Lunar Court. There are also a few history books. Cheshire will meet with us in the history section. I should, however, warn you about the Keeper of the Books, Gillie Dubh, and his tiny helpers, the hobgoblins," Fate began.

"Oh? And are the hobgoblins to be feared?" Alora uneasily asked, meeting his gaze.

"They are easily managed by Gillie. He only needs to keep them fed and well-directed. They have a great love of faerie wine, and once the day grows into the evening, their tempers do flare a bit. The tiny faeries dislike clutter. If your reading table grows messy, they will hurry to set it to rights, even taking the book you might be reading from your hands to reshelve. But keep berries or other treats for them in your possession to offer, and they will leave you alone most of the time."

"All right. I shall try to keep things tidy, but I haven't any idea where to locate sweets. Is there anything else I should know?"

"Gillie is a bit of a hermit. His home in the woods was destroyed when the Lunar Queen set it ablaze. That was some time ago. He is a kind old faerie, but he's developed a habit for the faerie wine. You can always tell when he's imbibed too much as he gets feisty and a wee bit wild. When he's in his cups, he doesn't mind the books as well as he should, and they tend to wander about."

Alora blinked at him. "The books wander around, or the hobgoblins?"

"Well, both in truth," Fate replied. "But the grimoires have fearsome teeth, so do be careful of them."

"How splendid." Alora shivered, then rubbed her arms with her hands while her reticule hung from her wrist, swinging back and forth from her movements.

Fate bent forward and, with his silver horn, twisted the star handle. He walked forward, then used his shoulder to push the door open. Standing still, he waited for Alora to walk past him into the library. She heard the door close after Fate followed her in.

Alora's breath hitched. The molded ceilings were high, and there were frescoes painted with brilliant colors of vivid scenes. Gardens with many colored vines and rioting shades of blues, pinks, and purples were depicted. Her eyes spied a watery world with mermaids and sea life in a dazzle of alluring hues. She wanted to view each brushstroke of every glorious piece of art. Alora's heart was rapidly beating as her eyes attempted to catalog the splendor.

Along the walls hung heavily gilded frames, which housed more art. Landscapes and still lifes were on display, and she longed to stop before each one. Hanging suspended within the air were circular orbs of turquoise lights as far as she could see. Padding softly into the room, Alora stopped at a trio of wooden tables that each had four chairs tucked under their rounded tops. Behind the tables were row after row of mahogany bookshelves that were home to more volumes than one would ever be able to read in one human lifetime. It was a very good thing that faeries seemed to live forever. What a shame it would be to perish before one who loves these dusty books had the chance to delve into each one.

"Ah, at last," came Cheshire's voice. Alora turned her head to the left. Perched upon a pale pink pillowed bench, rested a silver tray of pastries and a teapot with three teacups. Cheshire's grin appeared first, his head following. The sight made her flinch. She wasn't frightened of him to the point of letting out a scream, but her already excited pulse sped up.

What an odd cat. Floating aloft in the air...but if I have learned anything yet about Wonderland, it's that one must expect the unexpected and keep on one's toes. For this is an ever-curious world with beings both beautiful and frightening.

"I apologize for being late if I am so," stated Alora as she closed the distance between them. Gingerly, she sat down on the bench and then studied the dishes, which looked clean, but how would one truly know? Carefully, Alora withdrew the reticule from her wrist and set it down beside her.

"No surprises await in the teapot nor any unwanted guests," purred Cheshire silkily as he eyed her movements.

"And the dishes came from the kitchen?"

"Of course, Curious One! All freshly bathed and in soapy water." His bottle-green eyes were twinkling at her.

"How very kind of you," she beamed at him.

"I am not some drooly puppy that is slow to catch on or a card short of a deck. I shall strive to earn your good opinion, for I have a mind to continue to keep my head. Who knows how the Midnight Crown might alter you once we see you, or your father, sit upon the throne."

"I don't think either my father or myself will be altered so greatly should we rule. I hope you find that we are faithful and true to those under our care, no matter where we sit." Alora leaned toward the tea tray and reached for the teapot to pour a cup. "How do you take your tea?"

"Why, like all the best felines do: with a drop of sugar and a heaping of cream. Thank you," Cheshire grinned at her.

"You are most welcome." Alora tipped the tea into the cup and then added the ingredients to his tea before she handed it to him. With a spark of light, the rest of his body popped into sight. With a cream-colored paw, he took the teacup from her.

Turning to Fate, Alora addressed him, "Would you like tea?"

"I am on duty, Princess. As such, I must decline. But I do offer my gratitude for your kindness." Fate bowed his head to her.

"I do hope you have eaten your breakfast." Alora frowned.

"Just so. Theolf relieved me for a portion of the night. I

returned after resting and breakfast." Fate stood straighter in place.

"I am glad that you were looked after," she told him.

"You should eat something while I begin my tutelage. I think the best place to begin for the day would be a short summary of the Lunar Court." Cheshire set his teacup down, then rose into the air. In circular motions, he floated over to a small enclosed corner and called out, "Keeper, are you free?"

"Of course, of course," came a muffled masculine voice. When the small man came out from the corner, he smiled lopsidedly at the tabby. "How may I be of service to you?"

"I require *'The Courts of Faerie: Customs and Other Tidbits'* if you please," Cheshire said with a tilt of his head.

The Keeper quickly nodded, then took off in a rush toward the right section of the library. As he hurried, Alora found it curious how his clothing looked to have been created from golden leaves that shimmered in the lighting and moss that clung to his form. He wasn't indecent but was bordering on the line of propriety. If just one leaf fell or one bit of moss flaked off, he might be finding it a great deal cooler.

It took but a moment or two before the faerie returned with a large brown tome that had golden lettering along its cover and spine. He deposited the book into Cheshire's awaiting paws.

Alora's spirits sank into her stomach at the thought of having to read aloud from such a massive book.

"Is there anything else I can do for you?" the Keeper asked as he brushed a lock of black hair from his forehead.

"Not at present, thank you," Cheshire huffed as he moved back toward Alora. The book looked to be weighty; she wasn't surprised the tabby seemed to struggle with it. Cheshire reached her side, sinking down onto the bench. He leafed through the cream-colored pages, carefully turning the thin paper until he was halfway through the book. Clearing his throat, the cat began to read aloud.

"The Lunar Court was established by the sixth King of Faerie, Ceeven, who was a great dreamer. The Lunar Court was the last to be established, as it was the most unruly of the realm. King Ceeven had to battle his way to his throne and maintain control of a territory that did not welcome him. However, his rule was just as he was not easily tricked by the darker faeries who made his Court their home. He opened his lands to those who were oppressed and feared among their kind. His subjects came to revere and adore him. Ceeven was the first to prophesize the Oraculum as he foretold that one day a descendant would need to be ousted from power. To our knowledge, no such event has occurred.

"It should be noted that a true monarch of the Lunar Court shall always possess eyes of midnight blue, whether in Seelie or Unseelie form. Ceeven chose to sit upon his throne in his Seelie form and only took his Unseelie self when undertaking dream-weaving and other dreaming arts.

"King Ceeven could enter into the dreams of those who slumbered, altering them for good or evil. His dream-weaving was tied to the lands of the Lunar Court, and it was in the new lands that he discovered Faeriedust and its magical properties. He bottled what he could, then set about the task of hiding the veins from those who would misuse the potion. The exact location of the mine is unknown. The recipe to create the concoction has been handed down to the elves, who have been quite stingy with the ingredients.

"We can thank Ceeven for establishing dream divination and the FaeEclipse celebrations. The beloved ruler also invented a sleeping curse to strike down the enemies of the Fae race. Only the rulers of the Lunar Court may enact this feared curse, so a just ruler must be seated upon the obsidian throne at all times. For a ruler's heart is tied to the lands in which they reside, and in order to maintain the chaos of dreaming and the thriving of the kingdom, the monarch must have a pure heart. We do not know what would occur should the ruler neglect their duties or become corrupted. The lands would surely falter, and the faeries would once again descend into a state of madness that had long ago been eradicated due to Ceeven's reign."

Cheshire rested a paw atop the book's page and peered at Alora. "Do you understand now why we must put an end to the Lunar Queen?"

"I believe I do. So, a ruler was never meant to use the sleeping curse upon their own race?" Alora drew her bottom lip into her mouth and bit down.

"Never, it is blasphemy to do so, especially to one's own blood." Cheshire closed the book and set it down on the bench beside himself.

"What did my father do to anger her?"

"That is a tale best told from your father," the cat sighed.

She must hold such hatred within her heart to do such a thing to me.

"But trust that in other matters, your tutor, with style and sass, shall give you the information and put the tools needed before you to succeed, for we *must* succeed. Wonderland is losing what makes it filled with wonder. That shall never do." Cheshire lifted a front paw to his face, then proceeded to inspect it.

"Style and sass?" mused Fate.

"Of course, my very finest of qualities," Cheshire blinked at the alicorn.

"Oh, of course, you're correct. My humblest apologies for..." Fate trailed off, squinting his amethyst eyes. He looked as if he were searching for the right word.

"Cat got your tongue?" teased Cheshire.

"It would seem so," agreed Fate with a frown.

"What is the FaeEclipse?" wondered Alora.

"That is our holiest holiday, Curious One," said Cheshire as he turned to look at her. "Once a year, the moon eclipses the sun, and we have a full day of darkness. We feast, and we love, and we forge friendships in the dark. The dancing is divine as well. We also remain awake until just before the sun returns, and we drink True Dream's Delight. You'll fit right in with the merrymaking."

Alora let herself give a soft smile in response to the glee that flowed from Cheshire.

A day of celebration for all of Wonderland seems enchanting. I hope this year they can celebrate without the looming madness coating their hearts and minds.

12

A MAD DASH AROUND THE LIBRARY

"What is that delightful aroma, and why is your reticule hopping about?" Cheshire questioned with glee, lighting his eyes as he leaped up, pouncing upon her bag. His striped tail was rapidly twitching to and fro.

Alora was startled before she reached for her bag. But the tabby held it firmly gripped between both paws. A wicked smile full of pointed teeth spread across his face as his sharp nails quickly untied the cord. From between the cream fabric jumped the small tree frog. It leaped up high into the air and sailed over Cheshire's head. With a loud "Meow!" the tabby was racing after the runaway amphibian.

"Oh, good gracious, no! Cheshire! Please don't eat it!" Alora called out as she sprang up from the bench. She looked to her left, then to her right. Fate cleared his throat from behind her, alerting her once again to his presence. "Oh, Fate! What are we to do?"

"It's a very small creature; no doubt it can outlast the feline. Oh, there come the hobgoblins! They will soon put a stop to this, you'll see." The alicorn pawed at the dirt floor with his front hoof, seeming to be just as agitated as she was with this turn of events.

Alora twisted her body around to view the little hairy men who were running after the cat and frog, waving their hands in the air and shouting over each other. They were no taller than her knee and wore curious little brown animal pelts cinched at the waist with tan rope. Their coffee-colored legs were pumping furiously, attempting to gain upon the chase. Black beards that were so long the ends waved from the sides of their heads trailed in their wake.

A crashing sound made Alora jump as a gasp escaped from her lips. She bent forward to grab her hem and underskirt in one fist. Then she, too, raced after the noise with Fate's hooves clippity-clopping after her. As Alora reached the first set of bookshelves, she quickly veered right, then down a corridor of shelves. Her ears caught the sound of scuffling and then cries of alarm.

When the way was cleared to turn either left or another right, Alora came to a halt. She craned her neck to try to see which way she needed to go. Fate was no longer behind her. Alora stamped her foot, wondering where she had lost him.

"Not again," came an indignant shout from a teeny male form.

"Don't just stand there, run!"

"Ouch! Watch out, men, Gurdy has gotten loose."

Alora managed to distinguish the sentences of the little hobgoblins, whose voices had a musical lilt to them.

Then came a *ribbit* and a *meow*, which very much sounded like distressed calls. Alora's heart stuttered with an off-rhythm thud in her chest. Making up her mind to take the left aisle, she lifted a slippered foot, and before she could set it down, a little hobgoblin was crashing into her. They both fell to the floor in a tangled web of limbs.

"Apologies, Princess! But now is not the time to have a layabout. The grimoires have gotten loose, and it's not even noon yet. They're terribly unruly before twelve and even worse after," huffed the hobgoblin as he scratched his bulbous nose. He quickly unwound his legs from hers then climbed to his booted feet. He reached for Alora's arm, pulling it toward him in an attempt to convey the urgency he felt.

When she rose, Alora went to speak, but her thoughts were whisked away as a parade of hobgoblins came running toward them. She quickly turned around, fleeing back down the corridor with panting breaths.

As she ran in search of safety, she passed by Fate, who was locked in a battle with a huge, drooling, leather-bound book spewing blue liquid at him. His horn was thrusting in any direction the book moved in an attempt to thwart its escape.

Letting her eyes roam the chaos before her, Alora spied more puddles of blue fluid. Perhaps it was venom?

"Keep a steady pace and run in circles once you're free!" advised Fate when he spotted her. "The grimoires can't run in circles; it muddles their senses!"

"Will you be alright?" she called out to her protector.

"Of course, this is just another day in Wonderland, after all."

Looking over her shoulder, Alora saw that amongst the hobgoblins, the frog was being tossed about. From one to another, they threw the tiny creature.

"Please don't harm the little frog!" she begged as she brought one trembling hand to her mouth. Her legs wobbled slightly under her weight.

When Alora came to the second turn, she gave a shrill yelp as a leather volume latched onto her ankle with its vicious cutting teeth. A searing pain, making her vision flicker, coasted up and down her leg. She felt a sticky wetness and wasn't certain whether it was blood, venom, or spittle. Alora stumbled as she reached down and poked the little brown book in one of its many eyes. The book fell to the floor, stunned as its other beady eyes blinked rapidly up at her. Alora straightened and took in her surroundings.

Not wasting a moment now that she was back in the common area, Alora was able to do as Fate had suggested and run around the tables and chairs. As she did so, she was free to view how the others were faring. One of the last hobgoblins to run from the shelves was screeching, and as he listed to the side, Alora caught sight of the large black book that was latched onto his bottom. There were what seemed like hundreds of menacing little grimoires running amuck, with teeth flashing and pages rippling, terrorizing whatever was in their sight-upending other books, snapping at each other, spewing venom that crackled and hissed as it slowly ate away whatever it landed upon, and biting anything within easy reach.

Feeling as if she might faint when a cold sweat broke out across her skin, Alora once again circled the table. She was well aware she didn't have the stamina to keep running. Her limbs trembled as she tried to keep herself upright and continue moving.

A wizened little hobgoblin speedily rounded a bookshelf, and when he stopped for just a moment, he threw the frog at her. Alora halted and momentarily fumbled before she managed to grab the little amphibian, carefully tucking it into her bodice. The shuddering frog burrowed further into the lace that edged her neckline, nestling down for the ride. Alora's pulse thundered furiously as she fought to catch her breath. Searing pain lanced up her leg, hobbling her as she ran. A dark splotch grew above her hemline, staining her gown.

Blood. It was not surprising when their teeth made them such formidable foes.

Making a decision, Alora turned, withdrawing one of the heavy rococo-style chairs and gingerly hopping onto the padded cushion. She put her good foot on top of the wooden table, followed by her injured leg. Alora gathered her balance and felt a stitch in her side as she tried to breathe.

Cheshire was in pursuit of a grimoire chasing a hobgoblin. The grimoire was spitting black, inky liquid at everything it passed by. It was a nasty, horrid little creature, as all the grimoires were.

The tabby ran with a delighted look upon his whiskered face. Alora caught his notice by wavering her hand in the air.

"Nothing to fear, Curious One! We shall soon have this all settled. There is nothing quite like a good mad dash around the library." The feline winked at her, then took off again.

"Mad, you're all raving mad," she whispered. "Everything anyone does is mad!"

Fate ran before the bookshelves with one grimoire attached to his tail with its teeth while another was latched onto his silver horn. He was waving both his head and his back end in a frenzied manner, but the grimoires would not let their grip relax enough to be flung away from him.

What is happening? Where is the Keeper? Shouldn't he be here, attending to this mess? I shall have to brave this insanity and make my own mad dash to his closet to fetch him, but how he could possibly miss all this shouting and growling is unfathomable!

Alora flexed her ankle and grimaced at the movement.

"That way! We've got them on the run!"

"He bit off my button! I loved that button!"

"Look here, it's almost time for our mid-day meal!"

The little hobgoblins were all voicing their thoughts at once.

With a quick look around her, Alora slipped from the table then ran in the direction of the little office that belonged to the Keeper. She ducked her head as a grimoire came sailing over her head. It thudded onto the floor with a yelp, its spine open as its pages flipped one after another in fury. She didn't know where it had been thrown from and truly didn't care. Alora was surrounded in utter chaos, but she was nearly there.

Slowing her steps, Alora reached the office then rapped upon the door twice. She waited for a few seconds, but the door still remained shut. Reaching out, she curled her fingers around the knob and twisted. The door swung open, revealing a dimly lit chamber. Snoring sounded from a chair behind a miniature desk, and in that chair sat the Keeper, sound asleep. Or maybe he was passed out. Either way, it vexed her nerves. Everyone seemed so inept.

Alora tiptoed over to the faerie and reached her hand out to pat his shoulder. Instead of waking, a deafening snore came from his opened mouth. She leaped away from him in fright. With a hand to her racing heart, she looked around the room. On the floor was an empty green bottle.

Faerie wine? And so soon in the day? Well, there's nothing to be done except to ensure he wakes up to put everything to rights.

Bringing her two fingers to her lips, Alora let out a sharp shrill whistle. She cringed when the noise echoed in the small chamber, making her ears ring.

With a spluttering start, the Keeper shot from his chair and stood at attention. He gave her a look of pure outrage as his eyes narrowed and his fingers curled into fists, which hinted at his low opinion of her. Then, the Keeper tilted his dark head to the side. His gray eyes looked from left to right before he bolted to the door and, opening it, threw the door wide open. The faerie ran from the room like he, too, was being chased.

"Order! Order, I say! You nasty little things. Go to your places at once," he clapped his hands together. "Stop this madness!"

Alora lost sight of him amongst the mayhem. Little bodies and fluttering pages were in every direction her eyes scanned. There were puddles of goo here and there that she was certain was venom of some variety as the air above the mess simmered.

Cheshire appeared from the ether before her, and Alora

gave a cry of alarm. She quickly drew in a harsh breath and held it. Her hands reached for the neckline of her dress to ensure the frog was still secure in her care. When Alora's fingers landed on the rounded form of the tiny being, she let the air whoosh from her lungs. Thankful that, at the very least, there was one thing Alora could breathe easier about.

"How are you, Curious One?" Cheshire asked as he patted her cheek.

"As well as one could expect, I suppose," she answered.

"See, all is well. The Keeper is performing his duty most exceedingly well. I commend him."

"You realize this all began with your rash actions?" Alora perked an auburn brow at him.

"You should be thanking me. After all, hasn't this gotten one Hatter far from your thoughts? Besides, I never intended to harm your little friend. I just wanted to taste him. Just a harmless little lick." The tabby peeked out his pale pink tongue and ran the tip over his upper lip.

"That's revolting!" she shuddered as the very idea made her skin crawl.

"Perhaps to you, young one, but there are many who enjoy a frog leg in these lands. It's quite a delicacy. One shouldn't look down on others for their appetites."

Her mind processed his statement about Hatter. Alora bristled as her back straightened, and she spluttered. "And what do you mean by insinuating that my mind was engaged with thoughts of your friend, Hatter?"

"Oh, do cease with your useless protestations," drolled Cheshire as he rolled his eyes at her. "He has become an enigma, even to those who have known him since his birth. But with you, at the tea party, I began to see some semblance of the *he* that he used to be. You have met him before?"

"I have," Alora admitted in a small, timid voice. "But he doesn't remember me, and I have no desire to make him relive his past."

"You matter to him."

"He doesn't know me at all." She met the tabby's unblinking gaze.

"But he did once. If you could help him to find his way back to himself, I'd be eternally grateful. All of Wonderland would be."

"But if I was so important to him, if I mattered in the least to him, how could he forget me? How could his heart let mine go?" Alora felt a tear gather in her eye, and she let it course down her cheek unheeded. What was one more lost tear when she had shed so many?

"Fight for him. Fight for Wonderland. Fight for yourself."

"I don't know how to," Alora replied as her shoulders drooped, weighed down not only by the morning's antics but with a heavy heart.

The hobgoblins were busily rounding up the hideous grimoires. In relays, the little faeries ferried the books back to their shelves, where they belonged. Standing in the midst of the system was the Keeper, who quietly gave commands.

Fate trotted over to Alora and bowed before her. "Apologies for the delay, my Princess."

"It's quite alright, Fate. Thank you for aiding in the capture." Alora smiled at him.

The trio watched on in relative safety as the clean-up began. Alora offered aid where she could, upturning chairs and retrieving errant loose pages while her companions did what they could.

When everything was pristine and put back where it belonged, she sighed.

"There, a job well done," Cheshire purred.

"What's next?" Alora asked with hesitation.

"Luncheon. I am famished," Cheshire stated, and held out her reticule to her.

Alora withdrew the tiny frog from her bodice and let it

leap from her open palm back into the safety of the small bag. She eyed Cheshire wearily as he grinned at her.

"And then?" she wondered.

"Then we see if we can light a fire from the little spark resting within you," the tabby said as he walked toward the library's exit.

Alora looked up at the colorful garden scene above her, allowing her mind to settle from the chaos of the morning.

Is Wonderland truly wondrous, or just a silly impossible dream?

13

UNSETTLING CONVERSATION

"So, where did little Froggy come from?" Cheshire asked as he inclined his head while the little group made their way through the corridor.

"I can't exactly be certain. When I awoke this morning, there it was, perched atop my slippers. I believe we gave each other quite a fright," Alora answered, following after the tabby as they traversed the corridor to reach the dining hall for luncheon. Fate was just a few steps behind.

"Princess, we should address that nasty wound from the wicked tome that attacked you," advised Fate with a note of worry clinging to his words.

"We may stop at the infirmary; it's on the way," Cheshire remarked with a dismissive wave of his paw.

"It's not too terribly bad," Alora stated quickly. She disliked the idea of being a burden.

"Nonsense, you are limping. Besides, as your protector, and failing in that stead, it's my duty to see you made well again," Fate replied in a tone that didn't leave her room to argue.

Alora stayed silent as they continued to tread the corridor. She saw the sense in doing as bid. Her father wouldn't be pleased were the wound left to fester. She'd be absolutely no good to any faerie in that condition. In no time at all, Cheshire came to a halt in front of an elaborate set of obsidian doors. Without waiting for either her or Fate to catch up, he opened the doors and went in. Alora hesitated for a moment. She didn't want to intrude if there were ill faeries resting within.

When Alora timidly entered the brightly lit chamber, she blinked to adjust her sight. In the middle of the room was a little rosewood desk. Seated behind it was a curious female faerie dressed all in white. Her straight, long hair was snowy, and her skin was alabaster pale.

She looked up from the cream-colored sheet of paper held in her hand and met Alora's gaze. She smiled as Alora reached the front of the desk.

"How may I be of assistance to you, Princess?"

"Does everyone know of my presence here?" Alora asked as she furrowed her brows.

"Why, of course we do! It's not every day that a lost king and princess return to the realm of Faerie. Besides, Cormack is a well of gossip," she *tsked* as her pale brows drew together over her icy blue eyes. "Now, you are limping, if I am not mistaken?" The faerie patiently awaited a response.

"A bite from an errant grimoire, I fear. Nothing too dreadful," purred Cheshire, who sailed through the air toward them.

"Nasty beings. I have no idea why they are allowed to remain here. They do more harm than good since there are none powerful enough to read them. Well, let's get a look at your injury and have you on your way." The faerie stood and came from behind the desk. When she came to Alora's side, she gently grasped Alora's arm.

Cheshire and Fate were left behind as the two made their way to a dark curtain-enclosed alcove. Looking down, Alora discovered that the beautiful female had cloven feet.

"Make yourself comfortable, Princess. The cot isn't as comfortable as it could be, but it will do."

"Thank you," Alora said as she lowered herself to sit. The springs bit into her backside, but she managed to refrain from wriggling. She delicately placed her bag down beside her.

"My name is Faedora. I am the Head Healer here. May I remove your stocking to ascertain the damage?"

"Yes, of course!" Alora replied. She drew in a deep breath, wincing as the faerie removed the blood-encrusted stocking that had dried to the wound.

"I do apologize," soothed Faedora, and *tsked* her tongue yet again. Taking hold of Alora's ankle, she moved it around in a circular motion, closely examining the valley of tiny teeth marks that littered Alora's pale skin. "You've remarkable Fae healing abilities. The bleeding has stopped all on its own. I think perhaps a medical paste and a bandage should be just the thing we need. Honey is a useful substance and doesn't have an unpleasant odor."

"Wonderful, thank you, Faedora." Alora beamed down at her.

"It's my honor to serve our Princess," Faedora replied and rose to her feet. She turned and retreated from the alcove, leaving Alora for a few moments before returning. She arrived back with a silver tin and white bandages in hand and knelt before Alora again, settling her supplies in her lap. Faedora twisted the lid from the bottom and then set the lid to the side. In just a few moments, she lightly applied the golden, sweet-smelling paste before delicately wrapping the binding around Alora's ankle.

When Faedora finished her task, she rose gracefully. Alora picked up her reticule and then carefully rose as well, testing her weight upon her injured limb. Just a hint of pain in her ankle was the only tell that she had been injured. When Alora felt steadier, she took a tiny step under the guarded focus of the healer.

Faedora nodded in approval, then asked, "Would you like something for the pain?"

"No, thank you. I shall manage. I don't think being too relaxed while having luncheon in the dining hall would be in my favor."

"Wise thinking, indeed." Faedora took a few steps to the opening of the alcove and motioned for Alora to proceed with exiting the small space.

Alora looked up at the floating faerie lights as she walked out and into the greater room. There were several different enclosed areas. Her ears caught the sounds of laughter, sobs, and snores.

Seeing her pause, Faedora spoke, "The other patients. Some are in far worse condition. The last battle left many shaken and locked within their own minds. I am attempting to draw them out, but it's a tricky business, invading another faerie's mind."

"You can enter into another faerie's mind?" Alora canted her head in the healer's direction.

"I can. It's an imposing ability but useful nonetheless. And I take care never to misuse my gifts." Faedora leveled Alora with a piercing look.

Is she in my mind?

"I think your gift is amazing. Not one I would ever desire, but awe-inspiring all the same. I can't imagine the horrors you have been a witness to." Alora reached out, placing her palm onto the healer's arm in camaraderie.

"It has its challenges. If you would ever care to visit and spend some time with the patients, I think it would do them good. I know you care that Wonderland will have rulers who will stand for what's right and just. So many just want their injustices to matter to another, to know that what they've suffered has not been in vain. No one expects a perfect world or a flawless monarchy. But the hope of one smile shared, or a kind word spoken from the heart could mean the world to one who's lost their way."

For a moment, Alora stood stunned. Faedora had so much conviction in her being. She had so much wisdom and dedication, she humbled Alora. With a heart once shattered beyond all repair, she felt a tiny fissure mend itself.

Perhaps this is the way to heal those splintered pieces. Doing what this healer suggests could enrich my own heart and make me a better version of myself in the process. Thank whatever force brought me to this place in time, to this experience. I shall endeavor to deserve these faeries and let them guide me to where I may be of service to them, putting them first, as any ruler worth their weight should.

Beware, Grandmother, I am coming for you.

14

A DAUNTING DISCOVERY

Seated between Remius and Theolf, Alora regretted not making a visit to her bedchamber to deposit her froggy companion and to change from her soiled day dress. The blood stain marring her hemline seemed to attract the notice of the entire room. She hoped that faeries couldn't scent blood.

"Really, Cheshire, you need to use more forethought and caution when tutoring my daughter!" admonished her father for the fifth, or perhaps it was the sixth, time.

"With all due respect, Your Majesty, she needs to experience all that Wonderland is and all the dangers that lurk herein," Cheshire replied. Alora was impressed that he refrained from rolling his eyes.

"From a safer distance in the future!" bellowed her papa.

"And how do you suggest she train? Are we to remove the pointy end of the blade she uses as well? Honestly, Your Majesty, you cannot shelter her forever. The sooner she is introduced to the perils, the sooner she rises and accepts Wonderland, blemishes and all. She can't be blindsided, not if we want to win this war." Cheshire's eyes shone with determination.

What a surprising day this has been. Perhaps there are hidden wells of depths within us all; we only need to plumb them.

"Please, let us table this discussion for when we have all cooled off a bit," began Theodore in a placating tone.

All eyes landed on the White Knight leader, who didn't flinch one bit from the attention. He had a commanding presence and was every inch a commander.

Refusing to have his outrage be rejected, her father spoke again. "What good came from having the grimoires attack her?"

With a quick check of her reticule and the frog within, Alora sighed as she allowed her mind to wander. She didn't want to hear the endless debate surrounding her welfare. What she wanted was a break from her father's displeasure and to have the threat of doom hanging over all of their heads completely vanquished.

A pair of warm, golden eyes filled her vision. Alora bit into her cheek, fighting against the memories threatening to surface. Their dance, the way her body reacted to him, his scent…

Alora frowned at her unruly thoughts and made her mind recount the events of her morning. With determination, she recalled the grimoire that had nearly been intimately introduced to her head. Alora attempted to recall the words along its spine. What had it said? Her brows furrowed in concentration. Alora made the memory slow in her mind; then, she focused on the book. The lettering of the title swirled around in her head. She closed her eyes as the words began to make sense to her. There was no contorting or capturing the letters, nor slopes or shapes her mind needed to readjust to read.

How curious! Femfaeascent's Calamities and Curses!

Yes, that was it! But how had she managed to understand the language? At the moment, she was thankful for the fact that she had, but it seemed of much more importance to question its presence in the library. Alora opened her eyes and looked at her father.

"Why is there a grimoire here with Grandmother's curses written inside it?"

All conversation and bickering at the table ceased as Alora became the center of attention. She wanted to take back her question for a brief moment, or perhaps sink down to hide under the table. Alora straightened her shoulders and met her father's searching gaze.

"How do you know there is such a tome?" Papa's jaw went slack

"It almost hit me as it flew past my head. I was just thinking about it; then the name flittered into my mind. All of the letters just seemed to make sense." Alora looked around at the faces studying her. Theodore was examining her closely while Remius was grinning. Theolf sat across from her with his jaw unhinged. Ickburt gaped at her as an unseemly amount of spittle dripped from the corner of his mouth. Cheshire seemed to be preening; he looked like the proverbial cat who had gotten the cream. She heard Fate's hooves shuffle behind her. Cormack was shaking his head back and forth as if he was amazed.

"Oh, for heaven's sake! Why is everyone at sixes and sevens? What did I do?" she cried out when she could no longer stand their stares.

Theodore sprang from the bench seat, digging through his trouser pockets. He withdrew a white sheet of stationery and kept searching. "A pen? Does someone have a pen?" he asked as his green eyes glimmered with anticipation.

Cormack raised his hand as he held out the tiny vial of black ink and a green feathered pen.

"Do you always carry that around with you?" Theolf inquired incredulously.

"One never can say when something of importance will

happen that needs to be recorded," replied Cormack in a haughty air as he lifted his nose and sniffed dryly.

Theodore rushed over to him, taking the writing implements from the elf. He then scurried back to his seat, where he removed the cork stopper from the ink bottle and dipped the quill into it. His friends all waited as he meticulously wrote on the stationery. When Theodore was finished, he studied his work for a moment more before turning the paper toward Alora and holding it up for her to see.

"Can you read this?" he asked.

Alora began to shake her head, but her eyes refocused on the odd script before her. To her immense surprise, the slopes and scrawling lines didn't need a moment to make sense to her. She immediately knew what the script said. "'*Faerie Glamours and Other Tidbits.*' Why do so many of your books have '*Other Tidbits*' in their titles? Seems very unimaginative."

The males were silent until Remius gave a whoop and pumped his fist into the air. He reached for her fingers, bringing them to his mouth. He placed a reverent kiss upon the back of her hand. "I will follow you anywhere, Princess." Their eyes locked, and Alora felt a delicious thrill soar through her, making her heart flutter.

She couldn't look away from him. Alora saw so much admiration in his gaze but also… affection. That wasn't a discovery she wanted to unpack when an audience watched her every movement.

Mayhem ensued after Remius' boisterous declaration. Everyone seemed to talk at once, bringing Alora back to her senses. Cheshire's grin unsettled her as she switched her gaze to him. At the same time, her father clapped his hands together to regain order.

"My dear girl, you don't realize what this means, but it takes one very unique individual to decipher that particular language. Those wily and dangerous grimoires are written in an ink that is under a spell to change to the forgotten language." Her father ran a hand over his face. "And since you had reading difficulties from the English language, I never dreamed you'd be able to decipher another language at all. Most especially a long-forgotten magical one."

"Reading difficulties?" scoffed Cheshire."My dear king! Do you realize that she's Fae? Her mind simply desired to learn its natural language, that of Faerie. Not some lowly common tongue. Her mind shows excellent sense and judgment in merely wishing to read its own natural language."

"I'm not at all certain that that is how it works," stated Theolf with a frown.

"What do you know of such matters? You're not the one who's been assigned as her tutor. Trust that I *know* of which I speak. Her mind had to unlock a foreign language when it was inclined to read its mother tongue. Tell me, Curious One, who aided in opening the locked door to your mind?"

"Papa arranged for a tutor to teach me. His name was... What was it? Seemed curious at the time, but now that I am here where the unexpected is the rule, a name such as Faehelm seems quite fitting. I do recall inquiring why he seemed to have teeth like a rat and pointed tips upon his ears." Alora looked at her father. She shuddered, just thinking about how odd he seemed to her.

Chuckling, her father said, "Ah yes, Faehelm. Did he ever return to Faerie?"

"No, he left when you summoned him, and we all just believed that either he perished or was still in your care," Theodore scowled down at the table. "Eventually, we forgot about him."

"Faehelm was an oddity. But very good with names and dates. How did he unlock the secrets to your mind, Princess?" Remius asked as he peered intently at her. His notice made a blush rise to her skin's surface along her face and neck. Alora had to keep herself from fidgeting.

"Perhaps he threw Faeriedust in her face?" Ickburt spoke, then ran his forearm under his nose. Alora quickly averted her eyes, not wishing to see if anything wet would remain along his muscular arm.

"Nothing of the sort. He had different-sized lenses of different colors that he ran over each page until my eyes began to understand what they were seeing. Is that a form of magic?" Alora shrugged her shoulders.

"Being able to understand that which has remained hidden always has some brand of magic to it. You simply needed to let your eyes follow a different path," her father answered.

Alora thought about how far she had come. From never being able to properly read, to excelling at the task, and now, how she could read this new ancient language that few others could. The entire time of her difficulties, all she needed to do was switch to a forgotten Fae language. Nothing at all had ever been wrong with her mind. Alora was just made for more and that which she could not easily find within the mortal realm. Faerie was so deeply embedded into her heart, her mind, her very being, that all along it was where she belonged. A part of her rebelled that her home had not always been in Wonderland.

I wasted so much frustration and unhappiness when there was nothing wrong with me at all. How spectacular, she mused.

"Shall I be able to read the common Fae language with ease?" She looked toward Cheshire for her answer.

"I suspect so. Now that you can read such an ancient book, the real question is, what will we do with the knowledge you will bring to us?" The tabby excitedly twitched his tail to and fro as his whiskers quivered.

"And as you are pure enough of heart to read it, it is imperative now more than ever that we keep you safe.

There's an awful lot to learn from the library's collection of books. You can charm the grimoires and read their contents. They will flock to you in droves," Theodore stated before he stared at her.

"I don't think I want them to flock to me." Alora looked appallingly at Papa.

"But don't you understand that you have been bitten because you ran from them? That grimoire latched onto you to gain your attention," Cheshire explained as he batted his long lashes at her.

"You ran too, as did everyone else. What else was I supposed to do?" Alora threw her hands up into the air.

"Tomorrow, we will unleash them and wait to see what they will do. Do not fear them, or they shall overpower you. You must be in complete control, and we may just learn how to end this atrocious war," Papa said with a nod and a determined gleam in his midnight-blue eyes.

What an unappealing idea. To let the bloodthirsty books have free reign. What nonsense will they weave? Can they even be trusted? With everyone putting their faith in me, I feel as if I'm perched upon a great precipice. Any wrong turn can see my fall. How am I meant to be this faerie they believe me to be? Am I meant to face this destiny by myself? Or will I have friends by my side?

15

THE POINTY END OF A BLADE

"No, not like that. Like this," Remius said as he demonstrated the proper placement of her hands upon the sword's hilt. "Grip too hard, and the first blow could find your hands clutching the pointy end where you'll cut yourself to ribbons." He removed his hands from over the top of hers and stood back to observe her. "Widen your stance."

Alora adjusted to a wide-legged stance and nearly lost her balance; the blade was so heavy and unwieldy in her grasp. Endeavoring to hold the sword upright and level with her chin, Alora was breathless and her lungs struggled to inhale enough air. Simply attempting to hold the sword aloft in the air between them set her arms to shaking. Her knees wanted to buckle beneath the added weight. Though Alora's wound had mostly healed, the area was tender. How was she to ever master such a feat? If she was expected to don armor, then they were all quite doomed.

"Let's switch to wooden swords now that you have gotten a feel for the real thing. We can pick the steel back up once you've gained a bit more skill and a lot more confidence."

Remius relieved her of the sword, then strode to the stand to reshelve it. Alora's entire body wobbled in place.

Her fencing master reached for two wooden swords and examined them as he turned their tips in for inspection. He balanced each point on the tip of his index finger, then nodded. "Perfect. Now then, we shall resume our practice." Remius moved to her side and handed one of the wooden swords out for her to take. The grin he gave her made Alora want to swoon; she felt a force like lightning strike her heart as her breath was stolen away.

Alora grasped onto the sword and twirled the end of it around in a circle, forcing herself to redirect her thoughts. "It's much lighter and easier to handle."

"We begin all our young students with the wooden versions. I'd never entrust a sharpened blade to a beginner. Now then, let's see how well you follow my lead, for this will be a dance between you and me. Now, bring your weapon up between us. Be sure to watch my sword hand to see in which direction it travels. Also, take note of my body. Which way I lean, how I position my legs. It will all serve its purpose, and try not to be too mesmerized by my superior skill and physique." His teasing voice aided in allowing Alora to relax her stance.

The faerie was a flirt, but he was a capable teacher. He wouldn't stand by while she injured herself or another. Though, how she was to accomplish all of his instructions at once, she couldn't imagine.

"I shall do my best not to be distracted," she said as she cast a tentative smile his way.

"*En Garde*!" Remius struck his sword toward her head.

Alora ducked to miss the hit as the smile slipped from her face. She doubted he would do real harm to her, but this was Wonderland, and who knew when one would be carried away.

Taking a step away and to the side of him, Alora

attempted to put distance between them. He closed the empty space and circled her. She turned in place, watching his form. His body wasn't offering her any clues as to what move he would next make. When his sword arm extended toward her stomach, she thrust up her own wooden sword and blocked his blow.

"Very well done, Princess," he smiled at her. He then took a step toward her as their swords moved between them, clashing in the direction of his hit.

In moments, they were both in a flurry, parrying and blocking each other's moves. Their feet were moving perfectly in tandem; no matter how he tried to surprise her or throw her balance off, she was able to counter his attack. Just as he had said, this was a dance, this duel of theirs. It was almost as sensual as a waltz, only much more dangerous. But wasn't there danger hidden behind every rogue's flirtatious smile?

If, at times, Alora's dress skirts were in the way, they both stepped to untangle themselves. It was another bothersome trial to avoid while keeping in time with her opponent's strikes. Supplies were limited, and proper attire for her training lessons had yet to be smuggled in.

Alora's arms were growing weary as her muscles grew more sore; despite this, she continued to hold the sword in her hands, striving to best each slash and lunge of her opponent. Each jarring strike of their blades created a fiery spark from her wrists all the way down to the marrow of her bones.

"Tiring yet, Princess? I warned you I wouldn't go easy on you. You must protect the treasure at all costs," Remius said, allowing her to lead the battle as he tried to land a blow upon her dominant sword arm with a vicious downward motion.

Flinching from the near hit, Alora hissed at him, "And what is the treasure?" Mounting irritation made her skin heat as her eyes narrowed. She was peevish that while she had to use both of her hands to parry his attacks, he only ever employed one arm to hold his weapon.

Raising a blond brow at her, Remius answered, "Why, I rather thought that was obvious. You, my Princess, are the treasure." His statement caused her to pause her defense for a moment, and his sword circled hers, flinging her weapon away and off to the side. Alora's eyes followed its trajectory as strong arms came from behind her, crushing her back toward a firm, solid chest.

The sword soundlessly fell to the dirt floor as Alora's scrambled senses tried to ascertain how she had ended up in this manner. She was breathless as her chest heaved and her lungs struggled to suck in the air. But there was a thrill to it, a madness that encompassed her, and she liked it. Having never been subdued in this way before, Alora simply let her captor hold onto her. Color stained her cheeks as she thought of just how near her White Knight was. It wasn't altogether unpleasant.

A rivulet of sweat dropped from her temple down the side of her face, landing on the bodice of her dress. Her rapid breaths were fanning errant strands of Alora's hair that had come loose from the hairpins gathering the mass of her curls together. Alora had never been so disheveled before. She was thankful Miss Prickett was not in attendance to witness her in such a state of disarray. The dear lady would have been abjectly aghast, not hesitating to admonish her for violating every womanly trait that the lady had so prized.

Warm breath met her ear as Remius leaned his head toward her to whisper, "Now that you are caught, how will you escape me?"

A shiver descended along Alora's spine, pebbling her skin. She wondered what these feelings were and why she suddenly felt her heart rebel at the idea of breaking their embrace. Where were her thoughts on Phillip? Shouldn't she be thinking of him? Alora's feelings were waging war within her, and she felt as if she was left adrift in a roiling sea.

"Lost for words? My presence often has that effect on fair ladies."

Alora scoffed, "And how magnanimous of you to mention said *ladies*. I shall endeavor to escape their plight and earn my freedom from your charms." Alora leaned her head back to rest against his chest so she could stare into his burning bright green gaze. There were secrets and confessions lingering within his eyes, and she longed to draw them from his lips.

He's so very handsome…

The moment was heavy between them, weighing all their thoughts and feelings: what was right from wrong, and what was truth from lie? Hatter held her heart, but if Alora was not careful to protect it, this was a faerie that she could willingly succumb to. Hatter didn't know who she was, but this faerie before her did. Remius had seen her at her worst and at her best… and had ventured into another realm to save her.

If that was not heroic and worthy of my adoration, then what was?

"We leave you alone for no more than an hour, and this is how we discover you?" Theodore's baritone voice reached their ears from across the dirt-packed earth. He stood by the open door with Theolf trailing after him. Alora sought him out, noticing the displeasure lining his face.

She tried to move from Remius's locked arms and came up short. His hold was an unyielding force as his arm muscles caged Alora to him.

"Shall I give you a lesson on how best to free yourself from a situation such as this?" Theodore inquired as he stalked further into the sparse sparring room. Training dummies clad in various amounts of armor lined the walls. Next to the weapons stands, there wasn't much to take in. The room was dank and smelled of oil and sweat.

Swallowing the thick lump from her throat, Alora spoke, "Please do. I have been unable to move him at all."

"Oh, you've moved me alright, fair Princess," Remius darkly chuckled. Alora's brows drew together in question.

Rolling his eyes, Theodore clapped his hands together. "Now, enough of this. You must remember three things, Princess Alora. First, throw all of your weight onto his foot with your own, just on his instep. That will stun him. Second, bend your arm up and then thrust it back into his groin area. Do that as hard as you can. Lastly, when he has let you go, turn to him and bring your knee up with all your might to strike his nose, breaking it if you can. Remember those three basic techniques, and you will never be in a position such as you currently find yourself in."

Remius let his arms slip from around her.

Theodore held up a finger. "You do want her to train today, do you not? Why not allow her the tools to save herself?"

Alora took a few steps away from Remius and looked from him to Theodore. "I have no wish to injure him."

"Nonsense, Princess. Remius is happy to serve his *Princess* in whatever manner he may. Now, if you please, resume the stance and hold." Theodore waved his hand at them, waiting for them to comply. There was a reason why he was the head White Knight, and Alora understood she was witnessing his will, which was certainly crafted of iron.

Remius closed the distance between them and once again held her to him. Alora tried to still the thrill that went through her. They were training; this was necessary to learn if she were to remain safe in Wonderland. But she was loathe to bring real pain to Remius when he had done nothing to harm her. She took a few deep breaths, attempting to calm her racing pulse. Alora pushed the thoughts of his arm encircling her and his alluring scent far from her mind. Or tried to. What was Remius's scent? Something sweet and reminiscent of rain. Her mind pictured clouds as storms gathered. Yes, that was it. Remius reminded her of the sky just before dawn lights across the dark canvas; shadows and a hint of danger at what lurked on the horizon, in the hidden recesses.

Theodore held up his hand. He lifted his index finger. "One."

Taking a deep breath, Alora lifted her foot and brought it down over Remius's boot. She suspected he hadn't felt that one bit, but she was in no doubt the next blow would bring him immense pain.

I don't want to do this…

Her heart began to beat furiously as remorse settled into her.

"Two," Theodore lifted his middle finger, bringing it up next to his index digit.

Alora allowed her weight to rest against his arms as she brought her arm up and then thrust it backward in the vicinity of Remius's groin. He immediately let her go. A harsh whoosh of air escaped his mouth as he doubled over and clutched himself. Alora whirled around as her hands came up to clasp her cheeks in dismay. She had hurt him and felt like she was the worst sort of creature that ever was.

Tears gathered in Remius's eyes but had yet to fall.

"Three…" Theodore prompted. Alora turned her head to gape at him.

"He is injured enough, as you can see—"

"We have potions to offer him if his Fae healing does not speed his recovery. He has suffered far greater injuries in the past. However, you are delaying his healing by drawing this out."

"Oh…" Alora felt her own eyes mist as she turned back to Remius. Then, taking a quick breath, she brought her knee into contact with his nose. A sickening pop filled the air as she let her leg fall back to the ground before backing away from him. Alora curled in on herself and allowed the tears to fall.

Never had she purposefully caused pain to another, and seeing the droplets of his blood fall from his nose made her feel as if she'd run a blade through her own heart; her chest was tight with a series of sharp pains.

"This was a cruel lesson," she managed to whisper through her tears.

"But a necessary one. If given a choice in the future, I do believe our champion will gladly face the pointy end of a sword over self-defensive instructions later on," Theodore icily stated. Cold and unmoving. Alora tried not to hate him in these moments. He was, after all, in his position for a reason; surely, the faerie deserved his spot.

A leader must be hard and impassive at times. For who would follow one who was weak?

"Help him," Theodore gestured to Theolf, who remained quiet throughout the ordeal. Theolf strode over to Remius and lifted the faerie's arm over his shoulder. He helped Remius to a stool situated beside the weapons cache. Remius winced as he sat. He would not look in her direction.

Alarm beat through Alora's veins as she watched the scene before her. She would never allow him to get close to her again, not like they had been. He did not deserve such abuse, even if it was listed as training. This was complete rubbish.

"I believe we've had an excellent first day of training. You should expect to be sore as your strength builds in the muscles you've not used to excess before. Do not be alarmed. But remember, just as our muscles bend and break to build us up, so must our leaders. There are always eyes and ears waiting to suss out any weakness you bear. Do not give them any. For that is the surest way to fall here in the Lunar Court. If you must make allies, friends, lovers, make sure you are willing to risk them." Theodore's hard gaze met her startled one.

She felt her heart harden against the onslaught of anguish.

He was right. Alora had no business in messing with things she didn't yet understand. Alliances and allies were precious. Friends, true friends, were the real treasure and if her friendship was a real threat and it endangered them, then Alora couldn't afford to allow herself the luxury of friendship. Theodore was right to step in and put a stop to the thing, whatever it was, between his knight and herself. An excellent leader knew when to push and when to pull… when to soften their blow and when to let it strike true.

Alora met his unwavering stare and matched it. She inclined her head to him. "Wise words. Royalty should be above putting those under their care in danger. Thank you for your valuable lessons and time today." Without another word or glance around the room, Alora held her head high as she padded over to the door and opened it. Fate was on the other side, awaiting her presence.

"And how was your first day of swordplay?" he asked as he shook his silvery mane.

"Very eye-opening. I see there is much I have to learn," she answered and shut the door. Why did it feel like she was leaving behind a piece of her heart?

16

ENCHANTING FLAMES

The toasty bath water was heavenly as Alora rested against the back of the copper tub, allowing her aching muscles to soak in the warmth. She inhaled deeply as the scent of jasmine and vanilla filled her senses. Steam rose from the tub in curling wisps, hanging in the air above her.

Splashes met her ears, and Alora turned her head to see how her froggy companion was fairing in the bowl Meara had procured along with the copper tub. The frog had not stopped leaping and splashing about through the bubbles and purple water since. Alora spied what she believed was the hint of a smile upon his froggy face. Since the amphibian wasn't focused on her, she knew that her modesty had nothing to fear. Even if the frog was Fae in UnSeelie form, it was completely harmless.

From behind the other side of the screen, Meara hummed as she set out another dress for Alora to wear. "Princess, are you ready for me to assist in scrubbing your skin?"

"I can manage on my own, but would you mind washing my back? My arms are so sore, and I don't imagine that I will be able to reach around myself to accomplish the task."

"Of course," Meara answered as she rounded the screen. She knelt down behind the tub, then reached for the beige sponge and bar of pink soap with crushed flowers pressed into its form.

Alora turned her attention to the front of the tub and leaned forward. Meara began to rub her back in soothing circles with the sponge. Despite her careful attention, Alora winced.

"I do apologize, Princess." Meara's kind tone was sincere.

"No apologies needed. I must become accustomed to aches and pains if I am ever to be of real help here."

Meara began to wash Alora's arms, and Alora was happy to let her. When Meara was finished, she handed the sponge to Alora, who nodded her gratitude. Meara disappeared back behind the screen, waiting while Alora finished scrubbing her body.

"Where is the shampoo for my hair?" Alora looked around the lip of the tub.

"Just on the floor to your left, Princess."

"Ah, thank you. I see it now," Alora spoke as she leaned over the tub to reach for the small pink bottle. It was just at the tips of her fingers. She pushed her feet against the end of the tub to give herself an extra inch to reach for it. The action sent a sharp pain through one of her calves. "*Oaf*," the breath left her body on a harsh exhale.

"Oh, Princess, here, allow me," Meara coaxed as she knelt down, reaching for the shampoo. She had come to offer aid with a wry smile.

Sitting up, Alora bent forward to massage her leg. When the cramp began to ease, she let out a sigh.

"Just tilt your head back a wee bit, and we can quickly wash your hair. We shall make you comfortable on the bed or, perchance, in a chair before the fireplace." Meara poured warm water onto Alora's head, then began to lather in the floral-scented shampoo.

"I don't recall a fireplace."

"It's an enchantment. I will uncork a tiny bottle of magical fire and will it to loom in a corner to warm you." Meara poured more water over her head. Bubbles cascaded down her back, causing Alora to smile. She was content in this moment, and while not happy, being content was quite enough.

"How extraordinary! Can anyone cast the enchantment from the vial?"

"Almost any faerie can. But one must use care and caution. Fire is a powerful force that does not like to be mastered. If you are to use enchanted fire, you must possess some level of skill with compulsion." Meara dried her hands then helped Alora to rise from the water.

Trickles of water fell from Alora's body before Meara wrapped her in a plush towel. Alora carefully stepped from the tub and began to dry herself. Meara waited, and when Alora was finished, she placed a dressing gown over her slim shoulders. Alora cinched the sash at her waist, then followed Meara from behind the screened area.

"Compulsion? You have an affinity for it?" Alora asked as her curiosity grew. Should she be frightened that she could upset the maid, and then Meara might use her skills on her? Her unease dissipated, and the sudden tension flowed from her body. Meara was much too kind to ever cause her harm.

"I do. It's not as strong as it could be. I never courted it, preferring to excel in the art of divination. I like to attempt to see what awaits us."

"Curious, to be sure. I wonder, did you foresee me coming to Wonderland?" Alora inquired timidly as she tried to keep the waver from her voice.

"I did not. I did see a hero but never clearly saw their face. A dark suit of armor clung to their form. I wonder… could that be you?" Meara tilted her head to the side, observing her.

Alora clasped her hands together to keep them from fidgeting. "Perhaps."

"Well, let us get you warm and snug." Meara withdrew a clear vial from a hidden pocket of her dress.

"You have pockets? Like mortal men do?"

"Indeed. We faeries like to be practical sometimes, you know, and so much of the clothing human women choose to wear is impractical. Pockets are quite useful, and why shouldn't we ladies make use of them as well?" Meara perked her brows at Alora.

"We should! I think it's an excellent idea!" Alora was enthused as she watched Meara swirl the turquoise fire in the small vial.

"Watch this!" Meara winked at her, then closed her eyes. Meara bowed her head for a few moments, and when she reopened her eyes, she withdrew the tiny bottle's cork. Then, with gentle care, she upturned the vial, which allowed the fire to pour forth from its container. The fire settled in the corner, growing in size until the bright blaze was burning several feet in height. With a pleased smile, Meara turned to her.

"The fire will continue to blaze just as it is? No larger and no smaller?"

"Absolutely!" Meara beamed at her.

"How wonderful. I can already feel the warmth radiating from it to encompass the chamber. Why did you close your eyes before setting it free?" Alora held out her palms to catch the heat emanating from the flames.

"To bid the fire to do as I wished. To not have control over it before uncorking it would be disastrous. You must have it completely under your will before releasing it."

"How does one know when you've sufficiently compelled it?" Alora stepped away from the fire, padding over to sit at her dressing table. She watched Meara in the looking glass's reflection.

"You know in here," Meara answered as she touched her

head. "And in here," she said as she touched her heart. "It's as if a silent conversation is taking place."

"I can't help but wonder what abilities might be discovered within me. If I have any at all, I do hope they are as useful as yours." Alora cast her a smile.

"I have no doubt that you, Princess, have more residing within yourself than even any of us could possibly imagine. It only needs to be discovered and nurtured." Meara moved to her and picked up the silver-plated brush. She began to brush out Alora's damp tresses.

"Meara, how do you stand being cooped up? Do you never see the sun or feel its rays shine down on you?" Alora voiced the thoughts that had been plaguing her mind.

"I do well enough. As good as any faerie, I suppose. Though, did you know there is an enchanted garden? It's just past the library. It keeps in perfect time with the hour, so no matter what time you venture into it, it matches the Court above us. So one can soak up the sun or enjoy the twinkling starlight. You should visit it." Meara set the brush back down atop the dressing table.

"How delightful! I shall ask Fate to accompany me tonight after we have dined." Alora felt gratitude flood her being. Even underground and hidden, there were many things to be thankful for. Perhaps hiding out will prove to be very entertaining after all.

A croak sounded from behind the screen, and they both looked at each other.

"I guess that Froggy has finished bathing as well and has grown tired of waiting for us to fetch him," Meara reasoned as she turned and made her way to the frog. "I am coming to the rescue, Little One!"

17

TOWING THE LINE

Dinner was a quieter affair than their previous meals had been, at least at their table. Alora wiggled on the bench seat, uncomfortable and feeling miserable. In England, they had cushioned chairs, but the Resistance was not a place of comfort, nor was it supposed to be. They were all merely passing the time as they plotted for a better future and waited for the perfect moment to act.

Across from her sat her father, looking dignified in dark attire. Seated on either side of him were Theolf and Remius. Beside her sat Cormack and Theodore. Ickburt was blessedly absent. She kept trying to avoid staring at her sparring partner, and it seemed that Remius was committed to not paying her any attention at all. It was just as well. Nothing good would ever come from a flirtation. They would both end up heartbroken. With Hatter so deeply embedded in her heart, there may never be room for another. She didn't really want to injure Remius's heart, not for anything.

I shall tell my heart to stop longing for men it can never keep. Wondering what could be only leads to trouble. There's enough of that in spades already.

Couples were dancing in the open spaces of the dining room, hand-in-hand or scandalously pressed body-to-body, but they seemed to be floating on an undercurrent of unease. The air was heavy as doom and gloom clung to the shadows. Alora suppressed the shiver that wanted to dance along her spine. Her skin tingled, and her breath hitched as something in her very being alerted her to be on guard. Something horrifying was just on the horizon.

Even the clash and clang of breaking dishes was subdued, as they didn't seem to be thrown with quite as much enthusiasm. There were fewer shattered pieces of crockery and dinnerware discarded to the dirt floor to cast prisms of turquoise light into the air.

Behind the table where her party sat were a trio of smaller tables. Faeries of various sizes, shapes, and differing Fae traits made the room loud with their varied conversations. A lion-headed male was seated with his head close to his companion's, who was more birdlike than humanesque. It was, in Alora's mind, an unlikely pairing, but who was she to throw her unfavorable opinion their way?

"I hope they return with favorable news, though experience has often taught us that nothing good ever accompanies their return," stated Theodore, addressing her father.

"I do hope they greet us with good tidings," agreed Papa. He sat his mug down atop the table with a thud.

"Ickburt isn't the most diplomatic at the best of times. But he means well, and there are few who would stand in his way. I am sure he can suss out the situation in the Lunar Court as well as one of us," Cormack mused. He brought his fork, laden with some sort of brown meat, to his mouth and took small, delicate bites; he was meticulous with his manners.

Alora cut her meat into tinier pieces with her utensils. It was the first time she had felt real hunger without something unsavory to banish it away. Her exhortations from the day were catching up with her. She was no longer as sore, thanks to the vial of pink potion Fate had given to her before they set out for dinner. It had been sweet smelling and tasted of strawberries. Potions were not easy to come by, and she felt a twist of guilt settle into her stomach. There were those in the infirmary who had more need than she, but Fate had been insistent.

"How can one train and be at their best to learn all they can if their mind is preoccupied by complaints?" Fate had said.

"I don't expect any but those that have run mad to ever stand in the troll's way," Theodore spoke as he set his fork down.

"When do you expect them to return?" Alora ventured into the conversation.

"I cannot say," Theodore told her. He was no longer brisk with her, but he was still far from welcoming. His demeanor was always so serious and dignified, but tonight, his tongue seemed sharpened with his words to her. She felt the sting and bore it well, not once flinching. After all, she was the reason why Remius was hurt.

Once again, her eyes veered to Remius. He looked well. His nose wasn't swollen, and his posture was erect, showing no sign of any lingering pain. Remius must have taken the potion, and she was glad at the thought. She had no wish to see him still suffering. Alora wanted to rub the area over her heart, still riddled with pain. She mourned his friendship. Remius was always a welcoming face with distracting words when one needed to forget reality for a moment or two.

"We shall meet once they do return and form a plan of sorts. It's the best action we have from down here." Theodore ran his tongue over his teeth. The men around him nodded.

"Papa, may Fate accompany me to the enchanted garden this evening?" Alora inquired, gaining her father's attention. His kind eyes regarded her.

"Of course. If he is agreeable," he looked over at Fate, who gave a single nod.

"Cheshire is hosting a party there as we speak." Theolf grinned at her.

"Oh? Well, I don't wish to intrude then. I can visit another time," Alora was quick to say.

"No, it's a public place. And our Princess could never intrude when she walks into a room." Theolf dabbed the corners of his mouth with his napkin.

"You are much too kind. I am sure that is not always going to be the case." Alora set her fork down. She had managed to ease her hunger and was curious as to who the tabby would be hosting. Was there a chance Hatter would be in attendance?

Impatience was taking root in her body, making her jittery at the thought of meeting with the troubled faerie again.

"If you have finished, I am free to escort you, along with Fate, to the garden." Theolf stood, awaiting her reply.

She looked at her father, who smiled at her; then she, too, rose from the table. Alora took Theolf's elbow, entwining her limb with his. She cast him a shy smile and allowed him to lead her from the table and toward the exit. Just as they left the dining room, he spoke softly to her.

"Remius bears you no ill will."

"Oh!" she turned her head to look up at him. "I am so grieved that he was hurt and by my own doing. I would not blame him if he treated me like a viper."

Theolf chuckled. "He never would, never could, treat you in such a way."

"He would not even gaze toward me at dinner." She turned her head from him, letting it hang down in a burst of sudden weariness. She tried to stop her mind from dissecting all the ways she felt like a fiend.

"He is towing the line, as they say. He wants to ensure that there is no cause for Theodore to continue to watch him.

We respect Theodore, as he has more than earned our allegiance."

"He is a very good leader then. I don't wish to make anyone uneasy, and I certainly do not desire to place anyone's position in jeopardy."

They breezed down the dirt hallway, lost in their own thoughts. Fate was following behind them, his hoof beats matching their footsteps. The lit sconces made familiar shadows along the walls.

"No faerie thinks that you do. Remius is a flirt. He always has been; he's just never stepped out of line before. And at such a volatile time as this, any distractions could be disastrous. We all need to keep on our toes," Theolf said as they rounded a turn in the corridor.

Alora was silent. What could she say? It wasn't her wish to cause chaos or to get in anyone's way. She would do her best to keep Remius at arm's length for the good of them both.

When they passed by the turn for the library, they continued on for another minute until there was a fork in the pathway. Taking the left route, Theolf halted them outside an enormous wooden set of double doors. There were carved roses edged in gold all along each door. Circlets of thicker wood twisted through the flowers. Vines? Yes, they were vines. They were glorious, and Alora wanted to dance on her tiptoes with excitement. She wondered who the artist was because it was breathtaking. Or perhaps, was it a spell, like the garden?

Threads of excitement ribboned through her veins. She was ready to pass through the doors and see what magic awaited her.

Theolf pushed one of the doors, and it swung inward. The breath in Alora's lungs seized.

With a brilliant smile, Alora removed her palm from Theolf's forearm. She took a few more steps, letting her sight wander. Alora was in a lush garden bathed in beautiful beams of crimson moonlight. There were flowers in every direction. Roses, lilies, and orchids were just a few amid the vivid color scheme. Eyes took her in as leaves came up to hide busily moving lips. No doubt to gossip about the new visitor. There was not a weed in sight, and that made sense to her. Of course, they would have no place in this magical garden.

A gravel pathway was laid before her. With a tentative step, then a look behind her to ensure both Theolf and Fate were following her, Alora made her way further into the spelled chamber. The twinkling stars blinked at her from above.

The pathway took her along a straight avenue. To either side, interspersed among the flowers were statues of different animals. She spied various birdbaths placed in random formations. Alora stopped and stood on tiptoe to see over the climbing ivy.

Her ears caught the soft sounds of a small orchestra, and when Alora resumed her walk, she came out onto a rounded pavilion. In the middle stood a long rectangular table with eighteen chairs. Eighteen sets of eyes watched Alora and her companions as they ceased their steps, standing before the head of the table. Cheshire grinned at them as he waved a paw.

"Welcome to my little fête! I am so glad you deigned to join us."

Alora's eyes searched the faces that all stared back at her. With a sinking feeling, she realized that none belonged to Phillip.

"He isn't here tonight, Curious One. His mother had need of him," Cheshire explained as he locked eyes with Alora.

With a blush beginning from her chest to rest high upon her cheeks, Alora replied, "Whoever could you mean?"

"Why, my dear friend, Hatter, of course. Don't pretend

you weren't seeking him out." Cheshire gave a roll of his bright eyes.

Murmuring began from those seated at the table, and Alora's blush intensified. She felt as if her heated skin might melt from her bones.

Alora cast her eyes off to the side of the enclosure where a raised platform was situated. Six faeries were seated while they played their musical instruments. She trained her sight on studying all the many differences between them. A portly faerie held a violin up to his cheek with one long-limbed arm while the other held the bow and drew it across the strings. Atop his head sat a puff of purple fuzz resembling a wispy cloud. Alora's gaze was drawn to his bulging yellow eyes that seemed to have extra lids that were thin and clear with spidery webs crisscrossing along them. He wore a striped vest but no tailcoat, and his trousers were mint-colored. Seated to his side was a female faerie who wore magenta-framed glasses and had the palest shade of white hair Alora had ever seen. She was garbed in radiant golden silk with the most exquisite Brussels lace that edged the hem and neckline. In her long, tapered fingers was a silver flute that she held up to her pale pink mouth. She was stunningly graceful and held all the attributes of poise Alora had striven to master. Her one defining Fae characteristic was the cloven feet that peeked out from beneath her voluminous skirts. Behind the two faeries sat another two who were situated so close to one another that Alora could not tell where one ended and the other began. With a puzzled frown, Alora realized they were conjoined at the hip.

Alora had heard tales of humans who had been born attached to their twin. Never had she witnessed such a sight. These two males were beautiful, and instead of being frightened of their uniqueness, she was drawn to them. Faeries were always perfect beings, and that such a pair was before her highlighted that beauty came in many different forms, even when what at first seemed odd was viewed in a different manner. They were lively and engaging as they seemed to be enjoying the music their mandolins were creating. Their coal-black hair shone in the moonlight, and their sapphire eyes were lit with amusement as they casually returned her stare. They each boasted a set of mahogany antlers that reached high into the air above them. The one on the right inclined his dark head to her, and Alora fought another blush.

From behind the twins sat two more male faeries. One was slim, wearing black evening attire with a cleverly knotted cravat. His knee-high boots were polished to perfection, and were he amidst the cream of Society, he would have been a darling of the *ton*. From behind him waved a puffed tuft of silver hair attached to a long, thin tan tail. He could have easily hidden or glamoured away the appendage but instead chose to let it flit to the tune of the melody his golden-framed harp was casting into the air. The other faerie was not quite as statuesque, and the top of his shining head was completely hairless. His skin was umber-hued, and his eyes were a striking emerald shade. He was shoeless as his frog-like feet were busily tapping along with the tune of his clarinet. Such alluring differences they all possessed and the music they were making was magnificent.

"Perhaps you'd care to explore?" offered Cheshire, who brought her attention back to the party before her.

"I would, thank you. If that is alright?"

"You, my Curious One, may do whatever you wish," he purred as his whiskers twitched.

Alora looked over at Theolf and said, "You needn't keep watch over me. For what harm could befall me here?"

He scrutinized her, then after a moment, agreed, "As you wish."

Taking the chance to flee from all of the eager eyes assessing her, Alora turned for another pathway that led to an orangery. Rapid steps saw her to the orangery's glass doors, and she reached out to twist the curled handle. Fate was steadily in her wake, a faithful friend and protector no matter where she ventured. Her slippered feet carried her into the hot house, and she closed the door after Fate entered. Alora looked at the different trees that surrounded them. Most were ebony or mahogany with silver leaves at their trunks. A few had leaves in shades of pale pink and vibrant blues. All bore low-hanging fruit in a rainbow of different colors, shapes, and sizes. The entire orangery was lit with the soft glow of floating orbs of turquoise flames.

Fate trotted over to a tree that had purple fruit and then used his horn to spear one. He shook his head until the fruit fell from his horn and onto the ground. "These are a particular favorite of mine."

"Then you should enjoy them. I will explore for a bit while you savor your treat." Alora spoke to him, but her eyes were fixed on a pond where rippling waves of water were flowing, and koi fish were jumping up from the surface. Miss Prickett had told her of ponds such as this, but she had never before seen one. The gently rippling water was purple as it reflected the teal stars that shone down from the glass ceiling.

This is like a dream; here is a bit of Wonderland that truly looks inviting.

18

A DIP IN THE POND

Now that it was just the two of them, Alora gathered her skirts and sat down beside the pond. After arranging the dress's material to cover her ankles, she withdrew her reticule from her wrist and opened it. Gently, she set it down next to herself. From inside came the tiny creature with excited hops once it spied the welcoming water. Alora felt a moment of alarm as the frog reached the edge of the pond and dove in, splashing droplets of purple water onto her dress. Alora hastily rose to her knees, peering into the watery depths.

"Do be careful, little dear! I don't know whether the fish are friendly or sinister. They may try to nibble you whole!" Alora's palms came up to cover her cheeks with dismay. With quiet intensity, she watched the top of the undulating water. She spied the fish swimming around the new inhabitant, and after a moment, they ignored the amphibian. Releasing a sigh, Alora sat back on her heels. The swirling water reflected reds, blacks, and greens along its surface while tiny bubbles floated atop. This was perhaps a fitting place for the frog to make its home. It must seem like a paradise to one so small.

Would she be sad to part from Froggy? Chewing the

bottom of her lip, she pondered the idea. Alora truly wanted what was best for the creature. How could she ever properly care for the frog when she didn't spend her days by the water's edge?

Gazing up through the dark-leaved hanging vines toward the glass-domed ceiling, Alora made a wish that it was real. That what she was seeing was really the sky of the Lunar Court. Alora was curious about the Court. Though tales of madness and mayhem gave her pause, she really did long to visit the castle and to see it for herself. To take in the history and the architecture of the Court with her own sight. She also wished to know her grandmother, however unwise that might be. Could one manage to help the wicked queen heal the broken pieces of her soul? How had the faerie become so terrible? What if curing the Lunar Queen healed the land and banished the madness?

Alora directed her gaze to Fate, who was happily still munching away. The alicorn's silver mane was sparkling in the moonlight that filtered through the glass panes of the ceiling, and his white coat was given a pearlescent shine.

Raising her head, she wondered what it would be like to soar high into the clouds on Fate's back. Would that be frowned upon? Was it indelicate to even think about riding on the back of an equestrian animal here in Wonderland? Alora had so much to learn about proper etiquette in this intriguing realm.

Turning her thoughts to the orangery surrounding her, she noticed a single glass table set in a corner.

From Alora's spot on the ground, she thought she spied a plate. Straightening her spine, she stood, then made her way to the table. She looked down at it and smiled. Atop a lily-patterned plate was a tower of little pink and blue cakes no bigger than the palm of her hand. They were edged in golden icing. They looked decadent, and it had been much too long since Alora had last tasted something sweet. Her mouth watered just thinking about taking a little nibble. After all, she had missed tasting her birthday cake… surely one tiny bite couldn't harm her.

Beside the plate was a tempting handwritten note in golden lettering that said, *"Eat me."*

Since she, too, was a faerie, Alora couldn't fathom that a tiny peck would do her any harm. For who would leave a poisonous treat for any unsuspecting soul to happen upon?

Deciding she needed to be bolder, Alora reached for a pink frosted cake and brought it to her lips. She hesitated for only a moment before taking a small bite. Raspberries and cream met her tongue in an explosion of flavor. Were it possible for taste to make a color appear before one's eyes, the color would have been a blushing pink. Alora felt her skin begin to prickle as her stomach made a noise of dismay. Dropping the cake back onto the plate, Alora clutched her abdomen, looking in the direction she had last seen Fate. But he had disappeared from her view.

"Oh dear," Alora voiced aloud as everything around her started to triple in size. There was a curious feeling as if she were rapidly falling, but that was impossible as Alora's legs were very much still supporting her weight. Within a moment's time, she was encased in total darkness. She brought her hands up before her and felt around her surroundings. Soft material met her questing touch, and Alora frowned.

She climbed around in what seemed like a heap of satin, then noted it was a wonder that her skirts were not impeding her progress. When her hand met her bare knee, she was surprised. Was she naked? What in all the realms had happened?

Alora's hands felt her bare stomach next, and she swallowed the scream that wanted to break free. The last thing she desired was to be discovered. With widened eyes, her skin grew flushed with horror; her thoughts returning to the little cake. What had it done to her? Alora was completely nude, hidden in various amounts of satin and now she was certain of the fact that she had shrunken down to a very tiny size.

"Oh no, no, no, no, no! This is very bad!"

The air around Alora was cooling as fear sunk its claws into her body; chills wracked her as the violent emotion began to strangle her. Any breathable air was being suffocated by the voluminous fabric. The dark was one thing, but not being able to properly take a deep breath was entirely another matter. Alora's hair was a wreck around her shoulders. If she were going to attempt to help herself, she needed to subdue her unruly locks. Alora gathered her hair between her hands, then twisted it from the end until she had a suitable length and wound it in a knot at the crown of her head. Tucking in the last bits under the center of the bun, she let her hands fall back to her sides, commanding her labored breaths to slow to an even pace. Now that Alora had tackled her tresses, she was ready to fight her way to freedom.

With determination, Alora began to climb her way upward. It was not an easy task. The satin was slippery against her damp palms. Her abused muscles began to ache again as they protested her movements. Her bare feet were of no help in supporting Alora's weight against the slick material. But she would not give up. Alora deliberately inched her way up. In what seemed like ages, she finally saw the light. Pressing on, she reached the top of the dress's bodice, peeking her head out from it. Alora was closer to the pond than she remembered the table having been situated.

Looking around, she didn't spy a single soul. Alora felt like an ant amidst a forest of willowy flowers and mammoth trees. Never had she had reason to see the world in a different manner. How strange and dangerous everything looked when one was miniscule. The shadows were lurking monsters, and she hoped that nothing awaited within them to devour her. Was Alora now prey to some deranged butterfly or bird? She had not heard any birdsong but hoped that all animals or insects were fast asleep. If it were an enchantment, could she be harmed? The cake had altered her… this was Wonderland, and Alora reminded herself that anything could happen. What she needed to do was to think of her next steps.

The first order of business was to find a way to clothe herself. Alora couldn't wander around nude. Her body needed the protection just as much as her modesty did. Her searching eyes landed on the silver ribbon that edged the dress's bodice. Yes, that could work if she could free it. Alora scurried the rest of the way from the dress and hunched over the ribbon. She desperately began to tug upon it. It took all of her might to undo the threads from one section. Huffing out a breath, Alora continued to crawl along the length of the ribbon until she had managed to tear it completely free from the bodice. She felt a surge of relief flow through her core. Alora looked over her shoulder to be sure no one had noticed her yet. Turning her attention back to the ribbon, Alora studied it. It was much too long, but it was her best option. She took one end of it and held it to her chest. Alora spun in place, letting the ribbon wrap around her chest and stomach. Then she brought it down between her legs and spun again so that it wrapped around her backside. There was nothing Alora could do for her bare arms and legs. But this was a much better alternative than wandering the garden naked. There was still quite a lot of ribbon trailing behind her; at least a yard's worth.

How she was ever to locate Fate, or any faerie else for that matter, was a puzzle. Alora padded closer to the pond. The tiled foundation was her best option for safety. Attempting to tread the gravel walkway would be nearly impossible, but veering through the flower beds or tall strands of grass was a sure way to get herself into a more serious mess. What if she happened upon a flower that disliked her at first sight? True,

Alora had limbs to battle her way to freedom, but she didn't want to chance an altercation.

Alora took tiny steps, letting her feet form to the edges of the tiles. If she was very careful, she should be able to make her way across the rim of the pond to reach the other side of the gravel pathway. Her concentration was interrupted when one of the koi fish leaped up from the water's surface and then veered toward her. With a shriek, Alora fumbled to right herself. Her balance was restored, and she gave a quiet giggle of relief. That was much too close.

Patting the space above her heart, Alora bent to retrieve the tail end of the ribbon, which was now dangling over the side and into the pond. The purple water was soaking it, weighing it down.

Alora was about to gingerly pull the ribbon from the pond when a giant mouth latched onto the end of the ribbon, dragging it further down into the watery abyss. She only had a moment to think before a jolt on the other end of the length of the ribbon yanked her body into the pond.

Gravity pulled Alora under the surface, and she caught sight of the world underneath the water. Various finned and gilled creatures gazed up at her, some with astonished expressions and some that showed their utter boredom. There were far-reaching plants that swayed with the water's movement, much as her loose hair was now doing having come unwound. The fish had let the end of the ribbon go, and Alora couldn't tell which one had dragged her in. Feeling the lack of air, as her lungs longed to expand, Alora kicked her legs to reach the surface. Spluttering and waving her arms in an attempt to keep herself from drowning, Alora didn't see the other fish as it neared her. Her ears caught the sound of a wet collision as she whipped her head to the side to see huge black blinking eyes staring at her. Before panic could truly set in, the frog reached Alora with its webbed fingers, grabbing hold of her. In a moment's time, she was flung onto its back, clinging to it with fright. The frog leaped from the water, and they sailed through the air to uncertain safety.

"Oh, my stars!" Alora cried as the wind cut through her loose, sodden tresses and made them dance erratically around her. Alora's vision was cut off by her hair, and her heart was beating erratically at an unsteady tempo. Then, her circumstances caught up with Alora, and she was left breathless.

Heaven help me! Oh, certainly I have not been rescued from a watery death just to end up as dinner. How cruel of the fates when I've just discovered a world I belong to. A love that could be everything… or perhaps nothing at all. But… how I long to discover the answer.

19

RESCUED BY A ROGUE

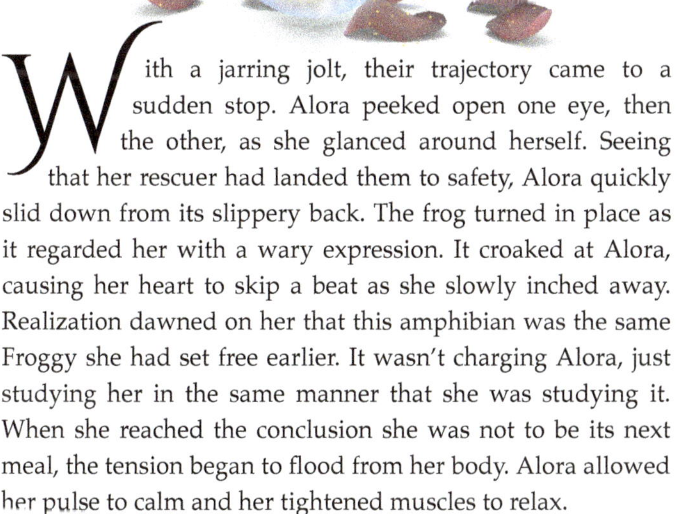

With a jarring jolt, their trajectory came to a sudden stop. Alora peeked open one eye, then the other, as she glanced around herself. Seeing that her rescuer had landed them to safety, Alora quickly slid down from its slippery back. The frog turned in place as it regarded her with a wary expression. It croaked at Alora, causing her heart to skip a beat as she slowly inched away. Realization dawned on her that this amphibian was the same Froggy she had set free earlier. It wasn't charging Alora, just studying her in the same manner that she was studying it. When she reached the conclusion she was not to be its next meal, the tension began to flood from her body. Alora allowed her pulse to calm and her tightened muscles to relax.

"Thank you," she said gratefully.

"Princess!" someone shouted loudly. Alora jumped, bringing her hands up to cover her ringing ears. Her lips curled down into a grimace.

An enormous white boot stepped just before her, and she wondered if it was going to squash her. Soon, the boot was changing into a knee, and then, a hand was reaching toward her. Alora held her breath as a large, calloused hand gently scooped her up. The hold was not alarming, but that did not stop fear from making her pulse drum faster.

Looking up, her gaze locked onto a familiar pair of bottle-green eyes. Remius frowned down at her. "There you are! We've been searching all over the garden for you." He had lowered his voice to a mere whisper.

"Are you not wondering why I am so small?" Alora raised her voice loud enough to be heard as she removed her hands from her ears. Water droplets were falling from her and landing on the skin of Remius's hands. She cringed at the sodden mess she was creating.

He doesn't seem bothered by it…

"I can only guess that you have eaten one of the party favors. Cheshire does love his tricks." He gave her a slight smile. "You look water-logged but gorgeous all the same. Can I keep you?" Remius winked at her, making her heart flutter.

"Don't be ridiculous. I am not much good to anyone this tiny!" She leaned forward to twist her hair, wringing out the water. The puddles seeped through the slits between his fingers.

"Massive or tiny, I adore you in all forms." He waggled his eyebrows at her. Remius brought his head closer to Alora and squinted. "What in all the realms are you wearing?"

"A ribbon, it looks like to me. Clever, Curious One," purred Cheshire as his feline smile floated in the air toward them.

"Can you make me, me again?" she shouted up at the wide smile, relieved that she was not alone with her White Knight.

While Remius wasn't leering at her, his gaze was steady upon her, making her feel slightly uncomfortable by his ardent attention. Had he not learned the lesson that flirting with such open affection was sure to bring criticism to himself? The last thing Alora desired was for her to be the cause of his suffering. The entire thing was a muddled mess.

She must do her best to ensure that they both towed the line of decorum.

"What a ridiculous question. You are still you, you know. You only need to grow a bit." Cheshire's lime stripes began to become visible as his cream body glimmered into sight.

"I rather like you this size, Princess. I could easily carry you around in my pocket with none the wiser. Think of all the adventures we could embark upon. All the discoveries we might make," Remius exclaimed with a grin.

"Have I been rescued by a rogue? Your attention, Sir Knight, is all in vain. I should think such adventuring would only place me in peril with no real way to defend myself," Alora teased back, shaking her head at him.

"True, and we can't have that," Remius dramatically sighed. "Very well, we shall cure this malady. But I am loath to let you go. Only think... With no one knowing where you are, we could continue along with our flirtation. You are absolutely enchanting, even in this petite size. Shall I whisk you away? Even for the evening? You can drink the cure in the safety of my bedchamber."

"You know, that's not such a horrible idea. After all, once you grow to your actual stature, you will outgrow that marvelous ribbon. And then...well, you'll have nothing in which to cover yourself. How scandalous." The tabby grinned as he twisted his furry suspended body in the air.

"Oh, I suppose the idea has merit." Alora crossed her arms over her chest. To be this size and partially covered was one thing. To be her normal size with not a stitch to cover herself with was entirely another thing altogether. Alora tried to keep the blush from her skin but felt the heat creep into her pores. Truth be told, the warmth felt wonderful. A chill had begun to descend along her skin in the places that weren't touching her knight. Goosebumps alighted upon Alora's skin and a shiver raced along her spine.

"You've something clinging in the stands of your hair,"

Cheshire noted as he floated nearer to her. His bright eyes quizzically peered down at Alora. The cat extended his paw, revealing one razor-sharp claw.

Alora felt him tugging until something pulled free.

"Oh, how marvelous! Fish eggs!" Cheshire's eyes filled with glee as his pink-padded paw moved to his mouth. His pale pink tongue peeked out to lick the dark substance from his nail.

With disgust, Alora gagged at the sight. She cupped her neck, willing herself not to be sick. After all, she'd be casting up her accounts within Remius's palm, and that mortification was not something she could *ever* live with. The thought of falling to her death as an alternative quickly passed through her mind.

Being tiny is so very trying. I am nothing more than a living doll.

Remius delicately maneuvered her body so that her front was lined up with his fingers. She felt a finger from his other hand rub soothing circles along her back. While his actions would be considered inappropriate, Alora wasn't bothered one bit. Instead, she was touched that he was being so delicate in his actions with her. Alora's lips wanted to pout as tears welled in her eyes.

"There, there, Princess. All is well. I do believe a bath is in order once we correct this situation. You've no idea how relieved I am to see you whole and unharmed. My entire world trembled when Theolf found me to tell me that you had disappeared." Remius paused as he swallowed. Clearing his throat, he continued, "Shall we be off?"

"Yes, please, at once," her muffled voice sounded from between his fingers. That Alora's calamity had caused him to worry made her feel terrible. Her already lowered spirits sunk further into despair as Alora's heart seemed to wither in her chest. She couldn't bring herself to meet his eyes over her shoulder.

Thunderous hoof beats filled the air, and Alora cringed at the volume they created as her ears rang. Fate's horn, then his face appeared over Remius's palm to study her.

"You are safe! Please forgive my lack of judgment, my Princess! I never should have allowed you to wander off unchaperoned. Dratted faerie fruit!" Fate huffed out as he stomped an irritated front hoof.

"I never should have allowed my eyes to make a decision for my stomach. I was perfectly fine until I was tempted by the little cakes. There is certainly no need to apologize, Fate," she told her guard.

"Just so, I have failed you," Fate hung his head in dismay.

"Oh, Fate! No faerie has stood sentry and protected me as you have. You deserve some time to enjoy yourself." Alora twisted herself around in Remius's hand and wished she was able to reach out to her protector to lay a comforting hand upon his muzzle.

"Our Princess is freezing, and while I could enfold her within my closed fist, I do not desire to squish her. Shall we depart for my chamber so that we may make her comfortable?" Remius looked at Cheshire and then Fate.

"Lead the way, White Knight!" Cheshire bowed his head to him as he waved a paw in the air between them.

Fate inclined his head as well.

A smallish croak came from below them. Remius leaned his head toward the ground.

"Froggy! We mustn't leave Froggy behind! Where is your reticule, Curious One?" inquired the cat.

"Over by the pond. Oh! We cannot leave my clothing behind! What would be said were they to be discovered?" Dread coated her words with a heavy weight.

"Fate, could you perhaps gather her things?" Remius pointed an index finger in the direction of the glass table and cakes.

"Yes, of course!" her guard said as he trotted over to manage the task.

Cheshire retrieved the reticule and held it open so the frog could jump into it. When Froggy eyed the feline, then the small bag, it seemed to give a small shrug of its shoulders before leaping into the reticule. Cinching it, Cheshire dangled it over his paw. "It's not really my style, is it?"

"I rather think it looks superb," quipped Remius. "The shade doesn't seem to clash with your stripes."

When Fate returned to them, the party of five journeyed from the orangery to the garden pathway.

"Are any of you able to glamour me and my clothing?" The thought occurred to Alora that if they could hide her and her things away, she would be much more comfortable as they made their way to Remius's bedchamber.

Remius brought his empty hand up to run through his hair, carefully avoiding his horns, as his fingers slipped through the silky tresses. "I can attempt it, though glamour has never been my strong affinity. Would you be able to, Chess?"

"I am afraid not. Those are not among my gifts. How about you, Fate?" Cheshire blinked his eyes at the alicorn.

"Not one of mine either. But perhaps we can stash her clothing amidst the trees? The flowers might not notice them there. And maybe if some faerie discovers their hiding spot, they will simply think an Unseelie wished to change forms?" Fate looked off toward the trees as he spoke. "It certainly wouldn't be the first time that forsaken articles of clothing were discovered."

"My dress is ruined anyway; what harm could come from the soil?" Alora agreed. However, there were other things to consider, such as her short corset and her slippers.

This was a lesson she would not soon forget.

Fate trotted off in the direction of the trees while the others awaited his return.

"Remius, perhaps you have a pocket you can tuck me into after all?" Alora asked as her body began to shiver in earnest, now that they had left the warmth of the orangery. Her teeth chattered.

"Of course, Princess," Remius gently smiled at her, reassuring Alora as his hand carried her down toward his pants. "I am sorry that this is the only free space for you, but it should warm you quickly."

Her world went dark again as she settled into the snug safety of his pocket. It seemed even white had shades of dark to it.

Alora began to warm as muffled voices met her ears. Soon, she felt movement, signaling they were finally on their way to where Remius slept. Alora fought the exhaustion that plagued her. She didn't want her mind to think of what atrocities she might face should sleep claim her.

Seconds turned to minutes, and those minutes felt like hours for them to reach their destination. Alora covered her mouth as a giant yawn consumed her. Her eyes grew heavier the wider she opened them. Being able to see nothing but darkness did not help one bit.

When Alora's head tilted forward, she was startled awake.

There is no way that I can possibly keep awake. Oh, Phillip, I hope that wherever you are, my slumbering brings me straight to you!

His expressive amber eyes filled her exhausted mind.

Will he ever look at me as he once did?

20

IN MY DREAMS

Masculine humming awoke Alora from her slumber. The melody was unfamiliar to her, but the rich tones of the voice filled her with comfort and peace. Though she didn't want to interrupt this moment of tranquility her body was lulled into, she blinked her tired eyes to adjust them to the low light. Alora gazed down at what was cradling her body and was surprised to discover that she was nestled within the wide, upturned brim of a black velvet hat. Raising her head, she saw a wide cobalt-colored ribbon affixed around the middle of the hat. The hat's center rose to form a high point. Rising onto her knees, Alora peered around its side to see the feather of the same shade of blue as the ribbon, standing tall and unwavering in the still air.

The honeyed sounds of the tune began once more as Alora stood from her spot to take in her surroundings. The hat rested atop a long wooden counter, polished to a shine. Beyond her were rows of shelves and hat stands with various hats made for any occasion. Some were grand in their design, with a wide variety of feathers and lace veils. Others were more refined, created for more of a mild taste. There were butterflies, flowers, eggs, and one enormous hat even had a ship with a full mast perched upon it. Tricorns, top hats, bonnets in straw, satin, and damask, as well as jockey caps, were on full display. There were pieces of headwear in every direction one could turn their head. Every available space within the shop was packed tightly. Looking glasses of different shapes and sizes hung along the side wall. Alora had to close her mouth.

An ornate window with golden, curving lettering took up one-half of the shop's front wall, located near the door. A brass bell hung just above the elaborate door, which must have sounded as customers entered to peruse the wares. Displayed within the establishment was a shelf filled with opulent colors to draw the eye of shoppers and passersby. There were three hat stands that stood sentry just behind the mahogany shelf.

To the other side of the door was a dressing table in the same mahogany shade with carved butterflies along the edges of the large looking glass that hung over it. The matching bench was padded in a sumptuous velvet scarlet. Shop patrons could sit and try on various styles of headwear with comfortable ease.

Floating faerie lights lit the shop, giving an air of enchanted beauty to everything their turquoise light landed upon. If she had the time and were properly attired, Alora would have loved to settle down and try on all the different styles. She had never been much of a hat enthusiast, but who could resist such unique beauty? She could envision spending many hours inside the haberdashery.

Turning herself around, Alora's eyes took in the back of the establishment. Behind the counter was a hanging curtain, concealing what was behind it. She supposed it led to a workroom. That was where the humming was coming from.

Alora looked down at her body to see how her ribbon was fairing. It was still secure and no longer dripping with disgusting pond water, though its end was fraying. While she was far from being presentable, she hoped her current state would not distress any faerie. Alora also hoped the faerie who owned the shop was friendly, for she didn't know how she was going to save herself from her current predicament.

The dark damask curtain fluttered before the humming male came into view. He strode from around the counter and headed straight for one of the hat stands. Placing the topper on an empty limb, he stood back to inspect his work. His left arm encircled his stomach while his right hand stroked his chin in thought. The faerie's back was toward Alora the entire time. His dark hair hung down just below his broad shoulders. Wrinkles had creased into his dark trousers and marred the elaborate waistcoat clinging to his muscular back.

When the Fae turned his head slightly to the right, Alora caught sight of his carved ear and gasped before she could bring her hands up to cover her mouth. The part of his ear that should have arched up into a point was jagged with a serrated edge instead. It was almost the shape of a human ear, though mangled. Hatter swiftly turned around and his heavy gaze landed upon her. Hastily, he reached for one of the top hats, which was dark brown and decorated with a bird's nest, settling it onto his head. Hatter stared intently at her for a moment before rushing forward, then ceased his steps before the counter.

"It's you again," he spoke softly.

"It's you, too," she replied, removing her hands from her mouth and letting them fall to her sides.

"Only, it's a very tiny version of you. You're lucky I'm Fae and have excellent eyesight, or I might have entirely missed you. Tell me, have you come to answer the riddle?" Hatter bent at his waist to get closer to her.

"What riddle is that?" Alora had to swallow to moisten her dry mouth. She was jittery and became nervous to be standing before him. Realization that he still didn't know who she was pummeled her, nearly making Alora crumble to her knees.

"Why is a raven like a writing desk?"

"I haven't any idea. Why?"

"I don't know. I was hoping you did." His bushy eyebrows furrowed in deep thought.

"I am sorry to disappoint you."

"No one seems to be able to answer it." Hatter frowned.

"What will you do if you can't find anyone to answer it?"

"I don't know. Though, I suspect I will never be myself again unless I can learn the answer." His eyes were filled with sadness and regret. "I fear I shall never remember you until I do, and that seems to be such an important thing to do."

"Perhaps you're not meant to remember me," she replied and turned her back to him to hide her pain. Alora rubbed the tender area over her heart.

"Were we something more?"

"I shouldn't answer that question for you. It's not fair to either of us," Alora said as her shoulders dipped forward.

"But I so desperately want to know. If I have forgotten you and I promised never to do so, that makes me a faerie not of my word. And faeries can't lie. Perhaps that is why, when I look at you, my heart aches."

Alora felt a tear fall from her eye. She allowed it to trail down her cheek and land where the edge of the ribbon began. "What do you say to beginning anew?"

"That sounds like a splendid idea if it is the only way to ease this pain lingering between us. I have no wish to upset you."

Gathering her resolve, Alora turned back around to face him. "I could use a friend. Could you?"

"One can never claim that they have too many friends. They make the tea parties so much more lively. Might I ask a question?" He looked hesitant.

"You may."

"Is this a new fashion? Ribbons for clothing? I rather like my trousers; I wouldn't want to have to give them up."

A laugh escaped Alora as her chilled heart began to thaw. "It isn't and really should never become fashionable. I happened to eat a cake that made me this minuscule size. There is a cure. Do you happen to have it on hand?" She couldn't keep the hope from her voice.

"Do you mean the '*Drink Me*' potion?"

"I suppose so. As long as I am the proper size again, that is all that matters. Well… as long as all that it does is to make me just as I was before." The last thing Alora desired was to grow a tail or suddenly walk on her hands. She shuddered at the horror her thoughts were leading her to.

"Oh, you poor darling," cooed Hatter as he delicately scooped her up and into his hand. "You are cold, I'd expect. Allow me to aid you. I believe I do have what you require, and though I don't have any lady's clothing, you are welcome to my dressing robe."

Hatter held his hand close to his chest as he made his way around the counter, then past the curtain. Alora felt safe and secure within his large palm as the beat of his heart soothed her. Her bare skin tingled where it met his, causing her to wonder if he was affected at all by their nearness. Hatter's hands were smoother than Remius's had been, but they were not the hands of a dandy or a gentle-faerie of leisure. No, they bore the signs of one who worked daily with their hands.

His face was just as handsome as her memory had recalled. Hatter's lips called to hers, and Alora wanted to close the distance between their mouths, but it was a ridiculous idea when she was still so small. And most especially when he didn't know who she was. Her heart gave a painful squeeze when Alora thought about what should have been.

Images of Remius, Fate, and Cheshire flitted through her mind.

What must they all be thinking? By now, they have discovered that I have drifted off once again. How dreadful! I do hope I have not disappointed them too much and that they are not scouring all of Wonderland for me. I am certain, once again, I have alarmed Remius. And that is an action I had wished to spare him.

Alora's notice was directed to the room before her as she learned she had been correct. They entered a work room with various bolts of fabric, and a few different sized head forms were situated atop the long wooden table. Her eyes caught sight of different sizes of scissors and needles. There were wicker baskets of different colors of thread. A single chair faced them from behind the table.

Hatter ascended a squeaky staircase to the right of the table. They came to a set of closed doors, and he opened the first one they came to. Inside was a small kitchen. There was a fireplace that rested in the middle of the room. Off to the side was a table and four matching chairs. Hatter walked to the table, then set the back of his hand down atop it. Alora took careful steps from his hand down to the table's cool surface.

"Now, you make yourself at home while I search for what we need." He turned on his heel and went to the counter, opening and closing the cabinets that hung along the wall.

Standing where Hatter had left her, Alora watched his progress. It was inconvenient to remain this size. She didn't want to have to depend on others to care for her.

"Huzzah!" came Hatter's exclamation as he turned back to her, holding a tiny blue vial aloft. "Now to set things as they should be. Allow me to escort you to my bedchamber, where you may drink the brew from the obscurity of the dressing area. You shall find my dressing robe within easy reach, hanging upon a wall peg near the corner."

"My hero," she beamed up at him as Hatter opened his empty palm for Alora to climb back into.

"Happy to be of service to one as beautiful as you, my lady fair," he replied, grinning at her. A lock of Hatter's auburn hair escaped the brim of his hat to rest against his forehead. Alora's breath caught in her lungs as the sight mesmerized her. It was such a boyish gesture and took her back to their moonlit night.

"You're distressed. Did I harm you? Have I errantly caused you grief?" Hatter inquired with alarm as his golden eyes grew large with uncertainty.

Shaking her head, Alora replied, "No, not at all. I was thinking of something that was dear to me."

"It's no longer dear to you?" Hatter exited the kitchen, closing the door behind them. Resuming his pace, he took them before another door.

"It's precious to me. A very treasured memory."

"I see," he said, and his whispered words seemed to convey his sadness.

Alora didn't want to look up at him. She didn't want to make Hatter unhappy or for him to witness her mulishness. She looked at the papered wall that was navy blue and covered with white spools of thread and sewing needles. The silver wall sconces were glowing with the turquoise flame.

Opening the door to his bedchamber, Hatter said, "Here we are."

A massive four-poster bed was the focal point of the room. Burgundy drapery was sewn onto the four individual posts attached to the frame. The coverlet was of the same shade, with a mountain of pillows at the head of the bed.

A rococo-style desk and leather chair were situated in a corner, while a marble fireplace took up the long wall to the other side of the chamber. The other corner contained a screened-off area that led to another smaller room. Hatter walked to the alcove and gently set her down on the stool that rested in the middle of the space. He then laid the glittering vial down beside her.

"You will find my dressing gown hanging just there in that corner." He pointed to the space. "You may take your time and avail yourself of my water closet, which is through there." Hatter pointed again after straightening back to his full height. He towered over Alora, but she was not afraid. How could she ever fear him?

Alora's cheeks heated as she recalled the pond water that she had last bathed in. Picking up a lock of her dry hair, she sniffed it. She quickly let it go as she tried not to gag. The fishy odor was repulsive, and the idea of more fish eggs or anything else unsavory clinging to her tresses was not how she wanted Phillip to view her.

Recalling that her last coherent thought before she had drifted off, was of Hatter, she only had herself to blame. From now on, she vowed to always carry the Faeriedust with her.

"Thank you for all of your many kindnesses. I shan't take too long."

"Take as long as you need. It's very late at night, and as I am a bit of a night owl, your presence is no bother at all. Indeed, I shall always welcome you no matter the hour of the night or day." He smiled down at her.

Her heart fluttered within her chest as Alora nodded up at him. She watched as Hatter left the dressing area, then waited a moment more as she heard him leave his chamber altogether. Taking a deep breath, Alora reached for the cork stopper of the vial and tugged it loose. It gave with a sudden pop, and she flew backward as the cork flew across the space to hit the wall with a dull thud.

Composing herself, Alora stood up and leaned forward to take a tiny sip of the sweet-tasting potion.

Blue light shone from her body as it lurched forward. She began to grow a few inches, but that was not nearly enough. The ribbon was straining against her body, pinching her here and there, so Alora quickly unwound it, letting it fall to the floor. Taking another sip, she grew even more.

After another two sips, Alora rose from her knees and set her feet down one at a time onto the thick Aubusson rug. She felt like she was her true height, but how was she to know for sure? Seeing a looking glass reflect light from the water closet, Alora padded that way and pushed the door, which stood ajar, further open. The room was tiled in white and gray. A curious-looking porcelain chair sat in the corner, while a counter with an inset sink stood in the middle against the wall. Turning her head, Alora spied the tub that had some sort of spigot attached to the top of the wall. It looked as if whatever came from the tiny sprouts would rain down on one if they were standing just under it.

"Curiouser and curiouser," she mused aloud. Alora moved to the rounded handles and turned them just the tiniest amount. Water began to fall down like a waterfall into the tub. Holding her hand out, cold water met her flesh, and Alora gave a surprised cry. Surely, with such luxurious comfort, it wasn't silly to think that the water might already be a warm temperature. Alora turned the other knob, and hot water began to fall. Smiling in bewilderment, Alora stepped into the spray. It was heavenly. Only in her dreams could this be possible, and yet, here she was.

Finding the scented shampoo and soap, she began to scrub herself clean.

At least when Phillip sees me next, I won't be such a complete wreck. Some time alone may make his memory return, and if not, then we shall be able to make new dreams come true. If only he is as willing to do so as I am.

21

A DANCE TO REMEMBER

Feeling fresh and reinvigorated, Alora padded on bare feet from Hatter's bedchamber to the first open door she came to. Peeking her head inside, her gaze landed upon the faerie who was reclined in a club chair near the glowing fireplace. In his hands was a leather-bound book, which he had angled so its pages could capture the light created by the fire. No other illumination lit the room. Alora silently stood by the door, content on just watching the Fae prince. Hatter's hair was made darker within the dancing shadows of the room. His bushy brows were furrowed in what looked like focused determination.

When Hatter made no move to turn the page after a time, Alora knew it was not the words on the page that held him transfixed; no, something was weighing heavily upon his mind.

Alora found that she wished she was free to soothe his troubled brow. To sit in Phillip's lap as she laid her head against his chest. But she could not, and the desire to do those things was slowly driving her mad.

She sucked in a low breath, the air gently whistling against her lips. Phillip's attention snapped up from his novel. He looked around and grew still as his eyes locked on her gaze. Hatter swallowed before quickly rising to his feet. With the book clasped in one hand, he addressed her.

"Feeling better?"

"Very much so. Your magical waterfall is wonderful," she enthused.

"Ah, yes. I had forgotten just the very basics are in use underground. I am happy that you have found comfort in my home." He set the book down on a side table and then closed the distance between them. When Hatter reached her, he held out his hand for her to take. Alora didn't hesitate even for a second to give her hand to him. They entwined their fingers together, and the brilliant smile that Hatter gave her made her pulse pick up its pace.

"Would you like some tea or perhaps a bite to eat?" He led her over to the settee situated on the other side of the roaring flames.

Alora carefully sat, mindful of the dressing gown. She should have been embarrassed or had the urge to flee to the other side of the room, far away from him. Propriety would dictate that even being unchaperoned with him, much less being alone in his house, would ruin Alora, making her a pariah of Society and cast away as bad *ton*. But in Faerie, social status didn't seem to matter one whit. Alora had never felt so far away from her home in England as she did at this moment. Yet, at the same time, she didn't mourn the idiocy of women as being inferior to their suitors.

Hatter smirked at her, raising a questioning eyebrow, standing before her.

Oh yes! He asked me a question. What was it? Tea?

"I am quite well, thank you." She shyly smiled up at him.

He nodded and sat beside her on the plump violet padding of the settee. Hatter laid his arm to rest along the scrolled back of the furniture and turned his head to gaze at her.

"You looked filled to the brim with sorrow just when I came into the parlor," Alora began the conversation.

"I admit I was deeply lost in my unsettled thoughts," he replied with a tilt of his mouth.

"Care to share your burdens? I promise not to spill them to a soul."

"That is very kind of you. In truth, I have very few secrets. What I was thinking about was you." Hatter picked up her hand and rubbed circles along the back of it with his thumb. "Your skin is so soft."

Alora watched his hand move over hers. "Why were you thinking of me and frowning?"

"Was I frowning? If I was, it's only because I wish to understand you better, to know you better. I have this feeling I'm not supposed to let you go, but I haven't the faintest idea what it is that I am meant to be to you. Am I to protect you? Am I meant to guide you? And if so, as a friend?"

"I thought we agreed to be friends," she said, nearly whispering. Alora supposed that Hatter thinking about her should not have caught her off guard, but it had.

Am I meant to fill in those blanks for him? Would there be ramifications for either of us if I did?

"Now you are the one who is frowning," he teased.

"I wish I knew how much I should tell you…"

"I don't see how knowing could be harmful."

Alora took a deep breath to steady her frazzling nerves. She felt breathless just being so near to him, and yet it was not nearly close enough. She leaned back to rest against his side, feeling the warmth of Hatter's arm against her neck.

He leaned his head down toward her ear, then whispered, "There is no being who can tell me how we met. Believe me, I have asked."

A shiver raced through her body as the heated breath of his words met the sensitive flesh of her ear and neck. It was a delicious feeling, and Alora longed for more. More time with him, more time to feel what Hatter's presence did to her, and to learn the effect she had on him, too. It would seem he wasn't quite immune to her being near him either. Alora felt her hair move as he quietly breathed in her scent.

"We met in England. I haven't any idea why you were attending a masquerade. Do you?"

"Not in the slightest," he shook his head.

"I was there, too, but I had snuck in. I wasn't officially on the guest list. I only wanted to attend to watch the dancing."

"And did you dance?"

"I did—with you…" Alora had to stop her words so she could contain her rampaging emotions. How many times had she replayed that night within her memory? How many tears had Alora shed because Phillip had never come back for her as he had solemnly promised?

Hatter leaned toward her, gently placing a kiss on the crown of her head. His action caused a tear to slip past her defenses. It fell down from her lashes to land against his dressing robe. Another followed in its wake, but this time, his index finger was there to catch it. The tear lingered on Hatter's finger, which he held still just under her chin. When Hatter lowered his hand, he looked down at the tear.

"I would never wish for you to cry. I am grieved I have hurt you; whether I remember what happened between us or not, I know enough to understand that for you, and I suspect for me too, it was a profound parting we had."

"It was. You made a promise you could not keep, and for the longest time, I thought it was because you didn't want to return to me. Now I know it's far worse than that…it's because you don't remember me at all." Alora turned her head to look up at him. Tears were swimming within her vision, but she saw the depth of hurt shining from his stare.

"I promise you that you are important to me. That you are special unlike any other before and no one could ever compare after. I have a sneaking suspicion, but for now, I'd like to keep that to myself." Hatter paused and looked into the fire. His contemplative gaze gave Alora a few minutes to gather herself together. She dried her tears on the sleeve of his dressing gown and wished that she had a handkerchief handy.

Alora sighed, her shoulders relaxing as peace washed over her. The fire crackled and popped, filling the room with a cozy atmosphere. She could live in that moment with Phillip forever. Alora had thought her wounded heart was grieved enough for what she had lost. But there had still been more to mourn. Now, beside Hatter, she could make different choices, and so could he.

Hatter straightened his spine and rose from the settee. He turned to her, then winked before he strode over to the mantle and lifted a tiny box from atop it. He wound the little golden key at its base, and a lively, joyful melody filled the air. Alora had never heard the tune before. Hatter returned to her and held out his hand again for her to take.

"May I have this dance, my lady?"

Alora's lips split into a radiant smile as she rose, allowing her fingers to meet his. Hatter walked backward, leading her to the middle of the room. Then he brought his free hand to rest against the middle of her back. Alora bent slightly to grasp the edges of the dressing robe so it would not impede their feet.

To and fro, they twirled in one direction, then another, waltzing in perfect sync. She lined up flawlessly with him, even without satin slippers to lift her height. In Hatter's arms, Alora felt as if she were home, a place she had only ever known once before. Her dearest wish was that the outside world would leave them alone and they could dance for the rest of time. Just existing to live within each other's warm embrace. His eyes would not break contact with hers, and in those depths, Alora spied hopes and dreams that enfolded her in their center. She wondered what it was that her eyes were reflecting back to him. Could they truly begin anew?

A luminous rose-patterned butterfly landed upon Phillip's shoulder, and the breath caught in Alora's throat. Her eyes searched the parlor, catching sight of at least a dozen of the fluttering insects. Then Alora felt a small brush against her hand that felt like delicate silky wings. Terror gripped her heart when she realized that this glorious dream come true was about to take a twisted turn. She wasn't yet ready to flee from his side, not when Alora had finally found her place in Hatter's arms.

A screeching sound interrupted the peace of the late hour. They were both brought back from the cloud on which they had been existing. When the noise sounded again, they pulled themselves apart, and Alora followed on his heels to peer out the window.

The cobbled street below was lit with torches as goblins and little beasties created chaos. They were setting the shops on fire with the glowing ends of their torches while others were casting venom at the streetlamps as the faerie lights within hissed and died. One ugly creature was throwing large rocks and breaking the windows of establishments, while a dog-like creature with the head of an eagle was tearing up flower beds and knocking down small trees.

"Oh, not again," seethed Hatter as he flew from the room. Alora followed on his heels, descending the staircase. The faerie tore through the workroom, then halted his steps just before the large window at the front of the shop. Hatter leaned down to hide himself and took in the mayhem outside.

When she came to his side, Hatter reached up for her hand, drawing Alora down as he settled her next to him, wrapping a protective arm around her shoulders.

"It's not safe for you here," he said with anger that made his gaze burn.

"Is it truly safe anywhere?" Alora saw a tiny pixie chasing after one of the goblins with a knife.

"I hope one day, it shall be. We need to hide you…" he trailed off.

"I don't think you can. My dream-self often meets peril. It's part of the curse."

"Then you need to wake up! Alora, wake yourself up!" Hatter begged as a torch came hurtling through the broken window. With a crash, it landed on a hat stand, setting the headwear near it on fire in a blaze of turquoise flame. It took only a breath, and the flames were leaping in every direction, consuming every surface they set upon. Broiling heat began to fill the space surrounding them, twisting the scene into wavering shapes.

Hatter hurriedly rose and pulled Alora to her bare feet.

"Nowhere is safe just now. We shall run to the back exit and make our way through town. Hold tightly to my hand; don't let it go." He cast her a determined look, then steered them through the burning embers of the shop.

Throwing the lock open on the back door, Hatter opened it. He peeked his head out, then pulled her after him as he fled. They ran in a straight line behind the other burning buildings. Ashes rained down on them and caught in Alora's flowing tresses. The brim of Hatter's hat collected embers and ashes as the nest atop it smoked. They hurriedly raced along and rounded a corner. A gust of wind created by a flying terror that was much too close robbed Hatter of his hat. His hands vainly grasped in the air, trying to catch the top hat as it soared over his head; it was either chasing the hat or continuing to take flight to safety. He took Alora's hand with a muttered oath as she attempted to match his running strides. Hatter slowed when glass met their pathway, encircling her around the waist. He lifted her up and over the rubble, carrying her to safety.

A hill soon met them. Hatter set her down so they could

more easily climb the incline as it rose up to tower over the town. Reaching the top, they both bent forward to collect their breath. Overhead were flying birds seeking shelter and protection. In the distance, a flame lit up the ebony sky, calling attention to the massive horned dragon that would soon ravage the town. A single black raven was circling over their location. His onyx feathers glittered in the burning embers that swayed with the wind currents.

Turning to her, Hatter gathered her into his solid arms to hold her to him. One hand came up to cup her cheek as he gazed into her eyes. A maniacal gleam lit in Hatter's eyes, which caused Alora's heart to skip a beat with fright, for she had never seen such a look on his handsome face before.

"Not again! Never again!" he raged as his body began to quake.

"Phillip, come back to me," she begged him.

"I won't let them carve me to pieces again! Do you hear what I'm saying?" Hatter shouted as spittle flew from his mouth.

"I hear you," Alora soothed him as her hand gently stroked his cheek.

"I see her killing him all the time. You don't blame me, do you?"

"For what?"

"For not stopping her from ripping out his heart? I was right there, so close! And I couldn't stop it. She'll rip out my heart and yours, too." Hatter laughed maniacally.

"Phillip, stop this! You are not yourself!" That he was lost in the horror of the past tore Alora's heart to shredded pieces. Hatter was not to blame for his father's death, nor would he be to blame for whatever fate awaited them.

"I am not myself? Perhaps this is the me that was always meant to be. She'll drive us all mad before she's through. Is it better that way? Succumbing to the madness before the wicked queen eats our souls away?" His eyes were looking at her, but it was as if Hatter had lost all sight of her. He seemed to be viewing past memories that were haunting him. Alora didn't know how to bring Hatter back to her.

Feeling around in his vest pockets, Alora located a tiny box. Withdrawing it, she opened it and saw the hat pins that were collected in it. Alora pulled one out and considered what to do. A tiny pin wouldn't save them; it wasn't mighty enough to do battle. But perhaps one prick might be enough to bring him back to her.

Alora didn't contemplate any further; she stuck the tip of the pin into Hatter's hand, and he withdrew from her with a bewildered expression on his face. A tiny droplet of blood wept onto his hand. Hatter peered down at it and then up at her with a murderous expression. Swallowing thickly, Alora took a step away from him. She hated moving away, but the way Hatter was glaring at her caused her real alarm.

Hatter erased the small distance that Alora had created, towering over her, crowding into her space. His dark look held her captive. Bringing a hand up, Hatter wrapped it around her throat but didn't squeeze. He seemed to be warring with himself as he shook before Alora, scowling into her eyes. Realizing that at any moment his sound judgment in not harming her could lose out to his sense of self-preservation, Alora laid a hand upon his cheek. Warmth flooded her core, and she let it flow up her body to rest in her hand. Alora willed Hatter to heal, willed him to come back from the past, willed him to be here in the moment with her. She sent all of her love outward to wrap around her beloved's heart.

A perplexed expression overtook Hatter's face as he continued to stare down into her eyes. He blinked, then focused on the sky and the dragon gaining distance toward them. Turning back to Alora, Hatter eyed the pin in her hand before he grabbed it.

Inspecting the tip of the pin coated in red, Hatter looked

back at her. Alora lowered her eyes to search where she had pricked his hand, but the tiny hole disappeared. How had it healed so quickly?

"If the prick can bring me back to my senses, then perhaps it can wake you up! For your grandmother must not find you here right now." Hatter leaned toward her as his warm lips met Alora's forehead.

"I will come for you! When next you need me, I will be there." Hatter vehemently swore his oath to her.

"But how will you know when I need you?"

He touched the area over his heart. "Because I will feel it here. Now, wake up, my darling. The time for this nightmare to end for you is now."

Alora stilled his hand with her own. "What will happen to you? I can't just leave you here!"

Hatter smiled sadly at her. "You must. Don't worry about me. I know where to find safety. But I can't do that with you here and in danger."

She closed her eyes and nodded. When the prick of the pin bit into her hand, she winced. Her eyes flew open; then she locked her gaze with Hatter's. Alora's vision became hazy, and everything went dark.

22

A HEART AT UNREST

"Princess, you have returned to us," Fate said, breathing a sigh of relief. "I knew it was likely after your ordeal, you might succumb to slumber, but it was not a certainty." The alicorn rubbed against Alora's stomach with his muzzle as his hot breath steamed the air around them.

Blinking, Alora brought a hand up to stroke his velvety forehead. As her thoughts caught up to themselves, she cried with alarm. "Oh, Fate! The town was in ruins! They need aid—"

"Calm yourself, Princess! Ickburt came bearing the news of the attack. The town is burning, and our Resistance has left to do what they can." Fate stepped back from her.

Nodding her head, Alora attempted to calm her racing pulse by taking deep breaths. When she felt steadier, she turned to see where they were. It was an unfamiliar chamber which held a small wooden-framed bed that was large enough to suit a full-grown faerie, and a small side table on which a lantern rested. To the side was a screened-off area where a rosewood cabinet stood sentry beside it.

"We're in Remius's bedchamber. He thought keeping to

the original convening plan was an excellent idea. When we couldn't easily wake you, he insisted we hide you away for safety," Fate explained.

Alora slowly rose to her bare feet as the sheets rustled beneath her. She expected to feel drained, and maybe even a dash of dizziness would assail her, but instead, Alora felt mildly tired and just a bit achy.

"We may return to your chamber if you wish," Fate said.

"I think that would be the wise thing to do. Tell me, how long did you try to rouse me? It didn't interfere with the Resistance leaving, did it?" Alora would feel dreadful if she had delayed them for even a moment.

"We attempted to wake you for no more than twenty minutes, and that was just to ensure you were unharmed and only deeply slumbering. Remius was more than certain he had not removed his hand from covering his pocket for the entire journey. His opinion was that you had simply fallen asleep, and nothing wrong had taken place to make you lose consciousness. When Ickburt returned with the news of the attack, they were ready to depart within five minutes." Fate shuffled his hooves.

"Five minutes was still much too long when I was the cause of the delay." She frowned. "Do you know where my father is?"

"He is helping with the recovery process. A steady stream of the wounded was trickling in when the Knights departed. He was not allowed to accompany them."

"I want to help. Let's return to my chamber so I may properly dress; then, will you please take me to the infirmary? At the very least, I can offer myself up to Faedora to instruct where I may best be of use." Alora strode to the door and opened it. She walked through it with Fate just behind her. After closing the door, Alora followed his direction to her bedchamber. They seemed to breeze through the dank corridor in no time.

When she raced through the door, Fate dutifully stationed himself outside of Alora's chamber, awaiting her return. Alora went straight for her clothing cabinet and began to pull articles of clothing from within. With her arms full, she located the single chair and then placed her things on it. Alora's hands came up to stroke the fabric of the dressing gown. While she didn't want to remove Hatter's robe because she felt she was discarding a piece of him, she pulled the sash open. It was curious that the dressing gown had remained with her.

Once Alora had donned a serviceable navy dress with little frills, she twisted her hair in a simple knot at the base of her neck. Alora stood before her full-length looking glass, inspecting herself. She was more than presentable. However, the ache in her chest from having parted from Hatter was not something she could easily dismiss. Was it her imagination, or was there some invisible ribbon tethering their hearts together?

Turning on her slippered heel, Alora went through her bedchamber, reaching for the black shawl over the chair. Draping it over her shoulders, she padded to the door and exited the room. Alora hadn't bothered wearing gloves since no one seemed to cover their hands or arms unless clad in sleeves. Not all of Faerie was enchanted by the fashions of the human realm.

"Just this way, Princess," Fate said as he guided her through the dirt corridors. They didn't exchange words as they moved along. The tunnels were filled with the sounds of anguish and suffering, though they came across no one. It was as if they were locked away in a dungeon; the air was so thick with misery.

A heavy weight began to settle over Alora, but she pushed it away as she breathed another deep lungful of air. Perhaps there was truth to the statement that each time she slept and the nightmares plagued her, she died just the teensiest bit.

I imagine souls cannot feel pain, but mine seems to.

The infirmary came into view, and Alora barreled through the double doors. The scent of charred flesh invaded her nose, and she had to force herself to breathe through her mouth, which wasn't much better. Inside was pure chaos. Injured faeries were lying on the floor as if they were discarded rubbish. Blood and various burns met her horrified stare. Among the masses were the young as well as the elderly. The curtained alcoves were a bevy of movement. Faeries rushed in and out from behind them, dragging the hooks of the curtains across the metal with shrieking sounds to join in the communal misery. Soiled cravats had been untied, stained tailcoats had been discarded, and torn stockings had been removed. Plenty of faeries were in various states of undress as well, some even more disarrayed, skimming the line of propriety. Having fled in their nightwear, some would have had little choice in how much they could don.

The thought of so many losing their wares, just as Hatter had done, didn't sit well with her. All of Hatter's beautiful creations going up in a wisp of ash and smoke wounded her heart. Would he be able to recover any of what had been lost? Would any of them be able to?

Alora caught sight of Faedora, who was giving instructions to a faerie with the head of a fish while possessing the body of a panther. When he rushed off to do as bid, Alora hurried her steps to intercept the healer before she could disappear from view.

"Please give me a task. I wish to help." Alora reached out with her hand to stay the healer's steps.

"Princess, this is not the place for you. Return to your bedchamber," Faedora patted the back of Alora's hand.

"I am not squeamish. I can help. Please, allow me to."

Faedora considered her momentarily before gazing at the wounded faeries surrounding them. "All right. Can you apply salves to the burns and bandage the wounds?"

"I can. Thank you," Alora replied gratefully, her heart swelling with purpose.

"No, thank you, Princess. Come this way, and I will give you the necessary supplies," Faedora said as she pulled Alora to the side of the room.

There was a cupboard where Faedora withdrew bandages and several small tins. Alora noticed an empty wicker basket and took a few steps away until she reached it. She picked it up and returned to the healer, who dropped the items inside. Silver scissors rested atop the bundle.

"There are plenty of injuries, and the worst are being attended to behind the alcoves. While burns can be terrible and become infected, they are not immediately life-threatening in most cases. You will see to the ones who just require a bit of aid." Faedora pointed to the left side of the room where the injured faeries huddled. "Treat those faeries first, then send them on their way. We need the space."

"Where are they to go?" Alora wondered aloud.

"That is not my concern. Do you need any further instruction?" Faedora stopped and turned to look at her.

"No, I can manage." Alora nodded at her.

Faedora hurried off to the opposite end of the room while Alora strode intently to her waiting patients.

Reaching a small boy with perfectly pointed ears and a pink, rounded, pig nose, and whose purple eyes were shedding fat teardrops, she knelt before him. He rested in the arms of an older female faerie's whose horns rose to curl around to cover the top of her head.

"What's your name, little one?" Alora gently inquired.

Hiccuping, he answered, "Gilbert."

"Are you hurt, Gilbert?"

"My hand is." He unfolded his arms, holding his hand up for her to inspect. A red wound ate the flesh from the back of his tiny hand. It looked painful.

"Oh, I have just the thing to take the sting away. Do you mind if I help you?" Alora gave him a timid smile.

Gilbert nodded and stuck his quivering lower lip out. Alora reached into the basket, withdrawing one of the little silver tins. Opening it, honeysuckle and some herbs, which her nose could not suss out but smelled pleasant, wafted into the air. She retrieved a wooden depressor with a rounded end and dipped it into the paste. Using the instrument, she applied the salve to Gilbert's hand with careful pressure. His tears slowly ceased as he watched her bandage his hand.

"All finished, little one," Alora said to the boy before looking at the older woman. "Is that all that you require?"

"Yes, you've been very accommodating," said the older faerie with a nod. She rose to her cloven feet, taking the boy in her arms. He waved as the two maneuvered their way from the tangle of bodies.

Turning to the elder faerie who was next, she winced when she saw the burn covering his entire left leg. His pants were singed, and it looked like his Fae healing had attempted to work, but the pant leg was hindering its progress.

"May I help?" Alora asked as her hand closed over the scissors. She pulled them from the basket.

"Aye, that would be faetastic," he grumbled at her.

Raising her eyes to his face, she noticed his eyes were milky-white, signaling his blindness. Alora would endeavor to be gentle and go slowly with his care. His frogesque feet twitched when she touched his injured leg.

"I need to cut away your trousers just above the injury on this leg." Her hand returned to lay against his wounded limb.

"Do what must be done," he growled out.

"Cutting it now, then." Alora bent forward as she cut away the tattered fabric. She had to give an extra tug in certain places, but he never made a peep. Alora cringed when the trousers freed his leg for her to view better. His flesh was blackened and crisps of skin rose away from his limb. She looked behind her for Faedora but didn't see her. Taking a deep breath, Alora fortified herself and then got to work. Applying the salve, she began to see its magic working as amber-colored bursts of light knit the skin, pushing the destroyed bits from it. Alora needed to keep adding more, but she was amazed it was healing even the worst burns. Alora talked her way through each action so the faerie knew precisely what she was about to do. When the salve stayed on his wound and ceased its melting, Alora unwound some of the bandages before wrapping his leg. She cut where it was needed, then tucked the end securely into place. Through the entire process, Alora willed the injury to heal. Her sole focus was on the well-being of her patient and her adamant desire to see him better.

"All finished. Do you have some faerie to assist you?" Alora looked to the faerie beside him, who shrugged.

"I don't, and I don't need none either. I can manage just fine," he grumbled as he rose and tested his weight on his injured leg. "Feels fine," he said, then bowed to her.

Watching him hobble away, she felt sorrow that he seemed all alone.

A cough returned her attention to the next faerie who required her attention. And so, the long hours of what remained of the early morning passed by. Alora picked up her pace, but there were always more wounded to squeeze into the empty spots previously vacated. Her heart was in unrest, fearing that at any moment, one of the faces she knew would be brought through the infirmary doors.

I wish the end were near so that it was time to dethrone my grandmother, for who could participate in this reign of terror and not have their heart bleed?

23

CALMING THE SEA OF TERROR

Sluggish steps were all Alora could manage as the tide began to change and the number of those who came through the infirmary doors decreased. None seemed to know that she was the returned princess. Then again, perhaps they simply didn't care. Alora's dress and hair were mussed and covered in ashes. Streaks of soot lined her face and clung to her shawl. Alora persisted even when the fatigue threatened to make her succumb to slumber as she stood on her aching feet.

"There you are!" thundered her father when the last wave of injured had been attended to. Alora was standing at the sink washing her hands when his voice wrested her from her thoughts.

He came to her, reaching a steadying hand onto her shoulder. "I knew you'd awaken and return to us, but I wasn't sure what state I would find you in."

"I am exceedingly tired, but well," Alora replied as she rinsed her hands. When she turned around, she gasped. There was a gash along her father's forehead that looked like it needed stitches. "You are hurt! Faedora must see to you at once."

Alora reached out, wrapping her arms around Papa. He gently patted her back. It was an awkward moment between them, but not one she would take back. Alora let him go, then stepped away.

"The healer is busy. Theodore said he had a potion to fix me, and I said I must find you first." Papa looked just as dead on his feet as she felt.

"Let me put the supplies away, then I'll leave with you." Alora spun around and began pulling the items from the basket to reshelve. She closed the last cupboard and placed the basket on the floor in the same spot where she had first located it.

Her father watched her as his eyes tracked her every movement. Once she was ready, he held out his arm for her to take. They took a few steps when a curtain of one of the alcoves fluttered, revealing Faedora, who came out from behind it.

"Oh, are you leaving?" She addressed Alora. She tucked unruly wisps of her white hair back into her upswept coiffure.

"I am taking my daughter to rest," Papa answered in a no-nonsense tone.

"That's a rather nasty gash. Shall we stitch you up before you go?" Faedora came closer to study his wound.

"No, Theodore has a potion that will cure it. He's awaiting our presence," he said with a wave of his hand toward the room's exit, impatient to be gone.

"Oh? I won't keep you here any longer in that case." She turned to speak with Alora again. "We are grateful you could spare the time to help us. Your skills have been put to the best of use. Anytime you wish to return and hone those healing abilities, I would be pleased to teach you."

A gasp bolted from Alora's mouth as her eyes grew round.

"You believe she has an affinity for healing?" Her father's brows were upraised in wonder as he peered at his daughter in silent appraisal.

"I do. When I treated the bite wound, I remarked she had a fast healing ability." Faedora nodded to the King before switching her gaze to Alora. "You have had no other complaints with it, have you?"

Alora frowned. "No, in truth, I had forgotten all about it."

"I have some theories I'd like to test." Faedora tilted her head to the side.

"That sounds both immensely intriguing and also frightfully daunting. But I am thrilled to see what I can do; if I have a gift to heal others, that's more than I could have ever wished for." Alora felt her heart lighten.

If I can help more heal quickly, we can turn this tide of terror even faster. Is that what brought Phillip back to me? Did that warmth I experienced flow into him, healing him, even just a little bit?

"When you have the time, I will happily show you all I know," exclaimed Faedora as she beamed.

"I can't wait to begin!" Alora enthusiastically replied. Could she perhaps heal the evil that festered in her grandmother?

Her father nodded at the healer, then together, he and Alora left the infirmary. Fate stood a few paces away from the double doors. When they began to walk, he was quickly on their heels. As they descended the corridor's twists and turns, they came to a section she had never been to before.

Papa pushed the door's handle open and swept them into the massive room. There was a sizable table in the middle of the room with maps tacked down with little red and white figures, much like the pieces from a chess board, sitting in different areas. The light shone down on them from a colossal chandelier created from the same black obsidian she had often seen. To the side of the room stood a rounded table with fourteen matching chairs. The table's surface was littered with papers. A few books were scattered about atop it. Faeries were rushing back and forth from the main table.

"Welcome to the War Room, the very heart of the Resistance," Remius told her as he came to stand by her side. Was it her imagination that she felt the back of his hand touch hers? She was winded by the walk she had just taken, not by the idea of his skin against hers.

"Impressive," she answered as she inspected him. Covered in ashes, Remius's former white and pristine clothing was now blackened. His golden hair was grayed, as was his face. But the sparkle in Remius's eyes was the same, letting her know he was physically unharmed.

"Was I right? Did I make you so comfortable you succumbed to slumber?" He waggled his brows at her.

"Remius," barked Theodore, who came from across the room, his tail twitching in irritation. His stern expression dimmed Alora's smile before it fell entirely from her face. Remius held up his hands as he backed away from her.

"My apologies," Remius bowed with a more reserved manner.

"We've all had quite a long day already," began her father. "Let's get some sleep and then reconvene this afternoon."

"Excellent idea, Your Highness." Theodore reached into his vest pocket. He held a tiny vial with shimmering silver liquid. "Here is the healing potion. Drink it all swiftly, Your Majesty."

Papa took the vial with a nod, indicating his gratitude, then uncorked it. Alora watched as he emptied the contents into his mouth; when her father removed the tiny bottle, a puff of silver emanated from his mouth before he closed it. Letting his hand rest back at his side, the vial was still gripped tightly in his grasp. Alora watched with wonder as the wound began to cast a soft silver glow. The torn flesh began to knit itself back together until nothing remained, not even a faint scar.

"Curiouser and curiouser," Alora breathed as she poked at

his forehead with her index finger. "Does it hurt?" This potion had worked even faster than the salve.

"Your prodding at me or the former wound?" Papa inquired with a slight upcurve of his lips.

"I am sorry; I didn't mean to," she began, removing her finger.

"Nothing to worry over. I am fine, it would seem; even the headache has vanished. How remarkable." He touched his forehead, prodding at the healed flesh.

"We don't often use our supply; however, as our leader, it's imperative to keep you healthy and ready for what awaits us at any given moment," Theodore explained in a droll tone.

"I take it there's a limited supply?" Her father frowned.

"Just so. So we are very thoughtful before doling any out," the White Knight leader said.

"Is there anything more we can do for the citizens?" Papa waved over to the map atop the table.

"Not at present. We can help by rebuilding, though it's only a matter of time before Femfaeascent destroys it again." Theodore rubbed his forehead. He looked just as worn out as the rest of them. They all required a bath and a few hours of rest.

"Very well. Then I am escorting my daughter to her bedchamber, then seeking my own. We can discuss this further later." Her father held his arm to her, and Alora entwined their limbs.

Alora turned to smile at Remius, but he just scowled at the ground before stalking off through the door before them.

I have bungled things. I need to show Theodore I am not some silly chit but have worth. It was never my intention to cause strife. We all must work together to do the right things for the Lunar Court. That is where the focus should be. I also need to have a chat with my surly, flirting knight. My heart has been in such turmoil, but spending time with Phillip has made me aware I could never truly give my heart to another, for every beat of my heart whispers Phillip's name.

24

SHRIEKING SCREAMS OF MOURNFUL FRIGHT

With a jostle, Alora awakened and tried to recall whether she had dreamed. Looking over at the small side table, she noticed the Faeriedust, then sighed in relief. She had remembered taking the potion following her bath. Meara had handed the vial to her before leaving the chamber. With determination to not be a bother to another soul, Alora had uncorked it, allowing tiny particles to fall from it into her mouth.

Alora sat up and stretched as she wondered what time it was. She needed to ask whether a clock could be provided; Alora disliked not knowing the hour. Swinging her legs over the side of her small bed, Alora looked over at the side table and then pulled the drawer open. Peering down, she spied Froggy nestled cozily within one of her discarded gloves. The frog's eyes opened and it looked up at her expectedly.

"I hope you rested well," Alora whispered.

With a croak for a reply, the frog hopped to the drawer's opening, then from there to the top of the side table.

"You wouldn't happen to know the time, I suppose?"

Beady black eyes rolled in their green sockets up at her.

"Right, well, let's begin our day. Or rather, afternoon? For it surely can't yet be dinner time." Alora climbed from under her coverlet and gazed down at her slippers resting on the dirt floor. She wanted to be sure no surprise visitors were awaiting her notice today. Her mind began to count down the days.

Three days?

How had she only been in Wonderland for three days? So much had happened. A lifetime of events had been crammed into such a few short hours. She had experienced so much more in the last three days than eighteen years of her life in England. Was her father right to try to hide her away from this chaos for all those years?

"Puuuurfect! You have finally risen. It's time for our meeting," groused Cheshire, who glimmered into view from his curled spot at the foot of her bed.

"Meeting?" Alora craned her head to look at him.

"The one in which we venture to the library and poke at the grimoires? To see whether you can tame them to do your bidding and read their contents? That meeting? Sound familiar at all?"

"Oh, yes. I forgot all about that. I shall ready myself at once, and we can get to it." Alora rose from the bed with her warm slippers in place and padded to the cabinet to retrieve her clothing. When her arms were laden, Alora slid behind the screen, setting her things down to dress.

"We are to meet your father and his retinue there. They wanted to meet with Gillie and be sure he isn't three sheets to the wind, in case we need him," Cheshire informed her.

"Excellent," Alora said as she brought her dress over her head, then slid her arms into the capped sleeves. In a few more moments, her stockings were in place, and her slippers were donned. They matched the teal day dress with a floral pattern in lime-green, transparent lace. The bronze ribbon high at her waist nearly matched the highlights in Alora's hair. Bronze lace decorated the bodice along the neckline. It was an enchanting ensemble. Alora felt both beautiful and graceful. Since her bare skin still pebbled from the chill that she could not cast away, Alora decided to retrieve the elbow-length white silk gloves from her cabinet's interior drawer. Though she didn't bother to put them on just yet, Alora brought them with her as she came from behind the screen.

Making her way to the dressing table, Alora sat down in the chair and set her gloves to the side. Picking up the silver brush, she ran it through her long russet tresses until her hair was tangle-free and shining. Alora gathered her locks between her hands, twisting the mass into a very messily arranged bun. Her curls wanted to rebel and pull from the coiffure, so she decided to let them have their way the tiniest bit. Twin tendrils of curling hair caressed the sides of her face. Turning her head from side to side, Alora took in the full image of her hair in the bedeviled looking glass situated before her. The style suited her. Alora was pleased that though it wasn't perfectly pinned in place, it was striking nonetheless. Her sapphire eyes sparkled as Alora let herself enjoy a quiet moment.

"Ahem," scoffed Cheshire. "But there are some of us who do not have the entire day to laze about admiring their own true perfection. Were that an acceptable pastime, I would never be budged from my looking glass. I am rather handsome, am I not? Do you not admire me?"

Turning her head to look toward the bed where the tabby was still perched, Alora nodded. "We are all in constant awe of you, Cheshire."

"As you should be! Now, Curious One, let us be off." Cheshire lifted himself from the bed to float along the air. His gaze landed upon the frog as he said, "You are to remain here. 'Tis much safer for you there, and you won't be such a distraction to those beings that so desire a taste. We shall refrain from mentioning any names." The tabby's face bore a serene expression as he clasped his paws together to his chest, over his heart. Alora fought the giggle that wanted to break free at his ridiculous display.

"That is an excellent idea, Froggy. I feel sure Meara will soon be by and see that you are well cared for. Take today to rest, Little One." Rising, Alora bent over to reach for her gloves, pulling them on before she made her way to his side. When she reached the door, Alora opened it and waved toward it. "After you, Cheshire."

"How kind of you," he said as he twirled through the open space.

Alora's lips quirked into a smirk, watching the cat as she followed him through. She turned, grasping the door handle as she pulled it shut behind her.

"Feeling rested, Princess?" Fate inquired, keeping in time with her steps as they set out for the meeting.

"I am, thank you, and how are you? Has anything more happened while I was slumbering?" Alora felt a dip of anxiety squeeze her heart.

"No, all was blessedly quiet," her protector assured her.

"Thank Heavens." She let a whoosh of air escape from her mouth. She was desperately in need of just a little calm today.

Within a few minutes more, the trio reached the library's entrance. Fate trotted to the door and then used his horn to push it open. Once again, Alora's senses were filled with wonder as she gazed up at the ceiling. She stepped over the threshold, and her companions trailed after her. The enchanted ceiling only grew more beautiful each time Alora saw it. Odd bits of color and details revealed themselves with each new visit.

"There you are, my dear," greeted her father, whose serious tone of voice commanded her attention. Her eyes sought him out, and she noted that, once again, he was dressed in dark colors; this time, he seemed to be entirely clothed in midnight blue.

"I am sorry to have kept you waiting," she answered, hurrying her steps to close the distance between them.

"Nonsense, you needed your rest. We have been talking with the Keeper, and he is agreeable to allowing you to try to tame a grimoire or two."

"Oh? Well, how splendid." Not wanting to prove to be a huge disappointment, Alora tried to be cheerful. If she could mask her anxiety perhaps some of the pressure she felt would disappear.

"Indeed, shall we further this escapade along?" Cheshire rubbed his paws together animatedly.

"You realize we don't actually wish for a repeat of the other day, don't you?" Alora raised a skeptical brow at the tabby.

"Are you not on your best behavior, Cheshire?" teased Remius, who came out from a curve of the bookcases with Theodore and Theolf by his side. Cormack hurried his steps to keep up with the longer-limbed faeries.

So every faerie is here, how marvelous… I shall either epically succeed or dismally fail, all under the watchful eyes of an audience.

"I shall have you know I am the source of discretion and moral integrity," sniffed the tabby.

"Oh, I must have forgotten that," Remius replied as he stroked his jaw in thought. Alora caught the twinkle of amusement in his gaze that he focused on the tabby.

"Let us begin, shall we?" Theodore interjected as his tail swished behind him. "Keeper, if you would be so kind as to present the grimoires that we may visit with, we can sooner leave you to your solitude."

Gillie nodded once, then hurriedly strode over to his little office and peeked his head into the room. He exchanged words with someone until he turned back to their group with two of the hobgoblins in his wake. The two hairy beings clasped a book each toward their chest with glum looks on their grim faces. Their guarded looks did not inspire confidence in Alora's abilities.

Once the trio reach the gathered group, the two hobgoblins set their charges down on the tabletop. The grimoires blinked their sleepy eyes up to survey the faeries who stood looking down at them.

"These are lower-level grimoires, and if you can master them and read their contents, you should, in theory, be able to do the same with the higher-powered ones," Gillie said to Alora as he once again scratched his chin in thought.

"Just do your best and at your own pace," advised Papa. "We are in no rush."

Alora felt all eyes upon her. She struggled with fear and then frustration that years of her being unable to read had gifted her with. Attempting to push those unwanted feelings away, Alora sighed as she reached her gloved index finger out to run across the cover of one of the grimoires. She tickled its leather-bound front, and the book somehow seemed to let out a wheezing giggle. Alora quickly drew her hand away and then looked over at Gillie.

"Go on, I would say that they won't bite, but you've been here before…" He prompted, gesturing to the grimoire.

Without another word and thinking about it overmuch, Alora caressed the cover and silently concentrated on willing it to open. The cover slowly rose up and then laid flat against the table. A thrill passed through Alora as she gave a small grin of glee at that one accomplishment.

Small beginnings can lead to grand things.

Stroking the first page, Alora ran her finger over the edge, nudging the page to turn. The letters resting upon the next page as it settled down were clear and effortless for her to read. "*The Tales Of Those Who Came First* by Ellifae Emmert."

A whoop of excitement sounded from Remius, and she looked up at him. He had come to stand opposite of her, behind the table separating them. Alora shook her head at him, but elation was marked upon her own features. It was almost as if she felt his pride brush along her skin.

Directing her attention back to the grimoire, for she didn't want it to feel neglected when she had coaxed it to reveal its secrets to her, Alora let her fingers encourage the page to turn itself again.

"'*In the beginning, there was no safety. All was dark, and those who roamed the forest were consumed with self-interest and survival above all other things. Monsters with vicious teeth and sharp claws prowled on silent steps to devour all who crossed their paths.*' How frightening the beginning of Faerie sounds." Alora shivered and rubbed her hand over the exposed skin where her gloves ended before her sleeves began.

Alora saw movement before her and looked up to see Remius removing his white greatcoat. He held it out over the tabletop for her to take. Alora reached for it, then nodded her gratitude to the knight. Bringing the garment to her, Alora slipped her arms through the sleeves and tugged it on the rest of the way. The scent of Remius met her nose as she deeply inhaled his leather and bergamot fragrance. Alora longed to bask in his scent, for it was a palpable, comforting presence.

A throat cleared with indignation, and Alora directed her attention to the grimoire once more. "Shall I try the other one now?"

"Go ahead," encouraged her father.

Alora reached for the open grimoire and gently helped to close it. Its eyes regarded her before they sleepily closed. Looking toward the next volume, she hesitated when it glared at her with open disdain. It was more than just a bit prickly.

Gathering her courage, Alora brought her hand down to rest upon the grimoire's corner. When it didn't fight her weight, she moved her finger to trace the golden filigree swirls on its cover. It made no movement or even any indication that she had touched it. Perhaps that was a good thing.

With a firmer insistence, Alora pushed the edge of the cover. The grimoire shrieked at her. Alora jumped. Her heart thundered in her chest, fighting to stay within her ribcage. She swallowed before taking a deep breath and obediently opened to the first page. The cream paper was wrinkled as if water had touched it at some point, to forever mar its crispness. Alora wondered if the crinkles caused it pain.

Alora coaxed the next page to present itself. The title of this one was nowhere to be seen. She closed her eyes and reached out to the book with her mind.

Please reveal that which is hidden. I do not seek to harm anyone nor to enact vile misdeeds.

She heard the rustle of the pages as it turned. Alora opened her eyes and gazed down at the page. Inky lettering stared up from the parchment. "*'Cursed Curses for the Cursed'* Well, now that is quite the twisty title." Alora nudged the next page to turn and greet her. "*'This is a warning to one and all. The contents herein shall do you no good but very much harm. Within lies the vilest of curses and tricks, information pertaining to unbreakable bargains. Should you not heed my warning, know that banshees will visit you shortly hereafter.'* Perhaps we've had enough of this one." Alora looked to her side, where her father was looking at the grimoire with dread.

"Yes, you have more than proven what you are capable of. I see no reason to continue on with this one," he agreed.

Alora reached her hand back toward the book and was about to push the edge of the book to a closed position when the next page flew open to reveal more inky words. She rushed to reach for the edge of the page to tug it closed when Alora's eyes landed on the words, *'Death comes on swift wings for you as she haunts you from the grave with malice in her heart as her wails split your soul in two…'* With a sharp inhale, she placed both hands on the edges of the book and willed it to close.

A shrill scream pierced the silence, filling the air with

dread and fright as Alora's beating heart grew simultaneously heavy and frozen with fear within her throbbing chest. Goosebumps alighted onto her skin as a black-robed figure appeared suspended over the table just above her. Mist emanated from its ebony form as a skeletal finger lifted out to point accusingly at Alora. The horror before her had no eyes, just an open maw that issued forth another cruel scream that settled into Alora's bones and made her double over in excruciating pain. Feelings of a deep loss made Alora's entire being mourn for what she couldn't quite discern. Her heart seized in her chest as she fought to stay conscious. Alora desperately willed her heart to beat again. A warm trickle wept from her ears as the floor rose up to greet her.

25

NOT EVEN FRIENDS

Rough hands grabbed onto Alora, shaking her with all of their might as she lay on the library floor. Her frightened gaze was locked upon the banshee, who was still wailing in her direction. Her father's face appeared, blocking the horrifying view of the banshee from her eyes, but Alora's hands climbed up to his as she attempted to claw his hands from either side of her forearms. Words formed with his mouth, but her ears could only decipher the tortured wails. Terror held her in its clutches, and all Alora longed to do was to flee away from the reality of the petrifying nightmare. There was no escaping from a night terror when one was wide awake!

Her father let her go before picking Alora up to cradle her against his comforting chest from his spot beside her. Plump, warm tears trailed down her cheeks as she shook her head back and forth. Alora's hands clutched at the fabric of Papa's waistcoat.

Fate stood rigidly before them, guarding them with his massive body. He didn't hesitate to let his snowy wings extend to their full impressive length in the library's mammoth dimensions. They reached out in an arc to shield his charges from certain dangers. The white downy feathers were ruffled and standing on their edges as alarm, and weariness made the muscles along the alicorn's flanks flinch.

Alora caught sight of her knights surrounding the table. Gillie ran up to Theodore, brandishing a golden sword, and shoved the ridged, dragon-scaled-like handguard into his awaiting palm. Then, the smaller faerie brought his hands up to his ears and ran in the opposite direction. The banshee's hold on Alora lessened as it focused on the trio of White Knights, who bore a greater risk to its presence.

Remius and Theolf waved their hands in the air, shouting words Alora could not hear. Remius turned his head to look at her. His face was darkly menacing as he regarded her. They locked gazes briefly before he broke their stare to shout and wave at the unrelenting banshee.

Fear… even he is afraid. What have I allowed to happen?

Theodore leaped onto the table's surface and brandished the glinting sword toward the banshee. The glimmer of light on the blade lit up the chamber. The banshee's obsidian hood tilted to the side before it let another sharp wail tear through the air. The sound seemed to hit Theodore with its full force. Blood wept from his ears, but he shook his head and charged for the creature with furious intent. Though the banshee dodged the first strike, it was not nearly fast enough for the second. Theodore's hit landed straight for its heart. The blade tip sunk into the robe, and a puff of vapor emanated underneath the blade's point. When the banshee next opened its mouth, a soundless cry came forth. It crumpled into itself as the mist enveloped its entire being. The banshee's shrieks reverberated around the chamber until it was no more. Silence settled into the air when the mist dispersed, and nothing remained of the haunting specter. It was almost too much to bear after the deafening noise.

"Thank all that is holy," Papa breathed out, his words slicing through the stillness like a sharp-tipped dagger.

"That was decidedly *not* delightful *nor* entertaining." Cheshire approached her side and patted her shoulder with his paw as she briefly wondered where he had hidden himself.

Fate shook his wings before refolding them, tucking them against his body as he relaxed his stance. He gave the tabby an irritated look.

Theodore heaved a great sigh and lowered his head, his chin sinking to his chest. Then he jumped down to land on the dirt floor with a resounding thump. The White Knight leader held the sword out to his side. A sticky, wet glob of inky substance clung to the sword's tip. Remius tilted his head to regard it.

"Rather nasty business. It's been ages since we battled a banshee." Remius folded his arms across his broad chest.

"I had rather hoped never to have to do so again," Theolf replied as he came to stand behind Theodore and rested his hand upon the other knight's shoulder, squeezing it before letting his arm fall to his side.

A chair slid out from under the table, scraping against the dirt-packed floor as Cormack peeked his body out before he climbed to freedom. The elf was scowling at nothing in particular. His disgruntled features landed on the trio of knights, and Cormack shook his head at them. "Why did no one foresee that happening?"

"How were we to even consider that occurring?" scoffed Theolf as he rolled his eyes.

"It's a miracle we are all unharmed. In the future, we should concoct a plan for any eventuality." Cormack nodded to himself as he strode from the library.

"Sounds utterly exhausting," Remius muttered as he turned to stride over to Alora and her father. He bent down and captured her gaze with his. "It's alright now." He tried to soothe her using a gentle tone.

"It's gone, forever?" Alora timidly inquired. She couldn't mask the tremors that wracked her body.

"Vanquished true and properly," he promised, running a hand over his chest.

"What an afternoon," her father stated. Alora turned her head to look at him. He had his head tilted back, and his eyes were tightly shut.

"I am never doing that again," she adamantly stated. Her heart was still beating erratically, refusing to agree with the idea that Alora was safe.

"I should hope not!" Cheshire agreed, lifting a paw to lick it.

"We should have some tea," Theolf replied.

"We should have a good stout nip from the bottle," Gillie said as he eyed the group.

"That too," agreed Remius. He held his hand out for Alora to take. He leaned toward her when she hesitated and whispered, "I will not let any harm befall you. Don't you realize that? I'll even bear the scorching flames of a dragon for you."

Alora met his gaze while her tears continued to fall. When had she started crying? She blinked, trying to clear her vision. She found nothing but sincerity and a warmth reflected from his eyes. Her heart belonged to Hatter, but he wasn't there with her. Was it so wrong to bask in the open affections of another? Would Remius accept her friendship, which was all Alora could give to him? What was the strange effect they seemed to hold over each other?

She tentatively set her hand into his, allowing Remius to help her rise while Fate pawed at the ground with one of his front hooves. Theolf came to their side and reached a hand down to assist her father to his feet. Alora leaned her head back to meet Remius's gaze.

"Friends?" Alora silently pleaded with her eyes, begging him to accept the boundaries that existed between them.

Remius nodded his head and gave her a grin. "But, of course. Always and forever," he vowed. Searching his gaze, she couldn't locate any sign of hurt or deception. That he could accept her friendship when so much stood between them was a monumental feat. A surge of gratefulness and relief flooded Alora's tired and aching body.

"You have something here," Cheshire said as he gently approached her to wipe her earlobe with a wet handkerchief, then turned to repeat the action with the other one. "Now, all better."

"Thank you," Alora told him as her eyes landed on the bloodied linen. How would she ever forget this haunting experience?

Alora tugged Remius's tailcoat tighter against her chilled body, dislodging his hold upon her.

Remius let her go, and Alora felt unsteady on her feet. She wobbled a little, taking one careful step after another. Remius tentatively reached for her, then tightened his hold and caught her as her knees gave out with the next step.

"Easy there, Princess," he said with a pinched expression.

Alora drew in a slow breath. She could do this. Straightening, she pulled herself to her full height, and Remius allowed his hands to slip away. Placing her arm in the crook of his elbow, Alora let her weight lean into him, grateful for his support. She didn't need to be strong for him, and now was not the time to tumble onto the floor again.

Rubbing his hands together, Papa spoke. "Let's depart and allow Gillie and his assistants to have the library to themselves. I think tea with some faerie wine would hit the spot."

"Truer words were never spoken." Cheshire rose to float along the air as he exited the chamber.

"Thank you, Sir Theodore!" Alora said gratefully as he walked toward them. He halted his steps and looked at her, then at Remius, and shook his head. Alora moved to distance herself from Remius, but Remius stopped her by placing his free hand over hers. She looked to where his hand was resting against her bloodied glove.

"We're friends, Theodore. That is all. Surely, you can't object to that," Remius stated with an exasperated shake of his head.

"I can, in fact, object. What happens when tragedy strikes and a decision has to be made? Who will suffer? Both parties, most likely. It's a fool's errand to make friends with one who you serve. Alora serves the faeries of Wonderland while you serve the Crown. Your place is in keeping her safe. It only takes a moment, one innocent mistake, and everything could come crashing down," Theodore admonished.

"He's right. I realize it, and so do you." Alora curved one side of her lips in a half smile. "It's alright," she told him as she slipped her hand out from under his and pulled away, putting distance between them.

With shaky but determined steps, Alora left the knights behind her. Fate was standing guard at the door, awaiting her. Alora nodded to him, then followed after her father, who had halted his strides to wait for her.

I will not allow myself to be the weak link in Remius's armor. I couldn't bear it if he came to harm because of me. Never because of me. And I will not be the cause of further angst between the knights. If we can't even be friends, so be it.

26

MYTHS AND MAYHEM

Alora carefully studied her reflection. She didn't look any worse from her ordeal. The blood from her ears hadn't even stained her capped sleeves or bodice, much to Alora's delight. She liked her dress and would have been saddened if it had been ruined. The dirt from her fall had been brushed off easily enough as well. Alora stood before the hanging looking glass directly along the wall's middle point. Meara had pulled her aside, tucked her into her bedchamber to set Alora to rights, and then escorted her to her father's chambers. With a fresh pair of white elbow-length gloves adorning her arms, Alora was ready and presentable to take tea.

The group had retired to her father's sitting room and were now sipping tea and eating cucumber sandwiches. The room was smaller than his study in the mortal realm, which he had preferred to preside over. Colorful tapestries hung by metal rods were stationed along the walls. Alora peered at them, discovering that they depicted battle scenes and were gruesome to behold. The blood, in particular, was a vibrant crimson shade. She shuddered as she turned away from them. The side table was loaded with icing-covered confections, but Alora steered far away from those tempting sweets. The last thing she wanted was to shrink down again or to grow too tall. She had had enough adventure for one day.

"Who knew Gillie was in possession of the legendary sword, Excalibur?" Remius raised his brows in question. He was seated in a burgundy-padded wingback chair.

"Don't look at me," answered Theolf as he shook his head from his spot atop the settee.

"King Arthur's Excalibur?" Alora asked with open curiosity. The legend had always entertained her, and Miss Prickett delighted in reading her tales of the mythical king.

"The very same," answered Remius with a wink.

"There is always a reason why humans can't locate a particular treasure," Theodore interjected from his spot in the corner. He was seated in a matching armchair.

"Not all items can exist on that side of the divide once magic has been imbued within them. Arthur bore Fae blood, and when the Lady of the Lake gifted him with the sword, she conjured it from Faerie. She fashioned it with magic, cunning, and even a bit of a dragon's breath. It couldn't exist without one powerful enough to wield it. All of Camelot exists in the Faerie Realm now. The entire kingdom came home once the legendary king was no more. The king created Camelot from dreams and faerie enchantment." Theolf sipped from his teacup.

"The entire kingdom? I seem to recall that bit of lore from my youthful studies," her father voiced quizzically, leaning his weight forward. Papa was perched in a rocking chair near the enchanted flames heating the sitting room.

Theolf nodded. "But how Gillie ended up with the sword is quite the mystery."

"Another puzzle of the realms," mused Remius.

Alora came to sit on the satin ivory padded settee next to Theolf. She delicately set her food down atop the long table before them as she withdrew her gloves, which she placed upon her lap, then retrieved her fare. With her teacup in one hand, Alora nibbled on the cucumber sandwich that she grasped in her other hand.

"When shall we delve into the higher level of grimoires? Maybe next, Alora will summon a dragon, which might not be the best choice as the library could easily go up in flames," Cormack said from around a bite of his sandwich.

Cheshire flicked an ear in the elf's direction. He was reclining on the settee between Alora and Theolf. "You wish to delve into the grimoires again so soon?"

"Might as well get it over with," Cormack said with a grimace.

"I, for one, do not wish to catch sight of another grimoire for quite some time," Alora replied, jerking as a shiver raced up her spine.

"But we shall take precautions," the elf cautioned.

"Must we? Must I have to learn how to master them?" Alora cast her gaze on her father, who considered her.

"I think not just yet. Perhaps we can focus on your training in other areas, such as self-defense." Papa's lips thinned into a firm line.

"I rather think that is an excellent idea. Most especially if she is to wield the Vorpal Sword, Alora will need to hone her skills to stand against the Queen's Jabberwocky and whatever other forces the wicked dragon throws into her path," surmised Cheshire.

"What is the Jabberwookie?" inquired Alora as she tilted her head.

"Not Wookie, Curious One, Wocky. And that is the vilest being in all of Wonderland. The Lunar Queen has complete dominion over it. Picture, if you can, a creature created from pure darkness with razor-sharp teeth and of a mammoth size, even larger than the queen's dragon form. It's said that she feeds it with the human flesh of those poor beings who venture into her kingdom. To make it more cruel, the queen keeps the poor monster caged so when she does set it free, it's in a frenzy to take down all it can before it returns to its savage lair." The glee in the tabby's voice sent goosebumps careening along her bare arms and the nape of her neck.

Knots twisted in her belly as Alora regretted the bit of sandwich she'd nibbled at.

To hear another tale of her grandmother's cutthroat tactics to keep her subjects in line was appalling and sunk her further into despair. Alora hurriedly rose to her feet, and stars filled her vision. Tugging her gloves back on, she made her way to the door. What she needed was a bit of fresh air, but just exiting the stifling atmosphere of the sitting room would do her well enough. Her companions' curious eyes followed Alora until she closed the door behind herself with a resounding thud. Her gaze took in Fate, who was as ever vigilant and stationed beside the door. Alora let her head fall back to rest against the door as she took a deep breath.

"Are you well, Princess?" Fate worriedly regarded as his amethyst eyes observed her.

"Very nearly," she stated, as a faerie who bore the head of a zebra and the body of a lion came sprinting down the corridor before them. He caught sight of the pair and reached out a paw with the tip of one of his claws extended. The odd faerie neatly cut off a few strains of Fate's silver tail before he began his drunken jog down the corridor in the opposite direction.

Fate indignantly shouted after his retreating form. "How dare you maim my beautiful tail, you Wobbly Crawl Creeper!"

"Well, go after him and enact some justice for yourself, Fate," nudged Alora with incredulousness.

"I can't very well leave you alone when chaos is running amuck," Fate said with an exasperated huff.

"Well then, I shall return to my father's sitting room at once. Go!" She encouraged him with steely resolve.

Fate looked at her and then down the corridor. His face set into a determined look as he nodded once. "Right! Into the sitting room with you!"

Alora turned back toward the door, placing her palm against the door's handle. Fate took off, galloping away after the rabble-rouser. Before Alora could turn the knob, he was out of her sight. A curious noise sounded from the corridor's other side, and she turned her attention to discover what was happening now.

A little white rabbit came into her view. It wore a little violet suit with white gloves and an orchid-colored top hat with a broad white ribbon. She squinted in thought. She was almost certain she had laid her eyes upon that very same rabbit before. But where?

An image of a white rabbit came to her, and she bit her lip.

That is the rabbit that came and interrupted my time with Phillip while we were in England. But if he is here, then perhaps Phillip might be as well.

The rabbit caught sight of Alora and squealed in fright as its beady pink eyes grew large before it turned, hopping back in the direction in which it had come from.

"Oh no, Mister Rabbit! Please don't go! Is Phillip with you? Is he safe?" When no reply was given, and it was almost out of her field of vision, she made a snap decision to follow after him.

He continued down the corridor, and Alora gave chase. After a few steps, she reached down to gather up her hemline so that she could move more quickly. Then Alora ran, noting how quickly he hopped.

The rabbit turned left and disappeared through the dirt-packed wall. It was an impossible thought that he had just vanished.

Alora didn't hesitate to let her strides take her right

through the wall. Tingles danced upon her scalp and chills ricocheted down her limbs as she came to the other side of the wall. Before her were three ornate doors, each one carved with blossoming rose bushes that looked to be dripping rain from their petals. It was a curious sight, and Alora wondered if it often rained in these lands. Something niggling in her stomach nudged her to consider that perhaps something much more sinister was at play here.

The very first door was just small enough to fit the rabbit's size, while the next door was large enough for her to pass comfortably through. The last door was massive, and Alora knew it wasn't likely the rabbit had chosen that one, for it looked very heavy. When she padded over to the smallest door, she knelt down and grabbed onto the handle, attempting to give it a twist, but it wouldn't budge. Locked, but where was the key? With the rabbit? Drat!

Alora looked around the room, noticing a tiny silver key resting atop a wooden table. The size wouldn't fit any other door but the tiniest. She noticed the glass dome beside the key. Underneath it rested a single bite of chocolate.

She looked at the door again and then at the piece of chocolate.

Forgive me, father.

Rising to her slippered feet, Alora quickly strode to the table. She reached for the key and slipped it into the top of her glove. Next, she grabbed onto the top of the globe where a circular handle rested, then moved it to the side. Eyeing the chocolate with dubious intent, Alora finally reached for it, bringing it up for closer inspection. If she truly wanted to follow after the rabbit, there was only one option.

Opening her mouth, Alora placed the chocolate onto her tongue; raspberry and cream flavor dissolved in her mouth. Within moments, she was shrinking down, but not too much. Just enough to crawl through the door on her hands and knees. Alora's dress was hanging upon her, and her gloves were loose along her arms. But her hair fared well enough as the pins did their job of holding the mass together. Alora withdrew the key from her glove with a secret smile, then moved toward the door on her hands and knees. Fitting the key into the lock and twisting the tumblers, the handle turned in her grasp and allowed Alora to push the door open.

Before Alora could even crawl an inch from the chamber, a harsh shout met her ears.

"Off with her head!"

Coils of dread consumed Alora as she crawled through the door and rose. She crept from the threshold and entered into another world. She had come this far; she wouldn't turn back now, not if there was a chance to see her Phillip again. There was little doubt within Alora whose voice it was. Her grandmother was near, and it seemed she was not in a very good mood.

27

DRIPPING ROSES AND SMOKE

Dark purples and blues collided in brilliant brush strokes, blanketing the evening sky and permeating countless glowing teal stars. The moon was crimson and reminiscent of a globe filled with weeping droplets of blood. Alora backed away from the door as she took in the eerie sight. She was careful to not so much as snap a twig or rattle an errant stone with the satin slippers that were a few sizes too large for her now tinier feet.

Before her stood a hedgerow covered with tangled vines of creeping ivy, a hurried glance to the right then left confirmed the row was unending; Alora would simply have to walk parallel with it until she came upon an entrance. The dim lighting was broken every few feet by lit torches whose turquoise flames reached up to tease the stars in a contest of luminosity. Alora gathered her hanging garments and wound them around her arm until she felt secure enough to begin the journey ahead of her. In the distance loomed a dark castle with turrets that soared to touch the radiant sky. There were glittering bits woven into the stonework along the castle's walls and roofing that made one's eye immediately take notice. If dread could have a dwelling to call its own, it would surely be that malevolent structure. It was best to keep moving, even if it brought Alora closer to it.

There was nothing of interest to break up the monotony of her steps for quite some time; how long, she couldn't begin to guess. Fallen leaves, which were not brown or crackled with age, littered the ground underneath Alora's feet. It was quiet except for the din of conversation that met her ears when she rounded the edge of the hedgerow.

Taking a deep breath to steady herself for what would next happen, Alora squared her shoulders and defiantly lifted her head. She would not allow herself to blindly walk into trouble.

One step after another saw Alora beyond the vibrant hedgerow and amidst a lush garden. Rose bushes were planted in circular patterns with red pavers marking their circumference. Even in the faint lighting, Alora noticed something was not quite right with the roses. They looked damp, but the surrounding ground was dry. It was a bizarre scene, almost as if they were shedding tears.

Spying no faerie about, Alora softly padded over to the nearest rosebush that towered over her diminutive height. She gazed up and cautiously reached out her hand to cup the rose just above her head. Alora slowed her movements when a plump droplet fell from a petal and landed on the paver just before her. Bending down, Alora's brows drew together in contemplation.

It looks sticky. Perhaps paint or something more nefarious. It couldn't be… Blood? Who would color the roses with blood?

Without touching the treacly substance or one of the unnerving roses, Alora straightened up and sighed. She didn't wish to stain her gloves, hoping to remain somewhat presentable for when she could locate the cure to her dilemma.

A clatter caught her attention, and Alora scrambled to hide herself to the side of the rose bush. Peeking her head out, her eyes landed on a male faerie clad in crimson armor. In his hand was a paintbrush, and dangling from his other arm was an obsidian bucket.

His pointed ears twitched in her direction. Alora quickly held her breath. She stayed as silent as a mouse. The racket of metal on metal rang out into the air as it neared her. With little choice, Alora released her breath, taking a few steps until she came into his sight. Her lungs burned, and she was thankful she no longer had to constrict them.

The faerie was breathtaking with rose-gold hair that gathered at the nape of his neck, held back by a dark ribbon that trailed down the middle of his back. Frosty eyes glared at her before looking her up and down. Then the fierce expression left the Fae's, face smoothing out his eyebrows and lifting the corners of his mouth into the resemblance of a smile.

"Are you Lady Faella?" his deep voice inquired as he watched her.

"I am not she," Alora decided to tell him the truth.

"How irregular. Why, then, have you ventured so far from the games?"

"I find that I have managed to get myself lost," she admitted.

"Is anyone expecting your return?" He glanced behind her.

Alora wasn't certain how best to answer the faerie. She didn't want him to think that she could be easily toyed with. She might be in danger. If he were harmless...well, that thought almost seemed a remarkable feat considering in whose garden they were currently standing in. What was she to do? Alora smiled politely at him before responding.

"I am expected to be in amongst the courtiers, but I stepped away to discover where a cure may be to restore me to my rightful height. Would you happen to know where I may discover that which I seek?" Alora met his stare without flinching.

"Aye, that I do. You may take a few bites of the mushrooms growing down the path just beyond these rose bushes. If you find that you have lost your way, call out to the caterpillar, who is sure to be awake. If he is in a festive mood, he may direct you to your quarry."

"And if he is not?" Alora frowned as she let her words wither away.

"Then best to avoid him altogether. What a silly little thing you are," the faerie scoffed as he dipped the end of the paintbrush into the pail.

"What are you doing with the paint?" She decided to ask that instead of taking offense to his rudeness.

"Why, painting the white roses red, of course. Do you always interrogate every faerie you meet? No wonder you find yourself lost out here," he mused, pulling the paintbrush from the pail and brushing its bristles against a spec of white that dared to defy his actions.

"Why not plant red roses to begin with? Surely that's easier than continually touching them up?"

"The queen commands it to be this way. Besides, just what are we to do with the blood of the slain if we don't coat the roses with it?" The Fae raised his pale brows in indignation.

Alora gasped, bringing her hands up to her mouth. So it *was* blood. She felt a burst of dizziness, and her stomach began to cramp as bile rose to the back of her throat. Alora's eyes began to burn and water because of the sting. Concentrating, she managed to swallow the bile back down.

"Here now, don't you dare be sick! I will have to be the one to deal with your mess. Be off with you! Scurry away! I have business to attend to. These roses won't paint themselves, you know, and we have such a vast collection of blood from last night's skirmish."

"I see," Alora whispered as more horror filled her. Each

drip belonged to a faerie that was not saved. Each droplet accused her of not being worthy enough to rescue them from such a cruel fate. Alora backed away from the queen's soldier a few paces, then made her way quickly past him and kept her feet moving. Could Hatter's blood be even now dripping from the petals?

Tears were glistening in Alora's eyes as her throat clogged. Each anguished beat of her heart was painful. She only knew to keep herself treading the dirt pathway before her. Alora's thoughts were an unceasing whirlwind, and all of them circled back to either Hatter or her own plight of fulfilling a prophecy she wanted no part in.

The air became thick with fog, and when Alora next took in a breath, she choked upon it.

Alora canted her head behind her, then toward the direction in which the path was taking her. If she could be helpful, then it was her duty to do so, even if she failed miserably. Her feet were tiring the more she walked; keeping the overlarge slippers on her feet was a chore. Alora was certain that blisters were forming from the friction, but she could do nothing to aid herself of the affliction until she could fit her feet into her shoes properly.

Though her eyes had not allowed a single tear to fall from them, and her stomach continued to feel hollowed out, Alora kept on the pathway as tree branches swayed overhead in the forbearing breeze. Shivers plagued her body, and goosebumps rose on her chilled skin. Her mind began to discard the mist that had shrouded it with the gruesome discovery of what clung to the white rose petals. Alora blinked and then took stock of her surroundings. While she kept to the path, in amongst the golden leaves and from around the ebony trunks lurked glowing eyes. They kept watch on her, and she tried not to pay them too much attention. But foreboding prickled at the nape of her neck. Whether they were harmless or not, she didn't desire to meet any more evil-hearted beings. Not when she was not yet her full size.

Alora's eyes scanned the neverending edges of the pathway for any growing mushrooms, and she didn't spy a single one. Dandelions met her gaze with cruel glares while little glowing insects crossed in front of her here and there. A few of the tiny bugs even stopped just before Alora to stare at her with open hostility. Was she so very odd that she stood out so much to them?

Feeling as if she had made a monumental mistake in venturing in after the white rabbit, there was nothing she could do at present to correct the error. She was once again lost and at Wonderland's mercy.

Alora let her thoughts wander, and she soon came to a fork in the pathway.

"Who are you?" came a raspy voice to the side of the pathway. Alora cast her gaze in the direction from where the voice had come, noting the various shapes and heights of the mushrooms standing erect just beside the pathway.

"I inquired who you are, you daft girl," seethed the voice with unguarded irritation.

"Why is everyone so unbearably rude?" Alora had had her fill with ill-mannered faeries and took angry steps until she halted before the mushroom where the tiny creature reclined. She staked her hands onto her hips in umbrage.

Resting atop the largest brown and white mushroom was a tiny cyan caterpillar puffing out tiny rings of smoke. In one of his many grubby hands rested the mouthpiece of a hookah. He wasn't wearing any practical clothing, yet there were minuscule sky-blue slippers on ten of his miniature feet.

"Perhaps you're the rude one, you unwelcomed interloper!" the insect snapped before taking another drag on his instrument.

"I don't wish to be here either. Kindly tell me which of the mushrooms will restore my height, and I will be on my way," she demanded with a glare in his direction.

"Why should I?"

"Because I can't be on my way until you do!" Alora removed her balled hands from her hips and crossed her arms over her body. She attempted to restore some warmth to her arms as her hands stroked up and down them.

"You could take a bite from each of them. Some are poisonous, you know. And as far as *I* am concerned, that would solve my problem just as well as pointing out the correct one and sending you on your way." A perfect tiny *W* floated into the air before the caterpillar from the smoke that left his mouth.

"Well then, perhaps I will just make myself comfortable, shall I? It's been ages since I had a nice, leisurely rest, and I do have so many thoughts about this land that I am practically bursting to share with some faerie or another." Alora sat down before the mushrooms to bring her face closer to his. "And you're as good as any other being. Where shall I begin my tales of woe?"

"Oh, please don't." The insect held out his free hand to stay her words.

"But we could become such wonderful companions. The night is young, and the stars are bright."

"I think I shall be sick." A green coloring overtook his face.

"Oh dear. I'm sure it's from your nasty habit of the hookah."

"I think not…" he trailed off.

"It all began on my eighteenth birthday—"

"No, no, no! I shall not become your listening board. You *must* take your leave," the caterpillar interrupted her.

"But, I don't want to. I wish to stay here with you." Alora beamed down at him.

"Good gracious me! Would you look at the delicious-looking mushroom just to your left? Isn't it sumptuous? Don't you long to take a nibble?"

"Not if it is going to make me ill or worse. Tell me, have you met Cheshire?"

"But, of course, I have! Is there anyone in Wonderland who has yet to meet him? Listen very carefully because I am about to dispense with some very helpful advice. Take two small bites of that mushroom, and you shall be as you were before." He waved his hands impatiently toward the plant.

"Are you certain that you wouldn't like my company for a bit longer?"

"Positive. Abjectly so." Picking up the hose to the hookah, he took another long pull upon it with his mouth.

"Well then, if I can't convince you to allow me to stay, I might as well do as you say." Alora reached out her arm and pinched off some of the mushroom's top with the tip of her gloved fingers. She eyed it critically once she held it before her face. Alora looked toward the caterpillar, who blinked avidly at her. She might as well…

Alora closed her eyes and popped the entire piece into her mouth. A vile bitterness accosted her senses and burned her tongue, which nearly had her spitting it out when her body flinched. Making herself quickly chew and swallow the sourness down, Alora felt her arms and legs extended before her body followed. In mere moments, she was back to fitting properly into her clothing.

Leaping to her feet, she twirled around in thankfulness and let her head fall back to gaze up at the sky. Relief coursed through her body.

"Now be off, little larger girl. I have no more time to spare for you," admonished the caterpillar as a cloud of smoke encircled his head.

"I believe I shall. Thank you for your assistance."

"*Bah*, just be gone; that will be sufficient enough payment for me," he droned with increasing agitation.

Shaking her head at the infuriated being and straightening up each glove along her arm, Alora waltzed back the way she had come. She was ready to face whatever came her way next. Hopefully, she would discover secrets within her grandmother's domain, with the faerie being none the wiser.

28

A HEARTSTOPPING GAME

After being restored to her normal size, Alora's journey to the Lunar Queen's garden was speedily accomplished. When her steps came to a stop before the pavilion where faeries were drinking from fluted wine goblets and nibbling food from the long laden table, Alora shook out her dress, then reached up to feel for any errant curls. When she felt as presentable as possible, she set one slippered foot down and then proceeded to do so with her other foot until her steps had carried her into the center of the pavilion. Vines hung from the rafters of the open skylight building. Sparkling stars shone through the tiny separations in the greenery as faerie light drifted overhead in a sea of blazing light.

Ebony marble constructed the pavilion, and toward the back of the space rested one enormous throne in the same matching shade. There were carved roses that clung to the top and sides and at the points of each foot's rose tip. The middle of the throne was straight and smooth. Alora felt a dip of disappointment that the queen was not atop her throne as she longed to stare at her grandmother from a safe distance. She wanted to gain her measure. To look upon the woman who had taken such a beautiful land and crushed its very soul. At any second, she might come face to face with her. Would the queen instantly recognize her? How would Alora react in such a scene?

The white rabbit came into Alora's sight and, with eager footfalls, Alora weaved her way between couples and those who closely conversed in order to keep her eyes fixed upon him. She hardly took notice of those she passed. Alora was causing a stir with her discourteous behavior, amusing her to no end as the blood-thirsty crowd surrounded her. Who would be willing to pay court upon the Lunar Queen if they did not desire to be there? Did they feel the call to shed blood, too?

A trumpet sounded and all of the faeries stopped talking, turning as one in the direction in which the notes had resonated. When the rabbit followed the same actions, Alora removed her eyes from his form and watched with a guarded heart to see what this interruption meant. The trumpet lowered away from the face of a small faerie whose head was that of an owl with glowing golden eyes.

"'Tis time for croquet, and Her Majesty wishes to choose her competitors herself," he called out, then stepped away to blend back into the observant crowd.

An eerie silence filled the oppressive air; not even the sound of fabric rustling nor the gentle cadence of breathing could be heard. A black-clad figure came to stand before the gathered mass and, turning, Alora caught her first sight of the Lunar Queen. The crown that sat atop her head stood out in contrast to the perfectly curled ebony hair and pale skin. Her horns were difficult to dismiss, and Alora tried not to stare at them. The queen was brilliant, breathtaking, and absolutely terrifying.

A flurry of feathers descended upon the queen's shoulders. Turning her head, the faerie queen allowed the raven to rub against her cheek. Cooing at it, she seemed pleased as it took to the air once again.

Alora watched it fly away to perch in the trees and turned her attention back to her grandmother. She needed to keep her wits handy to avoid the danger surrounding her.

The Lunar Queen's cold gaze raked over the courtiers until her turquoise eyes fell onto Alora, pinning her in place. Alora wasn't sure whether she could break eye contact and take the necessary steps to vanish into the night.

"I shall play against you!" the queen decreed as she narrowed her eyes to slits. Then, turning upon her booted heel, she strode off, descending the pavilion steps and toward a field where wickets were waiting. Wooden torches were placed in intervals that illuminated the area, casting menacing shadows that danced with dizzying delight. Were they really shadows or something much more ominous?

Alora felt a harsh shove into her back, nearly sending her careening to the stone floor. She turned her head to look over her shoulder at the insistent faerie.

"Take your place! For you do not wish to risk your head!" the faerie hissed as its forked tongue darted from its mouth to taste the air. The yellow eyes were widening at her inaction.

Looking around, Alora realized that she really had little choice. She would simply have to play this game under the close scrutiny of her grandmother. She made her way down the same route the Lunar Queen had taken, then halted her steps before a wicker basket of different colored hedgehogs, which were curled up to resemble little wooden balls. It was cruel, and Alora didn't want to strike the poor animals. While this was certainly not the worst the queen could do, this was among the worst Alora had ever been subjected to. She looked at the crimson hedgehog that lay upon the pale grass at the queen's feet and felt pity squeeze her heart.

Up closer to her grandmother, Alora let her eyes wander from the black boots up the same colored shiny trousers and corset that clung to the queen's voluptuous form. Faint lines crinkled the skin surrounding her eyes and at the edges of her mouth. She certainly didn't look like any mortal grandmother Alora had ever seen. Her attire was improper, and Alora wondered why the rest of the Court weren't donned to match their monarch. Were there rules regarding this which she was ignorant of?

"Choose your color! We haven't all night!" her grandmother demanded with impatience dripping from each word. Her glacial glare was taking in Alora, inspecting her for any perceived weakness. Alora would give her none.

Without a word, Alora bent low, then reached into the basket. She chose a violet-colored hedgehog and winced as its quills stuck into her gloves. Alora let the creature fall onto the ground before her. She said a silent prayer that these creatures were not Seelie faeries and that the *game* would not cause them any pain.

Furrowing her brow, she wondered where the mallets were kept.

The Lunar Queen snapped her fingers, and two courtiers rushed to stand before her. They bowed their heads, then lifted up their hands where one flamingo apiece clasped by its leg was held up for her inspection. She pointed at the one on the right, and the bird on the left flopped over in the courtier's hold to look as if it went limp or dead. The winning flamingo was handed over to the queen.

The remaining bird was thrust into her hands, and Alora blinked down at it. Its legs felt strong as its tongue peeked out from its beak. How was she meant to use the creature?

She gave it a shake, and still it remained floppy between her hands.

The queen promptly struck the crimson hedgehog with the head of the flamingo. The resounding crack made Alora flinch. The hedgehog tumbled through the grass and straight under the first wicket. Opening one of its beady black eyes, it squinted, then adjusted its course to sail through the next wicket and the one after it as well. A deafening cheer tore through the ether, disconcerting Alora. The Lunar Queen smirked over toward her Court before she solemnly regarded Alora.

"Your turn, my dear. Don't keep us lingering long."

Alora was entranced by the sight of the quills sticking out from the side of the flamingo's head.

With a determined stance, she carefully hit her violet hedgehog with the head of her droopy flamingo. The hedgehog gave a squeal, making Alora's heart squeeze, then race within her chest in equal measures of fright and sympathy. What a vile game!

The violet hedgehog clambered through the first wicket and then came to a slow stop. Its body flipped open, and it lay motionless upon the grass. Alora gasped as the queen's chilling guffaw filled the air.

"Better luck next time," she cooed to Alora as she tread to the next wicket with a smirking flamingo dangling from her hand.

Alora rushed over to her hedgehog and bent over it. Tenderly, she reached a hand toward it, stroking its bristled cheek. Its eyes flew open, and then it bared its pointy teeth and latched onto her finger, savagely biting down. Alora jerked backward, then waved her hand erratically to dislodge the animal. The hedgehog sailed through the air, smacking into a tree trunk with a *thawk*. Alora wanted to weep at this barbaric farce of entertainment.

Spinning around to see what the fuss was about, the queen sneered at Alora before shouting, "To the dungeon with you! We do not take kindly to cheating unless it's been sanctioned and you have been granted no such treatment. A night or two in the cold, damp prison will see you extinguishing those haughty airs."

Two armored guards with grim faces and malicious gazes

swiftly came to either side of Alora, taking hold of her forearms. They dragged her between themselves from the field and to the side of the castle, where a pair of gargoyles stood against the stone wall. Alora's gaze landed on their horned heads and traveled down to take in their long, tapered claws. They didn't meet her stare, but she thought her ears picked up a disgruntled huff.

A heavy, dark wooden door was flung open before the trio, as if by unseen magic, and they rapidly descended down a series of stairs. The air grew cooler and more chilled the further they progressed. Icy tendrils of fear crept into Alora as her feet sought purchase upon the stairs but were left to hang under her as she was escorted further into the gloomy depths of the castle. The lighting was dim, and for Fae, the low lighting was not an issue, but for a halfling such as Alora, it was daunting. Her hair came loose from its pins as she was jostled from one direction to another. Pings sounded behind her as the pins lost their grip, clattering to the hard steps as they continued on.

With her dark hair now a curtain before her face, Alora was surprised when the silent guards ceased their lumbering gait. With bated breath, she waited to discover what they meant to do with her. One guard let her arm go, and the guard on her other side grabbed onto her limb in a punishing grip. Alora tried to blow away the hair from before her eyes, but all she managed was to fluff it out before it came to rest back against her face. The brief view was not enough to give her insight into her surroundings.

The scraping of metal on metal resounded in the chamber until a small click met the air. What sounded as if it was a lock sprung free, and a shrill creak sounded just before where she and her captor stood rooted in place. Alora was roughly let go and given a shove from the small of her back, sending her tumbling ineloquently into the cell and onto her aching knees. Fire struck through her legs, and unending pain left her breathless as tears coursed down from her frightened, vacant stare. Her body began to shake as she eased herself backward to extend her legs so she could relieve some of the suffering. Scooting back as far as she could in a crab walk, Alora's back met the rigid, icy-cold wall behind her. She drew her legs up against her chest and clasped her arms around them, cocooning herself in protection. The ache in Alora's finger was forgotten.

Her captors left her to her doom as Alora's ears caught the sound of their retreating forms as they ascended the staircase. The stillness of the silence was the most terrifying experience she had ever endured.

"Is that you? You?" questioned a form as it rose carefully and crept toward her. The male faerie reached her side, lowering himself to sit beside her.

Alora immediately knew the voice and lifted her head to peer up at him through tear-dimmed eyes. "Phillip? It is you!" Unwrapping her form, she leaped toward him and wound her arms around his waist.

Hatter scooped her up to sit within the security of his muscular arms. He pressed earnest kisses into her hair atop the crown of her head. When Alora began to splutter inarticulate murmurings, Hatter hushed her as he held her closer to himself. The warmth of his body was seeping into her, offering comfort and protection. His scent of steeped tea leaves, vanilla, and sandalwood filled each inhaled sob that she made.

"There now, my darling. We'll get through this; just trust and see."

Alora was content to cry for the moment, allowing her fears to pour forth. Learning of the cruel way in which her grandmother ruled the Court was one thing. But actually, experiencing the terror she evoked was entirely another matter. Alora had nurtured the idea that she'd be able to reach the dark recesses of the queen's heart somehow. Even now, after interacting and being ill-treated, Alora still wasn't ready to believe that dream had died.

She didn't care what others were around to hear her; she didn't care if anyone was there to witness her crumbling into pieces. Alora had remained strong when she had needed to. Now, it was time to let another gather her close and whisper endearments into her ears and for gentle lips to softly caress her icy skin. In these moments, Alora didn't need to be the strong one.

29

TRUE LOVE?

"True love is lovely, is it not? If a bit odd to witness and really uncomfortable," spoke a tiny voice from the dungeon next to where Alora and Hatter were imprisoned.

"Indeed, but theirs is nothing in comparison to ours, my sweet," replied a masculine voice in the same direction.

The words thrummed through Alora with any icy chill, giving her a sense of alarming uncertainty. If strangers could so easily form their own conclusions, perhaps there was hope.

Alora's tears had long since dried up, leaving her feeling hollowed out and in a bit of a sleepy haze. But within Hatter's arms, as he held her so tenderly against his chest, she began to sense a rightness and belonging she had never quite experienced before. In his arms, nothing seemed as daunting as before. Enclosed in Hatter's warm embrace, Alora felt as if everything was a possibility, and though this bond she was experiencing with the faerie who had forgotten her was fragile and new, it gave her joy and a purpose. Here was something that could begin anew, that was, in fact, doing so with each new breath they took. They were building a bridge to all the tomorrows that would come.

"True love?" mumbled Hatter as he tilted his head to look down, thoughtfully studying Alora. His intense, dark gaze roved over her face.

"But, of course! You didn't realize the bond that ties you together practically thrums through the air between you two?" the female voice wondered with apparent skepticism.

"Is that true?" Hatter inquired as his voice took on a broken quality. His eyes were filled with wretchedness. What word could she offer that would heal all of the broken shards of his wounded heart?

"I don't know enough of this world to be certain of anything. But what I have felt since we first locked gazes has never withered, never allowed me to stop thinking and wishing for your return. To hold your hand, to sit and talk with you. When we are parted, it's as if a part of me is missing, and I ache for it to be returned. Nothing seems as it should without you." Alora bit her lip as she considered the emotion passing over Hatter's features and allowed the weight of her words to meet his ears and his heart.

Hatter rubbed his chest over the area where his heartbeat was and gave a single nod of his head before saying, "I didn't know what to think about the odd ache. How could I forget *you*? When you are so very precious to me? *You must forgive me!*" He reached for Alora's hands and enfolded them between his own as his eyes implored her to believe him. Gently, he brought their clasped hands up to his mouth and laid a reverent kiss along the back of her hands. His warm lips lit up all the dark spaces in her heart.

"You were rather distracted, and I understand the horrors you suffered have left lingering wounds. How could I ever find fault with you?" Her brows furrowed as Alora gave him a smile that wobbled.

"But you, if this is true, you would have turned my entire world topsy-turvy and inside out. I would have braved anything to get back to you…tempests, earthquakes, total annihilation. Anything. And yet, a rightness is enveloping my soul. I know that every word you speak is true. It's like all of these puzzling thoughts and pieces of myself are finally colliding together to create something unbreakably undeniable. You are my everything." His lips came closer to Alora's, and her breath hitched in her throat.

She was caught in a moment that she was both terrified to experience and terrified to deny. What would kissing him be like? Would Hatter's lips devour hers, or would their kiss be tender and sweet? The breath hitched in Alora's chest as her body became weightless with anticipation.

"You do recall that you are not alone?" whined the female faerie.

Hatter huffed out a laugh that cast warm air into the space between them as a chagrined look passed over his handsome face. Alora pulled away from him but was content to remain in his lap, even if it was the most improper behavior.

"Let them be," soothed the male faerie.

"Ick, no, thank you! And just who made you the boss of me?" the female's voice rose in umbrage.

"I am not trying to boss you, Fleur. I am only suggesting you let true love have its way," the male stated with slightly thinning patience.

"I am so...rrry," Fleur began, who seemed to be having great difficulty with her words. "My nerves are strained, and I am tired, and this entire debacle has not been easy. I left one Court on a mission, met you, and ended up imprisoned all in the span of one evening. I've reached my limit, Clement. Have you any idea how long I've watched my best friend and my king enjoy their mate bond and longed for the day that I met *my* fated mate? This was not how this day was supposed to go!"

"I am the one who is filled with sorrow! I have failed in protecting my mate," Clement grumbled.

"I can protect myself, or I could, and you too, if only that wicked witch hadn't had my dagger removed. She needs to meet its pointy end!" Fleur seethed.

As she hid the gaping yawn that consumed her behind her gloved hand, Alora had a moment to feel grateful that the angry faerie was held in another cell. It was becoming increasingly difficult to keep her swollen eyes from closing. The yawns overtook her body, sapping what little strength she was clinging to. If only Alora had not lost the Faeriedust along the way. Her nose crinkled at the thought of having to face a livid Cheshire. Alora was determined not to allow slumber to carry her away when the possibility of danger clung to the shadows.

Hatter's attention was focused upon her and not on the talking faeries in the next dungeon over. He was frowning as he rubbed circles along her back. His hands were gentle on her, keeping his hold delicate as if she would disappear before his eyes. And hadn't Alora done that twice already?

"Patience, my love. You will have your chance in ending her," cooed Clement.

"Not soon enough. My king and queen will be in a fit should I not soon return."

"Then it is a very good thing I have arrived," stated Remius with a smirk. His eyes were directed toward the lock of their prison as his hands worked a key.

"Remius! Whatever are you doing here?" Alora asked as she sat up and leaned away from Hatter. Was it a trick, some illusion to gain her trust? How was it possible that he was truly standing before her?

"Saving the day, which is what any White Knight worth his weight would do. Ah ha!" Remius removed the key and pushed the cell's door open. It whined as it did so, and Remius cringed. "We haven't much time."

Hatter assisted Alora to her feet, then quickly rose behind her. His hand rested against the small of her back. They made their way to the doorway, and Alora halted before it as she looked up at Remius. Her heart leaped in her breast, and she had to will her eyes not to shimmer with her tears. Though Alora was overjoyed to see him, giving in to her longing would only leave him with the wrong conclusions. No matter how her heart warmed in his presence, she was not his and never could be.

Tentatively reaching out a hand, she laid it atop Remius's arm. "Thank you for rescuing us."

"You are a complete surprise, Princess. My mission was to free the Prince, but I am happy to know you are unharmed. We really mustn't delay. Oh, you look as if you might be in need of this." Remius arched a pale brow at Alora, then dropped his sight to the ring that rested upon the middle finger of his left hand. With the fingers of his right hand, Remius pried open the top of the heart. Inside rested a few drops of glittering dust.

"Faeriedust?" Alora's relieved voice came out in a whispered hush. A rush of gratitude tickled her scalp and made her shiver.

"Indeed, upon Theodore's orders, select members of your guard will now be carrying the potion, as we never know whether you will have it on your person. Take it now, and whenever you cannot suppress the need any longer, you will be safe to slumber away." Remius removed the ring from his finger, holding it out to her. His eyes searched her, staring deeply into them.

Opening her palm to him, Remius gently rested it onto her gloved hand. Alora had dismissed the bite wound from the hedgehog but noticed that tiny holes marred the garment. There were a few drops of blood staining the once pristine white, but it was hard to make them out since dirt clung to the satin fabric as well. But since it no longer caused her pain, Alora guessed her Fae healing had once again healed her. She turned her attention to the band in her hand.

The ring was warm against her chilled skin, even through

the thin fabric of her glove. With no delay, Alora brought the gold heart up to her mouth, tipping its contents onto her tongue. A warm tingling flooded her being, and she felt as light as a feather.

"It's good to meet with you again, Your Highness," Remius addressed Hatter with a low bow.

"As it is good to see you again, too, Remius," Hatter replied with an open friendliness from his stance behind Alora. "Thank you for coming to our aid."

"It was my duty. We shall return you to your mother and then—"

"I won't be returning to my mother's kingdom. Not just yet. My duty is to my heart, and with my heart will I remain," Hatter interjected with determination.

"I see…" Remius looked from Hatter to Alora. His mouth pulled down into a deep frown before he set his face into a mask of indifference.

With reluctance and a stabbing sensation in her chest, Alora held the ring out toward Remius. The knight took it wearily, ensuring their fingers didn't touch.

"Let us not delay," began Hatter as he stepped around Alora, exiting their prison. "First, we need to free our army." Hatter strode over to the next cell as Alora came to stand next to Remius.

Silently, they both watched Hatter. Remius's warmth reached her in the space between them, and instead of moving away from him, Alora held her ground. There was so much comfort in being beside him.

"How do you expect to free so many, Your Highness?" Remius asked, shifting anxiously from foot to foot. It was as if he was completely ignoring her presence now. "We can't squire them all away."

"There are plenty of ways to hide in plain sight and many avenues of escape hidden interspersed throughout these castle walls. May I have the key, please?" Hatter extended his arm and waited.

Huffing out a breath and rubbing his free hand over his face, Remius closed the distance, depositing the key into Hatter's awaiting hand. "I hope you know what you're doing."

Hatter gave him a nod and then made quick work of freeing Fleur and Clement.

"It's marvelous to be free and stretch one's wings," Fleur rejoiced as she twirled in the air above them. Her red locks curled around her pale face. It looked as if her dress was created from the petals of a wilted and darkened rose.

"You realize at any time, you could have flown around in the dungeon?" Clement regarded her with a puzzled look. He wore a mossy-green fitted tailcoat and matching trousers. His coal-black hair was pulled back and tied with a ribbon that was a darker shade of green.

Scrunching up her face, Fleur spoke, "It's the principal of the thing. No one likes to be imprisoned. Chained to the icky walls and covered in rags."

"But—" Clement began. Fleur reached up and placed an index finger onto his lips, hushing his words.

"Best not to make a nuisance of yourself, darling," she cautioned him.

Alora watched the encounter with a bemused smile pasted onto her face, while Hatter strode to each dark hole, twisting the key in the locks, freeing a small number.

When their party totaled ten, Remius led them through a tunnel attached to the dungeon's end. The tunnel became visible when he held up the tip of his sword to the wall and uttered a few words Alora's ears couldn't quite catch. A shining golden light lit the space before disappearing to reveal a circular opening. The freed prisoners didn't waste a second in leaping straight into the portal. Remius stood sentry as Hatter went through it first; with a solid grip on Alora's hand, Hatter gently pulled her through the blinding white light and to the other side. Alora looked back to watch as the White Knight resheathed his sword and waved his hand in the air. The circle began to close, but Remius had time enough to make his way through it and into the dirt-packed tunnel to join them.

"Now what?" Fleur asked as she floated along the air.

"We traverse this tunnel and come out to the other side, which will see us safely ensconced into the Forest of Hidden Wonders. We best rest for a while before continuing along," advised Remius, regarding the group.

Hatter clapped Remius upon his back and beamed at him. "Excellent leadership."

"Thank you," Remius replied, and looked uncomfortable as he tugged at his cravat and cast his eyes toward the ground.

Alora felt as if a dagger was severing her heart into tiny pieces. Certainly, Remius's unease was not due to the praise. Hatter was standing so close to her and kept giving her little touches.

Oh, Remius's poor heart and mine too.

"Let us be off," suggested one of the freed faeries.

"Lead on, the forest awaits," called out Hatter. He wove his fingers with Alora's, and though her gloves prevented his skin from touching hers, it sent a delicious thrill up her arm, straight for her heart. The smile he gave her lit up his features as she quickly made a new memory to treasure.

Remius noted the tender action, then scowled. Alora longed to talk with him but now was not the time. Would it ever be the right time?

"Oh, what about your hat?" Alora brought her widened eyes to study the tips of Hatter's jagged ears. He was never without protection from prying eyes.

Self-consciously, Hatter mussed his hair so that his ears were covered. With an irate glower, he stated, "The queen stole it! One of her henchmen ripped it from my head, and she stomped it into the dirt. She likes taking my things." A dark look passed over his features.

Alora let his hand go to reach up to cup his cheek, the stubble was rough against her gloves. She reasoned her question had taken him back to the night his father died; when the queen had taken the tips of Hatter's ears.

"We shall find you another. You are so handsome; you don't need to hide away from the world." She attempted to soothe him. Hatter still had a distant light in his eyes, as if he wasn't really with her at all.

"She took his heart. Plucked it away…my ears are missing; have you seen them?" Hatter looked around them, but she didn't think his eyes were really taking in their surroundings. He began to grow more frantic as his arms waved in the air above them. The last thing they needed was to draw attention when they were so close to escape.

"Phillip," Alora entrapped his face between her hands. "You are not back there. You are here with me. We are safe at the moment, but if you don't calm yourself, we might not be for too much longer. You are safe, and you are here. Those are just memories, not your reality. Come back to me. Come back to holding my hand!" Alora came up on her tiptoes, leaning her forehead against his chin as her hands sought his. She willed him to be well, to be whole, to be with her in every way possible.

Be well, be well, be well, Alora chanted as warmth enveloped them both.

Hatter's frantic movements stilled, and his hands let hers go to frame her face with his hands.

"I am all right. I am…well. For the first time in a very long time, I feel well," he said quietly and swallowed thickly.

Alora's hands came up to rest against his as he continued to cup her face. Had she cured him? Was it a mere coincidence he had improved after the warmth had enveloped her?

Drawing her hands away from his face and regaining his full height, Hatter looked in the direction their party had taken. "We haven't much time." He again entwined their fingers before he set their pace to gain some of the distance separating them from the group.

They were back with their party in minutes, just slightly winded from the faster pace. Their troops tread through the tunnel single file or in lines of two for what seemed like endless hours. With only a scant few faerie lights to banish the darkness away, Alora felt far from content, even with Hatter staunchly by her side. She had pressing questions as to whether she had cured Hatter. And if she hadn't, could she? Then, there were the dark looks, or were they more of a tortured nature, that Remius was casting their way? Her heart understood how he must be feeling, but she didn't know how to set things right.

Remius brought up the rear, and she could feel his gaze burning into her back. Somehow, despite her weariness and the tears that threatened to fall, Alora kept walking.

How shall I correct this? This is not how things should be. My heart carries such deep affection for my knight, and I cherish his friendship. I must find a way to mend this rift between us, even though I have made it perfectly clear there is nothing more that I can give him. My heart can't bear to see him so upset.

30

THE FOREST OF HIDDEN WONDERS

When the lighting changed, signaling they had all safely reached the mouth of the seemingly unending tunnel, Alora wanted to swoon from relief. The damp air had become almost unbreathable for her the longer Remius stayed silent. Hatter had caught her eyes a few times, and his puzzled expression met her gaze. Alora felt as if she lacked the energy to have the discussion that needed to be held with Hatter, much less one with Remius. Would Hatter even understand that for a brief few moments, she had allowed her heart to long for another? Was it a betrayal? Would this damage the new beginning they were forging? Alora had never meant to deceive Hatter, and here, her two worlds were colliding.

When the exhausted group had stepped from the tunnel, and it was Alora's turn to join them along with Hatter and Remius, she finally exited the tunnels. Would they encounter friends or foes next?

Alora blinked, her eyes becoming accustomed to the brighter twinkle of the dazzling crimson moon. Teal hued twinkling stars peeked through the dense foliage above the towering willow branches that swayed with the gentle breeze that kissed her face and refreshed her senses. Tilting her head up, Alora let a smile break across her face.

From the crashing sound of water greeting her ears, she gathered that a waterfall was not too far away. When she let her gaze fall to the thick forest floor, glowing purple and blue petals stared up at her, their iridescent light cast onto the smaller things dwelling underneath them. Their little beady black eyes regarded her, but they stayed eerily mute, turning their heads to observe the newcomers. Mushrooms grew in abundance around the trunks of the mighty ebony trees in all shapes and sizes, with dark reds and browns topping them in color. Buzzing insects with translucent prism wings flew in zigzagging patterns, but didn't slow to pay them any attention.

"The camp is just this way. We can shelter there for the remaining night hours," explained Remius as he came from behind Alora to lead the way.

Hatter grew still, and Alora halted beside him. He was intently peering between the base of a trio of trees. His eyes lit up as he dashed over to them, and bending down, he reached for some dark object. When Hatter straightened, he held in between his hands a top hat. Smiling broadly, he turned back to Alora as he brushed debris from the hat's fabric. He beat the topper against his leg, then held it up to inspect by the moonlight. With a satisfied nod, Hatter promptly placed it atop his head.

"Everything seems so different under the wide brim of a hat. It's very relaxing," he stated as he took her hand, braiding their fingers together.

The hat wasn't too shabby, but it was far from new. From its high height upon Hatter's head, Alora couldn't tell whether it was stained or torn.

"You'll find the sprites to be very energetic and slightly chaotic." Hatter squeezed Alora's fingers as they followed, bringing up the rear of the group. He seemed to be much more at ease, so like he once was with her.

"I'm sure they're entirely lovely," Alora replied as she kept her gaze cast onto the ground. Little scurrying animals were darting in and out, cutting lines in the group's pathway.

The very last thing we need is for a princess to squash one of them. I do apologize for trampling your grandfather. I'm so sorry for kicking your baby brother's head. That would go very well for the first introductions.

"You've met two of their kind. Fleur and Clement are sprites," offered Hatter as he let her hand go and stopped to remove a hanging branch from their way.

"Oh my. Now I am truly—" began Alora as she allowed Hatter to reclaim her hand.

"Faemazed? Faestounded? Overcome with unwavering delight?" inquired Fleur, who came up to float in the air just before Alora's face. Her expression looked guarded as her sapphire eyes narrowed.

"Our princess hasn't yet learned how to speak all of the various Faeisms," Remius's voice rang out from the front of the group.

"Does anyone?" questioned Clement as he flew up to float alongside Fleur.

"I am one of a kind and very proud to be so," said Fleur as she fluffed the rose petals of her skirt. Her actions made some bits of the aged and discolored petals crumble as they drifted away on a cool breeze.

"That you are, my love," replied Clement as he leaned over to press a kiss to her cheek. A blush infused the tiny sprite's face.

"Now, *Princess* Alora, we really must educate you more efficiently. How long have you been in Wonderland?" Fleur folded her arms across her tiny body.

"This makes it three or perhaps four nights," Alora told her.

"Four nights!? And already you ended up imprisoned? I am impressed." Fleur regarded Alora as she pursed her lips in thought.

"Well, I shan't like to repeat that experience ever again," Alora answered as she carefully stepped over a fallen log with the aid of Hatter's direction.

"Stick with me, Princess, and I shall be happy to instruct you in all the delights of the faerie realm. Have you had any faerie to enlighten you on the perils yet?" Fleur kept pace aloft in the air next to the side of Alora's face as they trekked through the flora.

"Cheshire has been my appointed tutor—" began Alora.

"Oh! He's quite a good teacher, if insufferable at times, but there's nothing quite like a female to offer insight to another." Fleur tilted her head to the side. "I think I like you. We shall become fast friends, quite inseparable in no time."

"Oh?"

"Why, of course. And as your friend, it's my duty to offer you my sage advice. You must clear the air with Guard Grumpy. He looks cross enough to behead a few faeries every time he looks in your direction. If I am not wrong, there is a wealth of feeling he's masking away. It would be best to unearth his feelings so nothing untoward occurs and he doesn't embrace his darker nature, which is entirely possible now that nearly every faerie is going mad." Fleur gave Alora a demure smile before she reached over and grabbed ahold of Clement's hand. The pair shot off, outpacing Remius as they weaved a path through the trees.

The silence emanating from Hatter began to play havoc on Alora's nerves. He was concentrating on their pathway, but she sensed hurt lingering in the space between them.

"I feel as if an apology is in order," Alora began. Hatter kept his gaze lowered. "This is not how or when I wanted to talk to you about this."

"You may always tell me anything, sweet Alora," Hatter said as he raised his eyes to look at her.

She willed her eyes to convey the depth of her remorse, revealing to him the wealth of feeling she bore for him. Hatter deserved not to be kept in the dark, but Alora didn't want to break this delicate bond between them either. Hatter brought their steps to a halt, then reached his hand up to gently stroke her cheek with his free hand.

"How could I expect you would walk into Wonderland and not be charmed by the very beings who reside here? You are new to this all and a breath of fresh air to the faeries who have long sought to keep hope locked away within their hearts. You are the embodiment of all that is good and kind and a beacon to those who are seeking whom they may follow. I would be a fool to even believe for a moment you were not being pursued by more than just your guard," he paused to remove his hand from her cheek and rubbed it over his chest. "In here, I feel you. I know your heart. You do bear him great affection and esteem, but your heart is not embellished with his name. He is not your first thought upon waking, nor your last as you drift off each night. My name is. Just as your name is my savior and my ruination. We are forged together in blood, marrow, and truth. There is nothing that can sever our bond given to us by fate. How I didn't understand all of this when first seeing you again here in Wonderland is absurd." He reached for her hands and brought them to rest up against his chest, over his beating heart.

The thump of his heartbeats under her palms made her pulse race as warmth filled her core. Tears rimmed Alora's lashes as she tried to blink them away, focusing her watery vision onto his face. "I saw you and talked with you, and you didn't remember me. I felt all alone and with so much pressure upon my shoulders to be this unfailing being that I allowed myself to wonder what could be. And I can't forgive myself for this. How can I ever expect you to?"

"I will never forgive myself for causing you pain and uncertainty. That is mine to bear. Let us embrace our faults while we stitch together a new future." Hatter disentangled their joined hands and pinched the tip of her glove.

Slowly, he pulled it from her arm, away from her wrist, and off of the ends of her finger's tips. Alora gasped as the air met her bare arm, sending goosebumps to its surface, but maybe it had more to do with the strikingly handsome faerie who stood before her that physically affected her. Hatter's eyes had darkened and seemed to hold secrets she longed to draw from his sensuous lips. He brought her hand up to those lips and placed his warm mouth against her skin in a reverent kiss. Hatter allowed his mouth to linger as he stared into her eyes. Alora's mouth had gone dry as her pulse began to gallop in her chest. Her skin felt feverish and achy. Alora was even a touch lightheaded as stars danced across her vision. If Hatter had told her he was using some Fae ability upon her, she would have easily believed him. But in truth, it was just the effect his nearness had on her. He smiled at her as he slowly edged her hand away from his lips.

"You are very enticing, very alluring. I fear for my poor heart," Alora quietly confided.

"Never fear for your heart, my love, for it belongs to me, just as mine belongs to you. We shall guard them, nurture them, and revere them together. And as much as I'd like to keep you close by my side, you do need to fix things between you and Remius. Perhaps not this evening, but tomorrow. If you need me to be there by your side, then I will be."

Alora reached up to cup his face. She stood on her tiptoes to rub the tip of her nose along his jaw. Hatter's quick intake of breath made her smirk. She wasn't the only one affected by their nearness.

She readjusted her stance, then leaned in again to place a

soft kiss just below his cheekbone. The dark stubble on his face tickled the sensitive flesh surrounding her mouth. Alora then let her weight sink back onto the balls of her feet. She leaned her forehead against Hatter's muscled chest, deeply breathing in his fragrance of vanilla, steeped tea leaves, and sandalwood. His unique scent greeted her, filling her senses as emotions wrapped around her heart. Hatter enclosed her in his solid arms, holding her to him as he rested his chin on the crown of her head.

"As much as I wish I could whisk you away, we really should join the others. They will have noticed our lagging," Hatter advised reluctantly.

Alora groaned. "You're right." Drawing herself away from his comfort, Alora reached for her glove and pulled it on as he watched her. Combing her gloved fingers through her long tresses, she gave up when tangles kept snagging on her fingertips.

When she was certain no blush colored her pale skin and that she was presentable, she entwined her arm with his, strolling by his side through the trees. The closer they stepped to the camp, the more discernible the sound of the waterfall became.

I can't wait to discover just what a waterfall of Faerie looks like. And this is one discovery that I shall make by Phillip's side.

31

CURIOUS DISCOVERIES

It wasn't until Alora sat atop a fallen log with a cup of spiced cider in her hands that she realized how exhausted she truly was. The yawns from the dungeon had fled with the rush of being freed. Now, she was certain she could settle down amongst the flora and fauna and sleep for at least a week. When another giant yawn nearly had her eyes closed, Alora felt gentle hands pulling her up from the log. When she peeked her eyes open, Hatter stood before her, stooping to meet her gaze. When had she closed her eyes?

"You are almost in dreamland. There is no fear of your wanderings since the Faeriedust is still within you. Let's make our way to one of the tents and find a bedroll to settle you." Hatter leaned down, wrapping his arms around her waist. Alora stumbled as she took a step, but his arms caught her. She swallowed, fighting against the sleep that beckoned her, and smiled.

"Easy now," Hatter coaxed as he leaned down and gathered her legs to hang from one arm as his other continued its hold around her middle. His strong hands cradled Alora's body to his as his warmth and scent surrounded her.

Alora yawned, struggling to keep her eyes focused on the path before them. She trusted Hatter with her life, with her heart, and would allow him to carry her anywhere that he chose to.

When she heard heavy fabric rustling, she peeped open one eye as Hatter lowered her onto a navy bedroll. Alora allowed her body to extend forward, and she came to rest with her hands tucked under the side of her face.

"Sleep beautifully, my love," whispered Hatter as he drew something soft and snug over her body. Then she felt his body conform to the space behind her, his arms encircling her waist. Alora drifted away with a heartfelt smile on her face and a peace filling all the chambers of her heart.

"You suppose that she's dead?" murmured a voice next to Alora's ear. Her first inclination was to swat the irritating interruption away, then realized that might not be the best idea. So, she chose to ignore the being.

"She's breathing, you imbecile," pointed out another voice.

"Do dead things breathe?" another voice asked.

"I once heard a dead crab scream as it was put into boiling water," came a reply.

"You sure it was dead?" inquired a voice that sounded like Fleur.

Just how many faeries had congregated to watch her sleep? The idea caused Alora to shudder as she wondered if she had drooled. Alora covertly felt her mouth and the area under her head.

"Look, she's moving; dead things don't move."

"Well, technically, that's not altogether true—"

"Oh, for all the unfaely conversations ever held, this one has to top them all!" screeched Fleur impatiently.

With a smile, Alora opened her eyes and looked at her surroundings. She was still in the canvas tent with the navy bedroll underneath her. Hatter was missing, but she didn't feel alarmed by the discovery. He might have needed to see to things while she slept in.

"Have you ever slept on a pea?" asked a tiny sprite, who settled onto Alora's knee with legs tucked under her. The faerie was pale with coal-black hair and freckles that lined the bridge of her nose and the skin of her high cheekbones.

"Not that I know of," replied Alora as she carefully sat up. She didn't want to risk upsetting the tiny faerie's seat.

"Ah, but would you know if you had? Are you a real princess?" Skepticism met her gaze.

"Of course she is, Fiona! Look at her! Every inch practically states her station, while she is regal and noble and —" huffed Fleur.

"You just met her. Like literally five minutes ago," snarked another sprite who had magenta hair and wore daisy petals for a dress.

Fleur narrowed her eyes at the interruption. "Not *five minutes ago*, seven whole hours ago, and who made you the minute patrol?"

"May I remind you that I am significantly older than you and may, in fact, boss you around as I see fit?" The magenta-haired faerie popped the sound of the *T* in her last word. Her cold gaze alighted onto Alora, and Alora had to steel herself to meet the gaze teaming with diminutive judgment. Were they friend or foe, and could she really be sure of either, as the dualities in Wonderland's subjects was such a present force?

"This is why I have chosen to make my home in the Spring Court! To escape you and your all-knowingness," stated Fleur as she turned her back to the tent's occupants.

"We didn't miss you, you know! Not once!"

"That's not at all true!" Fiona rushed to say. "We did, in

fact, miss you. Maia is just salty and frigid and never offers a kind sentiment."

"So nothing new there." Fleur patted her coiffure.

"If I may be so bold, might we begin again, ladies?" Alora asked as she attempted to make peace amongst the tinier beings.

Maia's glacial stare only intensified. "I imagine that princesses may do whatever they would like to do. Since Fleur is your *dearest* friend, she may see to dealing with you. Come, Fiona, let's leave and see to our other guests."

"But I would rather—" began Fiona.

"Come along, now." Maia's demanding tone made Fiona's shoulders droop in defeat.

"You don't have to listen to her, Fi," advised Fleur, whose own gaze was shooting daggers at the older faerie.

"I do. I swore my loyalty to her. Promise you'll seek me out for a proper chat before you leave again," Fiona gently smiled at Fleur as she rose, then flew to the tent's opening, where she hung suspended in the air, waiting for Fleur's promise.

"Of course, I shall find you. You must meet Clement, after all!" Fleur told her.

Fiona flew from the tent with a wave of her delicate hand.

Fleur turned back to face Alora. She silently looked from the covered mounds of her slippered feet to the crown of her head.

"You don't much resemble a princess at the moment. We need to tackle that hair, and perhaps a change of dress would do wonders. Come along with me; we shall go straight to the waterfall and set you to rights." Fleur lifted into the air as her wings busily beat to float in the space before Alora's face. Her tiny hand reached forward to grasp an errant curl of Alora's, but she hesitated a moment before letting her hand fall back to her side. Fleur mumbled, "We do not grab onto friend's hair and lead them along."

Alora's ears caught the sentence nevertheless and wondered at the necessity of Fleur having to repeat it almost as if it were a mantra.

"I should like that very much," Alora said as she slowly lifted the blanket from her body, then herself from the bedroll. Standing, she winced at the soreness of her body caused by sleeping on the ground; the padding was not what she was accustomed to. A proper soak would do her aching body much good.

"Splendid! Just follow me!" Fleur flew to the tent's entryway and looked over her shoulder to ensure that Alora was indeed behind her.

Alora picked up the pacc, allowing Fleur to lead the way. Once they had exited the tent, a world of rich blues, verdant silvers, and stunning purples met her eyes. Cloud puffs in different hues of blue glided across the horizon into a melting pot of lighter blues and purples that swirled together like paint on a palette. Silver leaves swayed on the breeze as limbs gently bowed overhead. Alora had never longed for her paints more than she did at this moment. To capture the stunning world and the color's vibrancy would bring her so much joy.

The tents were situated in semi-circles around smoking fires where food turned on spits, roasting and being tended to by faeries of different sizes. Elves and trolls roamed the pathways while the air above their heads was clustered with faeries flying in zigging lines. In every direction that Alora looked, she saw beings of different skin tones and a bright, beautiful backdrop that highlighted them all.

Though Alora didn't see Hatter, she wasn't concerned. She would find her way to him again, or he to her. The memory of his strong and solid arms cocooning her as she slept filled her with pleasure, while butterflies fluttered in her stomach at the thought of him; she didn't mind their presence.

Following along the dirt pathway as she trailed after Fleur,

Alora found she couldn't take her eyes away from the stunning meadow to their left. Rich orchid flowers and pansies bobbed to and fro while yellow and lilac-colored bees pollinated them. Birds flew in circling loops as they tried to spy their next meal. She spied a fox observing her with its ears perked. Its amber eyes focused on every move she made. Bits of grass hung from the mouthful it was thoughtfully chewing.

It's almost as if I know those eyes, so familiar and warm they seem… Why, I am certain that Mister Fox must be a faerie.

The roar of the waterfall became almost deafening as the pathway twisted to the right, enabling a view of the breathtaking falls. Set against the craggy, ebony ledge, the amethyst water cascading down into the water pool was a dazzling site. The striking contrast between the rock formations and the water was extraordinary. Bubbles floated up from the lake in a display of translucent shades of the rainbow, arching from one side of the falls to the other.

"Just behind the falls is a secret lair known only to the sprites. We'll make our way through the water, and then we can bathe and dress you. It'll be simply faetastic! And there shall be no worries of prying eyes to see things they shouldn't." Fleur's gaze drifted over to the fox, who seemed to catch her words because he hastily dropped his head and ignored them.

How curious…

32

THE GUIDING HANDS OF FATE

Traversing through the rolling water didn't seem like such a daunting task to Alora until she found herself attempting to keep upright with the hem of her dress clasped in her ever-tightening grip. She risked a moment to cast an exasperated look at her guide, but Fleur only shrugged her tiny shoulders as she floated high above the tumultuous surface. Alora was on the winning side of the battle as she slogged her way forward. It was taking all of her concentration to not lose her balance as she became better acquainted with the gritty rocks. Delicate drops of spray rained down on her exposed flesh. Floating along in the air were translucent bubbles of varying sizes that glowed in alluring blues, purples, and pinks. Alora drew in a deep breath and slowly exhaled. She watched the bubbles float and pop with wide eyes, utterly enchanted by their grace.

As they drew near the falls, movement from Alora's peripheral vision caught her notice. Slowly turning her head, her gaze landed upon a set of tiny black eyes that belonged to a pale face bobbing along the water's surface. Everything below the curious eyes was hidden away by the frothy bubbles that coasted atop the water. When the eyes blinked at her, Alora felt compelled to change her course and meet with the new, interesting faerie. She forced her eyes away from the water faerie to locate Fleur.

To her delight, Fleur wasn't even looking in her direction; her sight seemed to be focused on where they were going, not what Alora was doing.

Surely, one little deviation from our plan won't hurt. I long to be up close to those eyes! Surely, a closer look won't hurt.

With her mind set, Alora changed her direction and began to labor toward the curious being. Her dress was becoming heavier, and it was a chore to hold up the drenched satin. But she was determined to satisfy her curiosity. She had to get closer!

Soft humming carried through the air to Alora's ears. It was mesmerizing, and though she had never heard the tune before, she hummed along with it in perfect harmony. Drawing nearer, she spied the body that belonged to the faerie, though the water's cadence distorted the image from being clear. Just below the water's surface waved tiny arms that ended in bony finned fingers with long, extended ebony nails. The body seemed to be covered in dark scales, and bringing her gaze back up to what she could see of the faerie, there were curious finned ears along either side of its face. Alora was no more than a few steps away from the creature when its mouth opened, revealing its many sharp, pointed teeth as it hissed at her. That gave Alora a moment to pause in her quest; she immediately stopped humming.

Something's not quite right. Why am I doing this? Being only a few feet away from the faerie is quite enough, Alora decided and began to turn from her path.

"*Princess, no!*" screeched Fleur as the sprite flew with a gust of speed straight toward her.

Prickles of fear began to trail its frosty fingers up Alora's spine as her skin pebbled and her breathing became strained. "Oh dear," she whispered. Frantically, she looked back to the rocky ground to freedom and relative safety. But the shore was too far away. Escape would not be easy.

"Back, you unholy beastie!" commanded Fleur as she withdrew a knife from her thigh holster and brandished it high above her head. Her trajectory was carrying her straight to the nasty water faerie.

With a high-pitched shriek reminiscent of the banshee, the malevolent creature dove deep into the water's recesses. A long thin ebony tail with delicate bones along its edges shot above the water's swell, then it was gone.

"Never, ever, simply do what a faerie wishes you to. You won't survive long if you're constantly putting yourself in harm's way. Nixies are particularly harmful and will drag you beneath the surface within mere moments to your most unpleasant, watery demise, crunching your bones as you descend. I don't recommend it; it's terribly unfaely." Fleur gave a deep exhale, then looked at Alora.

"I don't know what I was thinking..." Alora trailed off with a frown. Why had she blithely just gone off like she had?

"Being curious is not a bad thing if it serves to preserve your life. But inept curiosity will lead you to ruin. Come along. I see you need more of a direct hand, and that is exactly how I shall continue along with you." Fleur closed the distance between them as she resheathed her sword. Reaching down, she gingerly grabbed onto one of Alora's free locks and wrapped the end around her petite fist. "Now, let's be off to where you are supposed to be." Fleur gave a gentle tug to Alora's hair. Alora was quick to follow in the faerie's path lest the next tug be painful. She was no better than an animal on a leash, but perhaps that was for the best.

I feel so foolish, and after everything the past few days has presented to me, I really should take more care with my actions. Has following the white rabbit taught me nothing? And yet... I am here because I let my heart lead me...with Phillip, with Fleur, and in this haughtily enchanting place.

With little time lost, the pair stood before the waterfall as its spray soaked them. Fleur furiously blinked her eyes as her hand shot forward. Alora was blinking her own eyes in rapid succession. An opening was created in the middle of the falls, and Alora peered through to a rocky dwelling behind it. Fleur tugged on Alora's lock, and Alora readily climbed the stone steps that led up and into the space. Cream-colored candles were alight in every corner and crevice. They cast shadows along the damp walls with the swaying movement of their turquoise flames.

Fleur let Alora's hair go, then raised her hand to wave toward the opening in the falls. Silver magic flowed from her outcast palm, and the falls once again rained down in a harsh cascade.

Meeting her eye, Fleur pointed to the wooden shelves that lined the perimeter of the cavern.

"We shall have you looking fresh and rested in no time at all. I think honeysuckle and vanilla would be a wonderful combination." Fleur veered toward the nearest shelf and began to peer at the dark bottles. The little sprite was not much larger than the glass containers.

Letting her eyes adjust to the dim lighting, Alora caught sight of the enormous pool of water that rested at the very back of the grotto. Steam wafted up from the water's surface to glide along the air. It looked inviting, and after the past few days, Alora couldn't wait to soak for a few minutes, letting the tension and stress melt away.

"Ah ha! Just what we need. Go ahead and disrobe, then leave your things over there." Fleur pointed to a corner where a large empty wicker basket rested against one of the slick walls. "Towels are on the other side of the pool in another basket, and for the realm's sake, dispense with wearing those awful gloves. They are terribly unfashionable."

"As you wish, Fleur." Alora beamed with good humor as

she tread over to the basket. Her gloves really did little to keep her warm. What she needed was a fur-lined pelisse.

Her silk slippers were torn, stained, and utterly ruined. Nonetheless, Alora removed them and tossed them into the basket. Next, she removed her gloves, which were in slightly better condition but not by much. Alora had never seen gloves so dirtied before. Her stockings followed, then her dress and undergarments. Alora peered over her shoulder to see what Fleur was doing, but the sprite was busy gathering different bottles and setting them down beside the pool. Fleur didn't seem to have a moment's trouble with hefting the weighty containers from one area to another.

Alora padded over to the water to dip a toe into it. Warmth met her chilled flesh, and Alora clambered the rest of the way in as her eyelids dropped. Alora sighed with delight. The water was heavenly. Her thoughts turned to Froggy and how the frog would have enjoyed this hidden spot as well. She hoped all was well with the amphibian. Surely, being with the Resistance was much safer.

There were sloped edges along the pool's sides, and Alora chose one to settle onto. The balmy water came up to her neck. Auburn tresses floated atop the water, encompassing her shoulders and back. Closing her eyes, she allowed her thoughts to drift away.

"Here is soap; it has a pleasant smell and will make your skin glow with radiance," Fleur addressed her as Alora opened her eyes. The bar of soap was nearly as large as the sprite. Reaching out her palm, Alora allowed Fleur to drop the honey-colored soap into her waiting hand.

It smelled of honeysuckle, meadows, and fond memories as Alora brought it to her nose and inhaled. Spotting the towels, she noticed there was another wicker basket and swam her way over to it.

"We lather the sponges with the soap, then cleanse our bodies with them," Fleur explained from across the pool.

"Oh, how marvelous!" Alora remarked as she reached into the basket and picked through it until she found one that fit into the palm of her hand.

"The entire process is faetastic!" Fleur agreed.

Wetting the sponge with a dip of the water, Alora began to create a rich lather that scented the air. She thoroughly scrubbed every part of her body as Fleur disrobed before joining her. After their bodies were both cleansed, Fleur handed one of the dark bottles to Alora.

Dipping her head back, then straightening up again, Alora opened the bottle and poured its golden contents onto her palm. Scents of vanilla and honeysuckle wafted up to greet her, and she inhaled deeply. She worked the liquid into her tresses, letting her nails gently scrub through the thick bubbles to her scalp.

When both ladies were finished, they perched on the pool's edges, soaking in the summer setting. It was the most relaxed Alora had ever been.

"Do you think it's going to be hard to adjust your life to your fated mate? Easy to schedule him in? Do you think you'll always want to be by his side? I never want to be an extension of Clement. I want to continue along as my own faerie. But he's so clingy, and a part of me wants to bask in his presence, but another part wants to balk at the idea of never being alone again. Do you understand what I mean?" Fleur frowned down into the purple depths.

"What exactly does 'fated mates' mean?" Alora asked as her foot swished beneath the water. "I keep hearing you say that phrase, and yet, while I understand the general idea, it seems to be so much more than being forever tied to one another."

"Why, it's the other being who carries the other half of your soul. In all the world, in all the realms, there can *ever* only be one. *The one.* Some faeries live centuries without finding their fated mate. Some go a little bit insane by never having that connection formed. When you find your other half, you're stronger than you've ever been, but it also can be your greatest weakness. For who would ever allow harm to befall their beloved? And it's supposed to be the most magical meeting of your entire existence. I feel cheated. I waited so long to meet Clement, to know his name, and it wasn't magical; no stars aligned. It's all due to the evil queen. She was busy putting me in chains when my eyes locked with his across the courtyard. Clement risked his very life to come to my aid, and little good it did either of us as he was carted away to the dungeons with me. See, *not at all magical!*" Fleur huffed and folded her arms across her chest.

Alora took a moment to gather her thoughts. Hadn't she felt as if a piece of herself was missing without Phillip? Hadn't she felt as if the most magical moment of her life was when they locked gazes across the crowded ballroom as he made his way to her?

Fated Mates? That perfectly describes us. Even now, I feel this tether between us, reminding me of him, making me long to be in his arms again. Knowing that Phillip is near and missing me just as much. I could never tire of him, could never not want to be by his side... Poor Fleur, to always have this expectation and to have the moment completely obliterated.

"You have every reason to be upset, Fleur. It's often been my observation that one feels as they do, whether it's right or wrong. I am sorry that your meeting was not what you had hoped for. But is Clement *who* you wished for?" Alora tilted her head to better observe the sprite.

Fleur drew her brows together in contemplation before answering, "Yes, I rather believe he is. He has seen my stabby side and remained true and steadfast."

"Has he seen your softer side?"

"Not as much as he should. I was so disappointed; now I fear Clement may think I am disheartened by him and not the circumstances of our meeting." Fleur swallowed. "That's rather tragic."

"Yet, it's not unfixable at all. I won't pretend to know much about fated mates, but I do know how he looks at you. It's as if you're his entire world."

"I am, aren't I? He is mine, too."

"So, what are you going to do about it?" Alora asked, raising her brow.

"I am going to find Clement and throw myself into his arms. Then, I shall ask him to join me in a mating ceremony this very evening." Fleur's sapphire eyes lit up with tenderness and hope.

"Sounds perfect to me. One thing, though, what's a mating ceremony?"

"I suppose it's much like your weddings in England I've read of before. A couple joins their lives together, pledging their entire existence to each other. For faeries, there is nothing more sacred, and some would argue it's even more binding than an actual wedding. King Ezekiel and Queen Briella had both, which were equally as beautiful." Fleur ringed her damp, fiery hair out and then twisted and knotted it atop the crown of her head. Droplets of water cascaded down her pale skin.

"Is it a private event?"

"If you wish it to be. But as it's not every day one discovers their true mate, it's often a cause of great celebration, and there are many who wish to attend. The thought of my dearest friend in all the realms not witnessing mine hurts. But my queen would be thrilled for me." Fleur smiled sadly.

"I shall be happy to help you with any preparations you may need. Just direct me as you will." Alora's lips curved into a grin.

With a nod accompanied by a blinding smile, Fleur clapped her hands. "I accept! You are so very faederful! Let's dry ourselves and envision the perfect dresses and accessories from the enchanted cabinet, then go find our men!"

To Alora, that sounded like a perfect plan. She was missing Hatter more and more, longing to be by his side. Her thoughts strayed back to the fox with the familiar eyes.

I wonder why the fox has popped back into my mind...

33

A TEAR?

The enchanted cabinet was a curious wonder. All Alora had to do was envision the dress Fleur described and then close her eyes. In mere moments, Fleur threw the cabinet's door wide open and clapped her hands as she delightedly danced along the air.

"Well done!" Fleur chirped.

Alora reached inside the cabinet, marveling at the dress before her as silver stars pirouetted around the garment, coming to rest against the skin of her arm and hand. She waved her hand back, then forth, as her fingers slipped through the translucent stars.

"Don't dally. Go ready yourself while I do the same," instructed Fleur, who had already used the cabinet to create her attire.

Nodding her ascent, Alora moved to a wooden chair, laying her dress and trimmings upon it. She donned each item piece by piece. When she was finished, Fleur was as well.

"You really must take in the full effect. The looking glass is just over there." Fleur tilted her head to the right, and to Alora's surprise, a little alcove appeared, which contained a curtain and a full-length rosewood mirror. Alora wondered why Fleur hadn't directed her to the lovely secluded area for her to dress in. Nudity hadn't seemed to be an issue for the Fae, who showed such a lack of care toward it.

When Alora's eyes scanned herself through the glass, they widened with wonder. The forest-green muslin that clothed her body was beautiful. No matter which direction she moved herself, the fabric shimmered. Delicate bits of Brussels lace edged the modest neckline and trim at the hemline. The darker shade of green ribboned just under her bosom was embroidered in tiny golden flowers. Matching slippers boasted the same pattern.

"While these slippers are lovely, I think I would rather have sturdier boots in which to roam about. Silk slippers don't seem to hold up too well through the grass and gravel." Alora peeked one foot out from underneath her dress's hem, frowning down at it.

"Well, then, we shall put a tiny spell upon them." Fleur whizzed to Alora's side, intently focused on Alora's feet. Silver magic flowed from her hand to gently enwrap her slippers. "There, now they should do the trick. Let's move onto our hair."

Alora turned to follow the sprite over to a shelf that was inset into one of the brown walls. Resting atop the shelf were different sized brushes. Silver and gold hair combs were decorated with upraised filigrees of butterflies, hearts, and even flowers.

"This one for you, I think," decided Fleur as she reached for a gold comb with swirling butterflies upon it.

Alora weaved slightly as her lips pressed tightly together. Since coming to Wonderland she had developed an aversion to the tiny insects. While dreaming, they signaled when everything was about to change for the worse. Alora felt herself grow pale as the blood fled from her head, and her pulse began to slow.

To Alora's dismay, Fleur set the comb back down, "Whatever is the matter?"

"I don't like butterflies. They cause me to panic." Alora tried to still the thundering beats of her heart, which had sped up as she replied. She had attempted to hide her panic, but had failed.

"But they're completely harmless little creatures."

"Not to me…" Alora bowed her head.

"Very well, we'll skip the rose-decorated ones for very obvious reasons. How about this one with the two entwined hearts? It's rather perfect considering the circumstances." Fleur picked up a thick bristled brush, carrying it to Alora's hand. "Brush those gorgeous locks, then we can be on our way."

Taking the silver brush from Fleur, Alora began the task of taming her hair's tangles. When it was shining, Fleur flew up to the side of Alora's head, carefully tucking the comb into the cascading curls of her hair.

"It's lovely, just as you are." Fleur gave a decisive nod, then tended to her own tresses. Fleur's hair was left loose to hang freely around her shoulders and down her back in wavy tendrils. The little faerie looked stunning in her black petaled dress with matching slippers.

Grabbing onto Alora's pinkie, Fleur brought her back over to the looking glass, where they both took in their reflections.

"We're as perfect as can be," Fleur announced as she turned her head from side to side.

When Fleur had said earlier that the soap would make Alora's skin radiant, she hadn't been fibbing. A soft glow was cast over Alora's exposed flesh, making her midnight-blue eyes appear darker and larger, rimmed with long, luscious lashes that curled upward at their ends. Her hair draped around her shoulders then flowed down her back where the curled ends reached to her waist. It wasn't proper to wear one's hair down in England, but they weren't in that mortal world with those mortal morals and constraints any longer. She rather liked the sensation of her tresses hanging loosely.

Fleur tugged her toward the opening of the falls. With a shrug of her shoulders, Alora wondered if their efforts would be wasted as they hazarded through the water again. Before she could voice her concerns, Fleur let Alora's hand go before she lifted each of her own hands. The silver magic wafted from Fleur's palms toward the falls. A bubble was drawn from the water and began to grow. In seconds, the purple, glittering bubble became large enough to fit Alora.

With a satisfied smirk, Fleur motioned Alora forward. "Step into the bubble, and we shall float along until we reach the land beyond."

"Why didn't we just do that to begin with instead of risking drowning and dismemberment by the nixies?" Alora asked as her blood thrummed through her body, heating it with irritation.

"Because I am only a tiny sprite. My magic is not unlimited. I knew that we would need to save it for when we were fashionable and sparkling." Fleur rolled her eyes.

"I see, forgive me. Wonderland seems to always be at odds with what is easier, making every task much harder than needed."

"Forgiven. I am not a resident of Wonderland." Fleur impatiently waved her hand toward the bubble. "Therefore, my actions are usually straightforward and to the point; I have little patience to waste. I never really felt as if I belonged here…"

Alora lifted her hem as she brought one foot up to slide through the bubble, hoping it wouldn't pop and make the sprite even more annoyed with her. With success, Alora found that while the bubble was buoyant, it was also solid. She walked the rest of the way inside of it on surer steps. Fleur joined her, then lifted her hand. As she did so, the bubble gently rose to hover in the air. Alora flung out her hands to either side of herself in an attempt to stave off a fall as dragonflies flitted in her stomach. She felt a bit dizzy and weightless as she was lifted into the air.

"You have such little faith in me and in yourself. Believe in the magic and beauty that is Wonderland. Relax, Princess. I've got this well in hand." Fleur used her hand to guide the bubble from the falls and over the lake.

There were leaping fish and swaying water reeds beneath them as the bubble glided through the ether. Letting her arms rest to her sides, Alora looked down at the water and the meadow. The fox was no longer there. A crushing weight settled into her bones.

When the bubble floated down and came to rest upon the grass, Fleur made a fist, and the bubble dissolved. Purple mist floated down until it found the place where the air joined the water, settling in again from where it had been called; magic returned to magic.

"There you are!" came Clement's voice with joy as his wings steadily beat to meet them.

The smile that Fleur gave to him was timid and shy. Not once while in Fleur's presence had Alora ever seen the sprite behave this way.

True to her word, Fleur launched herself into her mate's arms, raining kisses down upon his forehead and cheeks, then to his eager lips. Alora felt herself blush, quickly averting her eyes.

Hatter met her gaze as he came to a stop before her. He enfolded her hand with his, then bent forward to press his lips in a kiss to her bare skin. Shivers wracked her body as delight filled her, leaving her to gasp. Hatter straightened with a gentle smile while his eyes teased her. He did not let her hand go; instead he tucked it into his forearm as he drew her to his side. Hatter set a meandering pace back toward the camp with a grin fixed upon his face.

Looking up at his profile, Alora spied something green

mixed in with his dark locks peeking out from under his discovered hat. While a brush had met his hair, he had entirely missed something. Alora shuddered as memories of fish eggs assailed her.

"Something the matter, my love?" Hatter quirked a coppery brow as he looked down at her with concern.

"Did you know that you have something in your hair? Just here." She halted her steps, and Hatter followed suit. Alora reached her hand into his hair, which was silky and soft on her bare fingers, and landed upon the intruding thing, withdrawing it. Bringing the blade of grass closer to her face, she examined it with a frown. "Phillip, are you a fox?"

With rich masculine laughter, he regarded her with weary eyes. "And if I were?"

"The fox in the meadow, was that you?"

"Indeed. Are you surprised? Or perhaps upset by that fact?" He avoided looking at her as he once again entangled their arms. He began to lead her back to the pathway.

"I find that I am not as surprised as I should have been. You know, when we first met, we talked of foxes?"

His brows furrowed as he replied, "Did we? Now, I truly do wish I had those memories returned to me. Did I give myself away?"

"Not at all. I think it was your eyes, even in fox form. I would know them anywhere. I painted your face back in England. I missed you so much. Your eyes always sneaked up on me, wedging into my thoughts."

"How horrible for you when I had all but abandoned you," Hatter lowered his voice as his bushy brows careened together.

"You had every reason to be preoccupied, and haven't we agreed to begin anew?" He stayed their progress, and she reached up to place a firm kiss along the underside of his jaw. Tiny pricks from the hair on his jaw tickled her nose. When Hatter was the one to shiver, Alora felt bubbly and light as a feather that she could also invoke his passions. A satisfied feeling unfurled within her core as a warm feeling caressed her heart.

"That we have, but I shall regret never having those moments back." He gave a half smile to her.

"He said yes!" Fleur gave a whoop and collided with Alora's capped sleeve. Clement was quickly following behind her.

"Congratulations!" Alora beamed at the couple.

"If I were a lesser faerie, I might feel emasculated that she was the one to ask me to have a mating ceremony, but I can't help but understand that my darling mate will always be upending my world." Clement cast a fond smile at Fleur.

"Congratulations!" Hatter echoed Alora's earlier statement. He looked at the couple and bowed his head.

"We have so much to do! There's seating to arrange, a menu to plan, music, and, oh, just everything else!" Fleur twirled in the air.

"Perhaps your sisters would like to aid in the cause?" offered Clement.

Fleur's smile fell away before she said, "Of course. I can't help wishing that Sabelle was here to see this moment."

"Sabelle? Who is she to you?" questioned Alora.

"Sabelle is my oldest sister. She used to live in the Summer Court. But things went very wrong, and she is not who she once was. There is no inviting her nor visiting with her ever again." A single tear fell from Fleur's eye, trailing down her pale cheek. "A tear? I never cry."

Clement gently drew Fleur into his arms as he whispered into her hair.

Hatter patted Alora's hand, gaining her attention. His gaze was locked before them. Alora swiveled her head to see what had gained his notice. Remius was looking their way with a frown, marring her perfect features.

"Oh dear," breathed Alora, even though she had suspected this was coming.

"Perhaps now is a good time to have that chat? Do you wish for me to join you?" Hatter looked from Remius to her. He studied her face as his eyes roamed over her features, reflecting warmth mingling with worry.

She shook her head. "I don't think that would be wise, but thank you. I need to fix this. Somehow…"

Nodding his head, Hatter allowed her to pull away from him. He didn't smile or say another word, but she felt his eyes on her, giving her courage.

When Alora closed the distance between herself and Remius, he looked down at her with searching eyes. She tried to rein in her tears and shrugged before finding her words. "We should talk."

Remius gave her a nod before he walked toward the camp. He hadn't offered her his arm, and it stung. Alora blinked her eyes before following in his wake.

This shall not be easy. Why did I allow him entrance into my heart? Why did I allow him to think impossible things? Perhaps my mortal side is a betrayer. Have I fallen for him with my human self? The feelings that I bear for each of these men are so contrasting and yet, so very similar. Remius is not my future… he's not even my past.

34

BROKEN HEARTS STILL BEAT

What words could Alora use to begin this daunting conversation? Her heart was aching as she sat down upon the fallen log in the midst of swooping willow trees. Bird songs interrupted the fraught silence; the buzz of insects punctuated the air between her quiet exhales. The gentle breeze carried the scent of lilac and honey. It was a comforting smell, but nothing was consoling about this situation.

Remius stood reclining back against the mighty willow trunk just opposite her. His gaze was focused on a line of marching ants that were in perfect formation just to his right, weaving between the fallen bits of decaying greenery lying on the forest floor.

"I think you should know that in all the world, there have been few beings that I have ever cared about as I do you. I have never had a friend before you, and I shall never have one quite as magnificent as you after. Your friendship has—" Alora's heartfelt words were cut off by the sad chuckle that issued from Remius. His mouth was twisted into a grimace that reached his expressive eyes.

"I am not upset with you, Princess," he began as he raked

his hand through his pale hair, carefully avoiding his horns. "I knew how this was to end. But how do you, how does any faerie, make their heart not long for more? It's something I have fought, absolutely unbidden. Yet, it remains. I have done my best to banish it away. I can't even name what it is..." He rubbed a hand over his chest, not daring to meet her gaze.

"I am sorry. So very sorry. I would spare you any pain for the slightest of reasons." Alora didn't bother to mask the tears from her voice or her eyes.

"I don't want you to be sorry. I want you to be many things, but sorry isn't one of them," he sighed; defeat was written in every pore of his stance.

"What can I do? What can I possibly offer to make this better for you? You must know that Phillip is my fated mate. I can't change that, nor would I wish to. But to witness this... Your hurting is not what I desire either. Tell me how to fix this, please!"

"I can't! If I knew, it would be done already. I don't like feeling like this. I have never floundered as I do now. Never questioned my motives and second-guessed myself. And yet, here I am. And there you are, perfectly infuriating, perfect as you are." He raised his eyes to take her in. His gaze was brutal in its intensity, as if he were memorizing and cataloging her every detail, every flaw, and yet still, he would not break his stare.

"So imperfect. I have erred and constantly done the wrong thing." Alora wiped at the tears on her face with the backs of her hands. It cut her deeply that he couldn't discern her intentions toward his well-being.

"You have erred, but you have learned so much more. You have a heart that only seeks to heal, correcting the injustices you perceive. If that isn't worthy of esteem, or love, of the purest form, then nothing matters." Remius shifted slightly, looking as if he wanted to step toward her, but decided against such an action.

"You don't love me."

"*Do not*. I can forgive you many things, but denying me of my feelings isn't one of them. Don't presume to know that which I feel. I may not share a bond with you; there may not be some invisible tether that ties my heart to yours, but you have it all the same." He shook his head and then lowered his chin to his chest. "I have watched you take on unimaginable things, I have witnessed you discover secrets and learn of your destiny, and, through it all, I have only held you in the highest regard. You have blown me away as if I weighed nothing more than a mere feather left to dance along the air. I know in here," he thumped his chest. "That you do not feel for me what I do for you. I understand well that we can never be, no matter what the future holds. Because in your own heart, you will always belong to another."

"Perhaps I should find a new residence. Give you time to sort your feelings out. Forget me if you must."

He scoffed. "How does one forget how to breathe? I could no more stop that than I could evict you from my soul. You can't leave the one place that offers you the most protection. But…I can."

Alora jumped to her feet, closing the distance between them in a breath. She held up her index finger, jabbing it into the space right before his face. "You can't leave. I forbid it!" Icy fear held her in its despicable clutches.

"You can't forbid me from doing anything." He quirked a blond brow at her finger, slight amusement dancing over his face.

"As your princess, I can! I do. Remius, you cannot leave the safety of the Resistance." She would instill her will into him if she must.

He didn't say anything to her as he studied her face. His bright eyes trailed over the planes of her face, and it was almost as if his hands roved over her. A sad, twisted smile captured his features. Raising his hand, he used his thumb to wipe away her tears.

"I can't exist in this unsettling limbo. It will destroy me. I can't watch you watching me as it devours all that is good between us. I won't be the cause of your distress by my mere presence. Be well, Princess." Remius leaned down with his warm breath heating her face. His lips found her forehead, and he left them there against her skin for a long moment. When he withdrew, his eyes were glassy, rimmed with unshed tears.

Alora tentatively reached out a shaky hand toward him, desiring to selfishly grab onto the lapels of his greatcoat, keeping him grounded to this moment, this spot before her.

Not like this! This can't be goodbye…and yet who am I to stop him?

As the quaking intensified in her body, Alora allowed her hand to fall at her side. Already Remius had taken several steps back from her, not meeting her pleading gaze.

Remius barely lifted his head, peering past her. "Take care of her. I know that you will, that my words have little weight to you." His tortured voice broke the ether between them.

"I vow that I will," came Hatter's firm voice from behind her.

Nodding once to Hatter, Remius glanced once more at her. His eyes were a deluge of sorrow and devastation coalescing together before she saw them harden with resolve. He took a deep breath before he turned and walked away from her, from the pain that weighed his shoulders down, from the bleeding wound his heart carried.

Tears dripped in a wild torrent from her chin to hit the expanding ground between them as she watched his form disappear through the ebony trees. When the last vestiges of white disappeared from view, her knees gave out, and she fell into Hatter's waiting embrace. He handled her as if she were made of fragile glass or was as delicate as the petals of a flower. His solid arms lifted her to him as he carried her bridal-style back to the fallen log on which he perched with her in his lap. Alora sobbed just as she had when her mother had passed away. Her heart was raw and weeping. At that moment, what she desired most was to be numb so that she would never again have to feel this way.

But there was Hatter, holding her to him, and she cried even more that he would console her when she was so upset because of another male. Hatter, who was perfect and here and all hers. Hatter, who was male, was robust and had a steadying presence. Who had vowed to love her for all of her tomorrows? Hatter, who would never leave her, even though he had, and Alora wailed at the thought of his leaving her again. That was something that would destroy her. Something that Alora could never recover from.

Hatter nuzzled his nose into her hair, breathing her in. His lips lingered over her head until his kisses met the rounded tips of her ears.

"You are my everything. Know that. I understand your feelings; you must know mine. I am agonized that you are feeling so abandoned. But I shall not forsake you. There is nothing and no being that will keep us parted. Alora, my love, you are my eternal happiness, joy, and purpose." The whispered words almost filled all the broken pieces of her soul as her tears began to dry. The sincerity of his assurances cast her in a warm glow, filling the hollow recesses of her that even she didn't know were barren.

"I do not deserve you." Alora inhaled his scent, burying her head further into his cravat. The layers of linen and lace were soaked with the traces of her heartache.

"It is I that does not deserve you."

"Phillip?" she tentatively asked as she hid her face.

"Alora?"

"When we are returned to my father, will you stay with me? By my side?"

"Have I not told you as much? We will not be parted. I won't allow that to happen." The conviction in his voice gave her the courage she needed. Alora withdrew her head from him to gaze up into his golden eyes.

"I won't let you go. I warn you now," she promised with an iron will.

"Good, because the idea of parting from you steals the very breath from my lungs and sends me into a rage."

"Then we are in accord." She looked from his eyes to his nose, to his mouth.

"Alora, when we are returned to your father, I plan to ask him for your hand in marriage. I know you have grown up with human customs. I long to see your mortal side honored. Would you consent not only to being my fated mate but to being my wife as well?" He swallowed, and she wondered if he was even breathing; he sat so still beneath her.

"Would you do those things for me?"

"I would walk through fire and brimstone for you. Marrying you, being by your side? That's the easy part; it's all the rest that gives me pause. But together, we'll reclaim Wonderland and heal our kingdom's wounds. Together." He linked their fingers, then bent forward to kiss the back of her hand.

"Together," she echoed. While her heart was sore, she allowed herself to feel the joy and pure bliss that being with Hatter gave her.

He was right. They fit together, and all the dangers pressing in from all sides could be dealt with together. Alora had never felt so contented in another's arms, not even Remius's. Even in her knight's arms, she had longed for Hatter. Hatter was the mate and soon-to-be husband that destiny had chosen for her; fate had taken one heart and cleaved it into two pieces, then separated them. She did feel deeply for Remius, but it was a mere shadow of her feelings for Hatter. But there was no denying that a selfish part of her wanted Remius in her life.

Alora made a wish that Remius would be sensible and keep himself safe because a world where he did not exist was not a world she could embrace or even force the desire to fight for. She *would* see him again.

35

WHAT A BEAUTIFUL NIGHT

The scent of honeysuckles and roses wafted into the air, greeting the mating ceremony guests as they took their seats on the rows of fallen logs resting in the middle of the meadow. The evening was upon them as the teal stars twinkled down on those that had gathered. In the first row, Alora sat against Hatter's side, his arm encircling her waist. Fleur's sisters, Fiona and Maia, were seated to her other side on an upraised dias.

At the end of the satin floor runner stood a circular marble and ivory pillar on which a silver goblet rested next to a white ribbon.

Excitement radiated from Fleur as she and Clement floated in the air just above the pillar. Before them, facing those who were observing, was a figure, clad in cobalt robes, whose face wasn't visible. Her figure was slim, and Alora guessed they were of a similar height. Her voice was musical and motherly in nature as she began the ceremony.

"We are gathered together to witness this mating between Clement and Fleur, bringing joy and happiness to not only the couple but also to their family and friends. We thank the Fates for bringing these two halves together. Fleur, do you accept

Clement as your fated mate? Do you vow to stay by his side and to allow your bond to flourish no matter what hardships you may face?" The robed lady paused to wait for Fleur's answer.

"I accept Clement and offer him my heart, my body, my dreams, and all of my love." Fleur beat her wings in a frenzy, then began to rise further into the air as a golden aura lit her from within. Clement pulled her back before him with their linked hands while smiling brilliantly at her.

"Do you, Clement, accept Fleur as your fated mate? Do you vow to protect her, provide for her, and make her the star in your sky no matter your hardships? Do you vow to accept your bond, nurturing it to flourish? To gently steer you back together should you drift apart?" The robed lady took a breath.

Clement cleared his throat and replied, "I accept Fleur and offer her my heart, which was hers the moment we locked eyes. I willingly gift her my body, my dreams, and all my love." As Clement smiled, he, too, began to glow in a rich golden hue. The two were like beacons of light.

The lady faerie lifted the goblet in the air and raised it high. "Let that which the Fates have paired together be fruitful and indestructible. Let your love glow in all you do for each other." She held the goblet out to Clement, who hefted it between his hands. He lifted the goblet to Fleur's mouth, tipping it toward her. When Fleur had taken a sip, she moved her hands to cover Clement's and helped him to take a nip. Taking the goblet back from them, the robed figure set it back down then retrieved the white ribbon.

Fleur held up her left hand, allowing the faerie to wrap the ribbons around her hand several times. The figure turned to repeat the process with Clement. Joined by the white ribbon, the glow from Fleur and Clement coalesced and traveled through their palms back toward their hearts, disappearing in a sparkle of gleaming stars.

Clement bent forward and placed a chaste kiss onto his mate's lips, then drawing away from Fleur, he lifted their fastened hands together into the air.

There was a loud *"Huzzah!"* from the gathered guests as they cheered on the ethereal couple. Fleur blushed while Clement beamed at her.

"They truly are splendid together," Alora gushed at the display of open affection.

"Indeed. I wish them many happy centuries together," Hatter replied as he leaned toward Alora and kissed the tip of her nose.

Wrinkling her nose, Alora asked, "What was that for?" She'd never been kissed on her nose and found the action strange. It wasn't an unpleasant sensation; it left her feeling treasured and cared for. It was a sweet gesture that warmed her heart.

"Must I have a reason?"

"I suppose not," Alora told him as she looked at those around them. No one seemed to pay them any attention. Yet another reminder that displays of affection were not frowned upon in the land of Faerie.

Couples began to pair off as strains of music filled the evening air. Alora didn't know the melody, but it was enchanting and perfect for the occasion with its romantic undertones. Metallic-colored bubbles drifted from the sky to coast down onto those who swayed in the center of the dance floor; they popped as they met the blades of grass or were kicked as a dancer took a step.

Hatter leaned away from her, then removed his arm from her waist. He stood and straightened his greatcoat. Alora looked up at him quizzically. He reached out his hand for her to take. "Will you dance with me?"

"I would love to," she replied and let him help her to her feet, towing her to an area of the meadow that was half in shadow and half in light. There was no faerie within the space as Hatter laid his hand on the small of Alora's back, then gently enfolded her hand in his. He began their dance by leading her backward, then forward again.

A waltz! How delightful. Nothing could be as romantic as this.

He brought her closer to him so that space between them hardly existed. Staring into each other's eyes, Alora felt the depth of promises of loyalty, forgiveness, and even love as her heart thumped a little faster. There was so much love being reflected from one to the other. She laid her head against his shoulder, basking in his warmth as she hoped it was always this way between them.

They continued to sway together for what seemed like hours, with their hands bare and merging in sensual intimacy. The other couples around them left them to themselves as they, too, seemed to be caught in their own moments of time. This particular dance was better than their first because of everything that they had both been through individually; this nearness was a gift. Now they were different beings, stronger than their former selves. All of the trials hadn't broken them apart, even when all had seemed lost. They had both been tested and stretched, and yet, their love was proving to be quite an unbreakable force.

A throat cleared. Alora unwillingly lifted her head from Hatter's chest. Fleur and Clement floated before them. She attempted to keep the blush from staining her skin but felt heat rush into her face.

"It's getting late, and Clement and I are retiring for the night. But we wanted to make sure to warn you that tomorrow we begin your intensive training. So rest well because I shall not go easy on you." Fleur gave her a determined look.

"But, I must get word to my father—" Alora tried to speak.

"Yes, that's been seen too. Have no worries there. Your father is quite happy that you are in my care with the full backing of the Spring Court." Fleur waved her hand in the air and was interrupted by Clement, who was frowning.

"The Spring Court?" Clement inquired.

"Of course! Do I not represent the Spring Court? After all, am I not their trusted advisor and ambassador? That position does come with some perks." Fleur smiled, baring her teeth.

"We're to remain here?" Alora asked hesitantly.

"We are. Forgive me for not letting you know our plans earlier," began Hatter, who still had her firmly locked in his arms. "Fate will arrive tomorrow, and we shall instruct you in the areas in which you'll need to excel. We're nearly as safe here as in the underground. And we have much more room in which to practice swordplay in the meadow. There is a pond nearby with healing properties should anything go awry."

"How marvelous. But what about the Faeriedust? Remius had the last little bit I know of with him." Alora bit her bottom lip.

"He passed it along to me while you were at the falls." Hatter gave her an apologetic look.

"So, you see, it's all taken care of. Nothing to worry yourself about. It's going to be faetastic, and you're going to be in fine form in no time at all. It's time for Clement and I to cement our bond." Fleur tugged on the ribbon that joined her to Clement, whose face was berry red.

Clement leaned into Fleur, "*You* can't say things like that aloud. Not to others that aren't *me*."

"Whyever not?" Fleur's sapphire eyes widened in surprise.

"It's nobody else's business what we do or when we do... whatever." He blushed an even deeper shade of crimson.

"Oh? Well, all right. We're off to go straight to sleep. No cuddling, nor kissing or hugging whatsoever," amended Fleur. Clement rubbed his free hand down his face, muttering.

Fleur turned around, speedily flying away from Alora and

Hatter as Clement pulled behind her, his wings beating in quick succession.

Hatter chuckled at the sight as Alora shook her head.

"Well, it's hardly the worst match ever made," said Hatter as he turned his attention to her.

"To be sure." Alora yawned, and from inside his coat pocket, Hatter withdrew a bottle of the golden dust, handing it to Alora. She smiled her gratitude to him as she uncorked the bottle, letting a few grains drop onto the tip of her tongue.

He really is quite perfect.

36

YOU CAN'T EXCEL WITHOUT ME

Standing next to Hatter with Fleur and Clement fluttering near their heads, the party watched on as the looking glass before them shimmered, casting a bright golden glow onto them. One white hoof came from the glass surface, and then the rest of Fate's body emerged. When he was standing firmly on the ground before her, Alora let Hatter's hand go and rushed to embrace Fate around his thick neck.

"It's a pleasure to be reunited with you, Princess," stated Fate in a dignified tone. Alora let him go, stepping away from him as she hoped her display hadn't offended him.

Fate hooved the ground before him and shook out his silvery mane.

"I am sorry, Fate, for leaving as I did. It wasn't my intention at first, but then, I was caught up in the idea of finding Phillip. I hope you weren't in trouble for leaving my side." Alora fidgeted with the folds of her dress. She had promised him one thing and then did the complete opposite.

"Your father was quite furious and with just cause. I neglected my duty not once but twice. The knights were angry, too. Poor Remius looked panic-stricken. But he found you." Fate gazed at her with a frown.

Fire engulfed Alora's heart, hearing that her absence had a cost for those she left behind. Not only had she abandoned her duties, but she had left without a trace. Of course, Alora's father and the knights had been concerned. If she thought about it, Alora would have suspected as much. But she hadn't taken the time to understand what her actions had done to those who she left.

Remius had been upset; she had caused him distress and anxiety. He had rescued her from the dungeon, even though his mission had been to free the prince. And after everything, Remius had been the one to leave her, ensuring she would be taken care of. Alora couldn't find fault with his actions; he had left her to guard his own heart, and she was glad they had parted before even more differences came between them. The less they could hurt each other, the better.

And it would be a very good idea, from this moment on, if she allowed herself to think of others before giving in to her selfish desires. Alora truly didn't wish to upset her father and cause others to worry.

The glow from the looking glass began to dim when a voice called forth to still its closure. "I say, that's most unfaely!"

"Cheshire?" Alora wondered aloud as her thoughts solidified. Her heart filled with equal parts joy and apprehension that her tutor would be joining them.

"Ooh no! *He* wasn't part of the bargain at all. You can't be here, you puffed up tabby! This is *my* role, not *yours*," Fleur admonished the feline as his smile came through the looking glass, followed by an unattached tail.

"You can't excel without me!" The smile spread, and within a moment, Cheshire's body glinted into sight.

"We can indeed, I assure you, manage quite well." Fleur folded her arms across her body.

Cheshire waved a paw through the air as if to swat at Fleur, but Clement shot forward and grabbed Fleur by her elbow, dragging her through the air and safely to his side.

"Cheshire!" Alora rebuked him.

"Calm yourself, Curious One. Why now, you have found my very dear friend, I see. Standing a little too close as well. My, my." The tabby grinned.

"You can stay if you can manage to behave and not get in our way," Fleur said, sighing.

The looking glass dimmed as a tiny troll with mauve fur hurried forward to redrape the black velvet curtain over it. He had two teeth that stuck out of either side of his mouth, with their tips curled inward to reach the midpoint of his cheeks. Once his chore was complete, the troll did an about-face and scrambled away.

"I could never be in your way, Fleur. And here I was suffering under the misconception that we worked well together." Cheshire posed with his head hanging slightly forward.

"We can all work together, and we shall so Alora may learn the best of what she needs in order to vanquish the evil queen," Hatter said with authority as the others bowed their heads to him in acknowledgment of his wishes.

Cheshire apprised his paw. "I forgot!" From the air, a burnished, copper top-hat appeared on his head. It looked to have been created from silk and had the same floral pattern across it that Hatter had worn to the tea party Alora had dreamed herself to. However, this one boasted a wide midnight-blue ribbon that wrapped around its brim as its loose ends hung from the back, extending several inches.

"My hat!" enthused Hatter, who removed the discovered top hat from his head and, with a flick of his wrist, sent it spinning in amongst the trees.

"My goodness!" Alora exclaimed with a perplexed expression.

"Back to the dust from which it came. No harm done; some small animal will discover the hat to make it their home," Hatter explained as he reached over to remove his topper from the cat's head. He brushed off the strands of cream and lime-green fur before he twirled the hat in the air, letting it trill down his arm. Leaning his head toward his shoulder, the opening of the hat came to rest atop Hatter's head. With a smile of triumph, Hatter remarked, "A hatter is nothing without his hat!"

Alora's thoughts were swept back to his shop and the fire. Here she had allowed her mind to push the harrowing night to the side when, all this time, Phillip had been mourning his establishment and all of the wondrous things it contained. Her stomach soured as her thoughts churned.

"Just so, my comrade. Now, tell me what's been happening since we last met." Cheshire floated over to Hatter, wrapping a furry arm over his shoulder.

Hatter reached his hand out to Alora, and she took it, allowing Hatter to lead them from the tent over to a fire that was encompassed with fallen logs. When Hatter perched along the edge of one elongated log, he tugged Alora down beside him, taking care to be gentle with her.

"Why do you keep such a firm grip upon the Princess?" Cheshire inquired as his body dangled upside down in the air next to Hatter.

"Because she is my sunset and my sunrise. She is the embodiment of my dreams, and all of my hopes are made flesh. The other half to my soul, my savior, and my healer," Hatter expressed his words in a reverent whisper. Then he brought her hand up to his mouth, turning it over, he pressed a kiss directly onto her palm, which struck her like lightning zapping through her in delicious waves. Alora couldn't contain the gasp that flew past her lips and risked a glance at the tabby to glean his reaction to such a display.

"You don't say," Cheshire drawled as his bottle-green eyes

rolled in his head. "You're fated mates! Took you long enough to put those pieces together, old boy."

"You knew?" Alora felt surprised by his statement.

"Of course. One look at the longing looks and covert glances, and I suspected as much. Of course, one can never be certain where a halfling is concerned. Were you both full Fae, one look into each other's eyes would have left little doubt in the matter. But…that's right, you can't recall that encounter, can you?" Cheshire frowned at Hatter.

Hatter shook his head in reply, his shoulders hunching in on themselves.

"But that's exactly how it was," Alora piped up. "We were standing on opposite sides of a ballroom. Our gazes collided, then he was making his way through the throng to me. And I remember that I couldn't look away, no matter how improper my staring was."

"I want that memory back!" Hatter banged a fist onto his knee.

Alora recalled two nights ago when she had brought him back to her in the dungeons. She had willed it to be. A thought occurred to her.

"Cheshire, what do you know about the affinity to heal?" she asked him.

"Not a lot at all," admitted the tabby.

"What are you thinking?" Hatter looked up and over at Alora. His ardent gaze was searching hers.

"Twice now, you have been lost to tragedy, and you have been brought back to me. I willed you to be with me with all of my heart. And a curious warmth poured itself from me and into you, chasing the madness away and bringing you back to me." Alora allowed him to form his own thoughts, not desiring to sway where his would lead him.

"Let me get this straight. You have a healing affinity, and I am just now learning this, and you believe that you healed Hatter?" Fleur queried as she came to a stop before Alora.

Alora's brows furrowed at the interruption to their conversation. " I don't know, honestly. Have I?" She turned her attention back to Hatter.

"I feel clearer and of a more sound mind. I still can feel the edges of…madness just within easy reach. But I feel more whole." Hatter caressed her hand with his thumb.

"And without any real training in the matter, it's no wonder," Fleur remarked. Her gaze rested upon Alora as she tilted her head to the side, considering her. "Think of what you could do if properly trained. Maybe even go so far as to repair lost memories."

"That should most definitely be a part of the training," purred Cheshire.

"Right, so sword-fighting and healing with history of the realms. That's quite doable. We should—"

"She can decipher, or rather read, the forgotten Fae language," interrupted Cheshire as he idly licked a paw. "See, you need me."

Fleur's eyes narrowed, "Does no faerie tell me anything useful?"

"We should go to my mother. She is in possession of the Oraculum. If it can give us any insight to aid us, we really must seek it out," Hatter told them.

"I thought the evil one had it firmly locked away," Cheshire said and pouted.

"Ickburt and Remius reclaimed it just the other night." Hatter grinned, making Alora's heart flutter, even though it wasn't directed at her.

"We will spend a few days training before we enter the White Kingdom. I like this plan." Fleur beamed as she nodded once.

"Of course you do." Cheshire grinned at her.

"Let's not waste time. Hatter is proficient in swordsmanship and will be an excellent teacher. It's a perfect morning for instruction." Fleur clapped her hands. "Up, up, up, let's make our way toward the meadow."

Hatter rose, then rested his fisted hands on his waist. "I don't know how useful I'll be. I don't relish the idea of putting my fated mate in harm's way."

"Nor will you relish the idea of putting someone else behind a sword pointed toward her. But I suppose Clement will do." Fleur turned to look at Clement. He quirked a brow as his mouth hung slightly ajar and pointed to himself.

"Me? Oh no." Clement gave a cautious look at Hatter, who was glowering at him.

"Why not?" challenged Fleur.

"I will instruct Alora," groused Hatter.

Alora rose to her slippered feet and took his proffered arm. It was vastly adoring how he disliked the idea of anyone harming her, even if by accident.

"We need swords," Hatter remarked as he steered them toward the weapons tent while Fate brought up the rear.

It was a large, imposing tan canvas monstrosity that Hatter led them to. As they neared it, Alora looked over her shoulder, watching as Fleur and Cheshire animatedly talked. Clement stood off to the side, observing them. Hatter let go of her arm and opened the tent flap.

"I think I'll wait out here. You go ahead and select what we need. Fate will guard me." Alora waved her hand toward the tent, feeling her stomach roil at the idea of so many weapons stashed in one place. Perhaps it was the healer in her that balked at the idea of wood and metal created to injure and kill.

Hatter peered into her eyes, then he nodded, passing through to the other side.

Alora had a moment to take a deep cleansing breath when she was approached by the cobalt-capped figure from the prior evening. The faerie had come from the other side of the tent.

"You need something special, I think," she stated as she looked Alora up and down.

"Come, Young One, let's go somewhere more private," entreated the faerie, extending her hand and wiggling her fingers.

Fate shifted beside her, and Alora looked at him.

"It's quite all right to do as she bids," he offered in his dignified tone.

If Fate said it was acceptable, then she was happy to do as bid.

"Lead the way." Alora cast a demure smile her way.

Alora and Fate trailed after the lady as she wound her way around the weapons tent, past the firepits. Alora looked for Fleur and Clement but didn't spy them. With a grin, she thought they might be off, *not* kissing or cuddling, which sounded much more entertaining than training.

When the robes in front of her ceased swaying, Alora looked up. They stood before another canvas tent, but it was one of the smaller ones that she had seen. When the faerie stood with the opening exposed, Alora padded straight into the area inside.

A large burgundy and cream carpet greeted her first. Then, raising her gaze, Alora noted the swaying chandelier that hung in the center of the tent. It held cream-colored candles, and though they were lit, droplets could be seen hanging onto the candle's bodies; the wax never seemed to drip onto the carpet.

The robed faerie briskly walked to the corner of the tent where a suit of ebony armor stood on its body form. The armor was shining and made of metallic material that held the silver sparkles that she had seen grace the castle and the underground dining hall. There was scrollwork along the arm and leg shields, and inset roses lined the middle. She was less than pleased to see the flowers. She arched her brow with dismay at the sight.

"This, you see, is your size. It was created just for you and none other." The lady brought up her hands, pushing the hood from her head. She blinked her large teal eyes as she stood, locking her sight onto Alora.

Alora stood staring at the figure with her mouth open. Had she ever seen another quite as beautiful?

The teal hair that cascaded down her back and around her shoulders was mesmerizing with its brilliant shine that seemed to be glowing.

The faerie closed the distance between them, and then, reaching up, she delicately closed Alora's mouth. "Of course, in Faerie, you are quite lovely. Your skin is exquisite, and your eyes are so captivating. It's of little wonder that our Phillip is so enamored of you. But then fated mates are often blinded by that bond. You don't say much, do you?"

"I... Um. That is, who are you?"

"Why, I have many names to many beings. None of them is more important than another. But, perhaps, I shall allow you to call me Weaver as I have weaved together this armor just for you. It was no easy task, gathering silken spider-webbing. But it was an adventure. Wonderland is filled with adventures, is it not?" The kind smile of the Weaver set Alora at ease.

"Thank you for the armor," Alora replied as she struggled for an answer.

"You don't like it? You had envisioned something else?" Weaver drew her delicate brows together.

"Oh no! It's just that I hadn't really thought about it. I think I would rather not think about it at all."

"I see. But, you must. For your destiny is much bigger than you know, and this enchanted armor will see you safe. In fact, you can't do this without it." Weaver shrugged.

"You are much more than just a weaver, are you not?" Alora felt chilled at the absolute conviction and certainty in the beautiful faerie's words.

"I am. But to you, for now, I am the Weaver. Let's get you into this chainmail. It can be quite tricky." The Weaver snapped her fingers and pointed to the spot before her.

Not wanting to waste another moment, Alora strode to her then awaited the next instruction.

Might as well do as bid and embrace this destiny that no amount of wishing can change.

37

UNPRINCELY BEHAVIOR

As it turned out, getting into the armor was a bit tricky, but the pieces floated into place thanks to the Weaver's silver wand. Alora felt the tingles of the white starry magic coasting over her skin and bemusedly smiled. If only she could wield a wand, then donning the armor would be a breeze. Alora wondered if a wand was mightier than a sword. But if that were so, couldn't one just wave a wand and vanquish all evil? Perhaps the task of that wasn't up to any one being; who's to say overtime that soul wouldn't become corrupted?

Standing before the looking glass, Alora turned one way, then another, to gain the full effect of her appearance. Despite the swell of her bosom, which nothing could mask unless she bound herself, Alora looked manly. No, that wasn't entirely correct. She furrowed her brow and leaned closer toward her reflection. Alora realized that there were elegant scrollwork and delicate feminine touches that gave the armor appeal. Her eyes moved to the auburn tresses that laid against her back and along her shoulders, coming to hang down to her waist, which lent a whimsical quality to her appearance. But quite impractical. Alora arched an eyebrow at the thought of an enemy whipping her around in battle by her hair or hacking it completely off. She was fond of her hair and didn't wish to lose her locks.

The Weaver lifted the helmet from the body form, handing it over to Alora. Gingerly taking it, Alora placed it on her head. The limited view the guard allowed was confusing; she felt discombobulated by not relying upon her peripheral vision. Removing the helmet, she tucked it under her arm. Alora sighed in quiet defeat. Placing a hand onto Alora's shoulder, Weaver came to stand behind her and observe their reflections from the looking glass.

"You know, you needn't worry so much about becoming all-powerful in battle, an unbeatable adversary. I'd wager that at the end, this chainmail and your training will be much more about keeping you safe and whole than feeling sorrow for your opponent. While it's all very well and good to hone your battle skills by learning to protect yourself, using your mind to determine how fate and justice are carried out is equally important. You battle just as much with your mind as you do your brawn."

Alora locked gazes with Weaver through the glass's reflection. The faerie was a puzzle, one of which Alora wasn't sure she could fit all the jagged pieces together. Did she even truly wish to try? There were secrets mixed with an all-knowingness and wisdom that swirled within the depths of Weaver's gaze.

"Worrying about what may likely never come to pass puts invited obstacles in your path. Think beyond what you're taught and how you may best use that knowledge." Weaver turned her head to place a gentle kiss upon Alora's cheek.

Holding up her wand, Weaver waved it in front of herself as white stars flowed from the wand's end, spiraling around her in a brilliant display of glittering light. Then she disappeared.

Alora's eyes grew larger as she turned upon her heel to

scan the tent, but she knew she would not find the Weaver anywhere. To wield such powerful magic, to have the power to persuade good or evil, what must her existence be like?

"Alora, are you in there?" came Hatter's cautious voice.

"I am," she replied as she stood facing the entrance to the tent.

The tent's flap opened, allowing Hatter's head to precede his body inside. With curious brows, he took her in.

Shifting uncomfortably from one foot to another, Alora bit her bottom lip, wondering what he must be thinking of her. Did he find her odd or perhaps foolish?

"You look magnificent! Like some ethereal battle goddess come to rule us all." Hatter came to a stop before her, giving her a sweeping bow with a teasing twist of his mouth.

"You don't think I look ridiculous?" Alora felt a blush creep into her cheeks.

"My love, you look like a vision of vengeance, and I must say, it's very becoming to your figure. Well…that could be a problem," he grimaced, stroking his chin in contemplation. "I don't desire the entire Resistance seeing your…attributes in such a stunning display. But I suppose it can't be helped, as I'd much rather you be protected than not."

"Am I terribly indecent?"

"No, I am just an unmated male who is overprotective and more than a bit sensitive to the fact we have not… What was it that Fleur said? Cemented? We've yet to cement our bond."

"Is that horrible for you? To not be fully bonded?" Alora gazed into his amber eyes.

"It's more uncomfortable; at times, I find myself panicking. I would feel easier if I knew at all times where you were, if you were well, how you were feeling. And before you think it's a control thing, I assure you, it's anything but. To have the bond secured means that I am never in doubt that you are well, that you are safe and breathing, and I can follow the tether between us so I may always find you. It's our hearts syncing and our minds linking. I can encourage my thoughts your way to tell you how much I adore you. To know in mere seconds if you have need of me or if sorrow is burdening you. To be bonded is so much more than just any singular thing. It's *everything.*" The sincerity and depth of his feelings made Hatter's voice waver. His words stole the breath from her body.

Mindful of the armor, Alora moved to stand directly before Hatter. Bringing her hands up to encircle his neck, she rose up to her tiptoes. She was barely meeting his lips with her own when Fleur glided into the tent, *tutting* at them.

"This is very unprincely of you, Hatter!" Fleur said with mock severity, or at least that was Alora's impression.

Hatter groaned as he dislodged Alora's grip from around his neck. When they were no longer touching, he reached up and adjusted his hat.

"Where did you spend last night?" Fleur queried with a suspicious look gracing her tiny face.

"I hardly see how *that* is relevant," stated Hatter as his lips twisted into a sneer.

"It's highly relevant! I am her protector and her mentor. You can't usurp me," whined Fleur.

"No one is attempting to question your place," began Alora. "I slept in Phillip's arms in the tent we first stayed in. We went to sleep and nothing more."

"We should separate you—" Fleur huffed but was interrupted by Hatter.

"No," was all he said as he narrowed his eyes at the sprite.

"But it isn't proper and not honoring her delicate sensibilities and those of her father's."

"No," he said again as he widened his stance, crossing his arms over his broad chest.

Fleur threw her hands up into the air. "You must give your word that you will not kiss or *anything else* until you've properly bonded. There's a right and a wrong way to enter into forever, and I mean to see that Alora gets all of her happily-ever-afters. Besides, I have more than one kingdom to be accountable to now, and that weighs very heavily upon my tiny shoulders."

"I would sooner drink tea with the evil queen than ever besmirch Alora's honor or mine. I mean to stitch a forever for us that will last through the ages. Never fear, Fleur, for I am a gentle-faerie and am true to my word. As faeries can't lie, my word is unbreakable." Hatter cast another dark look her way.

"Very well," Fleur took a deep inhale. "Let us begin with the swords to glean where we may improve her." She waved to the tent's flap, showing no reaction to the chainmail.

Alora passed her helmet to Hatter, quickly gathering her hair together in a messy braid that she wrapped into a circular knot atop her head. Spying pins on the small table near the looking glass, she retrieved them, then stood in front of the glass to watch herself secure her hair into place.

Hatter watched her with an intent stare that made warmth pool low in her stomach. When she had finished her chore, he grasped her hand in his. When her breath hitched, he grinned as they strode from the tent together out into the bright sunshine.

Fleur led the way to the meadow, with Fate trotting behind them. Alora tried to ignore the whispers and stares that her new attire caused. She disliked the constant attention and feared that, at any moment, Wonderland would find her lacking, and she'd be labeled a fool and a complete disappointment.

"You can either choose to be mortified or choose to be the princess and lead. A leader does not back down when their actions cause notice. You are their queen in the making; do not let them see you doubt yourself or show unease. You are *my queen,* and my queen rules in every step she takes. *My queen* commands in every breath she takes. You are magnificent; show that to them, and like me, they will follow you anywhere." Hatter's lowered voice in her ear as they walked bolstered her confidence. Alora felt her spine straighten and her resolve solidify. A shiver racked her body at his nearness, and she wished that she was free from her armor to bask in his warmth.

Nodding at him, Alora beamed with all the gratitude and love she felt. The warmth of the pink sun raining down on them was nothing in comparison to the warmth that filled her heart.

38

WE GO AGAIN

Panting breath stirred the tendrils of hair that had escaped Alora's braid. She was sore and tired and wanted to cleave Hatter's head from his body if only to wipe the smug expression from his handsome face. That even now she found him so attractive made her teeth grind together.

Why had I ever thought that his smile was alluring?

I hate him!

I adore him!

But why must he delight in vexing me so?

"Keep your arm up!" Hatter instructed her as his own sword stood posed and ready to parlay her attack.

Alora raised her arm and was furious when her muscles shook. She wanted to scream in frustration. For three weeks, there had been unending hours of training. Swordplay, history, and decorum lessons on ruling a kingdom took up all of her waking hours. She was slowly being turned into a person she barely knew. When each ingrained piece of knowledge joined the sea of its fellows, Alora knew it had all been for the better. There was power in knowledge, whether it be on how to cut down an enemy or how to outmaneuver a political foe.

Alora was so exhausted each night that she practically fell onto her bedroll face first. Her slumber was blessedly dream-free, and she began to feel stronger without withering away in her sleeping curse.

It must have been the defeated look on her face, but something caused the self-satisfied countenance to vanish from Hatter's features. He let his sword arm fall to his side as he silently regarded her.

"I think we're finished for today," he told their audience.

For once, Fleur didn't naysay him. "I think that would be a wise and relieving thing to do. We could all use an early break."

Alora's head bowed with relief as she walked over to the weapons stand, placing her sword into its place. Hatter followed behind her, and as he replaced his sword, his other hand settled against the small of her back. His breath disturbed the loose pieces of hair as he leaned forward to kiss her head.

"I am—" his speech was interrupted by Maia, who was arguing with Fleur.

The two faeries had been incessantly at odds, and it had further served to rattle Alora's nerves over the last weeks. Her shoulders drew up as she turned to observe the squabble.

"You are so hoity-toity. No one agrees with your silly decrees!" screeched Fleur.

"They most certainly do!" countered Maia.

"Can we not simply agree that every faerie has their own opinion—," began Fiona, whose words were shouted over.

"At least when the dust settles after you take your leave, I will still be here to correct your errors, much as I ever have!" Maia fisted her hands to settle them onto her hips. Her sapphire eyes flashed.

"You pompous—" Fleur was growing an alarming shade of red.

"Please!" interceded Alora. "Do not continue along in this manner. It serves no faerie and only widens the divide between you."

"Yes, I agree with the Princess. This ends now; you will set your differences aside and do so for the good of the kingdom," Hatter commanded, leaving no room for argument.

"Squabbling, again? Why even I have reached my limit!" Cheshire appeared aloft in the air opposite Alora.

"It's not my fault. I am accommodating as can be," stated Fleur with a venomous look at her sister.

Maia rolled her eyes and directed her remark to the tabby. "Did you need something?"

"Ah, yes. I come bearing news. The White Queen requests an audience with her son and our Curious One. Today, in fact." The grin stretching Cheshire's whiskers showcased every one of his sharp teeth.

"I am overdue for a visit. I'm not surprised in the least that my mother has taken to summoning me. Very well, we shall ready ourselves for a visit. Will you be accompanying us, Cheshire?" Hatter clasped Alora's hand in his, and it was as if all the rioting emotions in her body were immediately banished away just by his touch.

"Of course! I always love seeing my friends, and your mother is one of my dearest." The tabby bowed his head and waved his hand in the air with a flourish.

Alora allowed Hatter to tug her away from the others and through the gentle but downtrodden grass of the meadow toward their shared tent. Inside, awaiting her, was a copper tub with steaming water that wafted into the air, curling and evaporating. Alora wanted to cry from the kind gesture, wanting to eternally offer her gratitude to whoever had done this for her. The thought of having to trek to the waterfall made her want to weep. Coming closer toward the tub, she noted a curious fluff of lime-green hair clinging to the edge of the tub.

Cheshire's? He has done this for me?

"Bathe and soak for a few minutes; we can spare the time. I shall get myself ready and meet with you once you're finished." Hatter brought her hand up to his mouth and kissed it. Would butterflies never cease to unfurl their silky wings in her body at his nearness? She hoped they never did.

"Sounds perfect. I do hope I do not disappoint whatever rumors your mother has heard or any conclusions she has formed regarding me." Alora couldn't help being unable to mask away the unease in her tone. What if the queen despised her? Would there be an option to earn a second chance?

"She will adore you, my love." Hatter looked sad as he watched the emotions play over her face. "You needn't fear on that score."

"You don't know what she'll think or feel."

"I know she is not unjust nor unreasonable. My mother will love you as I do." He closed the small distance between them, enfolding Alora into his arms. Tucking her head under his chin, he sighed.

"You love me?" her muffled voice came from his cravat. Alora's heart took flight in her chest as she dared to rejoice at his words. Hope was as delicate as a wounded bird's wing. She didn't want to see it dashed to specks of dust.

"Have I not told you so before? I meant to. I should have, so often have I thought those words." His index finger curled under her chin to draw her eyes to his; he regarded her tenderly as love reflected from them.

"I've been waiting such a long time to hear you say that to me," she admitted with a smile as her body became weightless. A surge of happiness lit her from within. All of the strain of the past few weeks drained away in an instant as the bond between them heated, stretching and allowing it to take in all of their emotions. "Phillip?"

"Yes, my love?"

"Do you know how very much I love you? It's endless, and it's vast, and it's all-encompassing. I can't believe you are mine. That you love me, why, it's everything."

"You are my everything, my reason to hope, my joy in every extraordinary moment I get to be by your side. You are my heart and so very precious. Yes, I love you, you amazing girl. I'm so proud of you, of how you have taken what we have tried to instill in you and nurtured all of the best parts. You continually surpass all my imaginings and do so gracefully in your own style. We have pushed you, and you have borne it with poise and an unending well of patience. Who could not adore you?" He leaned forward to kiss the tip of her nose. Hatter's warm lips were gentle as they touched her skin. Frissons of pleasure flowed through her chest, all the way to her toes.

Wrinkling her nose, she replied, "You are always doing that. Kissing my nose. Noses are so unromantic, and yet, your doing so steals the very breath from my body."

Chuckling, he released her and stepped away. "I do hope my kisses never stop your heart from fluttering. Mine rattles along in my chest at the mere thought of you. The idea that after all the trials you'll still be by my side is the happiest ending I could have ever dreamed of. Knowing that you couldn't let me go, even after my appalling absence, my unforgivable desertion of you… It is I who must earn your love. Everyday. In every action I take." His lips downturned as he roughly swallowed.

"Let us not dwell on the past. Only look to the future. For I can see the horizon, and you're standing with your hand locked over mine for eternity." Alora felt emotions ripple over her features as she tried to reign in her sentiments that were oscillating back and forth.

"There is no greater honor than that, sweet Alora." Hatter gave her a lopsided smile that was filled with love and an open and raw tenderness. Clearing his throat, he added, "I shall return in a while." He pointed to the tub. "Enjoy that." Letting her go, he then strode from the tent.

Left alone, Alora closed her eyes as their exchange settled into her mind and heart, layer after layer. She hadn't realized how much it would mean to have Hatter's undeniable love. It had been easy to see that he cared for her, even adored her.

Words were the most powerful force in creation. They wielded absolute power to either build one up or tear one down. And their words of love were now part of the currents that would guide them.

Alora clasped her hands before herself as a laugh filled with glee escaped between her lips. This was what she had most wanted. This was the thing, the rightness she had been chasing when all had seemed lost. And hadn't Hatter moved into her sphere and upended her world twice now? How was one to cage their heart in their chest when all it longed to do was soar to the highest heights?

Alora had a queen to meet who might test her, and maybe some of her light would dim. But she believed that Hatter would stand by her side until the end of time. So, she turned her attention to the tub. Alora began to disrobe, starting with her pelisse and working her way to her slippers and stockings as she allowed her heart to dream.

39

THE WHITE KINGDOM

The soak in the warm bath had done a world of good to Alora's disgruntled muscles. As she was eager to be back by Hatter's side, Alora didn't linger too long amidst the floating bubbles. Slipping from the water and drying herself, she walked straight to the wooden rosewood wardrobe. Throwing the door wide, she perused her attire.

She bedecked herself in a robin's egg blue day dress with white lace and silver ribbons that tied at her waist and at the ends of her puffed sleeves. The slippers were soft on her feet. Sturdier boots had been Alora's daily staple whether she wore the armor or not, and she took pleasure in donning the softer material. Alora hoped she looked presentable enough to meet a Queen of Wonderland. Whether Hatter believed his mother wouldn't find fault in her, she had no desire to appear before the queen looking lackluster and dowdy. It had been so long since Alora had the affection of a mother; perhaps Hatter's mother would embrace her, faults and all. There really was no better woman to introduce her to Court life and all of the varied expectations. Alora would welcome any advice given.

Her shoulders drooped. What if the queen immediately found her wanting? Was she enough to keep her fated mate by her side? Was their budding bond enough to stack against familiar duty?

True, she had witnessed the strength of the bond between Fleur and Clement. Their devotion to one another gave her the courage to meet the challenges of the introduction ahead. She could do this for Hatter, for herself, and for all of Wonderland.

With a deep, cleansing breath and a warm hand pressed to her heart with gratefulness, Alora was ready at last to venture forth.

Stepping from the tent, Alora's gaze roamed the lively area enveloping her. The faeries were all busy seeing to their own responsibilities and didn't pay her much attention. Which was a relief, as oftentimes she looked an absolute wreck after her training with Hatter. With flyaway wisps of curls and sweat clinging to her face, she was quite far from presentable after every sparring lesson. Having them not notice her was wonderful, even if she was looking her best.

Fate's ears twitched as his gaze was directed to a faerie who was in fisticuffs with a hobbit over a loaf of bread.

Before she could act, the fight was broken up by a pail of water being tossed over their heads. The tiny peace-making sprite giggled as she righted the wooden bucket. Alora nodded her head once in approval. These beings were quick to fight, but she'd long since become used to that. Fists were often employed instead of words, and that seemed to be an acceptable manner of handling disagreements. That was one thing she resolved to put a stop to once she held the power to influence whoever next sat on a throne.

Alora's stomach gave a little rumble as she moved her

hand over it. It was best to eat a little something so she didn't inconvenience any faerie with having to see to her needs.

She had done her best to wait upon herself and not be a bother to those around her. But there were tasks that were beyond her, such as cooking over the fires or washing her and Hatter's garments. While Alora longed to give these chores a try, there were always faeries around who *wanted* to serve her. Hatter had taken her aside one evening when her limbs were shaky, and she could barely keep her eyes open.

Gently clasping their hands together, Hatter drew her to the inside of their shared tent and settled her down into his lap.

"You must understand that you are giving our subjects purpose when you allow them to aid you. They, too, want to fulfill their role, and some have felt very displaced with no true royalty to dote upon. It's not lowering them beneath your boot to allow them to assist you. Some faeries thrive on tasks; perhaps it's having to do with being long-lived. Whatever the case, there is no harm in letting them see what you need to have attended to while you are training to gain their freedom from lurking oppression and death. To some, it's the very least they can do to repay you, and since the system here works on bartering, this is more than a fair trade to the folk."

Alora allowed his words to flow into her, letting them come to rest in her heart. She would gladly hand over the tasks if she wasn't causing harm or asking too much.

And she had. There wasn't a single soul who seemed put out to do her chores.

When another rumble broke forth, Alora patted her abdomen. There was a table off to the side of the area where baked goods had been placed in differing baskets and tins. Quickly, she padded over to it, selecting a small ginger cake with her ever-loyal guard, Fate, following behind. Alora had no fear of anything being some sort of trickery and took a bite with relish. The taste of spices and sugar melted onto her tongue as she took a moment to enjoy the treat. While she hadn't been starving the last weeks, she did find that she was almost always hungry. Alora supposed it was due to her constant movement.

In England, ladies were creatures of comfort, better suited to drawing room activities. They weren't expected, or even encouraged, to pick up weapons and learn where best to place their hands upon an injury to better draw out poisons or to heal a broken bone more speedily. One thing was for certain: her time had been put to very good use. Alora's thoughts turned to her father, and she hoped he was fairing well.

Finishing the confection, Alora spied Hatter making his way toward her. She dusted off her hands on a linen napkin, then let it fall into the wicker basket that stood beside the table on the grass. In moments, a little green grasshopper no bigger than her hand was dragging the soiled linen away with a broad smile, happy to serve indeed.

"You look stunning," Hatter told her, drawing her attention to himself as he came to a stop before her, gallantly offering her his arm.

"Thank you, my dashing Prince."

After taking his arm, the two set off toward the tent where the looking glass they were to travel through was stationed. The tent was guarded by a pair of glaring olive-green trolls. The troll on the left opened the tent flap while the one on the right reached up a pinkie to pick his nose.

Alora's nose wrinkled, and then she brought one hand up to cover her mouth as her eyes widened. She took deep breaths to command the contents of her stomach to settle down as they entered the tent with Fate, allowing the canvas opening to slide closed after him.

Do not be sick! Oh, why were trolls always so preoccupied by their… bodily functions?

Hatter leaned toward her ear and whispered, "Nasty creatures. Now, where is Cheshire?" He looked around the tent with interest.

"I am here, just staring at the troll who is plumbing his brain. Rather a curious feat, you should see this, for I can't look away. Oh, *do help me look away,*" begged Cheshire with a feline whine.

"For the realm's sakes," muttered Hatter as he disentangled his limb from Alora's and tread to the tent's opening. He reached his upper half out, and within a moment, Cheshire was tugged into the tent, allowing the flap to once again fall back into place.

"You have my thanks," the tabby spoke as he grimaced. "Why, even I have my limit."

"If you're all quite ready, the White Queen awaits," reminded Fate with an impatient shuffling of his hooves.

"Quite right! Dilfae, would you do the honors?" Cheshire directed the sleepy faerie toward the looking glass with a wave of his paw and a twitch of his tail.

The diminutive, Dilfae, rushed forward, withdrawing the dark curtain from the looking glass. With a bow of his bald peach head and an incantation that Alora's ear missed deciphering, the glass began to shimmer, then glow. The radiant beams lit the tent's interior.

Cheshire drifted toward the mirror, directly floating through it.

Hatter led Alora over to the looking glass. "Just a small step, and you'll be through. I'll be right behind you," he encouraged her.

Nodding, Alora bent forward to pick up her hem so she could take the step to the other side. With confident steps, she made her way through the looking glass. Before she could take in the splendor that was the White Kingdom, Hatter and Fate exited and came to her side. She reached for Hatter's hand, interlocking their fingers.

"It's something out of time, like a fairytale," she drew in a breath at the beauty before her.

The White Castle was indeed a very lovely snow white,

glittering in the bright sunlight with a prism of rainbows casting reflection to the surrounding lush greenery. Tall towers rose high in the pink sky to touch the heavens as they seemed to signify a beacon to those who needed hope, entreating them to venture safely forth. Dark green hedges lined the exterior, and white fountains and stone pavings leading in different directions led to what Alora surmised was the opposite side of the castle. Bird songs met her ears as the creatures circled high above them. Alora wondered whether they were Unseelie. Multi-colored butterflies flitted through the air, unaware of the dangers the flying birds might create. Hatter was looking toward the lush hills rising just behind the castle.

"Where is the return looking glass hidden?" Alora turned in place, looking for a reflection, some glint of sunshine to clue her in.

"It's hidden and dwells inside the castle. While one can travel from it, one cannot travel to it. The protection spell upon the two allows for one to appear here before they ever reach the castle," Hatter told her. Alora nodded her understanding before she looked around herself again.

A sparkling purple moat, in which white swans swam in swirling patterns, offered protection to the castle's entrance. When a snow-colored armored guard walking atop the parapet caught sight of them, he directed the gate to be lowered. Alora stood between Hatter and Cheshire as she looked about them. The chains lowering the gate rattled and clanked.

The atmosphere was different here. It was calm and peaceful, and Alora felt her tightly coiled body relaxing. Perhaps this wouldn't be so terrible after all. For if this was the environment the White Queen nurtured, she really must be as wonderful as Alora had been told.

"Welcome, my Prince," said a stocky male faerie, rushing from the entrance to bow before him. He straightened just as quickly. Alora noted how his pearl buttons almost burst from his waistcoat with his movements. His eyes were kind, and his smile was warm and inviting. Alora immediately liked the faerie.

"Smith, so good to be met by you upon our arrival," greeted Hatter, nodding at him.

The shorter Smith beamed with pleasure, his brown eyes lighting up.

"Her Majesty awaits you in the drawing room. If you would please follow me." Smith stepped a few paces back and waved his hand aloft.

Hatter began to do as directed as Alora matched her steps to his. He seemed unconcerned that they had preceded Smith when they had been directed to follow him. The clip-clop of Fate's hooves sounded behind them.

Lessening his stride as Hatter always seemed to do when walking with her, he smiled at her with tenderness. It was one small way Hatter showed he cared for her, reassuring her that he was here with her. He had never made Alora run to keep up with him, well, except for the night of the fire. Alora had to steel her spine to keep from shivering at the horrific memory.

Hatter met her eyes, his mouth downturned as they walked side by side. The bond must be casting her feelings his way.

Giving him what she hoped was a dazzling smile, Alora once again turned her attention to the scene before them. He squeezed her hand in reply.

As they passed through the entryway of the castle gate, the lighting was a bit more subdued. Adjusting to the dimness, Alora spied faeries in all manner of attire, with some hauling materials or goods while others pursued the vendors' stalls that lined the circular pavilion to the right of the stone staircase leading up to the pale castle. Potted plants and flower pots rimmed the area in dazzling shades of pastels as their heads bowed and bobbed behind their leafed hands. Tiny orbs of light hung suspended over the entire area, casting a soft glow.

The further they entered the courtyard, the buzz of the communal chatter quickly died away. Hatter halted them in the midst of the staring crowd. He arched his eyebrow as he tilted his head to gaze down at her. Alora met his gaze, but she wasn't sure what her eyes were reflecting back to him.

The edges of Hatter's lips curved up as he continued to gaze at her. Then, he let his attention wander back to the faeries gawking at them. Whispers began to reach her ears, and Alora continued to grasp onto Hatter's hand.

"My dear faeries," Hatter began. "I am in no doubt that you are in suspense, speculating as to who is by my side. I won't leave you dangling along on tenterhooks. I have brought the Princess home to meet with our queen."

"Why?"

"Does the prophecy remain?"

"Will our kingdom finally be freed?"

The questions were being rapid-fired. Hatter held up his free hand for silence and calm.

Cheshire was silently observing the crowd. Alora guessed his perceptive eyes were taking everything in.

Fate stood guard at their backs.

"My friends, all of your questions will be answered in time. Allow us to formulate plans and seek the counsel of those above us in order to serve you better. We shall not fail in this last stand that *we must* undertake. I will stand with you, as will our queen. And with Princess Alora by my side." Hatter raised their braided hands together, kissing the bare skin of her fingers, which made the onlookers cheer.

Alora couldn't contain the blush that peppered her skin as she felt the many eyes inspecting her from head to toe. Hatter carefully drew her to his side against his firm body. His warmth enveloped her, doing nothing to calm her racing pulse. Hatter's distinct scent of vanilla, steeped tea leaves, and sandalwood met Alora's senses, making her long to reach up and run her fingers through his hanging locks.

Gently, he leaned down, pressing a kiss to her forehead. Alora closed her eyes to soak him in.

Even I know he is declaring his intentions to the citizens of Wonderland without uttering one word. He has publicly shown his intention even though he has yet to address his wishes with my father. Maybe in Wonderland, it's quite alright to do something backward as the situation arises. I certainly can't find fault with him so easily drawing me into his embrace. If only we could always remain in each other's arms within the safety of this castle.

40

THE QUEEN OF GRACE

Smith came rushing forth on stocky legs to usher their party into the White Queen's private domain. Huge crystal chandeliers hung from the vaulted ceiling adorned with frescos and molded plaster braiding along the seams where the ceiling met the wall. Ivory candles burned in tall, elaborate candelabras, their wax enchanted to never drip or mar the ivory carpet below them.

Fresh flowers in all shades were stationed throughout the large room in differing vases along small rococo side tables, their excited chittering creating a constant noise. Chairs in the same scrolling design were resting in their various spaces, but with their decorative facade, Alora fancied that at any moment, they might take a gallop through the room. Light danced along the air as specks of dust twirled, highlighted by the beams of bright sunlight that shone from the large bay window; lace curtains hung suspended from pale-roped rods along its edges.

The focal point of the drawing room was, no doubt, the large marble fireplace that sat along the side wall. Carved into the ivory stone were roses and cherubs with mischievous faces. Topping the mantle rested miniature frames that housed portraits of faeries with heads adorned with tiaras and crowns. In total, there were ten tiny faces to be gazed upon, and Alora was drawn to inspect each one, to discover what Fae attributes each one bore. But first, she took in the woman perched on an upraised, white dias in the middle of the decadent chamber.

The White Queen, whose posture was ramrod straight, regarded them all with an assessing and expectant air. The chair she sat in was golden with ivory roses carved into the headrest that towered over her diminutive form. It was strange that, even in her private rooms, she was set apart from her surroundings. The raised platform made her seem set adrift and all alone. Sorrow seemed to bleed from her heart, flowing into the ether.

Alora gathered her thoughts to execute a curtsey as Hatter and Smith bowed on either side of her. Cheshire's face alighted with delight as he began to purr while he, too, regally bowed to pay his respect to the queen. The silver horn of her protector glinted in the light as he followed suit.

It was the faerie queen's eyes that drew Alora's keen interest. They were a pale blue, reminding Alora of the pale starlight evenings in England. Kindness and sadness, which were so at odds with each other, reflected in her intelligent gaze. Lines marred the pale hue of the faerie's skin and were more apparent around either astute eye.

"Your Majesty, our Prince and Princess Alora have arrived along with the Cheshire cat," stated Smith as he puffed out his chest. He had come to a stop a few feet from the dias as he attempted to slow his rapid breaths. He withdrew a linen handkerchief and dabbed his slick forehead.

"Yes, thank you, Smith, that I can observe for myself. Would you be so kind as to have tea prepared?" The queen inclined her head to him.

Smith bowed in response and backed from the room, pocketing the soiled linen as he exited.

Rising, the queen shook out her ivory dress. The intricate design was in keeping with the Georgian style of courtly attire. Silver beading and embroidered flowers caught the eye with their shimmer. She took careful steps to reach the edge of the platform before raising a delicate pale hand.

Hatter unbraided his hand from Alora's and then closed the distance to reach his mother. He elegantly came to stand before the dais. Raising his hand up, Hatter allowed his mother to take hold of it. He helped her descend the three steps to reach the pale carpet. When he turned in profile, Alora spied the genuine smile that rested on his face.

The queen returned his affection with a kiss on her son's cheek as she cupped the other side of Hatter's face. "You have been missed." Her movements were dainty and elegant as she looked almost as if she was breezing about upon the air.

"I have had very good reason to have been absent for so long." Hatter pulled from his mother's embrace, turned, and returned to Alora's side, beaming down at her. "Mother, may I introduce my fated mate and future bride to you?" His eyes held Alora's in a fervent stare.

Alora's heart raced as a slight flush crept into her cheeks. Beside Alora, the tabby drifted in the air and rubbed his face against her cheek.

"Fated mate? Well, this is surprising, indeed! And she is quite lovely," enthused the queen. Her snow-white hair was coiffed in an upswept style that rested in several inches of height. Ivory bows were arranged to either side, tucked against her locks.

Hatter reached for Alora's hand and gently tugged her forward. They took a few steps; then, she was directly before the queen. Cheshire was at their side, grinning madly while a stoic Fate trotted to a corner and rigidly stood in place.

"She is the most beautiful being I have ever beheld," Hatter remarked with sincerity as Alora felt the truth of his words tingle along their bond and coalesce in her heart.

"I am pleased to make your acquaintance, my dear. We've had some very trying years pass. I feel certain the sunshine you bring into a room will lighten all of our hearts." The White Queen smiled, but the ever-present sorrow rimmed her eyes as she drew Alora into a warm gardenia-scented embrace.

Tightly, Alora closed her eyes as she attempted to keep them from betraying her emotional state. She willed herself not to cry. How many years had Alora gone without a motherly hug? Too many for her wounded heart to count. Warmth surrounded her.

Drawing away from her, the queen sought her hand, and taking it, she floated toward an ivory settee situated in front of the fireplace. Alora willingly followed.

Without letting Alora's hand go, Her Majesty sat, then looked expectantly at Alora with a silent invitation for her to take the empty spot beside her. Alora acquiesced and sat, arranging her dress modestly to hide her ankles.

Hatter picked up one of the armchairs, bringing it to rest before the settee with his back to the unlit fireplace. Once he was seated, his focus came to rest on his mother.

"Was there anything of importance that needs to be addressed?" Hatter politely inquired.

"Not at present. Let us set aside all talk of unpleasant things and instead chat about your future. I do wish to know everything there is to know about this stunning young lady." The queen's kind eyes rested on Alora once again. "Tell me, dear, of your mother. What was she like? Oh," she brought her free hand up to cover her mouth. "If you care to, I don't wish to impose."

"It's not an imposition at all, Your Majesty," Alora began, but the queen cut her words off with a wave of her hand.

"None of that title nonsense here. We are, after all, among family."

Alora cast the queen a grateful smile as she tried to dry the mist in her eyes.

"Mother is right; we should begin as we mean to go on," agreed Hatter with a wink just for Alora. Her insides fluttered with his gentle attention.

"You may call me Mother or Mother Queen or even Seraphina while no one is about if that makes you more comfortable," the queen offered, patting the back of Alora's hand. She let Alora's hand go, then smiled over at an upside-down Cheshire.

"Cheshire, how very faetastic to be graced with your presence again so soon after our last visit," the queen said, addressing the feline with a slight curve of her mouth.

The tabby continued to purr as he floated toward the queen's lap, promptly curling into a contented cat-shaped loaf.

The queen stroked his cream fur as her fingers threaded through the lime-green stripes. "The Enchantress must be missing her favorite companion," she cooed.

"The Enchantress?" Alora questioned as her thoughts piqued with interest.

"The original faerie; it's fabled. She is our benefactor and Cheshire's mistress. From time to time, she makes her presence known to those who have a key role in the future of the realm. You haven't met with her, have you?" the queen raised a single white eyebrow in question.

"I have not; at least, I don't think I have." Alora chewed her bottom lip.

"She tends to appear when the time is right. Often, she masks her true self away because, while she isn't meant to directly interfere in fate, she can nudge things from time to time," explained the queen.

Alora's thoughts immediately went to the Weaver. Hadn't the faerie's sudden appearance been rather odd? Wasn't it strange that Alora had never seen her again in the past three weeks? She felt her skin pebble along her arm as a shiver raced up her spine.

"Cheshire, wouldn't you know if your mistress were here?" Hatter asked skeptically.

"I cannot say, dear friend. You understand where loyalties lie." Cheshire hedged as he peeked one eye open to observe Hatter.

"Mysterious, but then, the most unexpected happenings usually are. Did you know it was the Enchantress who took this barren land and fashioned the castle and its surroundings?" The queen softly smiled at her.

Alora felt a rush of surprise as her brows drew together, and she wondered about Cheshire's mistress. "I confess I did not."

She didn't know if she should feel sorrow or anger. Who was this mistress; if she possessed great power, why hadn't she put a stop to the horrors of the evil queen? How could such a being show such benevolence and then turn a blind eye to the rest? But hadn't Alora just been told the Enchantress wasn't meant to directly interfere? Perhaps creating the castle was as much as she dared to do.

"Now, onto other matters. Oh, here is the tea tray," the queen announced as Smith entered with the silver tea cart wheeled before him. The queen didn't say another word, pursing her lips instead. There seemed to be some tension Alora had not noticed between the queen and her manservant, which was very curious to her.

Smith stopped the cart in front of the settee, then backed away to stand ready in the corner against the ivory-papered wall. His gaze was directed straight ahead.

"Would you mind terribly, my dear?" The queen gestured to her lap. "It seems such a shame to disturb him. I know how Cheshire adores his tea, but he looks so sleepy."

"Of course, Your—Seraphina." Alora stumbled over her address. The queen had been so magnanimous in giving

Alora options on how to address her. And Alora's reserved manners niggled at her mind to honor the female beside her. Alora leaned toward the tea cart. "How would you like me to prepare your tea, Seraphina?"

"Just a tiny dab of sugar and a thimble full of cream," the queen informed her.

Alora prepared the rose-patterned cup of tea before slicing the lemon-iced cake. With care, she transferred a slice onto a matching plate, then carefully handed both dishes over to the queen. With a benevolent smile, the queen took the offerings.

Returning her attention back to the serviette, Alora poured tea into a teacup for Hatter, adding generous amounts of cream and sugar to his cup. She made another slice into the cake, and when it was placed onto its plate, she grasped onto the tea dishes and rose. Taking the few steps needed to gain Hatter's side, she held out his refreshments to him. He took them, letting his longer fingers brush against the tips of hers. Electricity pulsed between them, igniting her heart and tingling along her limbs. Hatter was grinning at her, knowing exactly what his actions were doing to her. With a shake of her head, she locked eyes on him, willing him to behave. She didn't wish to appear flighty when she was being observed by his mother.

Somehow, Alora found herself seated back on the velvet settee. Blinking the daze away, she poured her own tea and cut a small portion of the cake. Sipping from the dainty teacup in her hand, her thoughts were in a tizzy. Alora managed to recall the question the queen had last asked.

"My mother was one of the best women I believe I shall ever know, but wasn't of Fae descent." Alora looked into her teacup to await what the queen would say about her bloodline.

"I feel sure anyone that dear father of yours wed was quite deserving and thoroughly captivating. I see features in you that must belong to her simply because they don't quite match those of your father's." The queen tilted her head.

"Mother, do you have a moment to spare in showing the Oraculum to us?" Hatter interjected.

Swallowing her bite of the lemon cake, the queen gave him a single nod. "Of course. You wish to glean what you can from it?"

"We have good reason to believe Alora may be able to read it," he said, pride evident in his voice.

"Indeed? Well, that is surprising; I am astonished. You really are quite unique, are you not, Alora? Let us finish our chat; then we can seek it out. I've had it locked away under guard in the library. It seemed the perfect place," the queen told them.

"That's a wonderful idea. I wonder, will you share with me what Phillip was like as a little one?" Alora shifted her focus to him. She saw his eyes alight with mischief, and she wondered why that was so.

"Oh, my dear boy was pure mayhem! Don't let his refined manners fool you. It took many years and a host of tutors to train him properly. But he has always had the largest heart of any faerie I know. And early on, Phillip learned that the way to earn his redemption was to shower me with flowers. So no matter the scrape he found himself in, he would bring me bright blooms to soften me up!" the queen chortled.

"Ah, he has not employed that tactic with me yet," Alora replied, sending a teasing smile over at him.

"That is because I haven't quite needed to resort to bribery with you *yet*," chuckled Hatter, winking at her.

The sudden vision of little boys with mud-stained trousers, grass-littered hair, and mischievous grins set in grubby faces flitted through Alora's mind.

Would they have his smirk, his teasing manner? What if they had children one day who were girls? Would they have his amber eyes and wit? No matter how they were formed, she would love them all, each uniquely and individually as they deserved. Her happily ever after was within sight. But first, she must take a long look at what the prophecy said in order to know how to bring about their love story because she wasn't ready to let such beautiful dreams wither away.

41

UNBRIDLED JOY

Once the last sip of tea had been tipped from the teacup, the White Queen directed her gaze to Alora. "Dear One, we should make our way to the library to see what you may learn from the prophecy. If you can read the scroll, the end might just be closer than any faerie suspects."

"Excellent idea, Mother," replied Hatter as he came to his booted feet. He gathered his dishes, stepping forward to replace them on the tray. Alora followed his lead, gracefully rising. She set her dishes down then turned back to retrieve the queen's. Placing them down, Alora took a moment to steady her nerves. No matter what some ancient scrap of paper said, Alora would ultimately do as she felt she must, for the good of not only the kingdom but for herself as well.

"Does the Oraculum ever change its writings?" Alora wondered aloud.

"A very astute question and one I can answer for you. Yes, it has happened, though how much I cannot say, as no one has been able to properly read it in ages." The queen peered at Alora through pinched eyes. "The squiggles and whirls have changed over time. But isn't that like fate? One's destiny is ever-changing."

Cheshire stretched his limbs before sighing his dismay. "I suppose this means my nap has come to an end."

'I'm sorry, dearest, but we have a kingdom to save." The queen clicked her tongue at him.

"Yes, I'm very well aware," the tabby grumpily complained. Cheshire rose from the queen's lap and looked about him. "I suppose I've missed out on teatime. How very unfaely."

"There may be a spot left," soothed the queen.

Alora made to reach for the teapot when Cheshire's paw stayed her movement.

"We simply haven't the time. Let's be off." With a feline smile, he glided through the air toward the drawing room's double doors.

Hatter offered an arm to each of his ladies while casting a saucy wink Alora's way. She shyly took his arm, braiding hers with his as his mother attached herself to his other side.

Alora felt a warmth caress her skin. Hatter was always finding ways to display his feelings toward her, even when in the company of others. It was one very perfect element of the bond. If it was already this strong, Alora had no idea how unbreakable it would be once they had fully embraced it.

Concentrating, Alora wished to return some warmth to him. She hadn't ever attempted it before. Hatter's Fae abilities were so much stronger than hers, and he'd had years more than she to hone them. Inwardly, she searched her heart for the invisible tether that joined them. It took a moment before Alora's mind discovered the golden chord. Tugging on it, Hatter's face took on a perplexed expression. Alora thought of how much love she felt for him, then imagined her feelings traveling along the golden ribbon between them. She knew she had succeeded when a knowing gleam lit his eyes, and a soft smile curved his lips. Alora felt glee unfurl in her chest and couldn't wait to surprise him again. She had to keep herself from bouncing on the tips of her toes. Hatter must've been waiting for her to at least attempt to project her feelings along to him. He never left Alora in doubt of his feelings.

Hatter escorted each lady, and together, they strolled in the tabby's shadow through the doors, then down the ivory corridor with Alora's champion alicorn in tow. They passed pale suits of armor and landscape paintings framed in milky frames with inset white roses. Wall sconces were lit with turquoise flames that cast shadows along the snow-white runners.

As they neared a turn, a portrait came into view from the wall directly before them. Alora's steps slowed as the painting became more detailed the nearer she came. Her steps faltered altogether when Alora found that Hatter and his mother had both halted as well. Turning her gaze from the portrait, her eyes sought Hatter's face first. His lips wore a brittle smile as his forehead creased with deep lines of sadness. His mother's face showed more grooves of despair in her taut expression as her own grief rose to the surface, devastation in every pore. Not desiring to pry into their feelings, Alora directed her sight back to the king.

The faerie king had the same long auburn hair as Hatter. He was lean but muscular and portrayed dignity and strength. Eyes that were kind peered back at Alora. It was such an odd feeling to have the impression that a portrait was studying one back, but so much of Wonderland had her reacting in unexpected ways.

"Shall we make introductions?" Cheshire asked as he backtracked toward them. The cat came to a stop next to Alora, and he, too, looked at the portrait.

"We haven't the time," the queen said briskly, giving Alora the impression that she didn't want to think about her husband. Or, maybe it was that she couldn't bear to look upon him when he couldn't truly see her.

"Five minutes won't change events too drastically, I daresay," Cheshire replied and reached into the air as his paw disappeared. When it came back into view, a miniature vial was clasped in his grip. "You see? Fleur thought ahead and left me some of her magic."

Alora's brows drew together.

What can he mean? And has he always been able to reach into nothing and produce things such as hats and magic vials? How utterly curious...

Hatter removed his sight from his father and locked his gaze on Alora. "Fleur's magic can bring a subject to life."

"But it's not really them." The queen brought a hand up, clutching at the beads of her pearl necklace.

"No? But it's, in essence, them. While it might not be their soul, it's very much a likeness of them. When animated, the subject reacts and speaks just as its bearer would have." Hatter swallowed heavily.

"Another time, perhaps, Cheshire—" Alora began not liking it at all that both Hatter and his mother were so dismayed.

"No, it's all right. He would have adored you at first sight." The White Queen turned her watery gaze to Alora. "Just as we all do."

Cheshire uncorked the bottle, then quickly held it up toward the king. "It won't last long," he cautioned.

A silver cloud rose from the bottle, shimmering and glittering. It floated along the air until it came to the portrait and leached into the fibers of the painting. Alora's heart skipped a beat at the idea of harm befalling the lovely tribute to the king. It would be horrid if anything happened, almost like losing him again.

The king blinked toward them as a robust smile broke out on his bearded face. "My family!" he greeted them in a rich baritone, much like Hatter's. The similarities between them were very marked. Rich, amber eyes shone with such life-like light. It was hard to believe there was no soul behind those eyes.

"Hello, Father." Hatter nodded to him.

"My son!" the king nodded back. Then he looked at his queen. "My darling wife!" and grief overtook his face as his mirthful features pinched together.

"My husband," the queen managed to say as silent tears dropped from her eyes.

"I never meant to leave you. You have my deepest apologies." The king's eyes glistened.

"It couldn't be helped, my love." The queen lifted a corner of her mouth until her lips trembled.

Switching his attention back over to Hatter, his father addressed him again. "I have always been proud of you. I want you to know that. Remember how much you mean to me."

"I do," assured Hatter through a roughened voice.

"And who is this pretty young lady by your side?" The king arched one bushy brow.

"May I present Princess Alora, my fated mate." Hatter smiled down at her, and the adoration swirling in his eyes made her heart flutter.

"My, that is wonderful news!" the king cheered. "I wish we had more time. I'd so like to know you better, my dear." The king's face began to shimmer.

"I am so honored to get to meet the man who's been such an important leader and even more pleased to meet Phillip's father. I'm sorry we didn't get to meet sooner. I promise to look after your kingdom and to cherish your loved ones."

The king's eyes softened as he peered back at her. Though he wasn't really there, she needed to voice these vows aloud.

"You have my eternal gratitude." He smiled at Alora, then turned his gaze to his wife. "I'm always with you. I left this world thinking of you. And in the quiet moments when you're most alone, know I'm right there by your side. Should you feel a gentle touch or hear the sound of a nightingale, know that's my doing." He raised his hand and expelled the silver magic from himself. He stilled and became nothing more than oil and canvas, but the silver magic continued to weave its way toward the queen, who stood still as a statue. The magic first brushed against her lips and then lowered to hover over her heart. It disappeared as it seeped through the ivory material of the queen's dress.

With a gasp, the queen closed her glittering eyes as unbridled joy brightened her face. "I feel the warmth of the bond again."

The atmosphere was quiet as the moment settled.

The queen opened her eyes and turned to look at them. "It's gone now, but for a moment, I felt my other half again and so much overflowing love. I haven't been myself in much too long; forgive me, my darling." She reached for Hatter and cupped his face.

"There is nothing to forgive," he stated. "Now that I have found the missing half of my soul, I can't fathom ever losing it, feeling it sever… I can't imagine the unspeakable anguish." Hatter's sight turned from his mother and landed upon his mate.

Seeing his attention veer, the queen let her hands drop from his face, then stepped away.

Hatter turned to Alora, framing her face with his hands. Peering into her eyes, he brought the tip of his nose against hers to gently brush his smooth skin against hers. "All of my days will be spent ensuring that you know just how much I treasure you."

Tears came unbidden to Alora's eyes, and she tried to blink them away. But it was silly; they weren't unhappy tears; they were completely the opposite. Love and joy fused in her chest and flowed to her fingers and toes, tickling her nerves along the way.

The bond between them grew daily. How much more

would they feel for each other? And more importantly, how would Alora survive if he was taken from her again? Alora quickly banished the dark thought from her mind.

I won't allow myself to think of any other outcome than attaining our happily-ever-after. Nothing less would do.

42

THE ORACULUM

Few words were exchanged as they began to make their way to the library once again. It seemed as if they were all lost in their own inner musings. It would have been surprising that even Cheshire was silent had anyone given thought to him. They were each caught up in tumbling waves crashing against the tender fibers of their hearts.

The White King had seemed so real. Surely, it wasn't just magic? Or the magic was indeed a piece of him, no matter how small. It must have been when he was able to cast the last vestiges of the magic from himself and into the White Queen. There couldn't have been any other reason. It had been genuine.

Alora felt a peacefulness settle into her at her conclusion as a comforting warmth traveled through her. Sometimes, there really were larger forces amidst them. Why waste time and energy trying to sort out that which was unexplainable? Living in the present was quite complicated enough.

A large, ivory, wooden door stood sentry before them. It was engraved with roses that climbed up a trellis, and on closer inspection, butterflies were hidden amongst the roses. The fluttering insects bore a rose pattern upon their wings.

Just like in her nightmares… this discovery was very unsettling. The tiny hairs on the back of Alora's neck rose as her skin prickled.

Feeling eyes upon her, Alora turned her head to look past Hatter and at the queen. She was staring at Alora with a knowing look, which made the blood in Alora's veins chill. This was another revelation, and she didn't know just what to do with it.

Is it possible I was so terribly wrong regarding the butterflies? Yet, they always heralded the approach of the beasts and carnage. Maybe they weren't an evil force, but instead one of good intentions? A warning that everything was about to go wrong before it actually occurred…

The queen gave Alora a demure smile and a slight inclination of her head, letting her know she was behind the butterfly invasion.

But why and how? For if the White Queen hadn't been the one to curse Alora, how had she altered the hex?

Thinking back to every encounter with the winged creatures, Alora had always had a sudden rush of adrenaline. Her heartbeat increased as her body prepared to encounter the next vicious event. It was always like that. The butterflies seemed to have presented themselves not only as a warning but also to ensure Alora had enough energy, and sense even, to ready herself for what horrors lay ahead. How had she not understood that before?

"You must hold to the truth that Wonderland is not always how it seems. There are friends and foes in the most unlikely of places, and they are all equally important. This wondrous land is built on dreams, but it's just as much a part of the nightmares as well. You can't have one without the other. It was meant to be a perfect balance." The White Queen winked at her, then pushed the pearl handle to open the door. She glided through it, pulling Hatter along, which, in turn, carried Alora's steps forward as well.

Alora's skin iced further as she shivered at the queen's words. Alora had a sense that she had just been given some very imperative information she must not forget. It seemed a riddle lay among the sentences, and when the time was right, Alora might need to draw the words from her memory.

Hatter perked a brow at her with a look of concern passing over his face. Alora attempted to smile at him, but it didn't feel genuine, and he knew it. Instead, she patted his arm.

Cheshire had all but disappeared; only his large, curved smile was visible. It floated in the air above their heads.

"I can't help but think you're lost somewhere that I can't reach." Hatter allowed his mother to part from his side as she wandered to talk with a short faerie who had magenta hair and large, silver-colored wings.

"I am never far from you; you only need to remind me that we'll get through this. All the battles that await us." Alora wasn't certain how she was feeling.

"We shall indeed conquer our foe and set Wonderland to rights. You needn't doubt that," he reached forward to press a kiss atop her head, just to the side of her curls.

"Darlings, Pheebs is ready for us. She's unlocked the case," the queen spoke from a few steps away.

"Very good," Hatter answered. "Shall we learn the secrets together?" He waited for Alora to answer him.

"We shall, together," she agreed.

Together, they strode over to the queen and the library's keeper. As they did so, Alora took a quick peek at their surroundings. This library wasn't quite like the one underground. The ceiling was ivory with carved angels and clouds adorning it. The wooden shelves were well stocked, housing many tomes, and matched the adorned table and chairs.

Alora's mind went back to her last venture into a library,

and she stumbled over her own feet as the screams of the banshee replayed in her memory.

"My sweet, is something the matter?" Hatter's eyes pinched together.

Alora swallowed the lump forming in her throat, releasing pressure so that she could speak.

"I forgot to mention the last adventure I had in a library. It involved a banshee, and the time before that, I was chased by grimoires whose spit was venomous." Alora quirked a half smile his way.

"How have you managed to remain uninjured? You've only been in this realm for nearly a month," Hatter shook his head. "You are *never* leaving my side again." He placed his hand over hers, which was still resting in the crook of his elbow.

His touch was reassuring, and she felt some of the tension melt from her body.

"My, what were they doing with you?" The queen asked with a hand on either side of her cheeks.

"Cheshire, you were looking after her, weren't you?" Hatter asked irritably.

The smile transformed into a glower as Cheshire's body materialized. "Of course, we had everything well in hand, I can assure you."

"Did I forget to also mention the bite I received?" Alora pursed her lips and looked downward, attempting to hide away her secret smile.

"*Cheshire*!" bellowed Hatter as a flush crept across his angry features.

"Now see here, you barbarian with the bond mush mind. I did my best to introduce our *Princess* to the wonders of the land. And I must say she did marvelously! Now, I shall forgive you for this one indiscretion. You are allowed that much, what with our long history and sound friendship. I may not be *bonded* to Alora, but I wouldn't allow serious harm to befall her, and you should remember that. *Everything happens for a reason.* You might also take a moment to remember her guards were all in attendance with her, not just myself. Besides, where were you during this time?" Cheshire's tail twitched back and forth, marking his dismay.

Hatter's face grew red with his anger, flooding their bond and saturating Alora. Little tattling zaps of energy prickled her heart.

From behind her, Fate leaned his weight from hoof to hoof, clearly upset at the situation. Alora felt a sting in her heart that he was made unhappy. He had been one of her guards, shadowing her during her time underground. Alora knew he felt some blame, even though she had tried to alleviate it.

"Boys, let us set our differences aside. We need to *attempt* to concentrate on the here and now. Now, let us take a look at the prophecy," the queen cajoled. When neither male made a move toward the glass display, she said, "If you do not abide me as a mother, you shall do so as your *queen*!"

That seemed to snap them all to attention; even Alora felt her posture straighten.

Wordlessly, Hatter took a deep breath, adjusted his greatcoat, then pulled his topper lower over his ears. He reclaimed Alora's hand and wove their fingers together. She reached up on her tiptoes, giving him a kiss on his cheek. When she lowered herself back to the balls of her feet, his eyes were free from simmering rage, and a grin animated his features.

Tugging him along, Alora padded over to the glass-encased display, halting before it. She felt Cheshire's whiskers brush against her cheek as he came to a stop beside her. The queen stood with her hands folded together beside her.

Laying upon snowy satin was the unrolled parchment. It was yellowed with age, and there were two golden knobs for handles. But it was the inky penmanship alongside the drawing that captured Alora's gaze.

The Oraculum...

She wasn't sure if it was awe or trepidation that had her bringing her free hand to her mouth. Alora exhaled, concentrating on what was before her. The swirls and loops shuffled, and then they shimmered into focus as she peered down.

"THE SAVIOR OF THE LANDS WILL NOT COME FROM THE REALM; SHE shall be set apart from her subjects. She will be linked with her fated mate, who shall battle by her side. The evil will fall, but all fates come with a price."

An image appeared as the words faded away. A female clad in dark armor wielded a sword. She ducked and weaved, changing her stance before she charged forward. The image faded out as a giant furred beast with razor-sharp teeth stared back at her. Saliva dripped from his large, open maw.

"But beware the beloved beast of the evil queen. For he shall seek to devour the savior whole."

Again, the words gave way to an image of the beast, but now it was crunching on a misshapen helmet.

"The dragon won't be easily felled. It will take skill and cunning to outmaneuver the rash reactions and misdeeds. The savior will need to guard not only her head but her heart as well."

A fire-breathing dragon transformed the words as plumes of smoke poured forth from its nostrils and mouth. Its vicious nails clacked the shining, diamond-like cobbled stones.

"Only a true hero will unmask the darkness and heal the lands. But beware of the choices the savior shall make. For one shall fail for another to rise. Things will not be as they were foretold."

In rapid succession, flashes of scenes played across the parchment-Hatter's face, the table set for tea-dissolving as butterflies flitted across the scroll. Their image was replaced with the Tweedle twins hitting one another before their attention was stolen by a white rabbit checking his pocket watch. Alora blinked, opening her eyes to an image of herself. Tears streamed down her alabaster cheeks, her eyes wide and horror-stricken. Then Fleur arrives, patting her shoulder.

The scene morphed again, replacing their forms with a crown upon her head. Stars swirl and bend, and then she's in Hatter's embrace, gliding back and forth in the steps of a dance.

The image before her stopped as words formed on the parchment again.

"Beware the untruths and events as they unfold. For nothing is as it seems. A betrayal or not will be the stone that propels the battle into action."

"I don't quite know what to think..." Alora blinked her dry eyes.

"What did you see?" the queen questioned.

"Random events, uncertain uncertainties. Alora garbed in armor and swinging steel that very much resembled the Vorpal sword. Of course, the Jabberwocky and the dragon herself were pictured. And then, it must be mentioned the friends and foes and truth that isn't quite true. Oh, and a betrayal that begins our last battle," replied Hatter ominously.

Alora frowned as she looked from the scroll to him.

"I think it's a part of the bond," Hatter told her. "I believe I viewed what you saw. Was I incorrect?" He frowned back at her.

Slowly, Alora shook her head. Words were tumbling around in her mind much too fast to sort them out. Likely, she would need a few minutes at least to make sense of the chaos.

What truths were lies? Past statements or ones yet to fall upon my ears? And what betrayal shall I face that would ruin me?

43

A KISS?

Arrangements were made for their little group to remain for the evening, then set out the next morning for the Resistance. For Alora, it was time to return to where the adventure had begun. They needed to form battle plans and prepare their army.

In an ivory bedchamber set in one of the castle's towers, Alora turned from her side to her back. She had slept little in the hours since she and Hatter had retired to take a rest. Sharing a bed was no different than individual bedrolls in the tent. Looking up at the ruffled canopy above them, she sighed.

Hatter peeped open one eye, peeking over at her. He was lying beside her with a bent arm behind his head. His cravat had been removed along with his ebony tailcoat and vest. Hatter's hair was tangled, and he was hatless, though his topper was never far from his reach. He'd stripped away his armor and shown her a vulnerability that her beloved covered away from all other eyes.

Her thoughts flew to the first night they had danced the dawn across the sky.

Hatter weaved her fingers through his as he led the way to their tent. Opening the tent for her to slip by, he followed her in. He helped her lower onto her bedroll and then sat down beside her, claiming his own spot. When Alora laid down, he'd carefully drawn the top of the bedroll up to cover her. She looked on with weary eyes as Hatter brought his hands up to either side of his hat. His fingers lingered over the silk fabric before he gingerly removed the topper. He cradled it to his chest with one hand while the other drew strands of his hair over his ears, completely hiding the destroyed tips.

Then he had risked a look at her.

Alora had cast him a gentle smile, watching as Hatter's shoulder slumped. He loosed a breath, his body relaxing, and stretched out beside her. He placed his hat down on his free side and turned to face Alora, drawing her close.

She wanted to close the space between them now and rest her head atop his chest, allowing his heartbeat to soothe her senses. Hatter was so handsome. How did he become more so every time her eyes came to rest upon him?

The bond tingled as Hatter smiled at her. He had both eyes open now as he studied her.

Alora wanted to return his smile, but she suddenly felt a cloud settle over her as her lungs seized. What if, after everything occurs, she lost him?

"Are you alright, my darling?" he asked, furrowing his brow. Hatter tilted his head to the side.

"I don't know how I'd bear to go on if I were to lose you again. If after the prophecy is or isn't fulfilled, what if we can't find our way back to each other? I lost you once..." Her words died out as tears gathered in her eyes.

Her mate moved toward her and braced himself on his elbows as he towered over her. Gently, Hatter cupped her face in his hands, his amber eyes burning into hers with a searing intensity.

"Hear this now. I shall always find you again if ever you're lost. There's nothing that can keep me from your side, breathing the same air as you, dreaming the same dreams. What we have...This doesn't happen every day." Hatter stroked his nose against hers.

When he pulled away, she spoke. "Fated mates? But I've seen so many mated pairs."

"Have you any idea how long it took for some of them to find their way to each other? We Fae are long-lived. It's quite common to go for centuries without meeting your other half. This love doesn't happen every day; in all the best stories, it's worth fighting for. And our love story shall rival them all. We will come through this trial together stronger, even if, in the end, we're changed a little bit."

"And if we've changed a great deal? So much so that we don't even recognize ourselves?" A tear slipped from the corner of her eye, falling onto Hatter's hand.

"Is that what troubles you? That you'll be unrecognizable to me? Impossible!"

"How can you be sure?"

A beautiful smile appeared on his face. "Because it's true love. Even fate would not separate us again. I'd follow the tether between us to traverse even beyond the veil to bring you back to me. Our story has only begun, and we've experienced our hiccups. Trust in *us*, my darling."

Alora allowed Hatter's words to fall from his lips straight into her heart. She endeavored to hold them close, tucking them safely away. She vowed to uncover them when her days became long, and her fears rose to the surface.

She nodded at him as she felt some of her worries lessen. Tears were still lining her lashes. The warmth of Hatter's body radiated against hers, causing Alora's thoughts to scatter. Was it so very wrong to desire a kiss from him?

His gaze fell onto her lips. The breath in her lungs shuttered. Hatter brought his head closer toward hers as his eyes heated into pools of deep honey. Alora's eyes slowly slid closed, and as she felt the whispers of a kiss touch her awaiting lips, he pulled away. The cooling air between them made Alora gasp as her eyes flew open with equal parts dismay and surprise.

Hatter's head was turned in the direction of the bedchamber's door. When the door handle began to turn, he leaped from the bed and stood sentry before it, his stance guarded as he waited to see who was about to enter.

When the door opened enough for Fleur to peek her head in, her eyes found Alora's.

"No time to laze about. We have come to have dinner and have brought a guest. Up now, for we must prepare for the evening's festivities!" Fleur flew into the room, clapping her hands once she reached the bed.

Rising and shaking out her wrinkled dress, Alora reached for Hatter's hand and squeezed it. She sent her love to him through the bond and, in return, felt his feelings reach out to caress her.

"Who has come?" inquired Hatter, freeing her hand as he strode to the bedside table. Reaching for his hat, he quickly donned it.

"It's the king, the other one, not mine obviously, but Alora's father, and he has accepted the White Queen's dinner invitation. He'll be spending the night here as well. Isn't a reunion always faetastical?" Fleur danced in the air.

"My father?" Alora asked with pleasure.

"Yes! Out with you, Hatter! We ladies need to prepare for dinner. It's to be a lavish affair, and I must see that we sparkle and shine." Fleur came to Hatter's side and reached for his waistcoat, tugging him along to the door.

Hatter wore a bewildered look upon his features as Fleur faerie-handled him from the room. He twisted the door handle that he was nearly shoved into and turned back. His gaze locked on Alora's as she silently mouthed an apology.

When the door clicked closed after Hatter, Fleur turned to her with a winsome smile.

"The maid shall be here presently!" Fleur glided to her, looking her up and down. "You have been behaving, haven't you?"

"Of course!" Alora blushed. She couldn't help herself.

Phillip had been so close to kissing me… A true love's kiss, and wasn't that the most powerful thing in all of the realms?

44

FOREVER MY HEART

Fleur had insisted on dusting Alora's cheeks with silver powder, then applying it to the ends of her tresses, which curled down her back. The effect was stunning, and it appeared as if the stars had descended from the sky to gift her with glittering kisses. Alora glowed. She had never felt more like a faerie before.

The maid had arrived with a rainbow of dresses in tow. The three of them had decided a periwinkle high-waisted dinner dress would look lovely paired with her dark locks and alabaster skin. The shimmering powder further accented her eyes and the plump shape of her mouth.

Fleur was attired in delicate, soft daisy petals that gave her a whimsical air. She was beautiful, and she knew it. Clement would have a difficult time keeping his eyes off her.

A knock sounded at the door, slightly opening to reveal Hatter covering his eyes. "Every faerie decent?"

Alora laughed and rushed to him. She tugged his hand away from his face, smiling up at him. His eyes grew large as he took her in.

"You grow more magnificent each time I gaze at you. You steal my breath away," he remarked as his face became serious. "How will I ever survive years of waking up to you? My poor heart, you must promise to take care of it."

Weaving their fingers together between them, she vowed, "I will promise to love you for all of our days and care for your heart as if it were my own." She brought their entangled hands up to her lips, kissing the back of one of his.

"This is all so entertaining, no, not really. May we please be on our way? I am famished. It takes diligent work to look this good." Fleur fluffed her fiery hair as she floated in the air, then looked at them expectantly.

"Of course," answered Hatter as he pulled Alora to his side, bringing his arm around her waist.

"After you, Fleur, I am certain you know the way we are meant to go," Alora replied.

When Hatter followed after the tiny sprite, Alora easily kept in step with him. It wasn't proper to be so close to him, and yet, she couldn't pry herself away. Never mind the fact she had been sleeping beside him for weeks. Her moral senses had completely deteriorated. Would her father be truly scandalized were they to appear before him thusly? She hoped not, but the fear was not enough to drive her from Hatter's side, from his intoxicating warmth.

They made their way through the corridor with the sound of Fate's hooves clip-clopping along the marble floor. Descending a grand staircase, they soon reached another long hallway. The second door on the right stood ajar. Voices from within met her ears. Alora could distinctly make out the cadence of her father's voice.

Alora's skin became heated as her breath became labored, and her nerves twisted her stomach into lava-like knots. Would her father be angry with her? Would he seek to discipline her for leaving the safety of the Resistance, leaving them all to wonder what had happened to her? It was a destiny Alora thought she might deserve. Her rashness hadn't been kind to him, most of all.

Hatter stopped their progress and leaned down to face her. "It will all turn out well."

Alora smiled at him, then gave him a nod. She allowed his presence to calm her racing heart as deep affection flowed between their bond.

Then, together, they followed after Fleur, who had already entered the sitting room. Once through the door, Alora took in the room's splendor. Pale statues of faeries in various forms were raised on marble platforms along the corners of the ivory-papered walls. Looking above her, Alora's eyes lit up with delight as carved wildlife pranced in the plaster of the ceiling. One large chandelier hung from the middle point of the room, casting a golden hue on the objects and beings below it. The furniture was white with ivory padding. The tiled floor was also the same unpigmented color that was the theme of the palace and was decorated with a floral design. The echo of Fate's clippity-clopping hooves filled the chamber as the voices within hushed.

"Here you are, at long last," Papa said, closing the distance between them. His arms reached for Alora as Hatter released her so she could settle into her father's warm embrace.

Alora looked up at him and could see it was not disapproval that resided in his eyes. Instead, there was tenderness and concern. She felt terrible for wondering how he would greet her. Since coming to Wonderland, her father had seemed to treasure her more than ever before.

He allowed Alora to draw back, but she was content to stay by his side.

"We are so fortunate our children have met and discovered what they are to each other," voiced the queen as she glided over to take part in the conversation.

"Indeed! I couldn't dream up a better choice for her!" her father exclaimed, nodding once to Hatter.

"Have you two spoken?" Alora inquired as she looked from her father to Hatter.

"Curiouser and curiouser," Cheshire remarked as his head rested in his upturned front paws. The cat really did have a flare for incentivizing dramatic events. His very presence created an air of mayhem and uncertainty; despite that, he was so very oddly likable that one couldn't help but desire the tabby to keep them entertained.

"We have indeed spoken," began Papa. "It was while you were busy getting ready for dinner. But we have known each other for quite some time. You see, Phillip used to visit our home from time to time. He kept me abreast of the happenings here."

"Why did I never meet with him?" Alora's heart squeezed as she felt cheated at never having been introduced to him.

"It didn't seem appropriate as he was pure Fae and you weren't. You must remember I was sheltering you from the harshness of this realm. I never could have imagined the boy who snuck away from the other realm would ever have any interests in you, other than as allies. The deft hands of fate often work these things out. I am happy to see its guiding force in bringing you two together. All's well that ends well." Her father rubbed his hands together.

"At least I am not the only one kept in the dark," Fleur spoke from a rococo armchair where Clement was seated next to her.

Hatter cleared his throat. "I have asked your father for your hand, and he was very enthusiastic with his blessing."

"A mating ceremony and a wedding! I couldn't be more thrilled!" the queen enthused as she gazed lovingly at the couple.

Hatter reached for Alora's hand, pulling her with him, guiding her to one of the silk-padded settees. When she was settled, he dropped to his knees before her, enclosing her hands between his. Her breath caught as she looked at her beloved, waiting to see what it was that he wanted to say to her.

"My darling, would you do me the very great honor of accepting my hand in marriage and joining our lives together forevermore? I promise to always cherish you and make you the heartbeat of my entire world. I will spend my hours by your side, ensuring you are happy and well-cared for. Together, we'll create the most magical moments as we let providence weave our threads into one strong and everlasting cord. Without you, there is no tomorrow worth pursuing. You are the twinkle in my eye and the cadence my heart beats to. Be mine in every way possible." Hatter swallowed as tears glimmered in his amber eyes.

With tears glistening in her eyes and a voice that trembled, Alora replied, "I would be most honored to be your wife. I cannot imagine a more perfect existence than belonging to you. You are my everything…my heart, my joy, and my delight. I can't wait to make more beautiful memories by your side, discovering all the layers our love will build."

All of her dreams were coming true.

The brilliant smile that lit Hatter's face made her own smile blossom. Through her watery vision, she surveyed him. From his bushy brows to the curve of his chin, she wanted to catalog each of his features.

This is a moment I never want to forget. His heartfelt words… the utter rightness and the love shining from his beautiful eyes. This could not have been more perfect.

"I don't have a token of my affection to bestow upon you," his auburn brows furrowed.

"You don't need to give me a thing other than your heart."

"Forever, my heart is yours." His gaze caressed her face. "You need never doubt. That is something even terror can never strip from me. I won't allow anything to part us again."

"Here, here!" came her father's joyful voice.

"My dear friend Hatter has found his other half. Soon we

shall have little ones to chase after." A delighted grin filled Cheshire's face.

Hatter coughed, then excused himself with a chagrinned expression morphing his countenance before saying, "But please, no gifts of the dead variety or soon-to-be such." He rose, taking the space beside his betrothed. His skin seemed to be slightly tinged pink.

"Spoilsport," the tabby huffed.

Footsteps alerted them to Smith's presence before the manservant entered the room and announced, "Lord and Lady Hubert are here." He stepped to the side, and in came a portly couple with smiles as they greeted the room's occupants.

In the next few minutes, various couples came through the sitting room door and were introduced as honored guests. The room became loud with the hum of conversation until Smith announced that dinner was served.

Alora felt as if she floated along the ether encased in a bubble. Giddiness and feeling as if she was as light as gossamer wings thrummed through her. Hatter continued to hold her hand and studied her face whenever there was a lull in conversation. She was so light, so airy, and felt as if nothing could diminish her happiness. Alora wanted to cling to these feelings as long as she could. If Wonderland had taught her anything, it was that everything was quick to turn havey-cavey, and in the blink of an eye, things could change.

She delighted in being on Hatter's arm, so firmly fixed to his side as he led her from the room, trailing after his mother and her father. Alora tried not to stare as they passed by an octopus couple, but when her eyes landed upon the Dumpty couple, she decided it was far safer to keep her eyes forward facing.

This shall be quite a dinner. I do wonder what will be on the menu as some faerie or another is certain to become offended by the fare.

45

DINNER AND A YOKE

The Tweedle twins were already seated at the long rectangular table when the dinner guests walked into the elegant dining room. They cheekily ducked their heads as they tried to scamper under the snow-white tablecloth, but a footman was quick enough to grab onto the dark collar of each boy. He dragged them away from the table and presented them to the White Queen.

"Naughty boys! Forever into trouble," the queen addressed them with a frown.

"It was *his* fault." One boy poked the other in his chest.

"*Ow*! It wasn't my fault. We smelled the delightful aroma of the steamed shrimp and couldn't keep away."

Fleur was beside Alora's ear and whispered, "The boys are allowed to run amuck. Their parents are terrible creatures who don't pay them nearly enough attention."

Alora felt a pang of sorrow in her chest for the poor, neglected, and unloved boys.

"Next time, I encourage you to wait for a proper invitation, but since you are here, you might as well enjoy the celebration dinner. Allow our guests to be seated first, then you may take your own seats," the queen decreed as she breezed past them, moving to her chair at the head of the table.

Alora's father followed behind her, taking the opposite chair from Her Majesty at the end of the table.

Hatter gallantly guided Alora to a chair on her father's right. He took the chair next to her instead of leaving her side to sit beside his mother. Alora felt her heart hammer in her chest, fearing the White Queen would not be happy with the seating, but when she caught Alora's eye, the queen nodded with a smile before turning back to the faerie she was conversing with.

Cheshire had taken the empty seat beside the queen. Fate stood sentry against the wall behind Alora's chair.

Alora looked down at her plate. The ivory napkin was fashioned in a swan with its elegant neck twisted to peer behind it. She disliked the idea of destroying the work of art, for it was so very pretty. Hatter wasted no time in picking the swan up by its neck and shaking the shape from the linen. He placed the cloth down on his lap. Alora followed his lead, retrieving the piece of linen and then shaking it out before draping it over her lap.

Scanning the other dinner guests, Alora noted that each was so very unique.

No dinner table in England would ever entertain such a variety of guests. It's quite an amusing thought. I imagine many a lady would faint as the gentlemen all blustered to share their table with such colorful beings.

The octopus couple was hard to look away from. Indeed, everything about them caused her to stare a bit too long. Their many legs were actively waving in numerous directions as they happily talked to their dinner companions. Never before had Alora seen sea creatures up close; she found them fascinating. Skin the color of mulberry with large, expressive, pine needle-hued eyes were certainly traits that commanded notice. The male octopus was named Henri and wore a monocle attached to a golden chain which was linked along the ruff at what appeared to be his neck. His wife, Octavia, wore golden shoes on four of her limbs and had a tuft of white hair curled atop her bulbous head.

Lord and Lady Hubert were seated at opposite sides of the table but seemed to be in good cheer. Where the male's skin was a duller pink, his lady's was a vibrant magenta. They each had bright lavender eyes and snow-white hair. Horns in a pale gray grew from the lord's head while his lady had none.

Fleur and Clement were seated toward the corner of the table near the queen. A tiny ivory table and chairs sat atop the larger table, complete with two miniature place settings. It was a thoughtful accommodation for the littler sprites and showed how much the subjects of the White Queen meant to her.

Smith stood off to the side of the chamber. When the queen smiled at him, he directed the ivory-liveried footman to begin serving the soup. The pale white soup was thick. Little bits of carrots floated along its top. Alora nodded at the frog-faced servant who ladled the creamy liquid into her bowl after serving her father. Alora and the other guests waited for the queen to dip her spoon into her bowl to taste it first. When the White Queen had nodded her satisfaction, each dinner guest took their own sample.

"I can't help but wonder how Mister Dumpty keeps his contents in when such a huge gash mars his forehead." Hatter leaned closer toward her as he spoke.

"Is it possible for his… yoke… to seep out?" The thought horrified Alora as she wondered how she would behave if that were to happen. Her eyes immediately flew to the egg-shaped oddity; then she felt horrible for thinking him odd. But even in Wonderland, egg-shaped faeries seemed fantastical. The short fellow wore a forest-green suit with a golden pocket watch.

Perhaps he isn't even a faerie, after all. Perchance, he's nothing more than an enchantment brought to life.

"I've no idea..." Hatter mused as he, too, observed the faerie creature.

"I say, you are new to our kingdom," a short lizard-esque faerie addressed Alora from across the table. His skin was lime-colored, and he, too, wore a suit, but his was white. Obsidian eyes stared at her, waiting for her to reply.

Alora dabbed at her mouth with her napkin, then she returned it to her lap as she spoke, "I have just recently returned to this realm."

"Do you find it tolerable?" The lizard blinked at her.

"I find it magical, and I do so hope to help lead it back to how it once was."

"We do mourn for the old days." A pale pink tongue darted from the reptile's mouth to reach up and lick his eye.

Alora nearly dropped her spoon in mid-air at the disgusting sight. The soup dribbled from the bowl of her spoon as it wobbled in her hand. She quickly placed it in her bowl. The fumbling of her fingers was badly done, but then Alora hadn't been expecting to witness such unsavory manners while dining with the White Queen.

"We won't have to mourn for much longer, my friend," Hatter interjected, saving her the trouble of replying as he caught her eye and winked at her.

Taking a moment to gather herself, Alora gazed at the papered wall. Ivory roses clung to trellises as butterflies with golden accents weaved throughout the design. The hanging chandelier was white with pale candles, which were lit, casting a turquoise light upon the room.

"That was mine," grumbled one of the Tweedle twins, who punched his brother in the arm.

"It was not!" returned the other twin, who grew rosy with anger.

"Boys, I won't warn you again to use your manners while

at my table!" the queen commanded with a firm tone.

Both boys bowed their heads, but one flinched.

Did the other kick his twin? How beastly they are! But if their parents largely ignore them, it's no wonder they are so ill-mannered and unkempt. I wish they felt loved...

"You were missed, my dear. I am glad you are safe and that you have been training to strengthen your abilities." Papa drew her attention from beside her.

Before Alora could reply, the footmen were retrieving the soup bowls while others were placing down ivory plates laden with white fish. Small potatoes and cauliflower were dressed in a colorless sauce beside the steaming meat.

"I am sorry for the way in which I left, Papa," began Alora. She was hesitant to ruin his good mood.

"You were always curious, and I was relieved to know no harm came to you. I have been busy strategizing the war efforts, so I felt that you were better off in the forest. How have your healing abilities been coming along?" Her father cut a piece of his fish and took a bite.

"We've only practiced my healing abilities a little. I so wanted to come back and learn from Faedora. I hope she will have time to teach me once we are back underground." Alora forked a potato, bringing it to her mouth.

"The Princess seems to be becoming quite adept at healing her own injuries. While she has not received any that have been serious, she had drawn on her gift to heal any minor ache or pain. That tells me she can heal rather quickly. I hope she can grasp more difficult injuries as she learns more from Faedora." Hatter addressed her father.

"Indeed, we haven't much time, but we must make that our priority once we are returned," agreed the rebellion's king.

"When is the mating ceremony?" asked a female faerie with iridescent wings that shimmered in the lighting and lilac hair that curled around her shoulder. Fair skin resembling cloud poufs, ruby bow-shaped lips, and a slender frame made it hard to easily turn away from her.

Alora gazed at Hatter, waiting to see what he would say. She didn't have any idea when they would be holding the ceremony or their wedding. Silky butterfly wings tickled her stomach when Alora thought about either day when she would be wholly joined to her mate. Would Alora feel differently? Like herself, but more once she felt the bond strengthen?

Hatter smiled at the beautiful faerie before he replied, "We are waiting to return to the Resistance and assess a few situations before naming a date, but I won't be content to wait for too long." His warm eyes moved to meet Alora's as the butterflies morphed into birds who flew to her heart, making it soar.

"I see; it is a true love match. I congratulate you both. How about a toast from His Majesty?" Raising her fluted goblet and tucking a long strand of her lilac hair behind one tipped ear, the faerie directed her attention to Alora's father.

"I quite agree that a toast to the happy couple is in order," Papa replied, beaming at Alora as he raised his glass and waited for other diners to raise their goblets before he began again. "Here is to the most perfect couple who exemplify both grace and courage. May we all wish them well as they begin this new adventure together."

"Here, here!"

"Huzzah!"

Many more shouts were heard echoing throughout the chamber. They all filled Alora's heart with joy and excitement as she wriggled in her chair. Their union would bring happiness to Wonderland and make her feel accepted and as if she had finally come home.

While Alora brought the wine glass to her mouth and was taking a sip, she caught sight of the canape that flew straight at Mister Dumpty. When it connected with his head, the fellow jumped from his chair, landing on the marble floor with a resounding crack.

Like most of the other dinner guests, Alora quickly rose to peer down at the poor fellow. A puddle of golden goo leaked from the widened gash on his forehead. Egg yoke was seeping onto the floor in a thick puddle.

"Oh no!" Alora brought her hands to cover her mouth.

"Boys, this is the last straw. You may not have dessert; straight home you will go!" admonished the queen, who looked just as horrified as Alora felt.

A trio of footmen rushed to upright a dazed Mister Dumpty as his shell turned a sickly green. Missus Dumpty rounded the table to stand before him.

"How bad is it?" inquired his wife as she wrung her hands in dismay.

"Only the White King could fix such a mess as this!" Smith remarked as he shook his head in dismay.

"But as he's not here, we're left with few solutions. I fear neither the king's men nor his horses could mend that crack and put him together again." The White Queen came toward the Dumptys. She raised a hand and waved Smith to her side. The two began to whisper as Mister Dumpty tottered on his feet. The two footmen on either side of him continued to hold him up by his elbows.

Fleur and Clement hovered in the air over the couple, gaping down at them.

"What a mess. You know it's very unfaely to let your inside's bubble out for all to observe," voiced Fleur with displeasure.

"It's hardly his fault," Clement replied, perking his brows at his mate.

"Still, it seems as if he needs to reside in a bubble of some sort. Learn a protection spell or better balance." Fleur shook her head, her red locks swaying down her back between her fluttering wings.

"What about a potion?" Alora turned to Hatter with pleading eyes.

"If we can get him there, then we can get one into him. But moving Humpty so far is quite dangerous for him," Hatter told her with skepticism.

"We should attempt it," Alora insisted.

Looking at the determined set of Alora's shoulders and the steel in her eyes, Hatter slowly nodded. "We will take him to the Resistance, where we can cure him. Let's not delay."

"Oh, my son, are you certain you wish to do this? It's nighttime, after all, and who knows what things are waiting to pounce upon travelers, even in the safety of the camp. After all, don't forget there are spies everywhere." The queen's worried gaze met theirs.

"We will be on guard and take weapons with us. Do not fear, Mother. We must be off." Hatter strode to Smith. "Have an armed guard at the ready and have torches lit. We will need to move quickly back to the Forest of Hidden Wonders to gather the rest of our party before we venture back to the Resistance."

"Why can't you go straight to the Resistance?" wondered the queen.

"We can't leave Alora's armor. It was specially crafted for her. There are essential supplies we simply cannot leave behind." Hatter rubbed his chin in thought.

"We could send a party back for the supplies." Alora's father spoke from beside her.

"I will escort the eggy couple to the Resistance. You can count on me," Cheshire patted his chest.

"It's a very serious task, Cheshire. Are you certain you want the responsibility?" Hatter asked doubtfully.

"Of course. We all are quite fond of Humpty." Cheshire grinned at him. "He has the best anecdotes, and his tap dancing skills are superb."

"Clement and I will go along. You need not fear a thing,"

Fleur interjected.

"Very well. We won't be far behind you. Smith, please see that Cheshire and his party depart at once," Hatter directed after a brief moment's consideration.

The portly faerie rushed forward to usher the Dumpty couple and their entourage from the dining room.

"Must you leave?" The queen closed the distance between them with worry reflecting in her sky-blue eyes. When she reached her son's side, she reached up to cup his cheek. "You've no idea how a mother worries for her child." She turned her head, holding out her free arm to Alora. Alora came to grasp her hand. "For both of you."

"We will be careful, Mother. But we can't stay locked away, doing nothing." Hatter's gentle words seemed to have an effect on his mother.

The White Queen nodded before she stepped away from them, allowing her hands to come to rest by her side. "They're so grown up."

"That they are, indeed," remarked Alora's father with pride overflowing in his voice.

Hatter leaned toward his mother, then pressed his lips to her cheek. "I will see you again, much sooner than the last time."

"See that you do." The queen's smile wobbled.

"We should be going. The later the hour, the greater the risk," cautioned Papa.

The other dinner guests were watching the unfolding scene from behind their chairs. A footman was busily wiping the yoke up from Mister Dumpty's place. A buzz of conversation accompanied the group from the dining room.

By Hatter's side, Alora felt safe. With the added protection of her father and the guards, she didn't fear a thing.

Besides, we're only traveling from one looking glass to another, and both are protected. What is all the fuss about? Surely, it's overcautious… nothing more than a mother's fears.

46

BETRAYAL AND CRUSHING HEARTBREAK

The journey from the dining room through the corridors was made in silence, as guarded eyes took in every shadow and corner in which a menacing foe might lurk. Alora felt frightened as her pulse raced and stars waltzed across her vision. Even in the safety of the White Castle, they needed to be cautious as they neared the secret location of the looking glass. When they rounded the last turn, Hatter paused before a large hanging tapestry. The threads looked worn and depicted a watery scene of faeries dancing along a meadow. Her mate looked down the corridor in both directions, past her father, Fate, and the handful of armed guards. He drew the tapestry aside with one hand while the other traced a palm along the stone wall. In moments, his fingers settled into a groove, pressing into it. With a heaving groan and a puff of dust, a small space in the stone moved backward. Hatter reached for a torch from one of the White Guards, then peered into the small space.

"Take the torch and enter. I shall be directly behind you and our party. I must secure the door before we leave." Hatter turned back to Alora, addressing her. He grinned as she reached for the torch, then she took a tentative step forward.

A breeze ruffled her tresses as she came to a stop in the confined space. Alora squeezed herself to the side wall with Fate coming to stand before her. Together, the pair silently watched as her father and the five soldiers pressed into the chamber. Sealing the doorway, Hatter joined them.

The room became bright with the flickering torch light of the five flames. Hatter leaned toward the stone wall behind the looking glass, rapping on it three times. Alora heard scraping as the stones moved aside. Her eyes caught sight of a tiny mouse that came from one of the opened spaces and jumped atop the looking glass's painted scrollwork. With surprise she realized the mouse was the same one she had met at the tea party.

"Door Mouse, I beg a favor from you," entreated Hatter. "Would you please be so kind as to activate the portal to the Hidden Forest? It's rather serious business, and we mustn't delay."

The mouse yawned before replying, "This has been a busy evening for me. I just allowed a group to use the portal, and now it seems I am needed again. Very well." A tiny gray paw waved in the air above the looking glass as squeaky chanting filled the ether.

A golden glow cast more light into the chamber and glinted from Fate's horn. Hatter gathered Alora's hand and moved them forward.

"Thank you, my friend," Hatter said as he stepped a foot through the looking glass, then quickly disappeared, taking her hand with him.

Alora quickly stepped along after Hatter. Within seconds, she was blinking as heat coated her skin, making it hard for her to catch her breath. Hatter was removing his cravat with jerky movements; then, he was pressing the cloth over her nose and mouth, dispelling the acrid taste and aroma of cinders. Her father came through next and was dazed for a moment until his eyes became wide. He began to cough, then brought his sleeve over his face to block the irritating air.

"A fire! They've discovered the camp's location." Her father's muffled voice held a hint of the panic that she felt rising even more steadfastly within her.

Fate next stepped from the looking glass to join them and immediately threw out his magnificent wings to wrap around the trio, cocooning them to his body. The alicorn's downy feathers couldn't block all of the acrid smoke, but they helped.

Blood-curdling screams from outside of the canvas tent rent the air in two halves as the sounds of battle ensued. Alora's heart beat furiously in her chest as her mouth went dry. It was odd that her skin was becoming sticky when the smoke was so oppressive. Fate's feathers could do nothing to banish the heat from their bodies.

When all five of the White Guards were standing on this side of the looking glass, attempting to quell their own coughing, Hatter peered over one wing and looked them over.

"We can't ignore this danger. We must take action." He swooped under Fate's wing and stormed to the tent's opening to peer out.

"Alora simply isn't ready to face the danger yet. We can't put her at risk," her father said before he raked a hand through his hair regarding her. His teary eyes showed vexation and even a bit of despair.

"Don't you think I realize that? When our bond hasn't been properly solidified, I might not be able to keep a constant eye on her. Those are our subjects out there! Fighting and dying to protect our lands. We can't turn our backs on them," Hatter remarked as he turned back from the opening.

Alora withdrew the cravat from her face, suppressing the urge to cough, and turned toward her father, encircling his waist with her arms. "I will be fine. I know it's risky, but you cannot coddle me here amidst this violence. We must take a stand."

He wrapped his arms around her and kissed the crown of her head. "I know you both are right. But, you are our hope. I can't stand to see that put in jeopardy. We will do as you wish and take action." He released her, removing himself from Fate's protection, and moved to stand by the guards. "On my signal, we rush from the tent and take out as many as we can. Use your swords and your wits."

"Papa! You don't have a sword! Neither do Phillip or I." Alora's heart thundered in her chest, attempting to escape her ribcage as she rose on her tiptoes to see past the edges of Fate's feathers. Sweat peppered her brow and slicked her skin from the intense heat surrounding them. The fire was nearing the tent. Soon, it, too, would be up in flames.

"I can handle myself. It's you and Phillip who need to take care. We will take out the enemy, then give you their swords. Stay here!" Her father strode to the tent opening, waving to the soldiers to follow him outside.

The cries of war, the hiss of blades being drawn, and the cracking pops of the fire consuming everything in its wake were so loud to her ears, they made her flinch. Hatter drew her from under Fate's wings, much to the alicorn's dismay.

Enfolding her in his arms, Hatter peered from the tent. Turning her head to look through the slit in the tent, Alora caught sight of the sky, which was heavy with black plumes of smoke. Turquoise flames leaped high to devour the tops of the trees and the tips of the tents, leaving hollowed-out pits where homes used to be. Tiny sprites brandishing swords, some even holding axes aloft, were valiantly soaring through the smoke and inferno to land hits upon the invaders.

A single raven sailed through the chaos, its wings coasting as it weaved through the fighting. Alora's skin prickled as she recalled seeing a lone raven before and wondered if it was the same.

In less time than she thought possible, two of their guards rushed forward, handing Hatter a sword each. They quickly retreated back into the battle. Handing her one of the blades, Hatter stared deeply into her eyes.

"You will use this only if you must. We will make our way straight to our tent to retrieve your armor. You must don it, and then we can do our part. First, we *must* protect you."

"I will follow your directives." Alora tried to show him that she was brave by smiling with feigned confidence, but her smile wobbled before completely falling away.

"It's quite alright to be frightened; I am." He leaned toward her and pressed a kiss against her forehead. He took a moment to breathe her in.

"I am trusting you, Fate, to keep her safe. Fly her away if you must." Hatter demanded as he pulled away from Alora.

"On my life, my Prince," Fate vowed, tossing his head.

Hatter brought his attention back to his mate, ensuring Alora had the proper grip on her sword. When he was satisfied, Hatter charged from the tent.

Alora swallowed, attempting to moisten her mouth, but ended up capturing smoke in her lungs and coughed. It seemed, so far, she was failing miserably.

With determination, she moved from the tent, dodging and weaving as she reached Hatter's side; Fate was behind her at every pace.

Hatter's sword was arching then swinging, adding more blood to the ground that was already saturated with it. Cringing, Alora adjusted her stance as her silk slippers soaked up the sticky fluid. The squishing sensation between each toe made her want to shriek, but Alora stood her ground, drawing on all of her fortitude to expel the feeling from her mind.

Hatter swung his blade over her head as a helmeted head went flying across the air behind her. Blood leaped up in a fountain from the jagged edges of the neck. Alora couldn't look away from the grizzly sight. As the body slumped forward, Hatter stuck his sword into the muck, grabbed her waist, and lifted her from harm's way. Once he set her down again, Hatter withdrew his sword, striking down a warrior who had attempted to surprise them, then began to run, pulling Alora along behind him.

Fate had fallen behind as his silver horn took out enemy after enemy. He was a whirlwind, stabbing and tearing a path toward them.

Upon almost reaching the tent, they were surrounded by four of the Black Knights. Two engaged Hatter while the other two leered at her. She held up her sword and corrected her stance, not allowing herself to look toward Hatter. Alora would not cower before either of the brutes.

"You think you can take us? You, a mere slip of a girl?" taunted one of her enemies.

"I don't think, I know. But if you're trembling too much to hold your sword, I'll allow you a quick death," she taunted back.

"Oh, feisty are we? Let's see what you can do!" His sword came slashing toward her right, but she parried the strike as she hopped back. She heard one of Hatter's opponents fall to the ground and internally cheered. He would soon be by her side.

The other knight came behind her. Alora ducked, nearly missing the swing of his blade, which sliced a few strands of her hair from her head. She watched in an absentminded manner as the loose pieces floated along the breeze. If she didn't wish to join them, she must do better.

Taking a deep breath, Alora stopped her defensive moves and went on the attack. She was a whirlwind as she landed strike after strike. She bent forward, plunging the tip of her blade into the first guard's stomach. His eyes widened at the attack as he fell heavily onto his armored knees. Alora felt the frosty fingers of hysteria creep into her mind and concentrated on pushing it aside. Now was not the time to fall apart. Before the other fiend could take advantage of her surprise, Hatter cut him down. The faerie joined his friend on the mucky ground. The first guard glared at Hatter as blood seeped from his mouth and from the gaping wound, she had given him in his stomach.

"Look away, my love," commanded Hatter, and Alora obeyed. She didn't want to watch another death take place. Closing her eyes, she heard the thunk of Hatter's sword sliding through flesh, then a dull thud as the faerie's head hit the bloodied ground. She willed herself not to be sick as that would hardly inspire their enemies to flee in terror.

"It's all right now. But we can't dally; more are headed our way," Hatter handed her sword back to her, then reached for Alora's free hand to tug her toward their tent. Their steps slipped, and they had to dig their feet into the mire to keep going.

When they were just a few feet from their tent, a flaming arrow hit the canvas material, setting the tent ablaze. Two savages came toward them at a running clip. Hatter immediately halted their steps, taking a defensive stance. He locked eyes with her, willing and waiting for her to mirror him. When she crouched into her position, Hatter removed his eyes from her to study his attacker. Alora did the same.

*The best way to block a blade is to see which angle it will be cast from...*Hatter's instructions rang in her mind.

Her blade met the tip of her foe's. Alora swung it away to strike at his sword arm. He dodged the blow, returning the gesture, but she was quick enough to sidestep the brute. He closed the distance between them as steel rang against steel in a clatter of reverberation. Alora fought with all of her strength to beat him, but whenever she seemed to have the upper hand, he improvised by moving either away or toward her; Alora constantly had to adjust her footing, even once slipping to one knee. The Black Knight swung for her head, and she catapulted to the side but couldn't regain purchase atop the muck. Her toes were sodden with sludge through her ruined slippers.

Alora's eyes briefly sought out Hatter, who had bested his attacker. He was on to battle another. The slick ground didn't allow any parlay; she slipped yet again, attempting to rise. Panic edged its way into Alora's heart as certainly as if she had been struck by true steel. Her enemy cast her a menacing grin as he sauntered toward her; his steps were sure and his boots never faltered in the path to reach Alora. The soldier brought up his blade to take her life when an axe struck his head, cleaving it in two halves. Carnage and blood poured from the faerie's upper half as he careened her way. She managed to scramble away before his body could pin her down.

Finding her footing, she looked in the direction the axe had come from but didn't catch sight of anyone looking her way. Could it have been an accident that turned in her favor? Behind her, the tent was completely engulfed in flames; there was no way to rescue the contents from inside. They were just possessions, not lives, but Alora did feel remorseful that her beautiful armor might not survive the heat.

She wasn't paying enough attention as she turned to aid Hatter.

"Watch your back!" screamed a voice coming nearer to her.

Alora spun around, bringing her sword arm up, but the foe before her was too close; she couldn't get far enough away to use her sword. Armored arms gripped Alora's middle with punishing force as the breath was forced from her body. Spots began to fill her vision as her heart frantically beat. If this was to be the end of her story, Alora wanted to find the words to tell Hatter how sorry she was to have failed him.

She was jarred forward and had to catch herself from falling face forward into the mire. Her elbows sunk into the squishy ground. Alora was lifted to her feet as gentle hands framed her cheeks. Looking up into the blood-stained face, she saw bottle-green eyes roving across her features.

"You're uninjured?" Remius questioned as he continued to cup her face.

Nodding, she cleared her throat, finding her voice. "I am. You saved me."

"I will always save you, Princess," he whispered as emotions whirled in his eyes.

"How are you here?"

He hesitated before speaking, "I came with the knights."

"The White Knights? Where are Theo and Theolf?" Alora's brows furrowed as she scanned the area.

"Not them," Remius admitted as her eyes flitted back to his. He looked away from her.

She spluttered. "But... No... How? You couldn't possibly do such a thing!"

"It's true."

Hatter came to her side, breathless and covered in sweat and gore. "Release her this instant, you coward!" Rage made the veins in his neck stand out.

"As you will it, my Prince." Remius roughly shoved Alora from his embrace, causing her to stumble.

Hatter caught her around the waist to steady her with one hand as the other pointed the tip of his blade at Remius's heart. "You blackguard!"

Fate galloped forward, leaping between them, creating a barrier, blocking Remius from Alora and Hatter. His purple eyes narrowed. "Traitor!"

Remius held his empty hands up, his face a mask of simmering anger. "You must listen. I don't have much time. I've spent the past weeks infiltrating the Lunar Court's army. Femfaeascent trusts me now. She knows where the Resistance is. You aren't safe there anymore; you aren't safe anywhere."

"You led her here," Hatter accused; it wasn't a question.

Remius nodded, but sadness reflected from his eyes. "A final test of loyalty. You weren't supposed to be here."

"So you would sacrifice your friends? For what?" Hatter was trembling with repressed fury.

"The greater good? The final war? You may think I have become the villain, but that is not so. I had to don a mask and reconfirm my soul to be what was expected of me. This?" Remius gave a dark chuckle. "Is nothing. The worst is yet to come. And I won't play a part in her mad game any longer."

"What do you mean?" Alora blurted out.

Remius avoided meeting her gaze as he addressed Hatter. "You must end me. Now, before her other knights see."

"No!" Alora screamed at him. Hatter let her go, and she skirted around Fate's flank to bang her fists against Remius's chest. "No, I command you to stop this! You can go back with us! You can be redeemed!"

Remius shook his head the entire time she assaulted him. His expression was sorrowful, but there was an air of impatience that clung to him. "She's in here," he pointed to the side of his head when her fists finally stilled. "I can't get her out. I can never be free! Not before she knows too much."

"But... there has to be another way!" Alora turned to Hatter, pleading with her eyes, her very heart, to discover another way to solve the stumbling block.

"We simply can't trust him, Princess," Fate's strained voice gained her attention. "He isn't the Remius you once knew. Your grandmother has twisted his mind."

"I don't believe that!" Alora's fists clenched as her teeth ground together. How could she bear to see Remius ended this way? He had a purpose to serve, a reason to still want to live.

"If you do not, know that Smith is awaiting my presence. Our orders are to slay the White Queen. Make a choice, Prince of Wonderland. If your conscience will not allow you to spill my blood, I will splatter your queen's viscera in her pristine palace."

"No!" Fate roared as his front hooves stamped along the mire.

Alora flew to Hatter and reached up on tiptoes to bring her face closer to his. She wanted to beseech for Remius, to offer any solution. Gazing into Hatter's tortured eyes, her heart plummeted. Alora's chest constricted as her throat painfully tightened.

"I am sorry, my love. There is no other way, no cure." Hatter admitted as grief twisted through their bond.

"I do not accept this! I can heal you," she said as she turned back to Remius. "If we can find a safe place, I will heal your mind. I will spend all my time devoted to the task."

"I cannot allow you to do so. Not while so many innocents are left to suffer. There won't be a Wonderland worth saving if you don't strike soon. I can feel the pull summoning me to make my way to the White Kingdom. I don't know how long I shall be able to resist." Remius looked at Hatter. The two held an entire conversation through their eyes.

Hatter nodded to Remius as Alora felt her heart turn to stone. "If you do this, there will be no us! I cannot allow you to do this!" Alora sent all her rage and heartache along their tether; molten lava passed from her core to his.

"Then so be it. I can't lose you, nor my mother. If he lives and becomes a vessel for the evil queen, I shall surely lose you both. I will wear the villain hat if I must; who else could carry this load but the Hatter? I don't relish his death, but I will celebrate his life by upholding his last wishes. I cannot ignore this request. Not even for you." He paused as he held her gaze. Regret and determination flickered over his face as the muscles in his jaw flexed. "If I must destroy us before we've even really begun, then perhaps this is the destiny we were never meant to escape. I love you with every fiber of my being, but this must be done in order to protect you."

Hatter moved to her side and reached for her hand. He braided their fingers together as he leaned forward to kiss her knuckles. He allowed his lips to linger, tasting her, then releasing her, he swiftly turned on his heel and drove his sword through Remius's chest.

Remius grunted as his eyes widened, then sank to his knees as blood gurgled from his open mouth. His pain-filled eyes sought hers. The top of Alora's head tingled as she dropped down beside Remius, pulling him into her lap and cradling his head to her chest. His eyes locked onto hers.

"It was always you. I was meant to save you. Did you know I dreamed of you long before we ever met?" Remius coughed, grimacing as the movement caused the sword to jar in his wound.

"You dreamed of me? I never knew." Tears fell from her eyes to crash against his blond locks and trail down his dark horns.

"I didn't want you to. I dreamed of my death…" he struggled for breath as his lungs began to rasp.

The sound struck her heart like a fatal blow.

"I have always known that I would leave you." A rush of blood fled from his mouth as he attempted to say more.

"Remius, I do love you." She wasn't sure why she felt compelled to tell him this, but she didn't second guess herself; she didn't have the time. It wasn't a lie…

He reached for her face, leaving a sticky trail of his blood to stain her skin. "I know… You have my heart now more than ever." His bright eyes became dull as they slowly slid closed.

Alora shook him, willing Remius to open his eyes, to grin up at her, to tell her this was all some horrible jest. She wasn't ready to let him go. She would never be ready to let him go. This parting, this final goodbye, was senseless. It was evil and cruel.

A buried part of her heart began to rage, to stir a tempest

through her veins. Her blood was a mix of anguish, disbelief, and bitter ashes.

Hatter bent forward and gave a mighty tug to remove his sword from Remius's chest. It made a sucking sound that brought Alora's locked-away sobs to the surface. She folded her body over Remius, acting as a shield in his death as she hadn't ever been able to safeguard him in life, letting her tears mix with his blood as her own battered heart hemorrhaged. No faerie would harm him ever again; she wouldn't allow it.

The sounds of skirmishes and the screams of those dying began to quiet, and Alora sensed that Hatter valiantly stood guard over them. He would protect her until his dying breath. That was the last thing she desired.

Alora forced the bond between them to wither; she couldn't deal with the wretchedness and heartbreak flowing from him and into her. True, he had lost a friend... But what was Remius to her? She had lost something so much more precious than a mere companion.

She felt a splinter of her soul fracture, floating from her body to ascend to the sky, where it joined the twinkling stars of the heavens. Her burning and swollen eyes grew heavier as her heartbeat thundered in her head. Alora was content to let slumber claim her as the sadness she bore was too great to suffer through. Her will to fight fled as all of the spaces in her mind that had been determined to thrive in Wonderland crumbled into dust. Feeling the pull of the curse taking hold of her, she welcomed the black embrace of oblivion.

47

NO MORE DREAMS OR TRUE LOVE'S KISS

Time was all-consuming; time was nothing. The world was dark.

Alora welcomed the peace as she gathered the splintered pieces of her heart and held them close. She knew she couldn't shove the shards back; they were broken beyond repair. There were moments when the sobs threatened to rip her entirely apart; then there were times when she was so utterly still she doubted if she'd ever really existed at all.

Alora couldn't bring herself to care where she was or what the strange limbo was that she was now a resident of. If this was death, she was content to remain just as she was with no new raw heartbreaks and no more painful partings. The grief was welcome; she felt as if she deserved her fate. Hadn't she been the one to push Remius away? What if she had given him hope? But… How could she have when Hatter consumed her?

Phillip…

Shutting off her mind from thoughts of him had been far easier than she had ever thought possible. Why hadn't she been able to master this feat when he had abandoned her?

It seems as if heartbreak was always to be my fate.

"You must do something! Anything!" commanded a voice. The sound came unbidden into Alora's mind, and she wanted to slip back into the blessed void where nothing could touch her.

She couldn't feel her body, wasn't aware of whether she slept or simply floated along in the ether. The voice was familiar, but she didn't want to remember who it belonged to. They seemed heartbroken, and she couldn't handle any more pain.

"My beloved, you must please attempt to draw away from this darkness. If not for me, for your father, who is wracked with grief. For yourself! You have so much to live for. I will leave you once I know you are here and whole if you so wish it. Forgive me for what I have done," another anguished voice pulled her from the peace.

It was curious that she felt a gentle tug in the area where she imagined her heart would be if she still had one.

"My dear, you've had enough time to yourself. It's time for you to wake up." Alora's ears perked up at the beautiful melody of the voice who spoke to her. She desired to discover who it belonged to because, suddenly, beauty was something she longed to revel in.

She longed to dance in a flower-filled meadow as twinkling stars lit the sky above her and iridescent bubbles tickled her skin.

"You can certainly do that if you allow this curse to be broken."

"How did you hear my thoughts?" Alora questioned in bewilderment.

"I am all-knowing and far more powerful than most believe me to be."

"Why do you wish for me to allow the curse to lose its hold over me? If you are all-knowing, then you must understand the tragedy I allowed to happen." Alora furrowed her brows and became alarmed when she felt the movement on her face. She didn't wish to go back, not when more partings would be catastrophic to her battered soul.

"You'll find that life is filled with sorrows, some monumental and some minuscule. However, there is also much joy and love to be found as well. You are *so* loved Alora. You are missed and mourned for. Your subjects and your family are holding out hope that you can be woken to rejoin Wonderland. While I could force the issue, the decision is up to you." The voice sounded closer to her this time.

Alora withdrew deeper into herself, not bothering to care about responsibilities or bossy beings who sought to force her back into an existence that she no longer fancied.

"We've tried every known and experimental cure, Your Majesty. I am at a loss as to how we should proceed." A heavy sigh filled the chamber.

"Thank you, Cormack. I appreciate all you have done. It seems as if we must simply wait."

"At least she's still beautiful! It would be terribly unfaely if her body began to rot."

"Fleur! You can't say things like that!"

"Calm yourself, Clement. I didn't mean any harm," the voice tutted.

Alora was intrigued to know who the voices were discussing. She allowed her mind to wake up, to grasp onto the tether tied to her heart. While she couldn't focus her vision, as her eyelids felt like leaden stone, her ears captured every sound.

Concentrating on her body, she felt a smooth surface beneath her. A sensation like fingertips was coasting up and down the back of her hand. She tried to twitch her fingers as she attempted to open her eyes. It was too much for her. Panic began to set in when she felt trapped in her heavy, chilled body. It felt like a hundred years had passed since she was last aware of her body. She would much rather welcome the nothingness than the prison of her own body.

"You should rest, Your Majesty," a tiny voice suggested gently.

"I don't want to leave her, Maia." The sorrow dripping from each word the man said was like a dagger to her heart that dug in further and further.

I know that voice…I'm here, Papa! I'm so sorry…

Her thoughts were erratically surging through her mind. Was she regretful for giving in to the curse? Wasn't it always going to play out? She had been dying for weeks.

The chatter of the voices pulled Alora from her ruminations. The voices began to resonate in her mind as she remembered who each one belonged to.

"We can bathe her and arrange her hair. It really should be done," Fiona timidly said.

"That's a faetastical idea," agreed Fleur.

Deep weariness was pulling her back to the bleak inkiness. Alora wasn't strong enough to fight it.

The curse, she realized. *It's still attempting to kill me.*

"I THINK YOU'LL WANT TO KNOW THAT SMITH HAS BEEN DEALT with. He was put to death for treason against the Crown. My mother suspected that he was not loyal, but she thought it best to keep the manservant where she could watch him. He was much too close from my perspective. I am only thankful he was stopped in time. They found the betrayer hidden in my mother's bedchamber, in her wardrobe to be exact." A hushed voice whispered close to her ear.

Alora knew the voice. It was once the most beloved one that she knew. No, that wasn't quite true, was it? A lance of pain stabbed her heart, and Alora reached for the darkness and succumbed to it.

"YOU SHOULD KISS HER!" FLEUR COMMANDED FROM NEAR HER head.

"Nonsense, that's a violation of her person," Maia interjected.

"Stuff it! She's practically dead; I think her rights have been suspended," Fleur huffed.

"Maybe a quick kiss on the cheek?" suggested Fiona.

"When have you ever heard of a cheek kiss breaking any curse?" Fleur asked with exasperation. Alora imagined that her eyes were rolling in her head.

"She wouldn't want me to," Hatter dejectedly replied.

"The truth is that none of us know what she'd want. It's not as if we can ask her!" admonished Maia.

The trio of faeries bickered over Alora's head, and she let her mind wander. Did she want to wake? If it meant that she was to exist in this state for the rest of her life, then the answer was a resounding… What?

Her heart hurt. She still felt every pain. Faeries were arguing over her, and Alora was helpless to put a stop to it. At least if she were awake, she could leave this chamber. Perhaps there was still good that needed to be done. Was she up to the task?

Her father was in pain if the ache in his voice had been

any indication to go by. Perhaps it was a good thing that she hadn't been able to see his face. That might have further broken her.

Alora felt delicate and weak. Brittle pieces of herself floated in emptiness. The complete opposite of what Wonderland needed from her. Remius had died because of her; that was irrefutable.

If only I had never chased the white rabbit, I could have stayed and learned how to harness my healing abilities. But then, I wouldn't have been reunited with Hatter. We made some of the most beautiful memories. Why do I always feel so torn between these two men who are complete opposites?

Did that matter when the bond was still and quiet? Had she completely obliterated it? Did the thought worry her? All of these musings weighed her down much more than her lifeless body seemed to. And she was so very, very tired.

WARM LIPS PRESSED AGAINST HER FOREHEAD, MAKING ALORA long to reach up and clasp the head closer to her. They lingered on her skin as the warmth traveled all the way to her toes, which wanted to curl in her slippers with delight. When the soft lips left her, she wanted to cry out, demanding that they return. Alora mourned for the comfort, the security the action had given to her.

The scraping of chair legs against the floor was like screams in the silent atmosphere.

"Did you know the first time I remember seeing you in the meadow during the tea party, the sight of you simultaneously stopped my heart and sped it up? I should have known then that you would be my entire world, my purpose, and my joy," Hatter dryly chuckled.

Boots shuffled against the ground as the chair squeaked.

"I can't imagine you never waking up, never gazing into

your exquisite eyes. I would give anything, do anything, to get you back, even if that means you hate me so much you never want to lay eyes on me again. I would leave you so that you could find happiness and flourish. I wish you centuries of joy and love, so much unending love. If only you would come back to us."

Alora's heart ached as unshed tears leaped to her eyes. She could feel his love, even without the bond; it was a living entity that filled nearly every crevice of her heart. Slowly, she reached out with her mind and heart, searching for any thread of the bond. Alora caught a tiny knot and slowly, diligently, concentrated on untying it. Each untangle cast off a flare of golden light that pulsed in time with her heart. Taking a moment, she listened for the heartbeats that echoed along the bond. Hatter's beat in tandem with hers, and gratitude flooded her. Even after everything, their hearts still beat in tandem.

It wasn't hate she bore for Hatter; it had never been, and it could never be. Alora hated that he had to be the one who stole Remius's life. Hated that the action caused them both to lose bits of themselves. Hated that she had allowed a severing between them. Most of all, she despised herself for putting doubt in either of their hearts and minds. Hatter was hers, and she was his. But how was the curse to be broken?

The bond thrummed from her heart straight to Hatter.

"My love?" he asked incredulously. "Are you returning to me?" Hatter loomed over her, having risen from the chair. His breath caressed her face as he hovered above her.

Concentrating, she gathered all of her love and sent it along the bond to him. His indrawn breath came out in a startled sound.

"We have used every method to wake you. Would you forgive me if our first kiss was not one you agreed to? I would never take liberties, but this is the last remaining hope. Hate me if you must, but I can't *not* do this." His plush, insistent lips came to rest against hers with gentle pressure. Then, with more certainty, he deleted any space between their mouths, holding still as their flesh melded together.

The tingling began in her fingers and toes, and especially along her lips. The bond was receiving his feelings of love and longing. Alora knew that what he most wanted was to vanquish the curse and return her to him.

Her lips curved into a smile as Hatter continued to press his lips against hers. Her arms lost their heaviness, and Alora was able to lift them; she encircled his neck with them. Trembling began in his shoulders as the rest of him followed suit. Hatter pulled away from her face, and he lifted her from the bed, then he sat with her in his lap to face him as shudders raced through him. Hatter hid his head against her chest, allowing his tears to fall.

"Shhh, I am here," she tried to soothe him with her voice as her fingers dug into his hair and unsettled his hat. She couldn't tell where she ended, and he began; Alora only knew that she never wanted to let him go.

Her heart was being mended; tiny stitches were being sewn back together. They both needed to cling to each other, needed to repair the damage that was done. How long the lovers remained locked against each other, basking in the love pulsing along the bond, she couldn't tell. Nothing mattered more than these moments with her other half and ensuring he knew she was safe and whole.

Hatter settled down, withdrawing his handkerchief from his vest. He wiped his damp face, then folded the linen. Taking a deep breath, he looked up to meet her gaze. Ever-so-gently, he brought the handkerchief against her skin and soaked up her tears.

Alora smiled at him. Her heart still had fractures, and an entire corner of it was forever lost. But she knew that, in time, all the cracks would seal. It would be whole again, except for the piece that belonged to Remius; that would never heal, and in truth, she never wanted it to.

Hatter was her future, and even though it pained her, Alora knew that she needed to make peace and let Remius rest in her memories, and when the sorrow hit, she would grieve for him. True love's kiss had awakened her, and true love's kiss would see her achieving her dreams.

Her thoughts flew to the kiss Remius had given her before he left her. It hadn't been strong enough to break the curse... But Hatter's kiss had been.

There were two dualities to her. One Fae and one human. Maybe it was her human half that was destined to love Remius. Her Fae heritage was just too strong to deny.

Two men to love in one lifetime, who loved me just as unfailingly back. How very blessed I have been. I will never stop loving Remius, and that is as it should be...

48

IT'S IN HIS KISS

"If you wish it, I will go," Hatter looked down at their joined hands, not meeting her eyes.

"Never. I could never wish that. I am so sorry that I..." Alora searched for the appropriate words, but they failed her. She wasn't sorry that she had mourned Remius. In those moments after Hatter took Remius's life, how was she to have behaved? She could explain it, but would Hatter be receptive to hearing the truth? Was it a kindness to him to reveal what Alora had discovered?

"You do not have to explain a single thought to me." He locked his gaze with her.

"I do! You deserve it. I think Remius was destined for me just as you are. But he was never meant to grow old by my side; that's your place and none others."

He waited patiently for her to gather her thoughts while he continued to rub soothing circles along her back.

"I cannot dispute what Remius meant to me any longer. It wasn't fair to him, and it's not to me either. I mean to honor him as I always should have done while he was with us. I believe there are two halves to my heart; while you belonged to the majority of it, he held a corner. I am half Fae, so it stands to reason my heart wished to honor that no matter what predicament or hardships were brought our way. Remius was always meant for me, just as you are. But fate saw to it that he wasn't the one I would share a bond with. He wasn't the one meant to break this curse. In the end, Remius said that he dreamed of me. His fate..." She looked away from Hatter because confessing this hurt her.

Reaching out, he brought his index finger up to tip her chin toward him. "That makes sense, in a way, I suppose. I could not have shared you for all of Wonderland. That would have been difficult. But, I never would have wanted to see you suffer..."

"So fate stepped in and made a path forward for us. I don't know how to... Would never have wanted to expel his place from my heart. But losing Remius after realizing what he was to me, I can't let that go. When I told him that I loved him, I meant it. Perhaps just not with my entire heart. Can you accept that?" She frowned as her shoulders drooped.

"I will accept it. I can't begrudge Remius for loving you, not when he gave his life to protect you. In the end, that's all that matters." Hatter paused and took a deep breath as he reached into his waistcoat pocket and retrieved something that was a golden color. "I removed this from his body while the slumbering curse held you in its clutches, with the express purpose of giving it to you once you woke. I hoped this would bring you some measure of comfort." He opened his palm, and resting in its center was Remius's heart-shaped ring.

Alora's breath whooshed from her body as a single tear wound its way down her pale cheek. Gingerly, she reached for it, staring at it. No words could form on her tongue.

"I thought perhaps you'd like to one day hold it in your hand, maybe dangle it from a chain around your neck." He gently told her.

Clearing her throat, Alora asked, "You wouldn't object?"

"I have no right to do such a thing. I stand by my earlier words. I only wish for you to find some measure of peace, and if this token can offer you that, then I am content. You're here; what more could I possibly ask for?" He tilted his head to better observe her.

"Here and yours. Please don't leave me. That I couldn't bear."

"Never. How many times, my love, must I tell you that you're mine and I am yours? Perchance another kiss might convince you?" His eyebrows raised and wiggled, bringing a lightness to the moment that her aching heart sorely needed.

"A proper kiss?" she teased.

"Was my curse-breaking kiss not memorable enough for you?" He brought a hand to his heart in mock dismay.

"It was very remarkable; after all, it brought me back to you. However, I always dreamed that when you did finally kiss me, it would be…more."

"More?" Hatter repeated, then cleared his throat. "Yes, a do-over for a first kiss is in order. I'm more than certain this next kiss will steal your breath as your toes delightfully curl."

The beaming smile was all the permission he needed as Hatter brought his lips against hers. He nibbled her bottom lip with his teeth, then moved over to each seam of her mouth as he fit his lips to hers. The warmth of her mate's nearness and the tingling along Alora's scalp and down her spine did, in fact, make her toes curl.

She sighed in wonder with delight as he moved his lips along her own. The tip of Hatter's tongue darted from his mouth as he tasted her. Alora couldn't mask the surprise as her mouth parted. Hatter was quick to slide his velvety tongue into her mouth as she instinctively opened her mouth wider for him. Alora chased his tongue with her own as the taste of tea and honey added to the overwhelming sensations. She became aware of her hands tangling in his silky copper strands, not bothering to wonder where his hat had fallen.

Hatter drew her closer against him as bright lights twinkled behind her closed eyelids. Alora's heart was filling with warmth as tears gathered in her eyes.

When he broke away from her, they were both breathing heavily. Alora was left lightheaded, and she relished in the delicious tingle of his lips that had permanently marked hers. Hatter laid his forehead against hers as their breaths mingled.

The door banged open, hitting the wall as Fleur's anxious voice burst the bubble of euphoria that had descended upon the room.

"Was I right? Was this what true love's kiss has done?" Fleur flew up before their heads, and Alora turned to look at the tiny sprite.

"It is," answered Hatter with a grin.

Fleur clapped her hands together as she merrily danced in the air. "I knew it! I am never wrong, you know. I should've insisted you kiss her sooner. What wasted time we've been plagued with. Now, I must inform you that you simply will have to partake in a mating ceremony this very evening if I can manage to arrange all the details. You can't go around kissing fair maidens, especially princesses, and not be brought to task." She wiggled her index finger at Hatter.

"I'm not a complete bounder, Fleur. I am a Prince of Wonderland, and my word is my honor, and my duty is to my beloved. I will happily agree to a mating ceremony." Hatter stood and settled Alora back onto the bed.

Through the opened door, Alora caught sight of her father making his way toward them. A smile lit up his face as he rushed by Fate, standing guard, to reach her side.

"My dearest daughter, you have been returned to us! It is a miracle! Cormack!" Her father turned his head to shout.

"I am here, Your Majesty," the elf assured him as he came to stand beside them. Reaching for her hand, his fingers found purchase on her wrist, and he was silent as he counted her pulse.

Everyone was silent, watching on as the elf let her hand go, then peered into her eyes. Cormack nodded and turned to address her father. "She's well. I see no sign of the curse. There is no darkness in her eyes, and her heart is beating unhindered. Her coloring looks good. I do believe that the curse is truly banished." Cormack looked to Hatter. "Well done, my Prince."

Hatter inclined his head. Alora saw her father's brow furrow as he studied her mate.

"How was the curse broken?" her father inquired as he crossed his arms and perked a brow at Hatter.

"Ah, well. It was Fleur who gave me the idea that a kiss of true love would wake her." Hatter shifted nervously on his feet.

"And are you in the habit of kissing slumbering maidens?" Papa frowned again.

"I am not, nor have I ever been, a rogue, Your Majesty. I have never, in fact, kissed another in any flirtatious or salacious manner. I was content to await my fated mate." Hatter held his stare.

"We were in the process of planning our mating ceremony before you discovered I had woken," Alora interjected. "Fleur had promised she could arrange things for this evening."

All eyes moved to Fleur, who was startled as she became the center of attention. "Yes, well, I must be off if I am to pull this all together. There are so many details to be seen to. If you'll excuse me, I shall take my leave." Fleur didn't wait for a response. Her wings beat furiously, carrying her from the chamber.

"Well, this is quite an auspicious day. I am pleased to know we have you back and will soon see that you are bonded before we have to battle the Lunar Court," her father said as his eyes moved to his daughter again. "I could not have parted with her to any other."

"I am not leaving you. I am simply fulfilling my destiny." Alora slipped to the edge of the bed and gingerly stood.

Hatter's hands came to her sides to steady her, and Alora gratefully cast a smile at him. When she felt as if her legs would carry her weight, she turned toward her father. Reaching up onto her tiptoes, she pressed a kiss against his cheek.

"You will always be important to me. Just because our family grows doesn't mean you won't be important to me. Besides, who shall lead Wonderland to the coming peace if not for you? I still have much to learn that only you may teach me." When she pulled away from Papa, he grabbed for a hand, tenderly holding onto her.

"You are the culmination of all my hopes and dreams. I could not have ever wished for a better daughter. Forgive me for forgetting that fact for so long after the passing of your Mama."

"Was she your fated mate?" Alora couldn't help but ask. She found the idea curious but believed she already knew his answer.

"I believe she was. Though she was purely human, our hearts melded together, and she was my shining star." His smile was dimmed by sadness as he gazed at her.

Alora patted the back of his hand with her free one. He squeezed her fingers, then let go as he stepped back.

"Well, let's get some nourishment into you, and then we can celebrate until the dawn. If Fleur has her way, she'll be back with dresses for you to try on in practically no time at all." Her father strode from the room with purpose and a smile on his face. It was difficult to believe that he was the same being when he was so very different.

Hatter reached for her waist, and she leaned into him as Cormack followed after the soon-to-be king.

"Are you well enough to walk to the dining hall, or should I bring something back for you? I daresay your father is ordering a feast for you either way." Hatter nuzzled the flesh of her ear, causing a shiver to travel down her body.

"I think I'd like to leave this room. I feel as if I've been here forever."

"Not forever, but two weeks is much too long to not see your smile nor lock my eyes with yours." He drew her hand to his forearm and escorted her from the chamber. "I can't believe after everything we've endured, there's joy ahead. That we'll be joined and bonded and I shall never have to guess how you're feeling or if you're in harm's way. That means the world to me." He bent toward her, placing a kiss on the crown of her head.

"You are all I've ever wanted or dreamed of. I can scarcely breathe from the idea that soon we'll be allowed to kiss without interruptions." Her voice was teasing as she stared straight ahead.

Fate trailed after them as they slowly traversed the corridor. Shadows danced across the pale walls as the wall sconces glowed.

"I'm especially looking forward to no interruptions," Hatter told her with a gleam in his eye, whispering so her guard couldn't catch his words.

I hope that we get this one night to ourselves without intrusion or bloodshed and that all will be safe. Just one night to know what it's like to lose myself to these feelings that are so much larger than I ever imagined they could be.

49

THE BUTTERFLIES & THE BEES?

The array of silks and the rainbow of materials that shimmered before Alora filled her with glee. It was the early evening of her mating ceremony, and Fleur and Meara were helping her choose what she would wear. Alora stood before her full-length looking glass as she held a copper-colored dress against herself. The color reminded her of autumn leaves as well as the highlights that glimmered in Hatter's hair. It was breathtaking; she couldn't wait to wear it. Her pulse sped up at the thought of matching her fated mate in any way possible, as this would be a tribute to her adoration toward him.

"It's quite stunning," Fleur enthused as she flew in a circle next to Alora's head.

"Indeed it is. You will look like a vision in that shade, and we can style your tresses in upswept curls, pinning it at your crown, then settling the tiara in the center." Meara came to stand behind her. "Soft curls to hang down either side of your face would be so romantic!"

Alora managed to stifle the squeal that wanted to burst from her. Tingles raced up her spine as a rosy hue stained her skin. Her eyes shone with joy.

"I can't wait for tonight. Is this really happening, or am I still trapped in the curse?" Alora suddenly felt a pool of simmering magma laced with uncertainty jumbling in her stomach. It completely erased her joy-filled thoughts. If this was all nothing more than a dream, she wouldn't be able to stem the tears once she woke. If she ever woke…

Fleur *tsked,* breezing to a stop right before Alora's nose and bopped it. "You are *not* still cursed. This is your preview of the happily-ever-after that awaits you. Take these moments and revel in them. They'll never come again. You deserve this taste of merriment. Everything that comes after tonight we will deal with together; you're loyal friends and steadfast subjects. Perhaps it's time to change the topic to what you may expect once you and Hatter are all alone." Fleur gestured to the dressing table with an impatient hand.

Alora followed her prompt, making her way to the satin-padded bench seat. Once she was seated, Alora waited to hear what the sprite had to impart upon her.

Brimming with joy once again, Alora let her friend's words continue to sink in as soft ripples waved in her heart. She was free and whole. No lingering death would steal any more pieces of her soul. No nightmares would ever again squander the moments of her dwindling life. Never again would Alora wander while slumbering. She could take comfort in the idea of being in Hatter's arms, safe, loved. They'd have a long life together, and that was all they dreamed of.

Fleur cleared her throat, bringing Alora's mind back to the present.

"Now, I know your mother passed away when you were still very young. It's my duty to have this conversation with you, to allay your fears and help you understand what occurs between mates in the privacy of their *special alone time,*" Fleur began as she crossed the space separating them. Clearing her throat again, not quite meeting Alora's eyes, she continued.

"You see, when certain feelings are involved, and you want to express those emotions…you take certain steps to solidify your bond. Hatter will likely understand what those steps are. You needn't really do a thing, unless you wish to. Remember that Hatter's heart is yours. He'd never do anything *truly terrible* to you. You might even enjoy the entire thing."

"I see," Alora gave a single nod. She was confused as the smile fell from her face.

"You know enough to get by," decided Fleur with a nod of her head as her fiery hair swayed forward.

"You're making a muddle of this entire conversation," Meara huffed as she regarded them. "You've probably frightened her as well."

"Have I?" questioned Fleur with regret, causing her eyes to widen.

"I'm not exactly frightened…" Alora trailed off as she studied her fingertips.

"You are." Fleur deflated as her shoulders slumped. "It's just, well, you know what occurs between the butterflies and the bees?"

"The what?" Alora perked a brow, looking from Fleur to Meara.

"Oh, for all the realm's sake. I haven't yet had my own mating ceremony, but even I know that it's nothing to be scared of. It's a natural and necessary conclusion to making the bond whole. To merge your heart and soul with Hatter's. What could be more glorious than that? Two beings loving each other enough to wade through the learning process of what makes each other tick," Meara said with confidence as Fleur nodded along enthusiastically.

"Exactly as Meara has stated. It's a beautiful experience and one you'll come to treasure. Need we say anything more on the subject?" questioned Fleur as her eye twitched.

"No, I do believe that will suffice." Alora smiled at her,

finding humor in the sprite's unease. It was such a juxtaposition to how Fleur usually carried herself: sure and commanding.

"Oh, thank the Fates! This has all been rather challenging. I think I'm a much better diplomat than a teacher of such things. If you ask certain faeries, I'm quite terrible with politics. That is saying quite a great deal." Fleur motioned to the dress that Alora still held clutched to her. "Let's make you sparkle, Princess. I can't wait to see you mated."

Rising to her feet, Alora went behind the screen and removed her robe. The scent of jasmine and vanilla clung to her skin from the bathwater she had soaked in. After Meara helped her to don her underclothes, she stood still as the coppery dress moved over her head and shoulders to hug her form as it slid to brush the tops of her satin-slippered feet. The silk felt like rose petals against her skin, making her feel like a princess.

Meara ushered her out from behind the screen, back over to the dressing table. When she was once again seated, Alora watched through the looking glass as Meara's adept hands arrange her hair. With twisted curls and many pins, her coiffure was soon complemented by the sparkle of the tiny rubies set in the golden tiara. Turning her head in one direction, then the other, the light reflected from the rubies, casting the illusion of flames waltzing in her hair.

"You are magnificent!" Fleur exclaimed, sitting on the handle of the silver hairbrush.

"Thank you, and thank you, Meara, for managing my hair." Alora smiled from Fleur to Meara, hoping she was properly expressing her gratitude. It meant so much for her to be able to let them know how much she appreciated and valued them. Alora never wanted to take advantage of kindness and friendship again.

"Now, some silver powder to offset all the copper and gold. You will completely steal Hatter's breath away," Meara stated as Alora closed her eyes to allow the powder to be applied to her face, neck, and just above the low neckline of her dress. She held her breath so that she wouldn't breathe in the residue.

Rising and returning to the full-length looking glass, Alora took in her reflection. How could this be her? She had changed so much in the time she'd been in the Faerie Realm. Her eyes were brighter; maybe that was simply due to joy, but still, they did seem larger.

Alora's gaze lowered to her fingers. They were more elongated, her nails naturally polished and longer. She felt radiant and sent her adoration and love along the tether to her bond with her mate. Within moments, Alora was receiving a return of his joy and love for her. It filled her heart, making her feel truly blessed.

How is this all real? I am as light as a feather; I could practically float to the ceiling. I never knew such happiness was possible and that Phillip would be mine for the long centuries that we'll live side by side. Please, dear Fates, don't let me have such short moments of joy to just take them from me in the battle to come. I cannot exist without him. Worse, should something happen to me, would Phillip return to the abyss that claimed all his memories?

When the knock sounded at the door, it was her father who turned the handle, peering in. His face showed equal sides of elation and trepidation. The smile on his face trembled, which caused Alora's steps to falter as she came to meet him. He reached for her hands.

"You look so grown up. How I wish your mother could see you now. But she's here with us in spirit." The shine of his eyes seemed to dim.

"I miss her every day," replied Alora as tears filled her eyes. She blinked furiously to regain the hold on her sentiments. Thinking of her emotions, Alora realized they were quick to change from one extreme to another. Hadn't most of Wonderland been the same way? Was it an attribute of the Fae race? Did faeries feel more than most creatures?

"We have our memories; they must be enough." Papa tried to console her.

She gave a single nod as she linked her arm with his. With his free hand, he reached to give her hand a gentle pat.

"Well, let's not dally. You have a mate to be bonded to." Fleur clapped her hands, then flew to the opened door, exiting the room.

With a curtsey, Meara followed the tiny sprite from the chamber.

"Are you ready?" her father inquired.

"I am. I feel as if I've never been more ready. It's all the things that come next that give me pause. But we shall do as we must and endeavor to free this kingdom." Alora took a deep breath, letting it slowly release.

Her father led her from the bedchamber with Fate's hoof falls sounding behind them. They traversed the dirt-packed corridor, taking twists and turns until they came to a stop before the doorway.

"Through that doorway lies your destiny. Being bonded to your fated mate is the most special event that will ever happen to you. All the stars align, and even the ebb of the waters in Faerie will still for the moments that you accept each other, promising all of your tomorrows one to another. Are you certain that you're ready?" Papa looked down to meet her eyes. Swirling emotions of sadness and loss were mingling in his midnight orbs.

"I am," was all Alora said as Fate came around them to push the massive doors open, using the tip of his horn.

Alora's breath caught in her lungs as the beauty of the garden was revealed to her. It had been spectacular before; now, with ribbons and more twinkling lights, it was paradise.

Matching her steps to her father's, they entered the garden as butterflies in a variety of colors flew through the air. She had a moment of panic at the flittering omens, but immediately she felt Hatter's love and assurance flow to her. These weren't here to harm her, nor were they a harbinger of doom.

The fragrance of a mixed bouquet, and all the scents combined along the air, brought her smile out in full bloom. Her heartbeat sped up as jitters coasted over her skin.

Crushed flower petals littered the ground, paving the way to a white trellis. Standing under the trellis was Hatter and, to her surprise, the same cobalt-capped faerie who had presided over Fleur and Clement's ceremony. Her eyes alighted onto Froggy, who she hadn't seen in weeks. Alora was delighted that her amphibian friend would be participating in their secret ceremony as well.

Just before Alora and her father reached the trellis, the White Queen canted her head to look at them. Her face flowered into a smile of pure joy, and Alora felt gratitude that such an affectionate woman was so welcoming to her. She would be such a gentle mother-in-law.

Cheshire grinned at Alora from his spot beside Fleur. Fleur waved a tiny hand at her, and Alora smiled back in return as her heart swelled with happiness and love. Clement gave her a brief nod.

There were so many of the faeries that she had come to know, now seated to watch her being mated to Hatter. She spied Gillie, a few of the hobgoblins, Meara, and so many others that she had only ever seen in passing, but had never been introduced to her. The kind eyes of many were on her, and Alora grew warm with unease at being the center of their attention.

Her conscience still plagued her that this ceremony was being kept such a secret from those they were charged with protecting. But secrecy has been paramount in the planning so that no word could possibly reach the Lunar Court. Alora didn't want her subjects to feel slighted or not welcomed at such an important event. Once again, Hatter calmed her by sending warm thoughts through their connection.

Hatter smiled so beautifully at her. All of his emotions were being cast her way, blending with her own feelings of euphoria. They were a symphony of love and adoration that flowed back and forth between them like the waters of the tide. She didn't care whether she looked like a love-struck fool; she could no more banish her smile than she could capture the moon.

"You're here," Hatter breathed as he reached for her hand once she halted before him. He was dressed all in midnight blue except for his black cravat and the copper top hat that rested on his head.

Her father released her hand, then leaned down to press a soft kiss onto her cheek. "You have been my greatest accomplishment," he whispered into her ear.

Alora turned her head toward her father as a watery smile blossomed on her face. They locked their gazes, and a surge of warmth wrapped around her heart.

When he stepped away from her, Alora watched him take his seat; then she redirected her attention to Hatter. He reached for her hand and drew her to his side. Together, hand in hand, they took a few steps to the table that stood central within the trellis. Froggy gave a cheerful croak toward them.

"We are gathered together to witness this mating ceremony between Prince Phillip and Princess Alora," began the lady. "Their union was predestined to bring peace to our kingdom. We, your family and friends, bear witness to this auspicious occasion. We thank the Fates for bringing these two halves together to make a whole. Princess Alora, do you accept Prince Phillip as your fated mate? Do you vow to stay by his side, allowing your bond to flourish no matter what hardships you will face?"

"I accept Phillip wholeheartedly. Every particle of my being belongs to him. I freely give him my heart, my body, my dreams, and all of my love," Alora whispered as her words carried on the gentle breeze to those who were watching them. She felt her throat tighten as tears filled her eyes. Hatter squeezed her hands as his own eyes shimmered.

How is such happiness possible?

"Prince Phillip, do you accept Princess Alora as your fated mate? Do you vow to protect her, to treasure her, making her the pearl in your seas, no matter what battles you will face? Do you accept your bond while nurturing it to flourish? To gently steer you back together should you ever drift apart?" The gentle-faerie took a breath to await his answer.

"I accept Alora and willingly give her my heart, which I lost the moment we met. I offer her my heart, my undying devotion, and my relentless protection. My dreams and all of my tomorrows are hers." Hatter swallowed, which, combined with the half-formed bond, left her in no doubt that he was just as affected by these moments as she.

A golden glow lit each of them from within, chasing the shadows away with the brilliance of their love. The light expanded to encompass the area sheltered under the trellis. Alora felt her heart being filled as the tether between them grew, knitting itself even stronger. How could one heart contain so much love?

The gentle-faerie reached out her hand to the pillar which separated them from her. Cupping the silver chalice in both of her hands, she raised it high into the air. "The Fates have brought you together. Let no force come between you, and let the glow of your love surround everything you do, one for another. Build your lives as indestructible fortresses where you will serve each other as well as our kingdom." She held the goblet out to Hatter, who nodded to her as he took it.

Bringing the chalice to her lips, Hatter tipped it so Alora could catch a drop of faerie wine in her mouth. The sweetest flavors of berries and chocolate met her tongue as she swallowed. Placing her hands over his, Alora helped to move the goblet toward his mouth. With a grin, Hatter took a sip.

The robed lady took the cup back once they finished, setting it back down. Next, she retrieved the ivory ribbon. Hatter reached around Alora's waist and wrapped his hand around hers, as the faerie weaved the ribbon in delicate knots, securing their left hands together. The symbolism of the dedication and acceptance gathered their individual lights as they traveled through their palms to their hearts. A shower of sparkling stars sprang from their joined hands; then the lights flared before dying out.

"Huzzah!"

"Well done!"

"At long last!"

"Ribbit!"

And many other cheers and congratulations poured from the ceremony's attendants as Alora blushed. She shared a delighted laugh with Hatter, who drew her to him. He grabbed her around her waist to twirl her around.

"Now I may breathe easier, knowing we are forever tied together and that nothing can ever separate us. How I love you, my darling Alora." Hatter's lips skimmed the shell of her ear as he whispered to her. Shivers of delight soared through her.

Dizzy with love and unending joy, Alora felt as if she was still spinning, even after he set her back down. Her father came to greet them, throwing his arms around them both as he brought them to him in an embrace.

"I am so happy for you both!" Alora's father enthused as he released them.

Before either could reply, a crashing boom filled the atmosphere around them. The ground shook as silver leaves and Fae lights rained down upon them. Hatter crouched, settling Alora between his legs and protecting her head by enclosing her in his arms. He quickly unwound the ribbon joining them together, allowing her to free her arms, which Alora wrapped around him, clinging to him as the entire world upended. Foggy leaped toward them, and Hatter reached out a hand to grab it, pulling the frog safely to Alora's lap, then tucked the ribbon into his waistcoat pocket.

No! Not yet, it's too soon! True, the bond is solid, but I wanted time to revel in our joining and to lock gazes as we danced under the stars. This night should never ever have been marred with the possibility of having to vanquish my own grandmother.

50

ENEMIES & ALLIES

When the sound of falling debris fell silent, and the dirt floor stopped vibrating, the White Queen gave a shouted order. "To the portals! Arm yourselves!"

Hatter rose, helping Alora rise to stand beside him. The ground shook again as bits of dirt began to flake from the walls and ceiling. A deafening crack rang out, and all of the enchantments surrounding them splintered and broke.

"Guard her with your life, my boy!" commanded Alora's father as he sprung to his feet. He turned on his heel, ushering the queen through the barren garden. A bevy of guards drew their swords and they closed ranks around the monarchs as they fled the chamber.

Faeries rushed to take their leave with unsteady steps as more explosions rocked the space. Some winged faeries coughed as they rose high into the air, having to contend with the falling dust. It was utter chaos.

Cheshire floated over to them with a feline growl. "This is so unfaely and boorish of Femfaeascent. On this evening of all." The tabby rolled his bright eyes.

The gentle-faerie threw back her hood, allowing tendrils

of her sea-colored hair to trail behind her. Alora gasped as the faerie hurried past them. Pointing to her back, Alora spoke.

"The Weaver?" Alora looked to Cheshire for an explanation.

"She is many things to many beings and often does not appear until expressly needed." Cheshire blinked his bottle-green eyes at her. His tail was twitching in agitation as another explosion rent the air.

"We haven't the time!" Hatter exclaimed as he tugged on Alora's hand, pulling her after him. She clutched Froggy to her chest and had to run to keep her mate's pace as they exited the garden. In the corridor, the dirt-packed walls were fissuring as the turquoise flames in the fragmenting glass of the lanterns licked the walls.

"We're all in danger of suffocating and being buried alive in no time at all; we must make haste!" Hatter told her as Cheshire kept by their side, floating chest-level with them.

More tremors made their journey difficult as debris and dust fell from the ceiling to coat them. Alora began to cough and had to stop for a moment to catch her breath. Hatter withdrew his handkerchief from his waistcoat, handing it to her. Alora hurried to bring it up to her face. He brought his arm over his mouth and nose, letting the sleeve filter his air. When Alora regained a breath, she tucked Froggy into the bodice of her dress, where she knew the amphibian would be safest.

They hurriedly began again to traverse the corridor. When they rounded a turn, she halted Hatter.

"What about those in the infirmary? They won't be able to escape!" She said in a muffled voice through the cloth of the handkerchief.

"There is a plan in place. An extra looking glass has been placed there for such a reason as this. We cannot afford another delay, darling. Please trust me!" Hatter entreated her as he got them moving again.

Alora nodded, allowing him to lead. Beside her, Cheshire's frown was the only visible part of him. It seemed bizarre in the shadows of the flickering light. Where did his parts go when he mostly disappeared?

She felt turned around until they reached the war room. Inside, faeries were packing maps and books into baskets as they scurried about. Every faerie seemed to have orders and were busily following them. Her eyes found Theodore and Theolf, and Alora was hit with a wave of grief to know Remius would never be with them again. How had she allowed her heart to completely block all thought of him? Tonight, of all nights, she should have felt even a tiny bit of sorrow at his death. Alora was such a dreadful creature, pushing all of her thoughts of Remius away. But how could her heart survive it if she didn't?

While Alora was busy questioning herself, Hatter spoke with Theodore, who didn't pay her any attention. That only added to her heartache.

Alora felt as if she was crumbling apart from the inside out. This was not the time, and she took a deep breath to settle herself. Both kingdoms needed her to be calm, and nothing could undermine all the diligent work that was being done, quite like a leader letting her fears reign over herself.

"Follow us as soon as you're able," directed Hatter, drawing her to the side of the chamber. They walked behind the dark, hanging curtain to see a looking glass that was shimmering with golden light.

Hatter kicked his leg up to enter through the portal, and with a firm hold of her hand, led Alora in behind him. After blinking her eyes, she took in the ivory surroundings, understanding they were now in the White Castle. Guards in white uniforms stood with swords drawn and scowls etched upon their faces. They relaxed their stances once they identified she and Hatter posed no threat to them or their castle.

A faerie with green-tinted skin and ivory tusks protruding from his upper jaw came to stand just before them. He gave them a bow and straightened.

"General Esmae! Have we been attacked here?" Hatter reached forward and clasped the faerie's shoulder.

"Not yet. The Lunar Court enemies seem to be hitting the underground the hardest. I have troops stationed and at the ready surrounding the castle. At the first sign of trouble, we'll know." The General frowned as he shifted his weight. He had an air of competence about him, and Alora was glad he was in a position to lead.

"Good, thank you, General," Hatter stepped away from him to survey the room. It seemed as if they had left one war room to enter another.

The central focus of the room seemed to be on the chess board that rested atop an ivory table. Opposing pieces of marble were moving in amongst each other. Some pieces had fallen over, perhaps signaling fallen soldiers. Hatter let her hand go, striding over to better observe what was taking place. Alora quickly moved after him. If what she was seeing was correct, their subjects were being mercilessly slaughtered. She felt, then saw, a striped paw settling onto her shoulder.

"We must strike the Lunar Court while the army is otherwise occupied. It's now or never," voiced the General.

"I agree. We shall don our armor and put an end to this living nightmare." Hatter took a moment to lock his eyes onto every member that came to surround the table.

Alora wasn't certain what Hatter saw, but it must have satisfied him because he reached for her hand, and then they were moving through the chamber. Fate stood at the door, and Hatter halted before him. In all the confusion in the garden, Fate had not been by Alora's side.

"Fate, would you escort the princess back to her chambers to ready?"

"Of course, Your Highness." Fate leaned his head toward the ground in a version of a bow.

"One more thing. Would you allow your princess to ride upon your back into battle? You can take her into the sky should things prove perilous." Hatter ignored her horrified stare, instead looking to Fate for his answer.

"It's my honor to serve as my Princess's steed. I will keep her safe." Fate's orchid eyes blinked at Hatter.

Turning to her, Hatter embraced Alora as he whispered into her hair. "Be safe. I shall see you in just a few minutes time, then we will depart. If anything should surprise you or you feel in danger, I will be by your side in an instant." He pulled away from her as he pressed his warm lips to hers in a chaste kiss.

"This way, Princess," directed Fate with a nod of his head, his horn pointing at the door.

Alora took a moment to take in Hatter. His lips were twisted into a frown that pulled at his taut features. His entire body was strung tightly. In her mind, Hatter was the perfect image of a fierce warrior. All brawn with alluring intelligence. How could anyone not wish to stand by his side?

"Cheshire, will you stay by my mate's side?" Hatter's attention was focused behind Alora.

"On my honor, my dear friend," Cheshire purred as his entire body appeared.

"He possesses the ability to make you vanish in thin air if the need arises," Hatter explained.

Alora felt a tug on her puffed sleeve. Casting one last glance at Hatter, whose intent gaze was lingering upon her, Alora straightened her shoulders, then turned and allowed Fate to lead her and the tabby through the door. She hadn't been able to summon the words for a parting from her fated mate. Did that make her a coward, or was she simply overwhelmed?

The trio speedily tread down the hallways and past

stationary suits of armor with hanging weapon displays lining the walls. Some of the pieces showed age and wear. Discolorations and dents were visible in quite a few of them. Did their warriors live to survive their battles? Or were these simply empty monuments to those who had fallen?

Her thoughts were tumbling, and she was content for the next few moments to let everything churn together in her mind. She would need to be decisive soon enough.

"Here we are. Meara, or perhaps another maid, should be awaiting your presence. Don't delay." Fate nudged her with his muzzle into the bedchamber she had stayed in before. His breath was warm against her bare arms.

"I shall guard the corridor with Fate. Have no fear for your safety, Curious One," Cheshire cooed to her as he came to pat her cheek.

She gave him what she hoped was a smile but was probably more of a grimace, then stepped away from her guards and into the bedchamber. Alora caught sight of Meara waiting next to the dressing area and rushed over to her. Meara reached for her hands, enfolding them within her own.

"I am so relieved to know you are unharmed. Are you well?" Alora looked from Meara's lilac hair to her slippered feet.

"I am! I am happy to see you are unharmed as well. Your armor was brought through the looking glass, so let's get you dressed and ready for battle." Meara pulled her hands from Alora's grasp and shooed her toward the screened-off partition. Her actions were a gentle reminder time was in short order.

Alora halted before her bed and gently freed Froggy from her bodice. She set the companion down on the plush pillow. "Goodbye for now, little one."

Froggy blinked up at her and seemed to bow its head in acquiescence, though she thought she detected a sadness reflecting in his eyes. She felt a tug on her heartstrings to have to leave Froggy behind again, but there really was no other option.

"Meara, would you please see that our Froggy is looked after while I am away? I dislike the thought of it coming to harm." Alora met her maid's stare.

"Of course, I shall. We shall get along quite swimmingly, I daresay," Meara agreed as she placed a hand on the small of Alora's back and guided her to move.

Once on the other side, Alora let her maid remove her dress and stockings after she removed her slippers. Keeping her underclothes on, Alora stood still as Meara began to buckle the dark pieces around her. Somehow, Alora felt stronger with her chainmail adorning her, and she drew comfort from being able to protect herself, at least a little bit. The restriction she imagined she should feel being outfitted in metal had never been an issue to her.

Meara's quick hands arranged Alora's hair into a knot at the nape of her neck, not allowing one errant wisp to escape.

With her gauntlets in place, Alora held onto her helmet. She would don that once they were ready to leave the castle.

"You look like a queen of vengeance. What's that?" Meara's brows furrowed as she reached for a cream envelope that sat on the stool. Bringing the missive up to her, she scanned it before handing it over to Alora.

Written in the flowery script were the words "*Princess of Wonderland.*"

They didn't have much time to dawdle, so Alora's metal fingers broke the golden wax seal. After removing the cream sheet of paper, she unfolded it and began to read.

I EXPECT THAT MANY SOLDIERS WILL WILLINGLY FOLLOW YOU INTO battle. Just remember that you are fiercer than you know. Trust your heart above all others. Lead with what feels right and cast your doubts to the side. When a moment arrives that you must take final action, know the path you chose was the one you were destined for.

—W

"Leave it to a faerie to be very mysterious," Meara remarked as she read the words over Alora's shoulder.

"Indeed. I suppose it's time to meet with our enemies and allies," Alora mused as she set the letter back down on the stool.

Come what may, I shall do my best to staunch my doubts and lead like the future queen of Wonderland. Nothing less will do.

51

I RIDE WITH FATE

"We battle for our homeland, for our traditions, and for our steadfast beliefs. We will reclaim the throne once again to make Wonderland that which it always was. A place of wonders and dreams. No longer will we allow fear to run amuck, travesties to continue unchecked, no more painted roses on display. For this is the night when a new dawn will come, one which unites us all in one purpose. Reclaim the throne. My brothers and sisters, are you with me?" Drawing his sword and thrusting it into the air, Hatter gave a battle cry.

The army before him beat their fists against their chests, stomping their booted feet as their chorus of agreement rang out into the air. Mist clung to the shadows and roved across the swaying blades of pale grass. Startled birds rattled the silver leaves as they sprang from their nests in bewilderment.

As the shouts died down, a liveried groom led a matte black steed past the soldiers and straight to Hatter. The horse whinnied and threw his massive head up in a show of dominance as his ashy hooves pounded the dirt. How was her Phillip to manage such a beast as he slayed their enemies? Would the hulking beast even allow him to mount?

Alora shifted her weight from one foot to another as a thorn stabbed her heart with icy prickles.

Hatter grinned as he took the white reins in one hand. He walked to the horse's head and touched its forehead with his own. Hatter whispered to the creature, who shook out his mane in impatience. He smirked at the horse and came up to his side.

"Phillip! Is he safe?" Alora couldn't keep the tremor from her voice. Fate rubbed his nose against her hand, attempting to soothe her rattled nerves.

"Quite unsafe, but he's never failed me. Though he is given to his wild nature, he is also my friend. We have an understanding. Do not fear for me. Cullen will protect me with his life." Hatter promptly climbed onto the white saddle.

He was dressed in his own obsidian armor, silver-tipped studs converging across his breastplate, greaves, and the gauntlets. A sword was strapped to his back. The top half of Hatter's tawny hair was gathered together and knotted in the center of the back of his head while the longer strands flowed untethered. Atop his head was a matching blackish top hat with a silk bronze ribbon tied in a double bow.

Alora's heart somersaulted in her chest at the sight of him. Hatter's muscles flexed and bunched under his armor, and it was then she realized it wasn't chainmail he was clad in but fighting leathers. While he looked magnificent, she hoped that an enchantment woven into his leathers would keep him safe.

"Mount up," Hatter called out to his warriors. Those with horses did so, while others gathered into wooden wagons, packed back-to-back and shoulder-to-shoulder. Their faces were set in determined lines.

Fate knelt down on his forelegs for Alora to climb to her ivory saddle. To the west, her father was leading his own battalion. Her mother-in-law was securing the White Castle. Alora took a moment to pray.

Please Fates of this Realm, let us live to celebrate when this is all over.

Cheshire was floating next to her as he scanned the field before them. Alora took to her seat, adjusting her feet into the stirrups. In England, she had ridden Wildflower many times, but never had she mounted without her sidesaddle. It was peculiar but also much more comfortable. Alora's range of motion would be a great deal better riding thusly.

Feeling eyes upon her, Alora turned her head to meet Hatter's earnest gaze. There hadn't been time for a final kiss, no parting words. When she had regrouped with him at the stables, they hurriedly made their way to the wildflower field. A sensation of love and adoration carried along the bond, and she smiled over at him while she sent her own feelings back to him. Who needed words when such overflowing love ebbed from one to another? Hatter knew her heart, and she certainly understood his.

She took the helmet from under her arm and placed it on her head. The slitted visor gave Alora a limited view, but she had trained with it; she could wield her sword well enough with it hindering her sight.

A trumpet sounded behind them, and it was their cue to begin their journey. Fate wasn't wearing a bridle, so Alora wound her hands through his silver mane, hoping she wasn't hurting him. Her protector brought her beside Hatter as they trotted over the field. Hatter's face was a mask of steely resolve, and she mirrored him.

The cold began to seep under Alora's armor, making a shiver race up her erect spine. Her breaths were coming out as puffs of steam dissipated in the air. Foggy breaths could be seen escaping helmets from all those surrounding her; even the horses' breath clouded the ether.

Overhead, the twinkling stars winked down at those below them as the full moon lit their way. It was eerily silent; the only sounds to be heard were those of wooden wheels and horse hooves. It was as if they passed through a shroud to come out to the other side. Everything was too lifeless. The lack of movement made the tiny hairs at the nape of Alora's neck stand on end. Alora surmised that they must have passed through the wards of the White Queen's protection.

In the distance loomed the obsidian castle. It towered over the land with its haunted beauty. Turning her head, she spied Cheshire, keeping pace with them. He wasn't wearing any protection, and she was thankful that he could disappear at will.

Hatter held a fist up into the air, and as he halted, so did the army behind him. He scanned the forest, then the sky above them. The air seemed thicker as danger lurked on the horizon. Hatter waited only a moment before he clicked his tongue to Cullen, setting off again, with Alora and the troops amidst them. They steered their mounts past rotting trees and around massive hollowed-out trunks. Luminescent mushrooms grew on the ground and along the bases of the trees, casting a soft glow in the denser areas. The fallen leaves became less clustered together, a sign they were almost through the forest.

As they neared the dirt pathway, whispered orders were given, and ranks were reformed to travel by pairs. Alora was at the lead, beside Hatter and Cheshire, while General Esmae was right behind them with his Lieutenant.

How curious it was that not even the flowers were speaking. There were not even any tiny insects to be seen. Could they tell tonight's battle would soon ensue?

Fate was twitching his tail as his eyes looked to either side of them. He was a steady presence underneath her. Alora tried to keep still in the saddle, but her nervousness made her flinch at the snap of twigs that lay along the pathway. They were impossible to avoid.

When the forest gave way to the field where the castle

rested, Alora could feel the unease coat the atmosphere. A bitter taste entered her mouth, and she fought not to gag.

"What in all the realms could that stench be?" Cheshire's mouth curled in disgust from beside her.

Alora shook her head, swallowing the bile down.

A sharp, shrill scream pierced the air as the sound of beating wings came from behind the castle.

"It's the Jabberwocky. Prepare yourselves!" commanded their general.

"What do we do?" Alora turned fearful eyes to Hatter.

"We ride hard and swiftly. To the castle!" ordered Hatter as he kicked his heels into Cullen's sides, and they practically flew over the field before them.

Fate was quick to match Cullen's gallop. Alora bent toward his neck to keep in the saddle. Wind passed by them in harsh bursts, threatening to steal her breath. Alora had to blink her eyes repeatedly to banish the tears from the biting breeze.

More fierce screams filled the air as the giant beast came into view. Alora craned her neck to take in its inky scaled body and the huge wings it pumped. The monster ducked down toward them. Alora threw herself to the side of Fate's flanks to avoid the jagged tips of its black claws. She caught a potent whiff of its breath and instantly recognized where the revolting smell was coming from. Tightly, she held onto Fate's mane to keep from falling.

"Hold on!" Hatter called to her as he steered Cullen to reach her. His hands came under her arms and helped to right her as the horses continued their racing pace.

The Jabberwocky continued along their group of soldiers, screeching as it did. They were nearing the castle when it came back toward them, opening its massive maw. Razor sharp teeth were bared as it spewed turquoise bile at them. Cheshire had disappeared, so Alora didn't fear for him, but there was an army behind her that tugged at her heart.

Cullen veered to the left, jarring Hatter. His hat flew from his head as a horrified expression morphed Hatter's face to one of pure rage. He pulled on the reins, meaning to change the direction, to rush back the way they had come.

Is he mad? I will not allow him to come to harm!

"After him!" she directed Fate, who was quick to comply, turning their trajectory on his hooves. Looks of surprise met her retreating form. Scowls and slitted eyes drilled into Alora's back. Silently, she begged them to continue on and not follow them. She didn't want them to even entertain the thought that they were being abandoned by their leaders.

The wind bit into the crevices of her armor as they neared Hatter. She leaned to the side, grabbing Cullen's reins. Hatter's head whipped to her, and she flinched at the wild look consuming him. With pleading eyes, he spoke to her.

"A hatter is nothing without his hat!" Hatter sounded broken as all of his confidence began to shatter.

"But, my love, tonight you are not the hatter. Right now, you are the Prince, and your people need you to lead them. I need you! Let. The. Hat. Go." Alora entreated as she first removed her helmet, then her gauntlet, freeing her hand. Tucking her helmet with the gauntlet tucked inside of it under her arm, Alora reached up to cup his cheek as she let all of her love twist along their bond. She took every ounce of her will to calm him, to heal those broken shards. Golden light shone from her heart and moved to encompass them in its glow. Hatter leaned toward her and pressed his forehead against hers. They stayed atop their horses, galloping through the mass of their soldiers. With a jerk, Hatter pulled away from her.

"You were so lovely; the very sight of you hurt. Here," Hatter said as he lifted his hand to run over the area atop his heart.

"What do you mean?" She questioned as her brows kissed.

"Our first meeting." He smiled at her with a new level of tenderness that pulsed along their tether.

Alora gasped. "You remember?"

"I remember it all. Every single moment," he said as he slowed Cullen. Fate matched the other horse's decrease in speed. Hatter turned Cullen back toward the castle as Fate kept them side-by-side. Alora hurriedly redonned her helmet and gauntlet.

"Oh, Phillip!" tears clogged her voice. Alora wanted to leap into his arms and rain kisses down upon his face as she felt his steady arms encircle her. She wondered why time never seemed to be on their side, but now was not the time to wonder.

Hatter grinned at her and then gave her one wicked wink.

"We'll soon have all the time in the world, my darling," he promised.

The Jabberwocky was flying overhead, commanding their full attention. Patches of grass hissed as they passed by, the venom having poisoned the ground. Screams still rang out, but they were fewer as the army made it safely into the castle's keep. Seeing them, the creature took a deep breath, then cast the venom straight toward them. With a burst of speed, Fate and Cullen made it into the castle foregrounds just before they were struck. Their slower soldiers behind them were not so lucky. Pain-filled screams met their ears. Terror had mist springing to Alora's eyes.

Cullen and Fate slowed their paces as they entered the keep of the castle. Hatter reached behind him and drew his sword from its sheath. Alora reached for her own sword and realized it wasn't the one she had trained with.

"Phillip! Is this the Vorpal sword?" Alora's voice was incredulous, her thoughts flying back to the visions the Oraculum had shown her.

"It is. You must be the one to wield it. It's the only way I could fathom allowing you to join in this battle." Hatter leaped from his saddle the moment Cullen stilled. He came to Fate's side and reached up for Alora one-handed. Alora swung her leg over the saddle, descending to the cobbled ground.

"I should take offense to your attitude, not trusting me to take care of myself," she said with humor, arching a brow.

The majority of their army was already dismounted with weapons drawn. They stood in huddled masses, inspecting the stairwells and murder holes.

"I know you are more than capable, and in a fair fight, you could do quite well. However, there is nothing fair about this battle, and, so, my trust rests on a very tiny thread," Hatter told her with tenderness.

"Glad to see you both returned," General Esmae interrupted in a disgruntled manner.

Hatter winced as he turned to face the faerie.

"My apologies, it shan't happen again." Hatter nodded his head.

With a grunt, the General replied, "This isn't right. They wouldn't leave the entire castle unprotected. Even the Lunar Queen isn't *that* self-assured."

"You think this must be a trap?" Hatter asked.

"I believe it may be," General Esmae's eyes continued to scan the courtyard. "Even our allies can become our enemies if provoked enough."

"What can be done?" Alora entered into the discussion.

A cruel-sounding laugh came from just behind them. The crowd parted to separate themselves from the mad faerie. He was rocking back and forth on his heels with a demented look marring his handsome face.

"What is wrong with you?" demanded Hatter.

"She's been waiting so long for her family to return to her. It's a pity you stayed away for so long, dear Alora. Now her anger will be a thousand-fold." The faerie smirked at her before looking at Hatter. "My queen will spare you and your soldiers if you leave right now. No harm shall befall you." He cocked his ebony head to the side to await their decision.

"Lies!" Cheshire hissed. Alora wasn't certain when he had reappeared.

"Very well, have it your way," scoffed the faerie. The faerie lit up with inky magic and transformed before their eyes. Dark feathers gleamed in the glow as the form of a raven appeared. The bird quickly rose into the air and gave a deep caw, flying past them and away.

"Phillip, I believe that raven has been watching us for quite some time." Alora's wide eyes stared at him.

"We've been in the dark queen's territory for quite some time; of course, she would have her spies about," Hatter answered her.

"No, even before that, when I was still in England, a raven would visit me, and its presence always incensed my father. I never understood why." Alora rushed to say.

Hatter regarded her warily, looking as if he were about to reply.

A drumming began to permeate the air. Its rhythm grew as its reverberations increased. With a start, Alora realized they were surrounded. From the shadows and down the staircase came obsidian-armored soldiers. The enemy army each wielded wooden shields that they were banging their metal fists against. The sound echoed all around them, growing louder and louder. Alora winced at the noise as it was almost painful in its intensity.

"They knew we were coming," Fate said and stomped the cobbles in agitation.

"Indeed," agreed General Esmae. "Steady now, steady on. We wait for the attack to come," he addressed his troops with his steely gaze.

There was no signal given, just a mass collision of bodies

converging, metal meeting metal as swords sang a greeting to their attackers.

Instinct prevailed, and Alora's stance widened as her sword arm raised to protect her from the focused warrior before her. He was relentless in the bruising force he used against her; each clang of their swords reverberated through her bones, making them ache. But her feet danced along the cobbles as Alora's steel clashed against her foe's blade; then he gave her an opening. She crouched forward and slashed sideways. In mere seconds, blood was dribbling from his mouth as he sought to form final words. The Vorpal sword lit up from within the slitted cavity of his stomach and then turned him to nothing more than ashes. With a stumble backward, a muffled sound escaped Alora as she studied the bloody sword in her hand, twisting it in a circular direction. The light glinted from it, and she narrowed her eyes with surprise as her breaths came out in ragged pants. Did no one notice its brilliant candescence?

A body knocked into her, bringing her attention back to the fight. Raising her eyes, Alora saw that two male faeries were brutally exchanging blows, and she ducked between their blades. Searching for Hatter, she saw he was slaying enemies easily enough; how he had veered from her side, she wasn't certain. It seemed an easy feat to be separated during the heat of dodging blows and cutting down foes.

Fate came into her line of vision, his silver horn stained crimson. He didn't hesitate to run his adversaries through. The alicorn's face was set in a mask of fury, and she knew he would easily hold his own.

Looking up at the towers and turrets, an idea came to Alora. Without overthinking, she fled from the fray and raced up the main staircase. She didn't pass any faerie, but Alora did spy several gargoyles scattered amongst the shadows. They made no move to stop her, and when she reached the top step, she faced a set of ornate, obsidian doors. Looking to her left and right, the corridor stretched on for some length with various entrances along it. But the glittering doorway before Alora looked the most promising.

I do hope you've prepared for a guest, dear grandmother.

52

THOUGHT I'D DROP BY

Pushing the heavy doors open, Alora glided through on silent footfalls. Her theory proved to be correct. This was the Throne Room of the Lunar Court, and when she met the cruel eyes of her grandmother, her resolve solidified.

This is my destiny. All of Wonderland is counting on me. Fail or succeed; this is the moment where I weigh and measure her.

From the obsidian throne, Femfaeascent perched with her hand stroking the fur of a strange beast with viciously pointed teeth. The terrifying gray and cream-striped animal was held in place by a silver-linked chain attached from the marble floor to the inky collar around its neck. It resembled a large cat with tufts of hair sticking out from its tipped ears. Silver whiskers appearing to end in sharp points could easily slice flesh to ribbons. The creature looked as if it could swallow her whole, but it was chained, and Alora drew a measure of comfort from the fact.

Quickly, she switched her attention back to the Lunar Queen. Where were the queen's guards? Was she such a formidable foe that she didn't need protection? Light reflected from the dark crown, topped with moon and stars, situated between her ebony horns. It was both beautiful and mesmerizing to behold under the twinkling teal stars. Of course, Alora had noticed it the first time they met, but it seemed to be thrumming with vitality now.

Feeling eyes upon her, Alora searched for who they belonged to. A furry gargoyle perched on its haunches was intently watching her. Its beady eyes were lit with intelligence, but it made no move toward her.

"At last, you have paid a proper call upon me, Granddaughter," the queen sneered, arching one elegant dark brow.

"It's not the first time I've visited," Alora told her as she came to a stop a few feet from the claw-tipped throne, still clinging to her sword.

"Indeed. How did you find my dungeons?"

"Quite dreary, to be honest. I wouldn't relish the idea of returning to them." Alora's eyes darted to the glittering walls and then the ceiling. The stars were so bright they nearly hurt her eyes.

"I'll have to relay your thoughts to my carpenter. Now, tell me what it was that brought you here to my home in the middle of the night. Uninvited," commanded the queen.

"Oh, you know, the usual. Fleeing from fiery infernos and the incessant noise. Oh, and the absolute and utter destruction that accompanies each of those. I suddenly found myself in the area. I thought I'd drop by. We've not had a chance to chat properly."

"Hmmmm. This evening was your mating ceremony, was it not? Did you like my present?" The queen quit stroking her pet along its forehead. The beast hissed at her, and its mistress swatted its massive head. Sea-foam eyes slit as it cowered beside her with an unhappy growl.

"Present? Honestly, I thought it was a bit dramatic. Did you feel so strongly about not receiving an invitation?" Alora smiled demurely as she removed her helmet, storing it under her arm.

"It's hardly the first time I've been excluded from family events." Her grandmother's black nails tapped impatiently on the arm of her throne.

"You must mean my Christening. Considering your gift of my curse, then, you can hardly blame me for the lack of an invitation this time. I hardly think you were truly wounded by the slight, if there was one."

"Wounded, no. But I do fear that a punishment is in order. Shall I take your head and mount it on my wall? Perhaps, your heart would be a more fitting tribute?" The queen slowly rose. "My prized roses could do with another coat of crimson."

Alora bent forward, then set her helmet onto the obsidian floor. When she straightened, she kept her face devoid of any emotion. "You may try to harm me, but I don't mean to lose anything to you tonight. Your time of ruination has come to an end."

Femfaeascent threw her head back, cackling as she brought her hand up to clutch at her chest. When she had composed herself, she replied, "You silly, stupid child. You aren't enough to beat me. I won't go quietly, and I have no intention of giving up the throne. You're just another usurper who needs to learn their place underneath my boot."

Before Alora could blink, the queen was standing right before Alora with her hand tightly wrapping around Alora's throat in a vicious grip. Her grandmother's eyes seared with hate as the turquoise in them bled into an ebony hue. The sword in Alora's hand clattered to the marble below.

Alora couldn't draw in any air as she felt the tips of her grandmother's nails cruelly digging into the sensitive flesh of her neck. Sticky, wet blood began to trickle down Alora's exposed flesh as blinding panic seized her heart. This could not be her end.

Taking her own nails to dig into Femfaeascent's hands, Alora sunk the tips in, meeting bone. Alora brought her leg up between them and used all of her weight to kick her grandmother's midsection. The Lunar Queen grunted in pain, but her hold didn't lessen. Black spots began to fill Alora's vision as rage; then horror flared in her bond with Hatter. She didn't have the strength to send any of her feelings back to him.

Despair and disappointment wrapped their claws around Alora's heart. Her grandmother was leaving her no choice. There was no redeeming the evil queen.

Closing her eyes, Alora concentrated on her healing abilities, dipping into the well of her golden power. Latching onto one thread, she pulled it, taunted, and twisted it, courting it to do as she bid. Alora reasoned if she could heal, she could also summon the power to harm. She took every dark thought, every horrible feeling she possessed, letting it coalesce into an angry dark mass, then sent the energy through her core to pour from her palms in a golden burst of light. Her limbs trembled as exhaustion made her muscles quake.

With a surprised hiss, the Lunar Queen loosened her grip. Alora fell to her knees, gasping gulps of air into her starved lungs.

Stumbling back a few paces, Femfaeascent hunched over. Swirls of inky blackness tinged with gold encircled her.

Alora watched on as the spots cleared from her eyes and her breathing began to steady. Her throat felt raw.

Throwing out her arms to either side, the queen took a deep, shuddering breath, then opened her mouth, drawing the darkness in with each additional greedy inhale.

Alora's eyes grew large with fright as she watched on. Her heart became a battering ram in her chest as her grandmother continued to devour every swirling mass.

Gathering her strength, Alora forced the fear to relinquish her heart and flee from her mind. She needed to fight harder.

The tips of her fingers brushed against the Vorpal sword. Its golden light surrounded her as if she were its beacon; Alora forced her arm to stretch. Her hand closed over the hilt as she rose on unsteady legs. If she could just nick the faerie queen, would such a wound be enough to turn her to ashes?

When there was not even a drop of the shadowiness encompassing her, Femfaeascent straightened, facing Alora. "So much darkness. I am impressed. It's quite a pity I have to end you. The things we could accomplish together… why it gives me goosebumps just contemplating it." With no warning, she pulled a dagger from her thigh-holster, throwing it at Alora's head.

Dodging the flying weapon, Alora held the tip of the sword toward her grandmother. "I'd sooner die than ever become one of your pawns. I have no wish to harm you, but if it must be one of us who survives, I willingly choose myself."

"To me," commanded Femfaeascent as a sword with a golden hilt emerged from the ether. "I shall relish this, Granddaughter." Without a moment's hesitation, she charged for Alora.

Their swords met in a clang of metal. Her grandmother stuck high, aiming for Alora's head. Alora ducked and spun away. Facing each other, Alora slashed her sword toward her grandmother's leg, but her blade was cast to the side by a parry before it could strike true. Femfaeascent snarled at her. Alora flinched under the weight of the next blow. All of Femfaeascent's weight rested on the sword that was attempting to drive Alora toward the ground. Her grandmother threw her head toward Alora, trying to use her horns to pluck Alora's eyes from their sockets. Alora gritted her teeth, holding her stance.

A commotion sounded from the entryway as the double doors were thrown wide. A tall, fearsome, blond male stood peering into the chamber at the spectacle of Alora fighting against her grandmother. Besides Hatter, he was easily the most handsome faerie she had ever seen as his mossy gaze locked onto her. Fluttering to the side of his head were Fleur, Clement, and a flock of sprites, all holding miniature swords and daggers. Cheshire wasn't wasting a moment in rushing past the doors to reach her with a wild, malicious look twisting his features.

Alora gasped as burning pain flared in her right calf. Her knees nearly buckled, but she fought against the agony soaring straight to her limb through the tear in her chainmail. Focusing her attention back to her adversary, Alora saw blood dripping from the razor-sharp tips of the Lunar Queen's nails.

"Never turn your attention away when in a fight to the death, dearest Alora," she cooed with a cruel twist of her lips.

Before Alora could react, the queen kicked her injured leg, causing Alora to wince and unexpectedly lower her blade. Alora's heart skipped a beat as she understood the mistake she made.

Fright and terror traveled along the bond as she sent her love to her mate. Alora willed him to know that in her last moments, she loved him; acceptance of her fate flowed from her heart to his. Sorrow and blinding panic were sent back to her. It was her fault they were separated. She had made the choice to leave him behind, and now, he would pay the ultimate price for her rash actions. Regret began to blossom in the pit of her stomach as she lowered her head for the killing blow. Now, Hatter would have to live with her mistakes.

The lethal strike to sever Alora's head never came. Hisses and the sound of tearing flesh tore through the silence. Looking up, she saw Cheshire with his claws savagely swiping at the queen's cheeks. Lines of crimson were welling on the faerie's stunned face as her sword clattered to the floor.

Her wild eyes were lit with euphoria as her bloodied face twisted into a sneer. Using her elbow, she struck Cheshire in the temple, his paws momentarily halted. The tabby shook his head as if he was attempting to clear a fog from his mind.

Femfaeascent used the moment to turn and run to one of the glass-paned windows. She threw herself through one, and the glass shattered around her with a violent impact. The handsome blond faerie was racing after her, but there had been too much distance separating them. He met the window and stuck his head through it, scanning the area.

"You poor dear! Does it hurt?" Fleur asked as she flitted down to examine Alora's wounded leg.

"Not as much. I think it's already healing," Alora answered as she bent to inspect her leg through the slit in her armor. The blood was congealing as the wound slowly sewed itself back together. Taking a deep breath, she concentrated on the tether, soothing the worry and trepidation wafting from her mate. It was as if a shuddering sigh twisted along the bond; she felt his relief and joy in every particle of her.

"That's a very handy power," Clement commented as he joined his mate.

"I suppose it's no surprise she fled. I am quite the foe to go up against," Cheshire said with disdain as he eyed his bloody paws.

Maia and Fiona led a group of sprites past the chained animal hissing at them and sailed through the window, brandishing their weapons as they passed. The large cat was curled up, but his eyes were as fiery as an inferno.

The serious-looking Fae came to join them. "Are you alright?" He withdrew a white handkerchief and passed it to the tabby. Cheshire began to incessantly wipe his paws with it.

"I will be," Cheshire hissed with distress. The blood was quickly staining his fur.

A high-pitched wail came from the window, drawing their attention to it.

"The Jabberwocky is taking out far too many of our soldiers." The curt tone of the blond faerie made her flinch.

"He should be dealt with," agreed Fleur, waving her tiny fist in the air. "Shall I lead my fellow sprites in a mission to end him?"

"No. I don't think Briella would be too pleased if she knew I commanded you into harm's way. The creature is no match for you, mighty as you may be." He frowned at Fleur.

"No, but he's no match for the Vorpal sword." Fleur switched her gaze to observe Alora.

"Excuse me, perhaps it's not the time to ask questions, but who are you?" Alora asked as she tested her full weight on her leg. She was pleased that it seemed to be completely healed.

"My apologies, I am King Ezekiel of the Spring Court. As my ambassador, Fleur has been keeping me abreast of Wonderland's happenings. I decided to see if you could benefit from my aid," he said cordially.

"Oh! Thank you so very much, Your Majesty, for coming to help us," Alora gratefully told him.

He bowed his head to her and replied, "The Spring Court has suffered its share of troubles. We long to see the entire realm free from abuse and hardships. My soldiers are aiding your army."

"Let's exchange pleasantries and backstories once we've rid the kingdom of the tyrant queen, shall we?" Cheshire remarked in a bored voice as he balled up the solid handkerchief and tossed it over his shoulder. "I assumed you didn't want that returned?" he asked King Ezekiel, who grimaced at him.

"I have an idea," Alora said as she turned for the broken window, making her way to it. Reaching it, she looked out and nodded her head.

Fleur joined her, then folded her arms, still gripping her tiny sword.

"While I don't know which way my grandmother went, I can still take care of one issue. The turrets look to have footholds in them, easy for ascending." Alora climbed through the window, quickly finding her footing. Cheshire appeared beside her with a scowl.

"Has Wonderland's madness finally captured you?" Fleur cocked her head to the side.

"She's completely bonkers," Cheshire said and began to swish his tail.

"Perhaps, but the Jabberwocky needs to die. That may serve to bring the queen back to face me." Alora placed her sword into its sheath and began to climb the steep roof.

"How may I be of service, Princess Alora," King Ezekiel asked as he poked his head through the window behind her.

Sparing him a look over her shoulder, she smiled at him. "Find Prince Phillip and help him in securing the castle?"

"I swear it shall be done." King Ezekiel nodded to her before retreating.

"Are you quite certain you want to do this? This way?" Fleur continued to look at her with uncertainty.

"How else am I meant to reach the skyline?" Alora began the slow process of climbing. Her fingers fitted into grooves as the toes of her boots pushed her up even higher.

"Perhaps I may be of service?" Fate offered as his downy wings pumped him into view.

"Marvelous! Yes, you may ride the alicorn!" Fleur danced in the air excitedly.

"Are you sure? I can't guarantee your safety." Alora halted her momentum, her limbs tired and aching, as her eyes pinched with anxiety. The idea of any of her friends coming to harm was like a sharp knife embedding itself into her heart repeatedly.

"There is no honor greater than serving my Princess," Fate said and came to her side and steadied himself, allowing Alora to slip into the saddle. Cheshire settled into her lap with a satisfied smirk. She held onto Fate's mane with one hand and the tabby with the other.

"Then we have a beast to vanquish." Alora was determined to end one of the nightmares that was raining down venom, injuring her fellow faeries. She felt fear for Fate and even Cheshire, but this had to be done. Her grandmother could be dealt with later. Alora needed to focus on taking down one vile-breathing maniac at a time.

When they rose higher into the air, Fleur called out, "Not without me! I am coming too!"

Clement reached for his mate's hand, and together, the pair flew to perch on Alora's armored shoulder.

"Well, now that I have an army with me, let's end this." Love and gratitude warred with the fear and uncertainty that had built cruel barbed mountains within her.

It was time to take out one enemy and up the odds of Wonderland surviving once this was all over. She took a moment to search the bond, discovering Hatter was injured. Alora also felt pricks of his unease that they were not with each other. Alora wondered if she should retrace her steps and return to him or continue to track the beast.

Her anxiety sent waves to Hatter, but he sent his love and assurance back to her, and it bolstered her confidence. He wasn't in dire need of her, so while he was dismayed they were separated, he was not demanding she return to his side.

He truly is perfect in every way…

53

DROPLETS OF VENOM AND BLOOD

Soaring into the air wasn't without peril. After all, the ground was such a long way beneath them; the faeries fighting looked like tiny specs. Should Alora fall, it would be to her death. Her companions would all fare well as they had wings, except for Cheshire, but with his ability to wink in and out of the ether, he could safely remove himself from harm. So Alora held on not only with her hands through Fate's mane but with her knees tightly clasped along his sides.

Flying over the turrets, Fate wasted no time in spotting the winged menace spewing his venom toward their army. A window had been broken in one of the tall towers, and as the beast hovered in the air, he turned his aim there. Hisses and pops came from the shattered glass as the venom ate away its fragmented pieces. A stream of the bile must have reached its target because, accompanied by the fizzing, were torturous moans. Alora carefully drew the Vorpal sword from her back.

"I think it's past time to vanquish this savage. Are you ready, my Princess?" Fate asked, twisting his head to eye her.

"I am, and I couldn't agree more," Alora replied, steeling her spine for the skirmish ahead.

The creature was massive, with little spikes raised from the crown on its head all the way down to the largest three prongs at its wagging tail.

"What's our plan?" Fleur asked as she tossed her dagger from hand to hand.

"Well, aside from slaying it, I hadn't really given it much thought. I'm not yet used to battle plans and forming them." Alora shrugged her empty shoulder.

"I say we go for its eyes. If it can't see us, it will be much easier to attack," Fleur offered with a bloodthirsty gleam in her eyes.

"You mustn't forget that the Jabberwocky has a heightened sense of smell. He can track us with that alone," Clement added as his ebony brows pinched together.

"Right, so, we destroy its sight, and we… What?" Fleur inquired with mounting impatience.

"The brain. All things are controlled by it, so let us deal blows to the thing's head. And if we have to make cuts along the way, so be it," Cheshire told them, as boredom warred with his own impatience to be done with the entire affair.

"Very solid advice," Fleur commended the tabby.

Alora peered down at the feline to catch him rolling his eyes.

"On the count of three, we'll each attack from different sides and angles. Fate, keep Alora close to you." Fleur rose to bop Alora's nose. "Where is your helmet? Oh no, we've left it behind! Clement! How could you not notice that?"

"Don't screech so loudly, my beloved!" Clement warned as he focused on the Jabberwocky. "I was not the only one with the princess! I did not realize my purpose was to track her helmet. You might have mentioned the task to me when you were prattling along your instructions at the castle."

"Enough!" Alora whispered with exasperation. "It was my choice to leave it behind. I simply can't see my surroundings with it as well as I'd like. Danger may come from any side, and I need to be able to discover its presence all on my own."

Fleur hummed.

Clement frowned.

Cheshire wore a delighted smirk.

Fate was silent, but she caught the muscle in his jaw flex as they drew nearer to the Jabberwocky.

When they were no more than a few inches away from the beast, Alora raised her hand to signal the others. Fleur and Clement rose to hover in the air as the tabby floated to the side. The sprites stealthily flew to the other side as Fate held steady.

Alora kept her attention on the head of the Jabberwocky as Fate came upon the hulking creature. On closer inspection, she noted it possessed many tiny spines for protection along its massive head. Landing a strike would be difficult as the tip of her blade was sure to meet with one of the spines. She resheathed the Vorpal sword.

The only way to ensure a direct blow is to get in between those little spikes. I can't do that on the back of Fate. One move of the beast and my blow could miss and alert it to our presence. We're all sure to become injured that way. I shall have to jump onto its neck and scale my way up.

Alora felt alarmed by the idea of falling, but she'd come this far and would not fail now. With wry amusement, she thought that perhaps having grown wings as a Fae characteristic wouldn't have been so terrible after all. Carefully, Alora tucked those feelings away, not wanting Hatter to know she was feeling inept and questioning their current path. It wouldn't do either of them any good to worry about the other.

Quickly, Alora slipped her leg over the saddle and to the side to meet her other limb. Taking care not to alert the others to her new strategy, she twisted her foot from the stirrup.

"Whatever you are attempting to do, I strongly caution you against it." Fate's lowered voice reached her.

"This is the only way. Trust me, please." Alora leaned forward to lock her gaze with his.

He frowned at her in reply before saying, "Very well."

The others were watching her with looks of dismay as she nodded her head and leaped onto the Jabberwocky's spiked back. With a determined nod from Fate, her companions all took action and sprang at the creature. Despite the beast attempting to throw her from him, Alora's hands found purchase, and she climbed. The deafening roar of the living nightmare wasn't a surprise, but it was much louder up closer to it, and Alora's ears rang. Pain-filled snarls rained down on her with punishing force. She wanted to curl up and cover her ears.

The monster was thrashing its head from side to side as it attempted to dislodge its attackers. Its cries of rage increased in volume, but Alora kept finding footholds as she stretched her hands to help pull her upwards. She could never allow herself to shirk her duty as her friends continued fighting on.

When acid whizzed by her head, Alora tracked its trajectory as it landed upon the Jabberwocky's own back. The venom had no effect on its toughened hide.

Reaching the enormous head that was still violently swinging, she concentrated on keeping hold of one of the spines with one hand as the other withdrew the Vorpal sword. Alora drove the blade through the tough, leathery skin, knowing it might take her many tries to slay the creature. Droplets of blood seeped from the hulking beast where she had pierced its hide. As the sword began to glow, wisps of smoke curled into the air from the wound, but it was not enough.

It's neck! That's the only hope to truly kill it quickly!

Backpedaling, Alora descended the spikes with the sword still secure in her tight grip. She found the creature's neck as its snout rammed into her side. Blinding light filled her vision as she gasped. Alora nearly lost her grip, but Fleur was there to distract the beast from her by viciously stabbing its eye.

The eye socket was a bloody mess and oozing out things Alora had never desired to see. Looking away, she had to swallow back down the acidic contents of her stomach.

Her side was aching, and Alora wondered if perhaps the Jabberwocky had broken one or two of her ribs. Knowing her healing ability would soon kick in, she dismissed her pain and got down to business.

The skin along its neck seemed to be smoother and not quite as leathery, with no spines to protect it. Alora drew her arm backward and then threw her weight into the action as the sword came down to land a heavy blow. The sword lit up the night as the blade came to life with an eerie glow as it sank through the flesh, taking Alora's forearm with it as inky blood spurted in time with the Jabberwocky's heartbeat. The monster's screams and hisses poured from its mouth, but it was no match for the fabled sword. From the racket above her, she knew her determined friends were also on the attack. With labored breaths she withdrew the sword and struck again and again. Each thrash was torturous, and her side flared with white-hot pain that brought silver stars to her vision. The stench of burning flesh surrounded her as the Vorpal continued to burn away her enemy with each collision of steel and flesh. Almost falling from her perch when the horned head finally severed from its neck, she looked down to watch as it plummeted to the cobbles far below them. Charred skin tissue clung around the fatal wound as blood and acid spewed from the gaping hole in pumping arcs to coat everything in sight with its visceral.

The body began to slowly fall and Alora gathered her wits to jump toward the window. Her free hand caught the frame and she used her elbow on her other side to pull herself through the casement. Her armor hissed as the venom coated her. Tumbling through the window, Alora landed in a heap on the dark marble floor with a moan. She quickly rolled from the puddle of goo and rose to her feet as Fleur and Clement tugged her to the side of the chamber.

"Help her!" Fleur's panicked voice erupted.

Alora was startled when larger hands gripped the gore-covered sword from her sticky hand. Alora allowed the blade to be set aside and watched as the faerie withdrew a handkerchief to wipe the blood from her hand. Stepping back to her side, the faerie began to loosen the buckles of Alora's chest plate. Looking at the faerie, Alora was greeted by a kind smile.

"Thank you for saving us," said the beautiful faerie with pale skin and onyx hair.

Nodding, Alora held stationary as another faerie came to her aid by pulling pieces of her hissing armor away. Alora felt like she could breathe better once the weight on her body began to be stripped away. It had never felt so heavy and suffocating before. Her mind was muddled, and she felt slightly dazed. Alora had to concentrate on pushing the horror of her latest kill aside as she allowed her mind to quiet.

When Alora was standing in only her small clothes, another faerie stepped forward and waved her hands before her. Alora felt invisible fingers coast over her skin, dissolving the carnage that had stained her. With rounded eyes, Alora watched as a forest-green dress materialized over her body.

"Thank you," Alora replied, shaking herself. "Thank you!" It was all she could manage as she fought against the tide threatening to drown her.

"You're welcome, Princess," curtsied the faerie, who had ivory horns and wore a lilac dress. "We hoped and prayed for a savior, never thinking that time would actually come to fruition. We are in your debt!" The lilac-gowned faerie reached for her hand and warmly held onto it.

"You are looking more than a bit dim-witted, Curious One," commented Cheshire as he sailed through the window.

She supposed she did appear out of sorts; Alora certainly felt so as exhaustion made her mind sluggish and her limbs heavy. Turning toward Cheshire, Alora spied Fate hovering on the other side of the window, his wings far too large to fit through. His face was set in a grimace as he took in the scene.

Fleur focused on the faerie with her dagger at the ready. Alora hadn't even noticed that her hand was still encased in the faeries's grasp. Alora perked a brow at Fleur, but her tiny friend just stared.

If they meant me harm, why bother to clean me up? Unless my grandmother is controlling their actions?

Movement alerted Alora to the presence of another in the room. There was a faerie on her hands and knees in the corner, scrubbing the venom from the cobbles. Her bent back was to them, but unease started to creep along Alora's senses as her skin pricked with trepidation. Drawing her awareness back from the recesses of her mind, Alora's thoughts began to spin.

Perchance, we're not safe here after all.

Reaching out to the bond, she sent a gentle nudge to Hatter. He immediately sent soothing thoughts to her. Alora felt him drawing nearer toward her.

"We should properly show you our gratitude." The ivory-horned faerie captured her attention, coming to lay a gentle hand around Alora's shoulders. The other faerie released the hold on Alora's hand.

Turning Alora, the beautiful faerie began to direct her toward the door of the chamber. Before Alora could react, her arms were wrenched behind her back as pain spiraled along her wrists to her shoulders, and flowing waves of nausea overtook her. Alora hissed in agony.

Fleur was hurriedly closing the distance between them,

her wings a blur of movement, but she was no match for the hand of the lilac-gowned faerie that swatted her into the wall.

Clement's eyes narrowed with hate reflecting in them as he hurriedly changed his course to fly to his mate's side.

The faerie brought a jewel-encrusted dagger up to meet Alora's gaze before cool metal grazed the skin of Alora's neck. It cut into her, and Alora bit back the gasp of pain that wanted to break free. Her eyes searched the room for her sword and landed on the faerie who had been hunched down, cleaning up the floor. Rising, the figure discarded the robe to reveal the Lunar Queen, smiling at her with vicious intent. The faerie queen nodded to the other faerie to come forward. With relish, the horned faerie moved to latch onto Alora's arms as she stopped by her side, grinning madly at her.

This time, Alora allowed every feeling to flow through her bond so Hatter knew how serious the situation was. She was ready for a rescue and for her prince to save the day.

I've saved myself countless times this evening. My strength is failing, and I am not too stupid to know that sometimes you don't need to be the hero. Sometimes, even the heroine of their own tale needs a rescuer.

54

A PRINCE OF HIS WORD

The Lunar Queen strode toward Alora with her hand poised in the air, her knife-like nails drawing close to Alora's face. "Now, how about a little reminder of our time together? I have a token, and so should you. Do stop squirming; I'd so hate to poke out an eye instead." Ragged scratches marred the faerie queen's perfect alabaster skin. Crusted blood flaked from the sides of her face as she spoke.

Alora tried to twist her head from the two faerie's grasps, but the dagger dug deeper into her neck as the hands holding her tightened to bruise her flesh. She was powerless to hold back the whimper of pain as rivulets of blood flowed from the laceration.

Before the tips of her grandmother's vicious nails could touch her, Cheshire appeared before them, clamping his sharp teeth onto the queen's hand. The queen attempted to wrench his hold from her, but he would not let go. The faerie queen took her other hand and buried her nails into the underside of the tabby's stomach. With an *oomph,* Cheshire opened his mouth. The queen used her forearm to bat him against the same wall Fleur had hit. His eyes slid closed as his body made contact with a sickening thud. Silently, he coasted to the floor.

Fleur was unconscious beside the feline as Clement held her, murmuring words, attempting to wake her.

Alora's eyes sought Fate through the broken window, but the alicorn was gone. Had danger found him, too?

An avalanche of sorrow bedecked with disgust crashed over Alora as she turned her gaze back from one battered body to the other, feeling all hope flee from her. She allowed the fight in herself to wither away. Her friends were in danger, and there was nothing she could do.

If giving in to her grandmother's demands would save her friends, then she'd willingly do it. Along the tether, Alora sent a plea to Hatter for him to hurry. The bond between them was strung taut as her emotions leaked to Hatter. She couldn't tell which one of them was more frightened.

"You look so human, so very *common.* How my blood flows through your veins is a complete mystery. How stupid of your father to fall for a mere mortal, bond or not. I shall remake this realm. I've very nearly succeeded here." The Lunar Queen circled Alora as the pair of vicious faeries continued holding her tightly between them.

"You won't win forever. There will come a day when your reign is over," Alora replied as she carefully watched her grandmother. She didn't wish to be taken unaware when her grandmother struck next.

"Posh and nonsense! That day will never dawn." The queen stopped before her and nodded to the faerie holding the dagger up to Alora's throat. The faerie removed the blade, handing it over to her queen, then backed away. "I shall make this quick. I don't relish the idea of you escaping your death yet again. It boils my blood."

Movement from behind her grandmother caught Alora's eye. Fleur was awake; she and Clement were inching toward the Vorpal sword. Alora quickly averted her eyes; she didn't want any faerie to notice what was happening.

The Lunar Queen raised the dagger and then drew it down Alora's face. Alora could barely repress the flinch from the cold metal. While the steel didn't break through her skin, it did leave an angry, red scratch from her temple to her chin.

With another victorious smile, the queen tutted at her and brought the dagger to Alora's heart. "Not even true love's kiss can bring you back from death this time. Say farewell, dear Alora."

Before her grandmother could plunge the dagger through, Hatter jumped through the broken window from atop Fate's back, dislodging more glass shards that crunched under his boots. His face was a mask of crimson rage as he surveyed the scene before him, withdrawing his sword from its sheath.

"You will not harm her!" he bellowed, his voice reverberating from the walls.

"You have no sway over me, Prince! Have you forgotten what you allowed to happen to your father? Perhaps, after I carve out her heart, I shall have it placed in a box and gift it to you." The queen cackled, sending chills along Alora's spine.

The evil queen was baiting Hatter with the cruel reminder of his father's death, which was not his fault, but Alora knew that he felt he bore the blame. Alora could feel his sorrow bleed between their bond at thoughts of his slain father. Sadly, she thought, he would always carry the guilt.

Hatter's gaze flitted from Alora to the queen. He seemed to be assessing the situation with care and control despite the lunatic threatening them. His hands flexed on the sword he held steady in his grip. He was coated with gore, but he had never looked more handsome to Alora. Hatter was every inch a warrior of Wonderland, and she had never been more proud of him. He was a force to be reckoned with, truly glorious with his righteous fury.

"I think not," he said calmly. "It's past time Wonderland had a new ruler, or even a few." He took a step forward.

"Ah, ah, ah, Prince. If you wish her death to be over in an instant, then by all means, do please continue along."

He locked his gaze with Alora's as a tear trickled down her cheek. She allowed her fear to subside, instead pushing love and acceptance through her bond. She didn't fear her own demise, but to exist in a world where Hatter wasn't breathing was her one true fear. Alora willed him to understand her death might not be in vain if he could vanquish the greatest foe that Wonderland had ever suffered.

"It will be alright, my love. End her quickly, even if you cannot save me," Alora told him. She let her most cherished memories of them flow through her mind, giving him a beaming smile.

Feeling eyes upon her in the crowded ballroom…Noticing the highlights in his hair… dancing in his arms under the stars. Seeing him look at her with a quizzical expression at the tea party. Being held in his palm at his haberdashery. The feel of his arms surrounding her in the prison cell. Dancing with him again in Faerie. Sleeping next to him in their shared tent in the forest. His declaration of love and adoration. His smiles and his kisses.

Alora cleared the tightness of her throat and said, "This is the only way."

Hatter empathically shook his head. "I do not accept this! You will live a long life by my side. I will not allow you to be harmed. This was never how our story was to be written."

With lightning-fast movement, Hatter reached them. Two things simultaneously happened. Fleur and Clement reached Alora and shoved the Vorpal sword into her hands while Cheshire's paws appeared, wresting the dagger from the queen's grasp. Hatter held his sword one-handed while his other arm came to encircle Alora's waist, pulling her away from the queen. The tabby and sprites navigated to either side of them as the queen's fury radiated in pulsing waves of obsidian magic leaking into the air.

"We go as one," Hatter instructed into Alora's ear. He sheathed his sword and wrapped his hands around hers on the hilt of the Vorpal sword.

Alora canted her head to look up at him and saw the determination shining from his eyes. There was also understanding. His heart knew that ending her grandmother would not be an easy feat for her. Gratitude permeated her heart. Alora broke eye contact; her foe was not to be trusted.

"I would have spared you. I would have let you grow old in the mortal world, stripped of your power. But you could have *lived*." Alora tried in vain to keep the waiver from her voice. She forced herself to take a deep breath and embrace the darkest parts of herself, to merge with the darkness, letting it wrap around her heart in a freezing embrace to accomplish this one vital task.

"A life kept as a pet is not worth living. No power?" Femfaeascent barked out a disbelieving laugh.

Hatter nudged Alora forward, and before she could register what was happening, the Vorpal sword was at her grandmother's throat with a trill of blood seeping from the beginning of her wounded flesh. Alora blinked and locked away her heart. The hiss of the sword as it seared through skin crashed into her ears. As her grandmother's eyes bulged, Alora spoke one last time to her.

"I forgive you," Alora whispered as she, with the help of her mate, sliced the glowing sword through the burning flesh. Her eyes wanted to shut, to close out this horrific event, but Alora knew she must bear witness to every agonizing moment the darkness in her wanted to witness. There was a single piece of seared skin attaching Femfaeascent's head to her neck. When it severed, her head tumbled to the cobbled floor, where a puddle of blood awaited it. One of her obsidian horns had splintered, its tip shattering at the impact. With a splash and one last rotation, the head stared up at them, open-mouthed as the smoldering flesh was doused out; it was hideous in its blank stare.

Tugging her hands free from underneath Hatter's, Alora turned and buried her head into his leathered chest. Silent sobs wracked her body, but within moments, Hatter was cradling her to him. He placed one arm under the back of her knees and circled around her waist with his other. Hatter carried her from the chamber as she continued to weep. The darkness fled from her heart in a torrent of whirling ebony threads. Alora's heart was better with its absence.

He truly is a prince of his word. Sheltering me from all the nasty things that saving Wonderland means.

55

A NEW DAWN

The tears Alora wept sapped her of any energy she had still possessed. Through every tear that fell, Hatter held her. She didn't even know to what chamber he had removed them. She was safe and alive, and so was he. Whatever wound he had endured was not serious. That was all her mind could fathom. She let oblivion take her as she nestled deeper into his arms, allowing his unique scent to cocoon her.

Delicate kisses rained down on her closed eyelids as a gentle hand stroked the hair from her face. She smiled as she let Hatter love her. The light was creeping through the black lace curtains, inviting the troubles of the new dawn to greet them. She didn't wish to move from the bed, not when so much had happened to rob her joy and burden her heart.

"Everything will be set to rights. I won't lie to you, not now or ever. Healing Wonderland won't be simple or easy," Hatter said as he leaned away from her. Alora peeked at him from under lowered lashes. He captured her hand and brought her palm to his mouth for a warm kiss, sending tingles throughout her body.

Grinning at her, he caressed her hand with his thumb. "Your father is growing impatient to rest his own eyes on you. He's sent servants, whom I have all promptly dismissed from the room. As much as I would love nothing more than to make you mine in every way possible, the kingdoms today must come first. But tonight, you are all mine. Only mine," he purred as a slow smirk appeared.

Alora brought her arms up to wrap around his neck. He moved over her, caging her with his forearms on either side of her. When Hatter's questing lips met hers, they both moaned. The bond between them was a raging inferno. He teased her with his lips and tongue, small nips to sensitive flesh that made her blush. When Hatter changed the angle of his kiss to better ravish her, a knock sounded at the bedchamber door, which did nothing to slow her thundering heartbeat. He drew his head away from Alora, and they both looked to the door. Hatter groaned as he ran a hand through his ginger tresses.

"Tonight is suddenly so very far away," he muttered as he rolled to the side of her.

"Princess?" questioned Meara as she peeked her head into the room.

"Yes?" Alora quickly replied, straightening her neckline. She reached a hand up to smooth her hair, but it seemed to be a hopeless mess as she absently wondered when the pins had tumbled from her tresses.

"It's the very early hours of the morning, but your parents are growing more desperate with their pleas to see each of you," her maid explained as she came through the door and closed it behind her.

"Oh, that will never do!" Alora exclaimed as she scooted to the bed's edge and sat up. The thought of her father or of her mate's mother in distress squeezed her heart. The idea of causing either of them more pain was heartbreaking after they had already experienced such cruelty and loss.

Swinging her legs over the downy mattress, Alora rose on stocking-clad feet. She followed Meara to the dressing area and entered the small bathing chamber. The porcelain onyx tub was massive, and she longed to soak in it for the foreseeable future. Twisting the dark knobs, the maid allowed the water to cascade into the tub as she reached for jasmine-scented bath salts. Alora wasted no time in disrobing. When the water reached halfway, she lifted her leg to bring herself into the warmth. Wisps of curling steam rose into the air. Alora sat against the lip of the tub and sighed with pleasure. The purple water steadily rose to cover her chest, and Meara shut off its flow. Alora could become accustomed to such mornings and evenings spent in such luxury. It was heavenly.

Alora brought her thoughts back to the present as she reached for the sponge to begin cleansing herself. The sultry jasmine scent enveloped her, and she felt the lingering tension ease from her.

Images of her grandmother's last moments replayed in her mind. Alora would have done almost anything to spare them both the thread of fate that had been clipped. She didn't feel less or even embarrassed by not being strong enough to vanquish the queen by herself. It didn't make her minuscule in the least to need the aid of her mate. Hatter existed to help her when Alora faltered or hesitated in doing what needed to be accomplished, just as she was created to support him when he needed her.

A perfect balance, two halves of a whole.

Alora finished her bathing, allowing Meara to wash her hair. When the last bubble was rinsed away, Alora rose as Meara wrapped her in a plush black towel.

THE IVORY SITTING ROOM GREW SILENT AS HATTER AND ALORA made their way toward the White Queen. The beautiful faerie rose from her throne, and Hatter moved forward to assist her from the dias. Alora let his hand go as the queen threw her arms around him and wept. The courtiers respectively drew away to the edges of the chamber.

Watching them, she didn't notice her father draw close to her. He reached out, cupping her elbow, and she canted her neck to look at him. His dark eyes studied her from the tip of her tiara to the silk slippers that peeked from beneath her muslin dress. The worry fled from his face as he tugged her to him, wrapping her in a warm and tender embrace. Tears came unbidden to her eyes, and she allowed them to fall. Could he understand that what she and Hatter had done had been forced upon them?

"I never wanted to be the one to end her," Alora muttered from the ruffles of his cravat. She hiccupped as her sobs increased.

"Shhhh. It's not your fault. I could never blame you for taking the actions you did. I only wish you could have been spared the burden of such a responsibility. My mother died a long time ago, back when she was still a child." Papa rubbed soothing circles along her back as he continued to hold her.

"But— you must have still loved her?" Alora's heartbreak made her stutter.

"I will always love the *idea* of her. Just because a person shares your blood, is even a close family member, does not mean they are deserving of your affection and time. Sometimes, the kindest thing one can do is to let them do as they please far from you, hoping someday, should you meet again, they will have grown and taken a different path. The older I am, the more I realize that choosing a new direction is the hardest thing one can do. My mother never chose wisely and, for too long, was left unchecked. I fear the suffering of Wonderland bears much of my responsibility. I mean to ensure, from this day henceforth, the Lunar Court has a monarch who will use his heart in ruling, in everything he does." Her father kissed her forehead, then peered down at her.

The tears had begun to slow the more his words made their way into the wounded places of her heart. Alora hastily rubbed the lingering wetness from her face and softly smiled up at him.

"You will assume the throne?" she tentatively asked.

"I will," Papa replied as he gave a decisive nod. A lock of his dark hair came to rest into his eyes. He blew a breath upward to dislodge it. "I have it on very good authority you and Phillip will be seated on your own ivory thrones in no time. The White Queen is ready to leave the burden behind and live in peaceful accord, tending to her white roses and hosting teas and luncheons." Her father's midnight eyes were warm as he regarded her.

"Oh. I wasn't certain the kingdoms would remain split. I suppose that is a wise decision. I never dreamed we would be ruling so quickly." Alora gazed back to Hatter and his mother, who was straightening as Hatter handed his mother a lace-embroidered handkerchief.

Hatter tilted his head to observe her before asking, "Do you not wish to lead the White Kingdom by my side?"

Alora reached for his hand, squeezing it. "I wish to do whatever it is that our kingdoms need of us. If you feel you are ready to lead, then I will stand with you."

"You will lead exceptionally and have no fear as to who will rule the Lunar Court in your stead. When the time comes, Remius will assume the position," Fleur interjected as she glided along the air into the chamber.

Alora stood dumbfounded at Fleur's statement, with her mouth hanging slightly ajar.

Remius? Could he truly be alive?

"What?" inquired Fleur as she came to stop, hovering in

front of Alora's face. "Oh, that's right! You haven't been sipping on True Love's Delight as the barrels have been making their appearances in the most unlikely of places. I have had the most faetastical visions! But let me put your wool-gathering minds at ease." Fleur looked at the other faeries in the room.

"Please do," directed her father with an impatient flick of his hand.

"I saw Alora with Hatter, cradling a tiny bundle, whom Cheshire addressed as Remius! You name your son after him; it's quite heartwarming, isn't it? But then another vision confirmed it as we picnicked on a hill, watching as our sons cavorted along the grassy meadow. They were shouting their names at each other as they played a game of Faerie, Faerie, Human. Your son is Remius, my son is Thaddeus, and the new soon-to-be-born princeling of the Spring Court will be named Lennox. They'll be all aged not too far apart, which means, should this vision prove to be a true possibility, we should all get cracking on the task of creating them."

Alora rubbed the tender area over her heart. She was to have a son?

Remius... his name rattled within her heart as her lips curved into a bittersweet smile.

If she could honor him in any way, naming her firstborn son after him sounded like the perfect way to do so. She looked to Hatter, who wore a softened expression. Remius had first been his friend. Alora felt his approval sail along their bond as glee overwhelmed him.

He does approve. I should've known that he would. He is always so caring and thoughtful.

Hatter bent forward and pressed his warm lips to hers, causing her to sigh.

~

A RIBBIT SOUNDED IN THE SILENCE OF THEIR BEDCHAMBER. Alora's pulse raced as she opened her bleary eyes and focused. She threw the coverlet aside and rushed to draw the drapes. From his spot in their bed, Hatter threw his arm over his eyes and groaned.

"Should I be alarmed and armed or just still and silent?" he questioned grousily.

"I think that, finally, Froggy has returned to us!" Alora lifted pillows and checked under each chair. She opened each door, peering behind every piece of furniture she could. Alora padded to the middle of their bedchamber and scowled, fisting her hands on her hips.

Hatter chuckled as he sat up in their bed to stare at her. He slipped from under the covers and rose. Prowling to their water closet, he peeked through its open door. "Ah, hello, little one."

At his words, Alora picked up the hem of her nightgown and raced toward him. When she, too, stood before the door, a relieved giggle escaped her.

"How did you know where to find him?" Alora asked as she bounced on her tiptoes.

"Do not forget I can shift to a fox in mere moments, my love. Foxes have exceptional hearing." He winked at her.

From the bathtub lazed Froggy, who was floating on a pink lily pad. The beady black eyes lit with joy as they took in Alora. Joyful croaks escaped the amphibian's curved mouth.

Rushing to the tub, Alora gently bent forward and scooped Froggy into her palms. She didn't mind its slick skin; her aversion had long since passed. Padding by Hatter, Alora returned to the chamber and sat on the chaise to better observe Froggy in the sunlight.

Froggy leaped from her hands and hopped to the table beside the massive four-poster bed.

"You want to sleep now?" Alora questioned. She felt

slighted as her heart pinched that Froggy wasn't content to visit with her. Had the little creature not missed her after all?

Hatter closed the distance, perked a brow at the amphibian, then opened the drawer. Froggy hopped into the drawer, rummaging around until he leaped from the drawer and into Hatter's open palm. Hatter moved over to sit beside Alora, and her heart missed a beat as she realized what object the frog held between its front legs.

"Remius's ring?" Her brows puzzled together. Alora had lovingly tucked the band away in the drawer for safekeeping to treasure for another day; she hadn't removed it since, too afraid to lose it.

Froggy nudged the latch but couldn't get it to spring open. Hatter took the ring, opening the heart-shaped lid before he looked down at the amphibian.

"I'm not sure what you want, little one," Hatter confessed as he set the ring down before the frog in his hand.

The frog hovered over the ring, dipping one hand into the small space. When it removed its hand, it was covered in glittering Faeriedust. Froggy's pale tongue darted from its mouth to lick the dust away.

Alora and Hatter exchanged a glance before a glowing burst of light called their attention back to Froggy. With a great ribbit, the frog began to grow. Its limbs lengthened, and silvery hair sprouted from its head. In mere moments, a naked little girl with bright blue eyes sat between them.

"Good gracious!" Alora squealed, as Hatter quickly drew his shirt over his head and settled it over the shivering body of the girl.

"That's so much better!" remarked the young faerie as she gave Alora a shy and timid smile.

"The whole time, you've been a frog? Why didn't you change forms? I suspect a hex of some sort?" Hatter gently prodded.

"I forgot how to change back. I'm only six, you know," the

young one told them. "I knew enough that the Faeriedust would force the change, but I never wanted to use it for myself 'cause I knew that it was so very important to the Princess."

"That's very clever, and how very brave you've been!" Alora smoothed out the silver tresses of the child. Her heart gave a painful squeeze.

I wish this little one had used the dust! Oh, her poor heart!

"Where are your parents? Certainly, they have missed you!" Alora bent to bestow a kiss upon the crown of the girl's head.

"The queen executed them, but I ran away before they got me, too." A tear slipped down the little faerie's face. She hastily brushed it away.

"Have you any relatives we can contact?" Hatter ran a hand over his heart. The bond was conveying how his heart was also aching.

"I wish to stay with you!" she replied. "Oh, please, may I? I won't be a bother or make a fuss. I don't think I can fit in a drawer anymore, but I will find a space."

Alora met Hatter's gaze over the child's head, and he gave her a slight nod. Their bond flared with gentle love, allowing her to know the decision was hers to make.

How could I turn a child away? We've enough room to house all the orphans and then some. But I still think I prefer her much closer to us. I have a treasure trove of affection in my heart for this little soul.

"Of course, you must make your home here with us. I couldn't bear for my little Froggy to leave me again." Alora gathered the child into her arms, placing her on her lap.

"That was always a silly name," giggled the little one.

"What is your name?" Hatter inquired with mock seriousness.

"My name is Rosalie."

"That is the most beautiful name in all the realms," Alora

said, smiling as tears of happiness misted in her eyes. "Welcome to your forever home, Rosalie. We're so delighted to have a daughter of our very own."

Rosalie lifted her head to meet Alora's eyes and gave her the most beautiful of smiles.

~

"STOP FIDGETING, DARLING," HATTER PLAYFULLY ADMONISHED. Alora let the ribbons of her bonnet go as she rolled her eyes.

"I'm just not certain I should be here," she hedged. She felt a distinct pain shoot straight through her chest at having left Rosalie. Alora realized she wasn't ready to leave the little one's side, and she hoped she was not already failing at motherhood.

"Nonsense, you will be their queen. Where else should you be, if not here, inspecting our troops?" When Hatter turned his head to look at her, he frowned before adding, "If your preoccupation stems from missing our daughter, never fear. We shall soon be with her again; we only have to perform our duty, and then we may return to her." He sent a wave of love through their bond, and Alora smiled at him.

Hatter's notice switched to Theodore, who strode toward them and bowed reverently. His tail hung limply behind him. An air of sadness clung to him, and Alora was in no doubt that, though their slain numbers had been great, Theodore mourned his friend most of all.

"Your Highnesses, General Esmae wished to be here, but he is still recovering in the infirmary," Theodore informed them as he regained his ramrod posture.

"That's to be expected," agreed Hatter.

"The army is ready and at attention, awaiting your approval," Theodore said to Hatter. He had not set his eyes on Alora, and her unease prickled her heart. She felt exposed and sensitive after Fleur's revelation of her soon-to-be son's name.

When Theodore made to walk away, Hatter placed a hand on his shoulder and addressed him in a hushed tone. "We value your leadership, Theodore. I have always treasured your companionship. If we cannot set aside the crushing loss of Remius, I fear we can not stand as strong as we should. Wonderland needs you; I need you. But I cannot allow you to dismiss my mate, your future queen."

Theodore blanched and replied, "My apologies. He was like a brother to me. I miss him."

"I miss him too, whether you believe that or not," Alora spoke, as her tears gathered in her eyes.

"I just need time..." Theodore trailed off, his eyes on something in the distance.

"You shall have all the time you need. Just remember that leadership comes with responsibility, and I don't need to remind you of that fact, do I? And that others will look to you when forming their opinions about our rule." Hatter's words were laced with iron.

"You do not, Your Highness." Theodore frowned and then looked at Alora. "I know it was not your choice for him to sacrifice himself in your stead. I have just felt that his heart was clouded with thoughts of you. And the situation brought him nothing but heartache."

"I well realize that. I can't change the past, but I will honor the future and him in any way possible. I know he did belong to me, just as a part of me shall always be his. I would like to sit and talk with you if you would allow it. You had so much more time with him than I did. Surely you have stories you might share with me?" Alora's hopeful pleading reached her eyes.

"It would be my honor, Your Highness." Theodore gazed into her eyes, searching them. He allowed a slight curve of his lips before he cleared his throat. "Shall we see the troops now?"

"One more pressing question, then we do as bid. Have your spies been able to catch any sign of the raven?" Hatter inquired as his features tightened.

Icy fingers gripped Alora's heart. In all the chaos, she had forgotten about the raven.

"He's slippery. My sources tell me he's not even in this Court anymore. They cannot track him. It's as if he's vanished." Theodore's scowl reflected Alora's feelings quite adequately.

"He may never return. What purpose does he have now? If his mind has not cleared from Femfaeascent's influence, I would rather he never reappears. But we must be vigilant that any foe to Wonderland be swiftly dealt with."

The captain nodded his agreement. "It will be done. Now, the troops? Shall we?"

"We shall," Hatter replied and nodded to him, matching his strides to his mates.

WITH HER FINGERS BRAIDED IN HATTER'S, ALORA TOOK A DEEP, cleansing breath. Already, the oppressive air was being chased away. Windows were open, allowing the sun to cast its glow in the chambers that had long been shut to it. Three days had seen monumental changes for the Lunar Court's kingdom.

While Alora hadn't been awake to see the sight of the many gargoyles taking flight, Fleur had informed her it had been quite a spectacular sight. It was the second time Fleur had witnessed a gargoyle migration. The Spring Court had seen the creatures leave as soon as the curse had been lifted. It seemed the dark beings favored chaos, or perhaps there was an altogether different reason for their being in the midst of darkness.

With the death of the Lunar Queen, the subjects of Wonderland slowly regained their sense of self. It was as if they were awakening from a long slumber, free from the constant nightmare that serving such a monarch had placed them in. There were those whose minds were just too broken to ever heal. The March Hare was one of them. It seemed as if he'd never leave the infirmary.

Alora had exhausted herself for almost two days, forcing her healing magic to work time and again. Hatter had marched into the infirmary and physically removed her. She had been nearly boneless with fatigue, and he had had enough. In the thick of things, Alora hadn't given thought as to how stretching herself would affect him and their bond. Hatter had given her strength, but his patience had reached its limit. He wasn't willing to risk her health any longer. With a promise and a yawn, she had acquiesced. Alora's conscience had plagued her regarding Rosalie and how much time she had spent away from her as well. Hatter was proving to be an exceptional father, but he, too, was new to parenting, and it hadn't been fair to ask him to devote so much of his time to caring for their new daughter alone.

The Throne Room was jammed with courtiers and those who wanted to ensure this coronation was in their best interest. Alora stood proud and regal next to her handsome mate, clad in an ivory uniform that stood out among the many shades of black. His ivory top hat boasted a white feather that weaved and bobbed with every movement he made. He was still the Hatter of Wonderland and would always be so, but now, he'd permanently left the mad part far behind on the battle field, after his mate had healed him.

Alora ran a hand down her own coal-colored gown to calm her nerves. She was still tired but had no desire to miss this event.

When the Midnight Crown was placed atop her father's head, she felt tears spring into her eyes. He looked every inch like the king he now was. Holding Court and sitting so gallantly on the rose-carved throne. His dark head of hair shone with the power the crown was casting off. He rubbed a hand over his chest and bowed his head.

"His heart is linking with the lands. It's drawing his intentions for Wonderland to the surface," Hatter explained from beside her in a whispered voice.

She furrowed her brows as she turned her head to inquire, "It doesn't hurt, does it?"

"No. But it's not pleasant either. The Court has suffered for far too long, and it will take time to nurture it. Your father is impressive; I have no doubt we'll soon see Wonderland returned to its wondrous state." He reached down to kiss her temple as the glow of their bond wrapped around her.

"I am so happy, I can scarcely believe this day has come!" enthused the White Queen, who stood on Hatter's other side with her hand clasped around Rosalie's. Tears rimmed her pale lashes. "This is all we've worked so hard to attain; your father would have celebrated for weeks!"

"We should celebrate every day, for each new day is a gift. It's a continuous fresh beginning, and what could be more wonderful than that?" Hatter beamed at his mother.

"Speaking of celebrating, I might have a surprise of my own," began the queen. "How does a wedding in three week's time sound to you? I, for one, am all for it and cannot wait to see you two dance the night away."

Rosalie gave an excited shriek as her feet happily danced in place. She was a bright beacon in their hearts that helped in healing the lingering pains.

Hatter turned back to Alora and grinned, "What do you say, darling?"

"I think it sounds like another dream come true. How do

you keep making all of my dreams come true?" Alora stood on her tiptoes and placed a kiss on his cheek.

"It's my official new role, that of making your every dream come true. I shall never stop," he teased.

When her father stood from the throne, he stepped down from the dias and came straight toward them. The smile on the Lunar King's face radiated pure joy. The midnight ceremonial robe trailed after him as it slid over the obsidian floor. The king's midnight eyes matched the floating Fae lights suspended above them. He reached for Alora, and she willingly went into his embrace. From over his shoulder, she spotted Cheshire's smile as he hovered toward the double doors. Pulling away from her father, she hurriedly kissed his cheek.

"I shall be right back. I have finally caught a glimmer of the elusive tabby, and I mean to chat with him. Would you mind terribly if we entrusted Rosalie into your care?" she asked as she caught Hatter's fingers and tugged him along with her. Without waiting for reply, they darted into the crowd that parted for them, passing by the Dumpty couple, who seemed in high spirits. Before Cheshire could exit, she called out to the feline.

"Cheshire! Where have you been? I have been wracked with worry!"

Turning to face her, the cat's body materialized as he regarded her with a tilted head. "I am sorry to have caused you to worry. I have been well, but I've been tasked with something of great importance. I was on my way to do my duty just now."

"You were going to leave? Without a word? Were you planning to return to us?" Alora felt panicked at the thought of a new Wonderland forming without the beloved tabby being a part of it.

"Wonderland is my home; I shall always return to it. But if

you must know, I loathe goodbyes, even temporary ones." His bright eyes blinked at her.

"I believe I do as well. But whatever it is that you are tasked with doing, will you be in danger?" She tried to be calm, but they had all survived what seemed like an impossible undertaking. The idea of more harm to befall him pierced her heart.

"I seem to have my share of lives; you needn't fear for me." Cheshire came to lay a paw against her cheek. "Hatter, you will look after our Princess, will you not? She's the heart of the entire kingdom."

"Of course," scoffed Hatter with indignation.

"Here we all are! Isn't a new beginning worth fighting for?" The Weaver came through one of the double doors to halt before them. Her cobalt robe was missing, and in its place was a flowing pale pink gown that shimmered. Dancing starfish glittered along the material and winked no matter which direction she moved. Her sea-colored hair was upswept with seashells and pearls woven through its thick curls.

"You are more than just the Weaver, are you not?" Alora turned toward her when Cheshire leaped onto the faerie's shoulders.

Dawning realization flooded Alora as her heart swelled. The mysterious faerie was the Enchantress!

"Why, of course, I am. But what you needed was a weaver, and so, that was what I was to you. I am many things to many beings. I wanted to express my gratitude to you both for your part in saving the realm."

"You have my sincere thanks for assisting us," Hatter told her with a bow.

"You always had the power to save these lands; you just had to believe in yourselves, what possibilities awaited you. You'll find that discovery of self is so important to one's personal journey. We Fae are long-lived, but some lessons can't be learned no matter how many centuries may pass unless your heart truly believes." The Enchantress smiled at them both.

"Cheshire mentioned he has a task. Is he leaving with you?" Hatter asked as he reached for Alora's hand.

"Indeed. We are needed to aid in another's quest. The survival of the realms depends upon it. Be well, my little ones, and never forget that darkness is never far away. The best way to keep it at bay is to love endlessly. And don't forget that a perfect balance of light and dark is needed in order to keep the wonder of these lands." She winked at them and turned away. As her steps carried her further from them, Cheshire disappeared, all but for his smile.

"Are you well, darling?" Hatter drew Alora's attention to him. She turned to face him and placed her hand over his heart.

"With you by my side, I am marvelous! I believe you promised me a dance," she replied and pressed a chaste kiss to his lips. When she was back on the balls of her feet, she looked behind him. "Don't look behind you, but Fleur and Clement are on their way to us."

"Shall we dance?" Hatter asked. His amber eyes were lit with mirth and love.

"I will follow you anywhere," she answered as their love wove knots along their bond, braiding the love together for eternity.

EPILOGUE

ONCE UPON A DREAM

Alora and Hatter waltzed across the ivory ballroom under the floating faerie lights and the glittering snow that was cast by the eternal snowflake. Each delicate flake was gorgeous amidst luminescent bubbles floating amongst the dancers. Her high-waisted wedding gown was shimmering, alternating between a royal blue and a pale green.

Fiona brought her hands to her ears and hunched forward.

"I told you, this is my friend, and you have no right to change her appearance!" Fleur screeched in such a high voice that the glass orb on the wall alongside them cracked.

"You don't have to always be so bossy! Queen Alora looks so much better in muted tones. Look at her skin; it's glowing whenever the pale green forms!" complained Maia as her eyes narrowed to slits.

"It's not the shade that is the cause; it's the White King! How daft could you possibly be?"

"I'm not daft, you imbecile! Just because you're so ridiculously happy doesn't mean the source of all joy rests in a completed bond!" Maia stomped her slippered foot, anchoring her hands upon her hips.

"You're just jealous! That's what's ailing you!" Fleur jabbed her finger into Maia's stomach.

"I am not!" seethed Maia, who swatted Fleur's hand away.

"Stop!" shouted Fiona, who rose to her full height, glaring at them both.

"What did you say?" Fleur blinked at her incredulously.

"I said stop. Stop bickering, stop fighting about all the stupid little things! You are driving me insane and widening the chasm between you! Sabelle is gone; I have lost my sister forever. Need I remind you that she is never coming back to us? You don't need to further break our family apart; our pieces are already splintered beyond repair. Just... Stop." Fiona's shoulders slumped as she gazed at her sisters, who were staring at her with open mouths of disbelief.

"Who are you, and what has become of my sister?" Fleur asked and shook her head slowly at her.

"She's grown a backbone at long last. I daresay it's the result of dealing with your insufferable ways for much too long," Maia rolled her sapphire eyes at Fleur.

"My insufferable ways? You can't be serious! You're the reason why I, too, left Wonderland," exclaimed Fleur with fury leaking from her form.

Fiona muttered under her breath and flew over the balcony to find better company. She just wanted one night where her two sisters didn't nearly come to blows or throw their magical essence at each other in a showy display. The dizzying effects of sprite dust were enough to give any faerie a headache.

They couldn't even contain themselves as they organized the arrival of Wildflower and the small odds and ends that had belonged to Queen Alora's mother, which the Lunar King and King Phillip were eagerly planning to give her the following morning. They had spent the better part of the day bickering over how to display the mementos. It had boggled Fiona's mind. At least they had all agreed that the horse's place was in the royal stables. That one detail had gone perfectly to plan. Wildflower had happily settled into her new stall with no complaint.

Seeing the White Knights, Theolf and Theodore, she floated over their forms as her tiny ears heard their quiet conversation. There were advantages to being overlooked. One of the greatest ones was gathering gossip that no faerie else could ever learn. Fiona never shared what she learned, but she figured that someone ought to be the secret keeper of Wonderland.

"She looks luminous," said Theodore with sadness in his voice.

"She does, and Remius wouldn't have wanted her to be any other way," Theolf replied as he took a sip from his goblet. True Dream's Delight slid past his tongue, tingling as it went down his throat, warming his insides and settling into his stomach. He took a moment to gaze at the hazy image that sprang to life before him. He saw himself leading a battalion in the Winter Court. A beautiful faerie was by his side, smiling up at him. He frowned at the scene. While True Dream's Delight didn't show one the future, it did show shadows of what could be. Theolf was unsettled, but leaving the Lunar Court made sense when he reminded himself that he was a soldier because he was good at it. He could leave his home if it meant saving others. Could he convince Theodore to come along with him?

Fiona raised her eyebrows at the vacant stare of the knight and flew over to the Dowager Queen, who held a sleepy Rosalie in her lap. The young one looked angelic with her silver curls surrounding her oval face. Her fluttering eyelashes showed just how worn out the day had made her. As the former queen stroked her head, it was evident just how much Rosalie had come to mean to her. There was a bond that tied the two together as surely as if they were blood-related.

When Fiona lowered herself and settled down on the domed butter dish on the table, the Dowager Queen nodded to her. Fiona returned the greeting and settled in the peace to watch the future of Wonderland dance before her. The midnight glow of the ballroom felt comfortable and like home. Yes, Wonderland was home once again to all of its subjects, whether they belonged to the Lunar or White Kingdoms. None needed to fear any longer. It had been faetastic to see so many of its residents return from the other Courts.

Her gaze landed on the other royal couple swaying on the dance floor. King Ezekiel and Queen Briella of the Spring Court curved together over the swell of the queen's stomach. The beautiful French monarch had blossomed in the Spring Court under the love of her husband and mate. King Ezekiel had been a fearsome ruler, but Queen Briella had seen through his bluster to the faerie beneath all the hurt. Their love story was still being whispered about over teacups.

"Long live the King! Long live the Queen!" Shouts rang out into the ether as King Phillip's and Queen Alora's lips met in a smoldering kiss to rival all others before and after it. Looking around herself, Fiona decided that, finally, the land was what it should be. Wondrous. And it was all due to a girl who dared to be different and do things in her own unique way.

"Did you hear that?" A bemused expression alighted on the Dowager Queen's face. Her granddaughter had finally succumbed to slumber in her arms and didn't wake at her words.

"Hear what, Your Majesty?" Fiona turned her attention to the kind faerie.

"Why, I do believe I hear the gentle song of a nightingale. Just as it was promised."

AUTHOR'S NOTE

Dear Reader,

Thank you for reading this book. It means so much to me that you did. I hope that you've enjoyed your time in the Lunar Court and have fallen in love with a character or, maybe, even two.

I'm on the fence about which direction to take my author career. If you loved this, let me know. I might get cracking on the third book in this series, or the prequel to Love At Last.

Supporting indie authors is important and appreciated. Self-publishing is a huge endeavor and the best way to support an author is to leave a review. Honest reviews can help others decide whether a book is right for them or not. Also, if you love a book, shout it out to the world. Share it with your friends and family and even with your book club. Books make wonderful gifts too. Sharing your love of reading inspires others and may even assist another with finding their new favorite author.

Happy Reading,
Michelle Helen Fritz

adorable version of Cheshire. He is simply faetastic, as are you.

Thank you to my sister Cathey who always adds thoughtful insight. Your attention to detail continues to be such a blessing to me!

Thank you Fandom Fealty! Your pop of Hatter is faederful and I adore him! Thank you for your friendship!

I can't end this without a huge well of gratitude to Paullett Golden. You have inspired me and lifted me up. You are exactly what I aspire to be. Thank you for allowing me to tag along in your author journey!

Thank you to all the social media peeps! Authors could not do what we love, if not for you! Every share, every post, and most especially each review brightens our world.

And finally thank you to my Creator who gifted me with one wild imagination and a love for unputdownable literature.

ABOUT THE AUTHOR

Michelle Helen Fritz began her literary career as a personal assistant to Indie authors. She enjoys being immersed in the process of turning an idea into a complete and published book. Michelle loves to write about dashing heroes and the compelling women that tempt them with a bit of intrigue and an abundance of romance, creating swoon-worthy characters and stories for her readers to enjoy. Occasionally, her characters talk to her and change the entire plot. Maryland is where her humble abode resides, housing her four home-schooled children along with her jaunty hero-husband who makes all her dreams come true. Michelle fully believes in happily-ever-afters and wishing upon stars.

Ways to Connect:

Facebook Reader Group

Instagram

Follow on Amazon

Follow on BookBub

ALSO BY MICHELLE HELEN FRITZ

A Bramley Hall Regency Romance

Love At Last

Love That Lasts

Love Ever Lasting

Shades of Bramley Hall Regency Romance

Love Holds True

Courts & Curses

A Court of Broken Dreams & Curses

A Court of Broken Promises & Nightmares

www.ingramcontent.com/pod-product-compliance
Lightning Source LLC
Chambersburg PA
CBHW070549310726
48982CB00011B/1518/J

* 9 7 9 8 9 9 0 3 8 1 1 1 7 *